House of Rayne

Also by Harley Laroux

The Souls Trilogy
Her Soul to Take
Her Soul for Revenge
Soul of a Witch

Losers
The Dare (prequel)
Losers: Part 1
Losers: Part 2

Dirty First Dates (short erotica series)
Halloween Haunt
The Arcade
The Museum

House

of

Rayne

Harley Laroux

KENSINGTON
PUBLISHING CORP.

kensingtonbooks.com

KENSINGTON BOOKS are published by:

Kensington Publishing Corp.

900 Third Avenue

New York, NY 10022

kensingtonbooks.com

All Kensington titles, imprints, and distributed lines are available at special quantity discounts for bulk purchases for sales promotions, premiums, fundraising, educational, or institutional use.

Special book excerpts or customized printings can also be created to fit specific needs. For details, write or phone the office of the Kensington sales manager: Kensington Publishing Corp., 900 Third Avenue, New York, NY 10022, attn: Sales Department; phone 1-800-221-2647.

The K with book logo Reg US Pat. & TM Off.

First Kensington Hardcover Printing: October 2025

ISBN 978-1-4967-5683-1 (hardcover)

10 9 8 7 6 5 4 3 2 1

Printed in China

Electronic edition: ISBN 978-1-4967-5622-0 (ebook)

Interior art courtesy of Claudiu Badea/Adobe Stock

The authorized representative in the EU for product safety and compliance
is eucomply OU, Parnu mnt 139b-14, Apt 123
Tallinn, Berlin 11317, hello@eucompliancepartner.com

*For all those still fighting the curses
handed down to them.*

House of Rayne

Prologue

Rayne

Winter's Coming

THE DEER HADN'T BEEN DEAD FOR LONG; RIGOR MORTIS HAD yet to set in. Fresh crimson blood glistened on exposed organs and clotted on shattered bone.

The creature hadn't been eaten. It had been shredded.

Hooking my pliers back onto my belt, I gripped the handle of my knife, surveying the wide open field. The wind howled through the crisp grass, a sharp chill in the air. The distant trees swayed.

Winter's first cold snap came early this year. The crops that hadn't yet been harvested had been frostbitten through the night, and reports said temperatures would continue to drop. Dark clouds churned in the distance. The ocean was as gray as the sky, as chilling as the fog.

A fly buzzed incessantly in my ear, and a cloud of them went up as I stepped closer to the corpse. Glassy, sunken eyes stared up at me. What had they seen in their last moments? Perhaps they'd never even known death was coming.

But I knew. I always knew. It had dogged my steps since I was a child.

Swatting away the flies, I trudged across the field toward my ATV. The fence was repaired; it would keep the Frontage family's sheep from wandering and getting picked off by coyotes . . . or worse.

The snap of a twig jerked my head like a puppeteer's strings. The pale colors of late evening blended into one another; grass, trees, fog, and shadow created a flat and eerie landscape.

Was it a pale, eyeless face I saw beneath the trees? Or only the tendrils of fog caressing the air?

Blinking rapidly and rubbing my eyes didn't make the strange visage disappear, and I took an unsteady step backwards.

It was a trick of the light. My eyes were tired.

I jogged, then sprinted. The wind had calmed but I swore I could hear movement in the grass behind me—something moving with speed, with purpose. Adrenaline shot through my veins and the flies were still buzzing, buzzing, buzzing—

I leapt atop the ATV, and the engine squealed as I cranked it to life. Blood rushed in my ears, but the field was empty. So were the trees. My fingers gripped the handlebars so tightly my knuckles were white, my palms sweaty.

Pull it together, Rayne. It's too early in the year. It couldn't be awake. It couldn't.

I knew better than to give myself too many assurances. Nothing was promised, and the rules by which I survived could change day by day. Death could adapt to any scenario.

"Hey! Hello?"

I froze, and I killed the engine. For several long moments, I waited. Listening.

"Hello? Who are you?"

A chill went up my back. The voice was *behind* me. It was high-pitched, like a young woman, but oddly flat. Devoid of emotion and inflection.

Barely turning my head, I searched for the source. The mist was messing with my sight, making it seem as if figures were sprinting between the trees.

"Who are you? Hello? Hello?"

Same words. Same tone. But louder. Faster.

Hungrier.

I cranked the throttle. Dirt plumed from the wheels as I accelerated, speeding down the hillside. There was no trail here; I had to navigate between trees, over rocks. All the while, that voice called behind me.

"Hello? Hey!"

Faster, faster. The fog grew thicker until I could barely see where I was going. Water soaked my pant legs as I drove through a shallow creek, constantly shooting glances over my shoulder. But that was my mistake. I looked away for a split second too long, and my wheel wedged between two large rocks. The shock wrenched the handlebars from my grasp, launching me from the seat as the vehicle flipped.

I barely managed to roll out of the way before it landed on top of me, coming to rest on its side against a massive fallen tree. Groaning, I lay on my back and gasped for breath, staring up at the swaying pines.

Get up. I needed to get up, *now.*

My chest hurt. My lungs were hollow. I rolled onto my side and shoved myself upright, holding myself there on shaking arms as I surveyed my surroundings. The fog churned, the illusion of constant movement making my aching head even dizzier.

"Who are you."

That voice drove a rod straight down my spine. The tone was cold. Empty. A mockery of human words.

I didn't dare turn around. Stiffly, I rose to my feet and started walking. Calm and steady . . .

"Who are you."

There was rustling. *Scrape, scritch.* Clawed hands dragging through dirt, clicking over a tree's rough bark.

"Hey."

A different voice. No less cold. *Keep walking. Don't look, don't look.*

"Hey!"

It wasn't even a word anymore. It was a snarl.

I stumbled out of the trees and onto a cobblestone road. Whipping my knife from its sheath, I whirled around and raised my weapon.

But nothing was there. The empty trees swayed in a soft breeze, the fog dissipating around my feet. But I could still feel eyes on me . . .

Mrs. Frontage stared at me from her yard, chickens squawking around her feet. "Are you alright there? Is that you, Miss Balfour?"

"Hi, yeah, it's me, I'm—fine." I barely hid a grimace as I returned my knife to its sheath, then brought my hand to my injured shoulder. I popped the limb back into its socket and her eyes went as round as marbles. "If you have an ibuprofen, that would be great."

Salem

No Names

TODAY WAS MY WEDDING DAY. BUT TONIGHT, I WASN'T married.

I'd biked nearly a hundred miles since noon, through long stretches of Pacific Coast forest. My back and legs were sore as I ate a quiet dinner of fish and chips, sitting in the bar across the street from my motel, alone.

When I went to bed later, I wouldn't find my loving fiancé waiting for me.

There was no fiancé. There was no country club wedding or honeymoon in Las Vegas.

There was me, my bike, and every single hour of vacation time I had remaining for the year. Just me and my desperate attempt to take back control when it felt like my life was falling apart. My companions were the bartender, a few grizzled strangers, and my ever-present anxiety—sitting like a cold, heavy block of ice on my chest.

The bar wasn't busy, despite being the only thing around that could pass for a restaurant. There were a few dockworkers hunched over their beers, engaged in quiet conversation. The bartender had been wordlessly wiping down glasses for the past thirty minutes, staring blankly at the bartop.

This was a liminal space. Between lives, between dreams.

But when she walked in, suddenly everything felt real again.

Her baseball cap hid her face as she strode inside, long brown hair dripping from the rain. She brought a gust of cold night air in with her, and her presence made the room shrink. When she turned her cap around, the neon lights hit her face and made her light brown skin shine like gold, revealing a long, thin cut on her cheek.

A fresh wound, cherry red.

The bartender gave her a nod and she gave him one back before he turned and grabbed a bottle of whiskey from the dusty top shelf. Her dark green eyes darted around the room, searching like a hawk, touching everyone but me. The sharp edge of her jaw made me stare, following the contours of her throat down across her strong shoulders to the soft curves of her chest.

As I sipped my drink, her gaze found me. I sharply inhaled, but instead of air it was beer, and instantly I was sputtering. Coughing frantically into my hand, I tried to hide my near choking from concerned onlookers and hustled to the restroom.

After coughing the beer out of my lungs in the privacy of a stall, I made my awkward return, only to find the seat next to mine was no longer empty. Oh, God. It was her. Her back was to me, but I couldn't doubt the strong shoulders, the way she leaned forward against the bar as if she owned it.

Sliding back onto the stool beside her, I clutched my beer with both hands and took a shaky sip. She dominated my peripheral vision. Her head was moving slightly, bobbing to the beat of the music emanating from her earbuds.

Listening closer, I recognized the song as "Talk to Me" by Stevie Nicks. Maybe it was just the beer catching up with me, but a ripple of excitement ran over me to hear one of my favorite artists, and my lips started moving silently to the lyrics.

At least, I thought I was being silent. But as I murmured along, there was movement beside me and a deep voice suddenly said, "Do you want to share?"

The woman had removed one of her earbuds and held it out in her hand, offering it to me. But I couldn't focus on the earbud, not when she was looking straight at me with those forest-green eyes, warm and gently amused at my expense.

"I, uh—yeah—"

Barely got a word out, but she understood. She exhaled sharply—a laugh?—and electricity shot through me when she pressed the bud into my ear, filling my head with Stevie's ethereal voice. The touch was so quick but it lingered in my nerves, imprinted on my cheek.

"I've been telling these guys to get the sound system fixed," she said, hooking her thumb toward the bartender. "I can't stand the silence, so I always come prepared."

She leaned toward me, slowly resting her arm on the bartop. She smelled like clover, burnt hash, and the salty ocean air.

Hastily, I said, "Sorry, I should have introduced myself. My name is—"

"Wait." Her hand shot out, and she pressed her finger against my lips. Sparks flew from that touch, and in a single instant, she had me. "No names. Let's keep it interesting."

She smiled, and my stomach fluttered. But this was no gentle smile; it wasn't an offering of friendship.

It was an invitation.

"You're not from around here?" I said. The rest of the room seemed far away. The neon lights danced in her eyes, and I was suddenly transported to the feeling of being at a county fair in summertime. The churning anticipation, the heat and desire.

"No," she said. "You're not either."

"Nope. I'm from San Francisco. I've been cycling for the past few days, that's why I look like this." I chuckled nervously, certain that my short hair had a serious case of helmet head and my face was sunburned.

But she wasn't looking at my bad hair or reddened skin. She hadn't looked away from my eyes, not even once.

"Damn, that's dedication." She scratched at the cut on her face, then seemed to catch herself, abruptly lowering her hand. "You must make good money to afford living there."

"Well, instead of going into tech like everyone else, I decided to pursue a dream and ended up working as an animator for a small video game studio, so . . ."

She nodded knowingly. "Got it, so you're a starving artist from San Francisco, you like Stevie Nicks, and you're gorgeous. You really were blessed with the whole Manic Pixie Dream Girl package, huh?"

It had been ages since someone made me laugh so easily. "The whole package and plenty of baggage," I quipped. The song changed, and we swayed together to the beat, simultaneously mouthing the lyrics.

She asked for my drink of choice, then ordered my gin and tonic, and a beer for herself. She tapped her glass against mine in a toast and said, "To new friends."

"To new friends." I took a long swig, hoping the butterflies in my stomach would settle. "I'm only here for the night."

"So am I." She took my hand, her thumb brushing over my palm. "So let's make it a night to remember."

"You're mine now, pretty girl. You'll never forget this, will you?"

Kneeling between my legs, she looked like she was praying. Knees on the grimy tile floor, eyes closed, skin bathed red in the neon glow of the Rainier Brewing Company sign hung on the graffitied wall.

A sinner in supplication, a priestess in worship, her tongue inscribing litanies on my flesh.

She was on her knees, but I was the one who felt small. Shrunken in her hands, legs shaking as she controlled my breath with her own mouth.

Sitting at the bar felt like a lifetime ago, now that we were crowded together into the single-stall restroom. We'd danced together, an earbud in each year, singing the lyrics in hushed tones into imaginary microphones. People stared and I didn't care. For once in my life, finally . . .

Her eyes opened, pulling me into their depths. My hand slipped as I tried to brace myself on the sink, but she held me up. She was drowning me and I didn't care.

That was what I wanted, wasn't it?

That was why I'd ridden my bike up the coast, every mile bringing me closer to the isolation I craved. Isolation, or obliteration. Feeling nothing, or feeling too much, was the eternal problem I faced. I cared too much about being careless.

I didn't even know her name. Was that careless enough? Was it enough distance to protect me from disappointment again?

Her tongue flattened and stroked, and my internal monologue became only a static tone. An emergency alert flatline that made my eyes roll back. Her fingers dug into my thighs, and with that deep, husky voice, she said, "Look at me. Let me see those beautiful eyes."

She was gorgeous in a way that was terrifying. Lean and muscular, with rough hands that made me shiver as they spread my thighs. She lifted my leg, hooking it onto her shoulder, and I had to tangle my fingers in her long hair for balance.

"Please—oh my God, don't stop!"

My fingers knotted in her hair and she groaned, grasping my hips as she murmured, "Pull harder. Show me how good it feels."

For a few moments, I wasn't thinking about the miles behind me or the miles ahead. I wasn't thinking about my ex-fiancé or the indent his ring left on my finger. I wasn't hearing the endless echo of him saying, "It's all too much. I'm sorry."

No, in that moment, I was entirely hers. Every tense muscle, every shuddering nerve, every inch of shivering skin. She possessed me with tongue, lips, and fingers.

I wanted to call her name, if only I knew what it was.

STANDING IN THE parking lot outside the bar, we shared a joint. The night was desolate and cold, the air sticky with ocean salt. We couldn't see the waves beyond the towering pines, but we could hear them.

"Do you come here often?" I wanted to seem suave and disinterested, but I sounded too hopeful. Too invested.

She took a long, slow drag. She was close to my age, somewhere in her late twenties, but there was a seriousness about her face that made her seem older. A hollowness to her cheekbones that looked tired and grim.

She was a closed book but I couldn't stop staring at the cover, tormented by the unreadable words within.

"You won't see me again," she said, winking at me as she exhaled. Like it was a reassurance, not a regret.

It wasn't until we said our good-byes and she walked away that I realized she never answered a single question I asked her. She was a nameless stranger, coming from nowhere and headed toward nothing. By morning, she'd seem like a dream.

She was the first person I'd been with since Colin, which meant . . .

Nothing. It meant nothing.

As I stood outside my motel room at 2 a.m., my mind was churning too much to sleep. I reached for my ring finger, momentarily filled with alarm when I felt the naked indent of missing jewelry. It had been a month since Colin called off our wedding. Twenty-eight days since he packed up all his things and left. Twenty-five days since he said he "just wasn't ready." Twenty-two days since I found out there was someone else.

Sniffling from the cold, I swiped my hand across my nose before inhaling another lungful of skunky smoke from my vape. The thought of going inside and lying in an empty bed, staring at the ceiling until sleep offered deliverance, made my chest tight. But so too did the thought of sitting out here until dawn burned through the clouds and the sun rose on a new day while I still clung to the last one.

Dry leaves rattled in the trees. The road was empty, traveled only by the fog. The bright blinking VACANCY sign, hanging in the front office window, tinted the damp air blue.

A sudden cry split the night, but it was only the shriek of a bobcat. Bloodcurdling, yes, but after a lifetime of camping trips, I'd heard it before. Still, my paranoia was exacerbated by the weed. I felt exposed, watched. A predator lurked somewhere out there in the trees, and I couldn't even see it.

But it could probably see me.

"Chill out, Salem," I whispered, hoping the sound of my own voice would make it feel less lonely out here. Spooky feelings aside, I needed to go to bed.

I had a ferry to catch in the morning.

Salem

Blackridge Island

B Y NOON THE NEXT DAY, I WAS SEATED ON A DAMP WOODEN bench at the stern of a boat, my bike braced against my knees as we rocked over waves as gray as the sky. Salty ocean air whipped across my face, the windchill cutting mercilessly through my jacket.

The website for Balfour Bed-and-Breakfast hadn't given any details about the ferry ride required to reach it; now I understood why. Planes, trains, boats, buses—I preferred my feet on solid ground, thank you very much. Or on the pedals of my bike. Every rolling wave felt as if it was going to launch my stomach up into my throat.

Besides myself, there was only one other passenger on board. A young woman, wearing a thin gray raincoat over her long skirt, sat huddled and shivering on the opposite side of the deck. She wasn't dressed warmly enough for the weather and looked miserable, so I dug my extra hoodie out of my backpack and approached her.

"Here, take this." I offered the clothing and she jolted, staring up at me with wide, bloodshot eyes. "It's okay. I don't need it."

She looked at the jacket but didn't take it. She huddled over again, arms wrapped around herself, ignoring me. She began to murmur, her words quick and frantic, "Our Father . . . hallowed be thy name . . . thy will be done . . . deliver us . . . deliver us . . ."

With a pit in my stomach, I returned to my seat. Her voice was drowned out by the waves, but every now and then, the wind would carry her words to me as she continued to pray.

Fortunately, within an hour, Blackridge Island's craggy black cliffs were visible on the horizon. I walked to the bow for a clearer look. It was a mountainous place, covered in a thick expanse of dark trees. The B&B's website promised fields of wildflowers, stunning ocean cliffs, creeks, and waterfalls.

But today, Blackridge was wrapped in a thin fog. Waves slammed against the towering ridgeline, churning in a dangerous riptide along the rocky shore. A lighthouse stood on a narrow outcropping to the west, but no light shone within. It was a sleeping sentinel above the stormy seas.

The ferry turned eastward, and the waves calmed as we entered a narrow bay. Wooden houses clustered along the shore, painted various shades of blue, white, and gray. The docks were surrounded by fishing boats, numerous gulls perched upon them. Their beady eyes watched me as we docked, their haunting cries echoing across the bay.

As I prepared to wheel my bike across the gangway, the praying woman rushed past me. She was panting heavily, her long hair soaked and wind-whipped. She sprinted down the dock and collapsed on the shore, weeping loudly.

I looked at the crew, but they barely acknowledged her or me, keeping their gazes focused on their work. A few passersby on the road glanced at her, but no one stopped. What was wrong with everyone? This woman was obviously having a crisis, and even though my hands shook, I hurriedly pushed my bike down the dock toward her.

But someone else reached her before I could.

A pretty woman with blonde hair stood over her. Her lips were moving, but I couldn't hear what conversation passed between them. The crying woman raised her head, her cheeks streaked with tears, and the woman standing over her smiled.

Something about that smile made me feel cold.

The distraught woman climbed to her feet and trudged northward on the road, the other woman offered no assistance. She watched, as did I, until the woman disappeared when the path curved into the trees.

When I looked back to the shore again, the blonde woman was now staring at *me*, and her smile was gone.

Thoroughly uncomfortable, I put my head down and pulled out my phone to check the directions to my lodging. I was right on time, with an hour to spare before I had to check in. I also had no cell service, which was . . . good. That was what I'd wanted out of this trip: a forcible break from life as I knew it. Reconnection with nature, with myself.

I didn't need to see Colin's social media posts featuring the new "love of his life." A love who wasn't crushed by the weight of anxiety, who loved the idea of a wild Vegas honeymoon and expensive clubs, who was spontaneous and carefree.

Someone who wasn't *me*.

Walking my bicycle along the footpath, I admired the old wooden shops perched along the rocky shore. A market advertising soda and scoops of ice cream caught my eye. There was nowhere to lock my bike, so I hesitantly left it next to the door as I went inside.

The market had all the usual supplies, with the distinct exception of any beer, wine, or liquor. A wood-burning stove crackled in the corner, a clowder of cats sleeping contentedly around it. A community bulletin board hung on the wall with printed fliers advertising chickens for sale, the schedule for the ferry, and a poster for the upcoming harvest festival.

There was also a handwritten verse thumbtacked to the top of the board: *For the wages of sin is death, but the gift of God is eternal life in Christ Jesus our Lord.*

Turning down the next aisle, I jumped in surprise to find the blonde woman from the beach standing there.

"Hello," she said sweetly, and a little too eagerly. "Did you just get off the ferry?"

Nodding, I said, "Yeah, just arrived. I'm actually heading up to the bed-and-breakfast—"

"Balfour Manor," she said, cutting me off. "It's quite a walk. Not many people come this late in the season, except hunters. I'm Ruth Miller. Is there anything I can help you find, Miss . . . ?"

"Salem. Salem Lockard." I extended my hand and she took it politely, although she grimaced a bit when she touched me.

"Salem . . . like where they burned the witches?" She smiled widely, and I wasn't sure what to say, so I laughed awkwardly.

"None of the accused witches in Salem were burned, actually," I said. Her eyebrows shot up, disappearing under her bangs, and I regretted bothering to correct her. Hurriedly, I changed the subject. "That woman who was crying, she came on the ferry with me. Was she okay?"

Ruth laughed lightly. "Of course. She was just happy to be home."

"Happy" certainly wasn't the word I would have used.

"She's a friend of mine," Ruth explained, although I hadn't asked. My eagerness to get out of this interaction was growing. "We grew up here together. She allowed herself to believe that the grass was greener out there." She stared beyond me, toward the door and the churning ocean beyond. "But God called her home, where she belongs. She will be fine. This was merely a lesson to be learned. As the Lord has commanded us, we must lean not upon our own understandings or be swayed by ignorant passions."

If she'd hoped to reassure me, it hadn't worked. Fighting my urge to scurry for the door, I said, "Well, I'm . . . glad . . . to hear that. Um, sorry, do you happen to carry American Spirits?"

Any semblance of a smile remaining on her face vanished.

"No. We don't carry cigarettes." Her voice was ice-cold and disgusted, as if I'd asked if I could piss on her floor.

"Does anywhere else around here—"

"No. Is there anything else?"

Her arms were folded, her thin lips pursed. I wasn't getting anywhere with her, and clearly she didn't have what I needed.

"No, I . . . no. Thank you."

"God bless!" she said, all cheerful smiles again as I headed out the door. I smoked weed far more often than cigarettes, but I still liked to have a pack on hand just in case. Especially lately, I'd been reaching for the cancer sticks more and more.

No better time to quit, it seemed.

THE BAY WAS swiftly swallowed by the forest as I cycled westward. The road was rutted with puddles that splashed my pant legs with mud, but I didn't mind. The air was crisp and clean, filling my lungs with the scent of pine and ocean spray. Birds twittered in the gnarled boughs overhead, and elk grazed among the blackberry brambles along the road. Occasionally, I would ride past someone out walking, or pull aside to allow an old vehicle to pass. Goats and sheep bleated from their fields, and dogs barked at me from farmhouse porches.

When the road forked, I took the narrow western path, following a wooden sign with an arrow that said simply, *Balfour B&B*.

My bike was equipped with mountain tires for the difficult terrain, and my heart raced with excitement as I navigated the steep trail. The higher I went, the colder the wind became, and the louder the roaring crash of the waves grew.

Rayne Balfour. That was the name of the woman I was supposed to check in with, the owner of the house. She'd been brusque over email, but the descriptions of the place on her website were more than enough to sell me on it.

A fully restored 1920s manor with beautiful gardens and meals served by an executive chef. For the next few weeks, I would spend my days biking through the forest and evenings curled up by the fire with a hot toddy and a good book. Two weeks of relaxation to reset my brain and let me get back to living.

Grabbing my brakes, I skidded to a halt before two pale stone pillars. They framed a black gate with an iron archway reading *Deus Videt Omnia*. The driveway beyond was short, and a meandering stairway led up the terraced hillside. The manor itself was hidden beyond the trees; only her sharp spires could be seen above the swaying pines.

A sudden sense of trepidation settled over me as I entered the gate. My tires crunched on the gravel path until I stood at the foot of the long narrow stairway leading to the house. With a sigh, I propped my bike against the wall, collected my bag, and began climbing the hillside like a long-suffering pack mule.

The steps were slippery with moss, a dip worn into their centers from decades of feet traversing them. The terrace gardens overflowed with fragrant flowers and vibrant ferns. Massive old pine trees clung to the hillside, their twisted roots making ripples beneath the soil.

As I crested the hill and emerged on the other side of the trees, the Balfour house revealed itself in all its intimidating glory.

It was tall and dark, with a facade of gray stone cloaked in ivy. The roof was steeply pitched, crowned with chimneys leaking tendrils of white smoke and spires adorned with birds' nests. Cherubs and gargoyles were carved into the stones around the entryway and decorated the fountain in the middle of the courtyard. Narrow windows lined the exterior, peeking out from the vines.

Those windows were like eyes, watching me as I craned my neck to look up. Making my way slowly across the courtyard, I paused to stare into the fountain's murky depths. The water wasn't flowing; plants and algae had overtaken the basin.

Distracted, I almost shrieked when I rounded the fountain and came face-to-face with a wolf, staring me down with pale blue eyes.

"Oh God, um, hello . . . hi . . ." I froze as the big black dog snuffled its wet nose against me. Okay, maybe it wasn't a wolf. It was a giant, fluffy shepherd of some kind. He had a thick leather collar on, and after giving him a few moments to figure out if he liked how I smelled, I caught hold of his tag.

"Loki," I said, reading the name engraved there. "Are you my escort?" He seemed friendly, although not particularly enthused, so I put on my best who's-a-good-boy? voice and said, "Such a big gorgeous boy, aren't you? Aren't you?"

That got his tail wagging. He let me ruffle his fluffy shoulders before he trotted away toward the front door, and I followed.

By the entrance, a copper plaque was affixed to the wall, inscribed with the words *Balfour Manor began construction in 1919 following Henry M. Balfour's return from World War I. Originally intended as the Balfour family's primary residence, it is now a bed-and-breakfast, welcoming guests from around the world.*

The door was massive and made of solid wood; I assumed it had been there since the place was built. It creaked loudly as I pushed it open, and the dog shook himself off before trotting in ahead of me.

I scraped my muddy boots on the doormat before entering. The foyer was warm, scented lightly with woodsmoke and nutmeg. The gleaming chandelier reflected off the waxed wood floor, and paintings and old portraits covered the papered walls. There was a stairway on my right, the wall lined with even more art and photography, and a hallway straight ahead.

Reception was to my left. Behind the large wood desk, a dozen old skeleton keys hung from the wall beneath a series of yellowed photographs. There was machinery too: a radio of some kind with a handheld microphone, and an old computer that looked straight out of the '90s.

No one was here. At least, until a door behind the counter burst open, thrown back by a teetering tower of cardboard boxes. I scrambled away as the boxes hurtled toward me, then were loudly set down by the tall, muscular brunette carrying them. Her hair was bound in a ponytail, and her back was to me as she ripped open one of the boxes and rummaged around, muttering weights and numbers aloud.

Awkwardly, I cleared my throat.

I'd never seen someone turn around so fast. One moment she was burrowing into the box; the next, she whirled around with a string of curses, holding aloft a potato as if to launch it at me.

For a moment, I stared in stunned disbelief. Not because she was holding a potato, but because I knew her.

The stranger from the bar.

The nameless woman who'd drawn out my soul with her tongue and swallowed it whole.

3

Rayne

Unwanted Guest

"**O**H, HI!"

Oh, no.

There was no denying it was her. Wide hazel eyes, the same color as rich summer honey. Short chestnut brown hair, ruffled from the wind. Pale skin, sunburned cheeks, and a freckled nose. Lips the color of a blushing peach. She was smiling at me as if she was about to disintegrate but was sorry about it, as if the bright red embarrassment flushing her face was a personal fault.

She couldn't have known her embarrassment was making this worse. Her wide eyes took me straight back to the last and only night I'd met her.

Looking up at her in the lights' neon glow as she fell apart on my tongue. Listening to her whimper and moan, a song just for me.

Like a fever dream. Or a nightmare.

Dreams were supposed to stay in the night, in the dark space outside of reality. They weren't supposed to waltz up to you in broad daylight with a blush and a smile.

"I'm here to check in?" she said, her smile shrinking with worry. Hurriedly, I tossed aside the potato and ripped my earbuds out. "My reservation is under Lockard. Salem Lockard."

"Salem," I repeated, her name tingling like candy on my tongue. Her face lit up—

Whoa.

There it was again: the same bizarre feeling I'd experienced when I saw her across the bar the other night. A feeling of recognition, an incomprehensible draw.

Static buzzed loudly from the CB radio, making us both jump. A youthful voice crackled over the speaker: "Seahawk to Dragon! Come in, Dragon!"

Muttering an apologetic "'scuse me" to Salem, I slid into my chair behind the counter and grabbed the mic.

"Rebecca, I'm a little busy right now. Is everything okay?"

Try as I might not to look at my unwanted guest, my eyes were inevitably drawn back. She was wearing skintight biking shorts over thick leggings, everything in a mismatched pattern of earthy colors. It was fascinating, distracting, irritating—shit, looking at her was a whirlwind of feelings I wasn't prepared for.

"Noooo, not Rebecca!" the little voice responded. "I'm Seahawk, remember?"

With a sigh, I gave Salem my very best customer service smile. "I'll be right with you in, just, uh, one second." Speaking into the microphone again, I said, "Seahawk, this radio is only supposed to be for emergencies. *Is* there an emergency?"

A long, guilt-laden pause came before she answered. "No. But I'm bored!"

"The radio isn't a toy, Seahawk. Go play with your sister, okay? I'll check in later. Dragon is over and out."

Cranking down the volume, I paused to take a deep breath before I turned around. Salem was beaming, rocking from her heels to her toes. Her tiny dangling mushroom earrings swung with her. Loki had already taken a liking to her; the big ham was at her side, nuzzling his wet nose into her hand.

There was a gargantuan elephant in the room, and if I didn't acknowledge it soon, it was going to crush me.

My heart sped up as I found her name in the reservations list. Salem Lockard. My lips silently formed the name before daring to speak it out loud.

"Miss Lockard?" I confirmed.

She eagerly nodded. I cursed as I waited for my ancient booking system to load, resisting the urge to slap the side of the PC. It was always slow, but with her standing there looking at me, I swore it took a million years.

"This is such a crazy coincidence, I mean, what are the chances?"

Oh God, she kept talking. Her voice was shaky, quick and nervous as she tugged at her coat sleeves. There were frayed threads sticking out of the fabric, as if that was a frequent habit.

I wasn't prepared for this. This was why I went to the mainland to hook up: so I would never see those hookups again. So they wouldn't show up at my doorstep wanting to spend the night.

I smiled at her. Sort of. The expression was smile-shaped and felt mildly friendly, at least. "Welcome to Blackridge, Salem."

Her expression changed. It softened. As if a little of her nervousness disappeared. I suddenly felt like I was back in elementary school again and had just been handed a gold star

25

sticker. Frowning in an attempt to smother the weird sensation, I spread several pamphlets on the counter before her. "This is a map of the island, and this is a map of the trails. The only one currently closed is the Lighthouse Loop. It's too late in the season to go out on the peninsula."

She collected the maps, wrinkling them as she stuffed them into her jacket. "Is it true that the island closes down in winter?"

"Not exactly. The ferry closes down, so no one is coming or going. Starts in autumn, not winter. You're staying here for two weeks so . . ." I frowned. Why the hell had I booked her for these days? Talk about cutting it close. "You'll be catching the last ferry off the island. Make sure you don't miss it."

"I guess I'll have a pretty cool place to stay if I do miss it, right?" She laughed. It was the kind of laughter that was contagious, that almost made me giddy.

But it was too loud. It echoed off the walls and I flinched, half anticipating hearing a yell in return.

Pull it together, Rayne.

"No one stays past November first," I said. "No one wants to either, if they know what's good for them. The weather is harsh. There's rain, sleet, and snow. The waves get big enough to slam any boat that gets too close against the rocks. The wind is strong enough to down a chopper, and there's nowhere for planes to land. So don't miss the ferry."

Her throat bobbed as she gulped. "Got it."

Snatching her key from one of the hooks behind me, I came around the desk. "You'll be in room six."

I held out my free hand expectantly. Without missing a beat, she grasped my hand, giving it a shake.

"Your bag," I said, and her face fell with embarrassment. "Do you want me to carry it?"

"Oh, um—right, sure, thank you." She hurriedly handed it over, ducking her head.

The warmth of her palm left an imprint on my own, and I flexed my hand on the strap of her backpack as I carried it up the stairs.

"Dining room is past reception, down the hall, on the left. Big room, you can't miss it." I said, giving my usual new-guest spiel. "Breakfast is served from six a.m. to nine a.m. Dinner from six p.m. to nine p.m. Pantry and microwave are available twenty-four-seven. If you feel like walking or riding to Marihope, there's a restaurant there, a couple cafes, and a market."

I reached the top of the stairway; she didn't. She was still on the landing, staring at a massive portrait of a dark-haired priest.

"Henry Balfour," I said. "My grandfather. He built this place."

"He was a preacher?" she said as she hurried to catch up with me.

"A soldier first. Then a preacher. Men of the cloth run in the family. My father was a preacher too."

If only holiness were as hereditary as greed.

"Is there someplace I can store my bike?" she said. "I left it in the driveway at the bottom of the hill."

"I'll put it in the shed for you. Do you plan on riding while you're here?"

"Yeah! Mountain biking is kind of my thing."

She'd mentioned at the bar that she'd spent the last few days cycling up the coast from San Francisco. Meanwhile, the farthest I'd ever been from home was the Washington coast. Like so many who'd grown up here, Blackridge was a part of me I couldn't escape. As if the roots of these trees had grown into me, and try as I might to break free, their hold would stretch but never snap.

They would always pull me back.

"The trails here are pretty advanced. They're dangerous, so . . ." My warning only made her smile widen. She was clearly capable of taking care of herself, despite her bouncy, nervous appearance. Her backpack was heavy enough to make my shoulder ache as I led her through the upstairs hall. "I'm sure you've noticed the cell service out here is spotty at best. I suggest carrying a satellite GPS. It's easy to get lost in the forest. If you don't have one, I have a spare you can borrow."

I stopped outside her door, upon which was fixed a copper plate with the room number, 6. The old key clicked loudly as I turned the lock and opened the door. It was a corner room, and I was pleased to hear her gasp of awe as she took in the view.

Across the churning waves, the Blackridge lighthouse stood tall and proud on the forested peninsula. Fog hugged its white walls, waves crashing against the black cliffs upon which it stood.

"It's been out of commission since the eighties," I said as she rushed to the window to look out. "So don't worry, there won't be any light to keep you awake." Crouching in front of the fireplace, I stacked some wood and got it lit. "There should be enough firewood for your first few days, but if you need more, just ask. The house has a furnace, but the nights especially can get cold."

With the fire crackling and warmth slowly filling the room, I stood to find her sitting on the bed, watching me. Her legs were too short to touch the floor, and she leaned back on her palms as she said, "Thanks for doing that. It's been a while since I lit a fire myself."

"No problem." My voice cracked. Brilliant. Why the hell was I just standing there like moss on a log? What was I waiting for? For her to fling her clothes off and welcome me into her bed?

God, no, bad thoughts, those were *bad thoughts*.

"Keep in mind, the house is old," I said, lingering. But she looked at me with rapt attention. She hung on my words and I didn't know whether to be flattered or terrified. "There's weird noises. Bumps, groans, creaking. With the forest around us, you'll hear some bizarre things. Just don't be scared." I headed for the door, but almost immediately turned back. "If you need anything, just use the landline next to the bed to call down to reception."

Okay, time to go.

Nope, I turned back again.

"And if I'm not at reception, you can come to my room. On the third floor. Second to last door on the left."

I never told guests where my room was. It was none of their damn business.

Even once her door was shut behind me, I didn't go. I stood there, listening but telling myself I wasn't, for far too long.

The pipes rumbled as water began to flow. She was filling the bath. Part of me wanted to press my ear against the door and listen for the soft sound of her clothing dropping to the floor. For the gentle splash of her feet entering the water.

But at the risk of acting like a perverted shut-in, I hurried away, softening my steps out of fear she'd hear me go.

She was only here for two weeks. I could act normal for two weeks, couldn't I?

THE SMELL OF her haunted me. Jasmine and lemon. Even after stripping off my clothes and stuffing them angrily into the laundry basket, her perfume remained, hovering around me.

29

Wearing only my underwear, I sat on the bench seat before my open window as I rolled a joint. Goose bumps prickled up my arms. The night air was bitingly cold on my bare skin, but it would make crawling into bed that much more comfortable. Pleasure was nothing without pain.

The crickets' song joined with the distant crash of the ocean. When I was a child, I would pretend the sound of the waves was a tiger roaring in the distance. The fantasy helped distract me; a distant enemy was less frightening than the ones in my own house.

Holding the joint to my lips, I lit up. The thin trail of smoke seeped out the window, vanishing into the night sky.

Was Salem looking out her window too? Did she treasure the moon's light, the cold gaze of the stars? Did she stare at them and feel small, inspired, intimidated? Did she wonder if it was worth trying at all, when this world was so vast and humans knew so little?

Pressing in my earbuds, I pulled up my favorite playlist on my phone and let Fleetwood Mac fill my ears. For a few moments, my world was at peace.

Then I saw movement reflected in the glass as my bedroom door swung open.

The back of my neck prickled. I didn't turn. The hallway outside was dark; in the reflection, it was nothing more than a black void.

Slowly, I removed my earbuds. Eerie silence greeted me, far louder than the music.

A floorboard creaked. Then another. My mouth was so dry I could barely swallow as I got to my feet and faced the open door.

The creaking came steadily closer, and I stared into the empty space until I swore I could see a silhouette in the dark.

Harsh breathing, as if every gasp was whistling through rotten lungs, emanated from the emptiness.

Prayers rushed to the tip of my tongue, but I didn't give them a voice.

"Come on," I hissed. I took another drag on the joint, forcing myself to stand strong. "Move. *Move.*"

Every step toward the door was painful. My heart threatened to burst through my ribs. A familiar smell hit me—pungent mold and rotten blood. The knob was freezing as I grasped it, pushed it closed, and turned the lock.

For several suffocating seconds, I listened to the harsh breathing on the other side. The sound was persistent, unending, like nails on a chalkboard. I only found relief when I snatched up my earbuds again and put them in.

Only then did I release my breath. But I still stared at the door as I climbed into bed, pulling the blankets around my shivering limbs. Only when my joint had been reduced to nothing more than a roach did I start to feel a little better.

I couldn't allow Salem to distract me, especially not now. The nights were growing longer and the cold was deepening. The sheriff thought I was crazy, but I knew it already wasn't safe to be out after dark, no matter how early in the season it was.

If the angel wasn't awake yet, it would be soon.

Then hunting season would begin, and whether I was predator or prey, I wouldn't know until it was too late.

Salem

Bear Season

IOR THE NEXT TWO WEEKS, I WOULD BE LIVING WITH A woman who had tongue-fucked me in a bar bathroom stall. A woman who had so thoroughly corrupted my soul that even two days later, thinking about what we'd done together made my knees go weak.

"Rayne," I whispered her name aloud as I lay in bed that morning. I wanted to test it out, to see how the syllables felt when I spoke like a lover, or moaned like a whore.

God, this was bad. I was the *worst* in awkward situations. The moment I saw her face, I was so flustered my filter disappeared and I started babbling nonsense. Considering her stoicism, she probably thought I was too loud and annoying. Which was totally fair. It wouldn't be the first time I'd scared someone off with my lack of social skills.

It didn't *mean* anything. Sex was just sex, and I was raised not to be ashamed of my ethical slut activities.

Yet as I walked to the dining room, there was a tickle of excitement in my stomach. Would Rayne eat with the guests? I wanted to see her again, but I had no idea what I wanted to say. It was that giddy, bubbly feeling of a crush—a sensation I didn't think I was capable of experiencing anymore.

But it still meant nothing.

The dining room was spacious. The ceiling was crisscrossed with timber beams, and a great chandelier hung over the tables, of which there were a dozen scattered throughout the space. Floor-to-ceiling windows looked out upon an ornamental garden at the back of the house, the yard so thick with flora it was like gazing into a jungle.

Several other guests were already seated. The savory smell of eggs and bacon hung in the air, and my stomach snarled for food. I was able to get a glimpse through a swinging door into the kitchen, where staff bustled around a steaming stove and pulled fresh bread out of the oven. A tall, bald man with a thick French accent, who introduced himself as Albert, appeared to take my breakfast order. He was graciously patient as I gasped with excitement over the food choices.

While I waited for my meal to be cooked, I served myself coffee and orange juice before choosing a small table for one next to the windows.

The sky was clear, pale blue. Birds bathed in puddles on the lawn, fluffing their feathers as they sang. Beyond a tall hedge, I could barely see the steep glass roof of a greenhouse. A stone stairway covered in moss led beyond the hedges and out of my sight.

"—heard she's been missing since last week, you'd think people would be talking about it—"

The hushed words dragged my head away from the garden, and I sipped my coffee as I surveyed the room. It was one of a group of hikers that had spoken, but they lowered their voice again and I couldn't make out the words. There were a few couples and groups of three and four seated around me; I was apparently the only solo traveler here.

Two middle-aged men in large camo jackets and pants were seated at the table directly next to mine. Their plates were scraped clean, and they were both sipping mugs of coffee. The one closest to me was polishing something on his lap, and I leaned over to get a better look.

I nearly tipped backwards in my chair when I realized he was holding a rifle.

The men glanced up at the noise. The one with the rifle gave me a friendly smile.

"Well, well, a new guest, eh? Good morning!" Following my gaze, he said hurriedly, "Oh, don't you worry, miss. Ain't never loaded at the table. Can't be neglecting her though." He patted the butt of the rifle affectionately. "Out there, this is the only thing between me and meeting the good Lord before my time."

The other man shook his head. "Don't let him scare you. I'm George. This is Martin. You just check in?"

"Yesterday," I said. They reminded me of my uncles from Montana, and I immediately felt a liking for them. "I'm guessing you're hunters?"

Martin nodded deeply. "Yep. Black bears."

I almost snorted coffee out my nose. "Bears?" I squeaked. "There are *bears* on this island?"

But another voice interrupted, "Martin, George, stop scaring my guests."

Every head turned as Rayne strode through the dining room. Worn leather boots were laced up to her knees, and her camo coat was unbuttoned, fluttering behind her like a cape as she walked. Loki trotted at her heels, seemingly oblivious to all the delicious food around him.

Did she realize her presence snatched the air straight from my lungs? Did she hear how much my heart quickened?

"Yes, mother," Martin grumbled, putting the rifle down under the table.

Rayne didn't pause. She passed me with barely a glance and poked her head into the kitchen, calling out something in French before she was answered in kind. Moments later, Albert returned with my order, along with something I didn't expect.

A gin and tonic.

"Our apologies for the wait," he said. I hadn't waited long at all and was going to say so, but he disappeared as quickly as he'd arrived.

My cheesy, vegetable-stuffed omelet looked perfect, and I was about to dig in when I got the distinct feeling someone was watching me.

When I glanced over my shoulder, Rayne was standing there and my heart leapt into my throat.

"Did you have a good night?" she said. She had one hand on the back of my chair, and the other she leaned on the table, mere centimeters away from my fingers. That closeness was like an electrical current tingling through my skin.

"It was good. Really comfortable. I stayed warm too; thanks again for the fire."

"I'm glad to hear." Her voice was low, loud enough for me and no one else. She reached inside her coat, frowned for a moment, then withdrew a shiny silver key and held it out to me. "This is for the shed at the bottom of the hill. You can store your bike there as you need. I'm the only other person with a key, so no one will mess with it."

"Thank—you." Before I could even finish the sentence, she'd turned away and walked off again, Loki obediently following.

"Well, I'll be damned." Martin chuckled. "Haven't heard that woman say more'n a sentence since we arrived. Wonder what makes you so special, little miss?"

With a shrug, I tried to drown the butterflies in my stomach with more coffee.

THE THIRD FLOOR of the manor was off-limits to guests, but that still left me with plenty of house to explore. The common room was farther down the hall on the first floor, the walls lined with book-covered shelves. Comfortable chairs and couches sat on thick rugs with elaborate designs. I would have stayed, but several other guests were already seated there and I felt awkward intruding.

While the manor's individual rooms were comfortably warm, the hallways were freezing. As I climbed the stairway, I could see my breath clouding when I exhaled. Not even the clear skies allowed the sun's warmth to reach us.

Emerging to the second floor, I softened my footsteps as I walked past the guest rooms. The entire place was impeccably clean. Not a single picture frame had dust; there wasn't a speck of dirt on the floorboards, or a smudge on a single window. It didn't have that classic old-house smell either. I suspected there were scented filters in the air vents.

But as I was passing the stairway to the third floor, I got a whiff of something horrendous.

Abruptly covering my mouth with my hand, I stared up the dimly lit stairway. A large marble statue stood on the landing above, depicting a veiled woman with clasped hands. It was difficult to see, but the beautiful wallpaper behind the statue appeared water damaged, with strange ripples and blooming patches of black mold.

Alarmed, I narrowed my eyes and stepped closer, ascending several stairs. It must have been a trick of the light; the mold melted into the shadows, disappearing entirely by the time I laid my hand against the wall.

Confused, I brushed my fingers across the pristine wallpaper, searching for any sign of the rot. But nothing remained. *Strange.*

Suddenly, loud footsteps charged down the stairs toward me. I startled, nearly stumbling as I ran back down the steps to get out of the way of whoever was coming. Gasping, hand on my pounding heart, I reached my bedroom door in a matter of seconds. With the key in the lock, I stared back toward the staircase to the third floor.

No one appeared.

I waited an entire minute. Then two. No footsteps ascended, and no one came down. Were they waiting on the stairs? Why? Who? I'd seen no one.

Cautiously, I approached the staircase again. I sincerely expected to find one of the guests playing a trick on me, but when I looked, only the statue was there.

Salem

Fantasies and Faucets

M Y SHOES SQUELCHED ON THE WET GRASS AS I WALKED
across the garden, carrying a mug of steaming tea. A
chorus of birds rustled in the bushes, shaking droplets of rain
from the leaves. The sun was sinking beneath the horizon, all
that remained of its fiery glow now hidden below the ocean
cliffs.

My phone pinged with an alert, but it was just an event
reminder for tomorrow. Swiping it open, my heart dropped
when I saw the notification: *Flight to Vegas—Honeymoon
Time!!!*

The pit inside me grew deeper.

It wasn't that I missed Colin; I'd mourned our relationship
at first, but now, I was mourning the future I thought I'd have.
The life I'd built up in my mind had crashed and burned, and
part of me still felt like it was my fault.

With a heavy sigh, I sat on a stone bench in the middle of the garden and stared up at the house. The windows were aglow, and there, in her bedroom on the third floor, was Rayne.

She didn't see me—or at least, she wasn't looking at me. Her hair was down, long and loose like it had been at the bar. Her lips moved, singing along to music I could faintly hear.

She swayed slightly, rubbing the back of her neck. Like she wanted to dance, but it was too embarrassing in her own presence.

In one smooth motion, she pulled her shirt off over her head and tossed it to the floor. A black sports bra covered her, but she reached for that too, and I—I should have looked away.

I didn't.

Her back muscles flexed as she lowered her arms. Her skin looked soft and warm in the meager light, and I imagined what it would be like to touch her again. To caress her arms, kiss her neck. Make her moan like she did to me. Her hair swept her lower back as she ran her fingers through it, then turned to the side . . .

She hadn't taken her clothes off during our time together at the bar. The sight of her made something desperate awaken inside me—something starving.

I'd gone through my fair share of romances and heartbreaks. After Colin, I'd convinced myself the foolish part of me who could give away her heart was dead.

Apparently, that part was dangerously alive and kicking. Lust wasn't love, but it was still too damn close.

Rayne stepped out of my line of sight, and the spell was broken. I got up abruptly, so flustered I left my mug of tea behind as I hurried out of the garden.

I MAY HAVE been unexpectedly single for the first time in three years, but that didn't mean I wasn't prepared to take care of myself. Frankly, the universe owed me some orgasms at this point.

My waterproof vibrator and the claw-foot bathtub in my room were about to become my best friends. With the air full of steam and comfortably hot water surrounding me, I imagined it was Rayne's fingers trailing down my chest instead of my own. Her hands squeezing my breasts, rolling and pinching my nipples between her fingers, talking to me sweet and filthy, "That's it, pretty girl. Does that feel good? Do you want more?"

I groaned, imagining her husky voice whispering in my ear. Switching on the vibrator, I gasped when I pressed it against my clitoris and tingles exploded through my nerves. My legs shook, overwhelmed for a moment . . .

"Such a good girl. Take it for me."

Waves of need roiled my stomach. On my knees, I leaned over the edge of the tub. One hand held the vibrator between my legs while the other supported my chest. Eyes closed, I imagined her behind me, fingers teasing me.

"That's it. You look so fucking sexy, Salem. God, I could eat you alive."

A whimper exploded from me, unbidden. Colin had once bragged to me about what a "freak" he was in bed, but that man was as vanilla as they came. My uncertain requests for kinky play were usually taken as complaints—blows to his ego—and then brushed off as disturbing or dangerous.

Rayne had no idea what I liked; she barely knew me. But for a few minutes, I imagined that she did. I imagined that I admitted every desire to her, and that when I did she gave me a dark grin and said, "Anything for my needy little slut."

My legs shook, and it was as if I wasn't in the bath at all anymore. In some wicked plane of my imagination, I was on all fours with Rayne curled over my back, her fingers inside me, one hand around my throat. Panting, pleasure building, I cried her name aloud and barely opened my eyes . . .

Someone was standing in the bathroom. A tall, red silhouette with long, dark hair, who seemed to subtly change and sway with the swirling steam.

A rush of cold air surrounded me. The light flickered. The figure moved, and I swore I caught a glimpse of a gaunt, bloody, corpse-like face—rotten lips pulled back from blackened teeth.

I screamed, flailing backwards. I tried to brace myself on the faucet but it broke away from the wall, water blasting from the broken pipe and pouring over me as I slipped and fell on my back—

"Fucking Christ!"

Rough hands pulled me from the tub. I was held—carried—out of the bathroom and dumped onto the bed, very wet and entirely naked. In the seconds it took me to sit up, one arm wrapped protectively around my chest, Rayne was already back in the bathroom, having turned off the water and now staring at the broken faucet.

"There was someone," I gasped breathlessly. "A person, there was—in the bathroom—"

Slowly, Rayne reached into the tub and pulled my vibrator from the water. Oh, God, now would be a perfect time to melt into the ground. She turned it off and set it aside on the sink, then grabbed a towel from the rack and brought it over, wrapping it around my shoulders as I shivered.

"Someone broke into your room?" she said, her tone skeptical.

I shrugged helplessly. "I don't know! Someone was standing there, but I didn't recognize them!"

Her hand rubbing slowly on my back, she said, "Are you hurt?"

"No." A lie. My pride was aching. "I swear I saw someone. I opened my eyes and they . . . they were there . . . right there." I jabbed my finger at the exact spot on the floor where the figure had stood.

Rayne entered the bathroom again. She drained the tub, she looked behind the door, in the cabinets. She even searched the closet. With every passing second, I felt more and more like a child crying about a bogeyman under my bed.

I could practically hear Colin's voice telling me, "It's in your head. It's your anxiety talking. Just pop a pill and chill out."

Silly, anxious Salem. Scaring herself again over nothing.

My chest was tight, and adrenaline bloomed behind my ribs. She didn't believe me. She thought I was a liar, I was making things up, I was *crazy*. My throat constricted, eyes stinging. Goddamn it, I didn't want to cry in front of her.

"I know what I saw," I said desperately. "Something was there."

"I believe you," she said gently. "Can you remember what they looked like?"

Desperately casting my mind back, I shook my head. "I don't know. It was foggy. They had long hair. They were wearing red, I think."

Of all things to get a reaction out of her, I hadn't expected it to be that. But she stiffened, and finally looked at me. *Really* looked, as if there were secrets written on my face.

"Did they say anything?"

I shook my head. My fear was slowly dissipating, leaving exhaustion in its place.

"Well, whoever they were, they're gone now," Rayne said, sighing heavily. "And I'm sure you don't want to stay in a room with a broken bathtub." She glared at the faucet, rubbing the back of her neck. "There's one other room with a similar view. It's on the third floor, so guests don't usually stay there, but it'll have to do. I'll give you a minute to get dressed."

I would have rather just gotten on the next boat and gone back to the mainland. Leave all my humiliation right here on the island and pretend this had never happened.

Instead, I collected my bruised pride and dressed myself. It felt as if her hands had left imprints on my body: The places she'd touched me when she scooped me up felt so warm. I tried to come up with something clever to say, some kind of joke I could make to ease the tension over breaking her things—but my mind was an embarrassed blank.

Had I simply seen a shadow and scared myself? Try as I might to recall a clear image of the intruder, I simply couldn't. Was I just tired? Hallucinating?

After dressing and gathering my things, I found Rayne waiting for me outside the door. She gave me a strange look as I emerged, staring at me as if she was imagining something else in my place.

"This way," she said, and I followed her down the hallway to the third floor. She walked ahead of me, marching like she was on a mission. She was only wearing socks, sweatpants, and a long-sleeved black shirt. Her hair was somewhat damp, wavy and loose, the fresh scent of shampoo wafting behind her. The certainty that I'd ruined her relaxing evening made me feel worse.

Still, it was a little exciting to follow her past the Employees Only sign to the third floor. Like the floor below, it was spotlessly clean, lit by the sconces lining the walls. There were no portraits here, however, unlike the rest of the house. The walls were entirely empty.

"I'm really sorry about the faucet," I said, unable to keep the apology back any longer. "I'll pay to fix it—"

She stopped before a closed door, rummaging in her pocket. "Don't worry about it. Shit breaks all the time. One of the fun perks of living in an old house."

Withdrawing a key, she opened the door and flicked on the lights inside. The room was larger than my previous one, with a view of the lighthouse to the northwest and windows overlooking the garden and greenhouse to the south. However, the furniture within wasn't as modern. There was a distinct smell of dust and the soft vanilla scent of old books.

"I usually don't put guests in here, so pardon the dust," she said. "The decor is a little dated, but it's all clean and functional. I'll get a fire going for you."

She didn't go far to collect some wood. She opened the door next to mine, and I got a glimpse of the room within. There was a big bed with green blankets, upon which Loki was sleeping. A bookshelf covered in old vinyls stood beside a record player and set of speakers. It was Rayne's bedroom.

Directly next door to me.

She returned with an armful of split logs as I dumped the contents of my backpack on the bed. As I organized my clothes, she got a fire going, and I kept sneaking glances at her over my shoulder. She took her time, tending the flames until they were crackling and the chilly room began to warm.

"I'll be next door," she said. "If you need anything."

"Okay. Thank you . . ."

She stood in the open doorway, hesitating, as if there was something she wanted to say. Her mouth twitched with something dangerously close to a smile. Then she reached for my doorknob, and as she pulled it closed, she said, "Have a good night, Salem. Try not to use up too much water with your shower fantasies."

6

Rayne

Specter

T HE SECOND FLOOR HALLWAY WAS SILENT. THAT SHOULDN'T have been unusual at 3 a.m., but I keenly knew the difference between silence and quiet. Quiet was normal.

But silence? The absence of breath, not a single creak from the boards beneath my feet, no howl of wind outside. As if this space was enveloped, cocooned outside of reality. But within cocoons, something usually lived.

Salem's previous room was ice-cold. The fire had gone out, and the humidity from her shower was gone. Not even the scent of her perfume remained. Instead, the aroma of mold and vegetal rot hung in the air.

Ingrained habit made me reach for the cross around my neck, tugging it back and forth along its chain as I stepped into the bathroom. Water was splashed all over the tile, the faucet lay in a puddle beneath the dripping pipe. Honestly, the situation was almost comical.

If it wasn't for something Salem said.

They were wearing red, I think.

Squatting down, I stroked my fingers over the boards where Salem claimed she saw the figure. They were wax-smooth, but a strange discoloration caught my eye. It was only visible from the right angle: the faint damp imprint of bare feet.

The bedroom door slammed shut, and I leapt to my feet. Hitting the light switch did nothing. How many countless times had I checked the wiring in this damned house? How many hours had I spent replacing and testing sockets and bulbs? Only to have them sapped, continually. As if light couldn't live in this place.

I knew one thing for certain: Salem's door had been locked when I tried to get in. Luckily I'd had my master key on me, otherwise I might have broken down the door when I heard her scream.

Whatever she'd seen couldn't be stopped by doors and locks.

With a sinking feeling in my stomach, I approached the door. The knob was ice-cold when I grasped it. My breath fogged in the air.

It was locked. The knob wouldn't turn.

Swallowing around the knot of tension in my throat, I pressed my ear against the door.

Tap. Tap. Tap.

As if someone was softly, continually, tapping their fingers against the other side.

The tiny cross dug into my palm as I gripped it tight. Prayers choked me, struggling to be given voice. But my tongue couldn't form those pleas anymore. There was no faith to carry them.

Out the window, across the water, the lighthouse glinted. As if its fire was still lit, as if it still had enough life to be a guide in the dark. A guide . . . or a trickster. Countless lives had been lost in the seas around Blackridge. Some said the ocean surrounding us carried more human bones than our own graveyards.

Then, as if someone had pressed their lips to the crack of the doorframe, the whispers began. Harsh, gargling, choked. I imagined blood foaming around cracked, rotten lips.

"To the bones, to the bones, to the bones, to the . . ."

On and on it went, and I dared not move, or scarcely breathe. But slowly, like a balloon losing its air, the whispers grew weaker. Fainter.

Then, it stopped.

The lighthouse was dark. The hall was quiet. When I turned the knob, the door swung open easily, and I stepped out into the empty hall.

But the cold still lingered.

"Leave her alone," I whispered. "It's not her fault. She has nothing to do with this."

Goose bumps prickled up my back. I heard nothing. Saw nothing. Yet I was entirely certain that someone was standing directly behind me.

I could feel their cold breath on my neck. Determinedly, I started walking. Fists clenched, head refusing to turn. When I passed the window, the moonlight cast my shadow onto the floor. It cast another shadow too.

Behind me. Looming over me. Hand outstretched as if to touch me.

I shook. I didn't turn.

"I'm not afraid of you. Leave her alone."

The shadow leaned closer. Rancid breath touched my cheek. Harsh, cold words grated from a rotten tongue: "The blood . . . the blood . . . in blood . . . do I . . . call thee . . ."

Don't look.

Don't run.

One foot in front of the other, I held my breath until I reached the stairs. Only then did I look back.

And I was alone. So very alone.

7

Salem

Watcher

THE DIRT TRAIL TWISTED AHEAD OF ME, NARROW HAIRPIN turns keeping me on high alert. My arms ached, my limbs tingling with adrenaline as I sped through the forest. Low-hanging tree boughs whipped by overhead, the air cold and fresh on my face. The path was craggy; rocks, puddles, and debris made it all the more difficult to traverse.

The forest felt clean and cool, pungent with the scent of loamy soil and fallen pine needles. Speeding through the trees, always on the edge of teetering from the path, wheels flying over every bump and dip, I could forget about everything else for a while.

I could forget about completely humiliating myself in front of Rayne. It was bad enough that I broke her bathtub. It was even worse that she'd found me naked and screaming with my vibrator. But the cherry on top was that the only explanation I had to give her sounded completely made up.

Of course she didn't believe me. I didn't even believe myself anymore.

As I sped around an embankment, then swooped through a dip, my tires left the ground. My stomach dropped, the incredible feeling of flying overtaking me before gravity sucked me down again. Breathless, I pumped the brakes just a bit as the trail turned sharply and became a steep grade, twisting and turning through moss-draped pines.

The trail forked, and I chose the narrower route. The signs meant to mark the trails were still standing, but the old wood was weather-eaten and rotten, the words long since washed away. But it was midday, and I didn't care where I was going. There was a map and compass in my pack if I truly got lost, and enough snacks to keep me going.

All I wanted was this feeling of freedom—even if it was full of risks. I swerved around a tree, realizing too late that I'd made a wrong turn and gone off the trail.

"Shit!" My tire struck something and twisted, and I couldn't catch my balance quickly enough. I plunged to the ground, knocking the wind out of myself as I rolled a short way through dirt and leaves.

For several moments, I lay still, flat on my back, staring up at the trees. Gulls cried as they swooped through the sky, their eerie calls echoing from the sea, and wind whispered through the crisp pine needles.

With a groan, I got to my feet, dusting away twigs and leaves. No injuries other than a few scratches and bruises, luckily. My bike was tangled in the thorny tendrils of a blackberry bush, so it took me a while to free it.

My tire was popped, putting an end to my ride for the day. Grumbling to myself about how badly these trails needed to be maintained, I walked back up the path, searching for the object that had pierced my tire.

Something pale gray and jagged jutted up out of the dirt. Squatting down for a closer look, I observed its porous interior and immediately knew what it was.

My tire had been popped by a bone.

It was deeply buried, but the soil was loose. Giving the bone a tug, I was able to pull it free. It was about half the length of my forearm. I was by no means an expert; I certainly didn't know what kind of animal it had come from, but it had to have been fairly large.

It didn't look very old, either.

"Welcome to the wild, Salem," I said, before tossing the bone away into the trees.

Wheeling my bike alongside me, I chose to take another fork in the path down to the beach. I didn't know much about bears, but I'd never seen a bear on a beach, so it felt safer. Waves crashed against the large rocks jutting out of the ocean, blasting spray dozens of feet into the air. Massive pieces of pale driftwood littered the sand, washed ashore from some faraway forest. The sun peeked through the clouds, nearly at its zenith.

For a minute, I stood there and savored the wind and sun on my face. The waves lapped against my shoes, mounds of foam floating on clear water. My face reflected back at me, a blur of pale skin and short brown hair. The trees loomed behind me, wavering sentinels at my back.

The waves receded . . . and rolled back in. This time, when I gazed into my reflection, something had changed.

Someone was standing on the ridge behind me, just outside the trees.

Turning my head, I searched the ridge. The trail ran close to the edge, so if anyone was walking past, it would be fairly easy to see them.

But no one was there.

My mouth was suddenly dry, my hands clammy. An icy wind whipped across the beach, drawing my attention to the thick gray clouds gathering on the horizon. The sooner I got back to the house, the better, but it wasn't just the impending storm making me nervous.

Someone was watching me. The back of my neck prickled, and out of the corner of my eye, I could see that figure on the ridge again. Motionless. Watching.

I didn't dare turn my head. Some deep, primal fear screamed at me to *move*, so that's what I did. The sand made my steps painfully slow, as did lugging along my bike. The temptation to drop everything and sprint was building.

I'D RIDDEN EVEN farther from the house than I'd realized. The blue skies had turned gray by the time I walked in the front gates and stored my bike in the shed at the end of the driveway. Luckily I'd brought a repair kit; I could patch the tire tomorrow.

The rain began to pour as I climbed the stairs. I was soaked by the time I reached the front door and rushed inside, shivering and anxious.

After changing into warm, dry clothes, I went outside to the covered walkway that ran along the back of the house next to the garden. Rain dripped between the stone archways as I lit a

joint and slowly inhaled, hoping it would burn away the paranoia lingering inside me.

But I couldn't shake it. That feeling of being watched was
still there, so much so that I kept glancing left and right, expecting to see someone standing there. I smoked and paced,
paced and smoked—until I turned around and almost smacked
face-first into Rayne.

"Jesus!"

"Fuckin' Christ!"

We both exclaimed at the same moment, and she braced her
arms against my shoulders as she stared at me. "Are you good?
Didn't mean to scare you."

"I, um, no . . . sorry, I'm . . . I mean, I'm fine . . ." I was out
of breath, and my hands fluttered nervously as I tried to collect
myself. "I was out riding and I saw . . . I don't know . . ."

Her eyes were narrowed, and she was still holding my arms.
"What did you see?"

A cold wind whipped through the walkway, making a chill
run up my spine. I moved closer to her instinctively, and she
stepped closer to me too. With my back close to the wall and
her body close to my front, it was significantly more difficult to
remember what had frightened me in the first place.

"It was . . ." God, why did she smell so good? I could smell
her wet leather boots, the rich vanilla lotion on her skin. She
raised one eyebrow, and her fingers dug into my arms with
anticipation.

"It was nothing," I said quickly. "I just heard something
weird and scared myself."

She didn't let go, not right away. She stared at me like she
knew I was lying, searching my face. I suddenly wasn't cold anymore. Quite the opposite; I was sweating with nerves.

"Nothing?" she said. "You sure about that?" Her frown deepened, and she brushed her thumb against my jaw. "Did you get hurt?"

My heart was still racing, but whether it was from fear or something else, I no longer knew. I hadn't bothered to look in the mirror upon my return, but I could feel the sting of an abrasion beneath her finger.

"Had a little fall," I said. She nodded. But still, neither of us moved.

I offered the joint, and she stared with an expression I couldn't read, prompting me to say hurriedly, "Sorry, I should have asked if I can smoke out here—"

"Relax, pretty girl." She laughed softly, took the joint, and inhaled. "I don't usually smoke with the same girl twice. You've shaken me up a little, Salem."

It was difficult to imagine anything "shaking her up." Frankly, the woman seemed unshakeable. She passed the joint back, and instantly it was like we were back in the bar parking lot again. Just two strangers in shared intimacy.

"I take it one-night stands are your thing?" I said, and she gave me a roguish grin.

"Yeah. Not really any other option, living out here. It's not like I'm going to manage to drag some mainlander back here for anything long-term."

"There's no one on the island you like? Not even a little crush?"

I offered the joint to her and our fingers brushed as she took it. Our eyes met, and for a split second I swore she gave me her answer without words.

"I'm a bit of a black sheep around here," she said. When she broke eye contact, I sucked in a breath I hadn't realized I needed. "Most of the other folks here . . . they're like family. I may not particularly like them, but they're what I've got. We take care of each other."

She leaned against the wall beside me, her shoulder brushing mine. Birds had come to bathe in the garden puddles, and we watched in silence for a while as they splashed and twittered. But against my better judgment, my gaze was drawn back to her.

"So—you've never been with the same girl twice?" The words escaped, and I instantly wished I could swallow them again. I was never so bold. Something about her prevented me from thinking straight.

"Never," she said, as casually as if we were remarking on the weather. "Are you trying to be the first?"

"I—uh—I mean—"

"Are you scared of me?" Her voice was almost a whisper, her gaze pinning me to the wall. What was *wrong* with me? I hadn't felt like this since I was an overstimulated, hormonal teenager.

"Yes." My voice cracked, but her serious expression didn't.

Her lips wrapped around the joint, and she didn't break eye contact as she slowly inhaled. Smoke flared from her nostrils, and she said, "Do you want me to stop?"

"Please don't."

8

Rayne
What You Like

ASMOLDERING CHERRY PLUMMETED TO THE FLAGSTONES, AND I crushed it beneath my boot. When I looked up again, Salem's eyes were fixed on the charcoal smudge, her expression impossible to read. I wanted to open up her head, see what made her tick, watch the inner machinations churn.

"If I scare you," I said, "then why do you fantasize about me?"

My thighs clenched at the thought of last night, the memory of her naked, all slick skin and blushing cheeks.

"I'm . . . I'm into, um . . ." The words almost choked her. She still hadn't lifted her eyes. "I'm into being dominated. I like, um . . ." Her cheeks flushed bright red and she finally looked up. The implosion threatening to consume me went supernova, overtaking my logic as I looked quickly up and down the walkway, then took her hand.

Guiding her down a few steps, we slipped into a small alcove that sheltered us from view. Yellow and red leaves swirled around our feet, crunching beneath our shoes. As we crowded together, desire locked my chest around my hammering heart, threatening to crush my lungs as I was torn between fear and desire.

I'm not supposed to do this.

"Take a deep breath," I said, as much to myself as to her. "Inhale while I count. One . . . two . . ."

She nodded, breathing with me. Her chest pressed to mine, and I could feel her nipples through her shirt, pebbled from the cold. Her breath was as warm as her eyes, inviting me closer, silently begging for more.

I need to walk away. Leave her alone. Don't involve her.

God, but I was weak. I touched the scratch on her face again, my fingers too cold, too rough. Like touching silk with sandpaper. But her lips parted with a soft breath, and she leaned into my touch like she wanted it, like she was eager for it.

Barely above a whisper, I said, "Tell me what you like."

"I like domination," she said. It took all my self-control not to shove her back against the wall and kiss her. She couldn't have known how those words would affect me, how her desire would sing to mine like a siren song. "I like feeling a little afraid. It's like a freefall. Like diving into the ocean."

"The ocean will swallow you alive," I warned. "You'll drown, and the deeper you go, the darker it will get."

Don't do it, Rayne. She deserves so much better than you.

"I don't care," she said. "I know what I like."

Her mouth was so close, her body—I didn't dare touch her, not yet. Part of me wanted to shake her and say, *God, please don't tempt me.* The other part wanted to rip through those little buttons on her cardigan, tear through the shirt beneath, and take her right there. The idea alone was torturously arousing, and I was sweating despite the cold air.

When she looked up at me, I swore she could see into my soul. I'd always been a closed book, but she was reading me anyway. She unbuttoned her cardigan and shrugged it off her shoulders, and I groaned in defeat.

"I can't promise you anything good," I said. "There's a reason I don't bring people back here, Salem. There's no light at the end. There's no happy ending."

"I don't need empty promises," she said. She touched her finger, the one with the imprint of an absent ring. "And I don't need another ending."

She loosened the belt on her waist, popped open the button on her trousers. My sharp inhale was painfully shallow, but I couldn't manage to draw another breath as I watched her. Stepping closer, pressed against her, I cupped my palm around her throat. Her heart sped up, pulse pattering against my hand.

Fuck.

I shoved her back, pinning her to the wall and pressing my forehead to hers. Those sweet honey eyes stared up at me as she smiled, eager and wanting.

"Then what do you need?" The desperation in my voice caught me off guard, my words strained and tight. She'd asked for domination, but it was me who was wrapped around her little finger, ready to obey her every whim.

"You," she said, striking a match that lit fire in my veins. "All of you."

I laughed softly, humorlessly. My self-control was gone—now I was simply toying with her, savoring every moment of watching her squirm. "You're not ready for that."

"Try me. Show me why I should be afraid."

"What are you trying to do to me?" I squeezed her throat for just a moment, enough pressure to make her smile widen and her eyes flutter. She reacted to my touch like it was made for her. "You're a dangerous woman, Salem. You have no fucking idea . . ."

"I think you're the dangerous one. You know, I . . . I like to ride." She reached for the top button on her shirt and popped it open, slowly baring her soft skin. "Sometimes, I'll find a trail that makes my stomach drop. One that has caution signs around the entrance, and people look a little nervous when you ask about it." She traced her painted nails down her chest, pushing her shirt open, revealing the perfect slope of her bare breast. "But those are the best rides. They make you feel alive."

"So you ignore caution signs, and everyone's warnings, and you do it anyway . . ."

"Yeah. I do." I looked at her mouth, and watched her drag the corner of her lower lip between her teeth. "I do it because it feels so damn good."

A split second of heavy silence passed between us. I took one last cautious look over my shoulder into the empty garden, ensuring no one was around to see. I was selfish. I wanted her all for myself.

"You want to feel good?" I said. "Touch yourself for me. Just like you were in the bath."

Slowly, she slipped her hand into her pants. She shivered, and I smirked at the thought of her cold fingers igniting her nerves, her pleasure building with pain.

"You've certainly found a creative way to pay for your stay," I teased, and her breath hitched. "Such a beautiful little slut for me." I tightened my fingers, holding her throat right beneath her jaw, keeping her face tipped up to look at me.

She groaned, grinding on her hand. "Please . . . please, touch me, Rayne, I—"

"Did I give you permission to use my name?" A little flash of fear lit up her face like lightning. "If you want a chance to orgasm after you've edged on those cold fingers, you will call me Madam, understand?"

"Yes, Madam," she said quickly.

The honorific sent tingles all over my body. She was making soft sounds, little whimpers and gasps, her lips parted in the most beautifully sensual expression of pleasure.

"Let's see what that mouth can do," I said, my fingers fumbling as I tugged my belt out of my jeans. Nervousness and desire made my words shake, but I hoped she didn't notice.

There had been plenty of times I'd hooked up and never taken my clothes off at all; I'd slept with people and barely let them touch me. My body was a tool, not a temple—I was more comfortable putting it to use than caring for it.

But she sank to her knees, grasped my hip with one hand and continued pleasuring herself with the other. Her eyes went round and wide when I tugged my jeans down to my mid-thighs, underwear going with them, and she let out a breath that made my insides churn with desire. She let me loop the belt around her neck and pull it taut. She nuzzled her face into the dark hair between my legs, and I braced my hand against the wall as I watched her.

"Go on," I said. "Show me what a good girl you are."

The anticipation felt even better than my fantasies. She lifted her gaze to me as her tongue slid between my folds, and I gasped at her touch. She moaned, mouth opening hungrily when she tasted how wet I was. She closed her eyes, her hips rocking slowly and her body moving with them.

"God, you feel perfect," I murmured. I held the belt wrapped around my hand like a leash, but I swore the noose was around my own neck instead of hers. Her tongue lapped over me, tracing poems of ecstasy into my flesh.

I was going to break. My vision tunneled until only she remained, the light on the other side of my little death. Her eyelashes brushed her reddened cheeks, her soft lips and curling tongue making my legs shake. I grasped the back of her head, grinding against her mouth.

My knees almost buckled. Everything went still, the world coming to a halt as my brain shuddered and my core tightened almost unbearably. She was watching my face, moaning against me, tongue drawing out every last second of ecstasy as I came.

Finally able to breathe again, the belt dropped from my hand and I leaned weakly against the wall. She drew back, lips and chin shining with my arousal, a sloppy smile on her face.

She lowered herself further, until she was straddling my boot. She rocked slowly on the well-worn leather, clinging to my thigh.

"Madam, may I come?" Her voice was so sweet, pleading and soft.

"God, yes." I stroked my fingers through her hair, palming the crown of her head. "Shine that boot for me. Fuck, that's it, just like that. How does that feel, pretty girl?"

She moved from slick leather to rough laces, grinding faster, harder.

"S-so good . . . you feel . . . so . . . good . . ." Her words became whimpers and moans, her movements clumsy. Her nails dug into my bare thigh, leaving crescent-moon marks in my skin.

She leaned into me, panting, and I stroked the back of her head, tracing my fingers along her nape.

"Breathe deep and slow for me," I said. "I want you to feel every second of this orgasm. Keep grinding, don't you dare stop. Press your clit up against the laces—make it hurt, I know you want a little pain, don't you?"

She nodded mindlessly, staring up at me as if she was bound to my every word. She shuddered, holding tight to me as she came. I could feel the orgasm wash over her in waves of shaking, her hips bucking against me until she slumped and went still, breathing hard.

"That's it, that's a good girl," I said. I traced my fingers through her hair, slow and steady, the motion soothing me. I loosened the belt from around her neck, tugged up my jeans, and threaded the belt through the loops, my hands trembling.

Now was usually the time for me to run off, to disappear. But I didn't move; I didn't pull her up or tell her to go. Instead I just kept staring down at her, half in wonder, half in fear.

I wanted to pick her up, hold her close. I wanted to take her into my room, into my bed. I suddenly wanted to do all the soft, silly, useless things reserved for those with far simpler lives than mine.

Salem lifted her head and smiled, and my stomach fluttered. "I like that title," she said softly. "Madam . . . it's nice."

Usually, outside the desperate heat of sex, the name almost repulsed me—it made me feel ashamed, reminded me of the desires I worked so hard to ignore. But not when she said it.

"It's been a while since I've let anyone call me that," I said. I offered her my hand and helped her up. She stumbled slightly and I steadied her, one hand grasping her arm and the other wrapping around her waist.

I wanted to hear her say that title again. Perhaps whisper it in my ear, speak it softly with gentle kisses against my neck. I wanted her warm hands in mine. I wanted—

Too much. Far, far too much.

I thought of the ring missing from her finger, and raging jealousy filled me. Envy, that someone else had been granted her love and loyalty, then had the gall to lose it.

She didn't need empty promises, and I wouldn't give her any.

I raised my walls. Slammed my doors, locked them, and swallowed the key. I helped her pull on her sweater, but I was distracted by the faint red marks my belt had left on her beautiful throat.

"I hope it was a good ride," I said, and winked before I turned and strode away. I wanted her to call me back, call me an asshole. I wanted her to fight my carelessness.

But she didn't.

Salem

Warning Bells

FWIP-THUNK!

Rayne paused, her ax buried in the thick stump as the log she'd split tumbled to the ground. She wiped her brow with the back of her hand, her shoulder muscles tensing and swelling as she lifted the ax again.

Fwip-thunk! Another log split beneath her blade, and my stomach tumbled just like the pieces of wood as they fell to the ground.

It was unfair to my mental well-being, frankly, that she was so distracting. Her long hair was tamed into a ponytail beneath her cap, and she wore brown cargo pants and a black shirt so tight I could count her abdominal muscles through the fabric.

She had no business being that hot. Wielding an ax like it was nothing, throwing around logs.

My fingers were numb from the cold, so I was clumsy as I worked to get the old tire off my bike. I wanted to ride into Marihope and explore the town, but it was hard to get any work done with Rayne nearby. She'd been out here since I awoke, clearing away the overgrowth at the bottom of the hill. There were no gardeners to help her, and so far, other than the cooks, I hadn't seen any other employees managing the manor.

I could only assume that meant she did the gardening, the landscaping, and the housecleaning all herself. It was no wonder she never attended meals.

That didn't stop me from looking for her though. I ate alone, or made small talk with the other guests, but it was Rayne I wanted to see.

She picked up the water bottle near her feet and took a long sip. A drip streaked down her chin, and I followed its trail over her throat, along her chest . . .

She noticed me watching. Hurriedly, I focused on my bike again, but I wasn't going to get away with it that easily. Footsteps came up behind me, and her shadow fell over me.

"Where are you headed?"

She seemed particularly tall when I was on my knees. She had her ax resting against her shoulder, her arms bare despite the cold weather.

"I was going to ride into Marihope," I said. "Explore a little, check out the place."

"I can give you a ride," she said. "I'm going into town anyway to pick up some things to get that faucet fixed."

"Sorry again about that." I stood up, wiping my hands on my leggings and smearing myself with grease before I even thought about what I was doing.

"Don't worry about it." She turned away, but talked as she walked, so I assumed I should follow her. "It would be a pretty boring season if a guest didn't break something."

She led me back to the shed where my bike had been stored, opening both doors wide. Pulling back a tarp, she revealed a muddy ATV.

"You won't find many vehicles besides these on Blackridge," she said. She grabbed a helmet from a shelf, curling her finger at me to come closer. "Most of the terrain is too rough, and the roads wash out almost every winter."

She fit the helmet on my head, and I let her.

"Sounds like the island doesn't want to be inhabited," I said. I was surprised when it actually got a small laugh out of her.

"Sure seems that way, doesn't it? Hmm. Your head is so small..."

She tucked her fingers beneath my chin, tipping my head up so she could adjust the chin strap. She checked to ensure it was secure, muttering softly as she did, "Good girl. That's perfect."

Thank God for the helmet's visor hiding my blush.

WE DROVE DOWN the steep, narrow road, riding over stones and through icy creeks. It was too loud to talk. I kept my head tucked down against her back, my arms tightly wrapped around her. Loki ran with us, either close behind or beside us, loping through the trees with his tongue lolling out.

It reminded me of being on my bike, whipping through the trails. That feeling of exhilaration, of freedom, when nothing else mattered except the tires beneath me. Only this time, I wasn't alone.

Rayne was warm. Her jacket smelled like pine sap and floral soap. Her heart beat hard and steady, quickening when we went through a large dip or careened around a corner.

We passed quiet farmhouses and old barns. Horses, sheep, and goats watched us drive by, raising their heads from the grass. Eventually, we reached a fork in the road and Rayne pulled to the side. She parked the ATV between an old truck and an overgrown fence, clipping the keys to her carabiner.

"I've got you," she said, batting my hands away as I fiddled with my helmet. She unbuckled it and peeled it from my head before removing her own. I didn't know what to call the feeling it gave me, but it was giddy and bubbly, like a bottle of champagne ready to burst behind my ribs.

The forest was lush beyond the fence, so thick and wild it would require the assistance of a machete to walk through. Down the road's left fork, the path turned to gravel. Steep-roofed cottages and brick-sided buildings sat beneath the trees.

Hurrying to catch up with Rayne, who had already continued down the road, I said, "It's so quiet here."

"It's Sunday," she said. "Church is in session."

Still, I expected to see someone. *Anyone.*

Every window was shuttered; the roads were quiet and vacant. Even the dogs, sleeping on front porches behind small wooden fences, didn't bother to bark at Loki as he trotted ahead, peeing on bushes and following random scent trails.

As old as the town obviously was, there was some unexpected modernity. Almost every house was equipped with floodlights. Some had obvious security cameras. Streetlamps lined the roads, and I spotted a metal sign affixed to one of them.

Winter curfew begins November 1st. Please be advised that all persons under the age of 18 must be indoors no later than 4 p.m. All persons, regardless of age, must remain indoors between the hours of 6 p.m. and 7 a.m.

"Winter must be really rough here," I said. "Curfews? Really?"

"There's places with harsher weather," she said. "But it's not the cold that will get you. When you're out here alone in the dark, all the trees look the same, and the snow covers your footprints in a matter of seconds." Her mouth was set in a grim, hard line. "You're vulnerable. You can't see shit. But shit can see you."

We turned onto a wide cobblestone road. We passed a small coffee shop, the sign in the window declaring, *Closed on Sundays! See you tomorrow!* Trees lined the street, and cats watched us pass from their rooftop perches. Chickens meandered across the path, scurrying out of our way as we got close.

Reaching a small shop called Andy's Hardware, we had to shoo a brood of chickens out of the way before Rayne opened the door and called out, "Morning, Andy! You open yet?"

She ushered Loki and me inside, even before a muffled response was shouted from upstairs: "I'll be right down!"

The shop was small, but well stocked. It smelled distinctly of fresh lumber and sawdust. A few mounted animal heads adorned the walls: deer, rabbit, pheasant. A plethora of home improvement goods were available, from nails and screws to piping and electrical wiring.

Suddenly, there came a rapid pattering of footsteps and an excited squeal. A little girl with long, wild brown hair came flying down the stairs behind the counter and ran straight into Rayne's arms.

"What's up, munchkin?" Rayne said, playfully swooping the girl into the air before setting her down.

"No, silly, it's Seahawk, remember? Not munchkin!" The girl giggled as Loki licked her face, then spotted me standing nearby and waved excitedly. "Oh, hi! I'm Rebecca! But you can call me Becca. I'm eight years old, and my sister Rachel is only four. That's why I'm the more responserber . . . um, wait . . ." She scrunched up her nose. "Respible . . . respopable . . ."

"Responsible," Rayne said, slowly enunciating the word. "This is Salem. She's one of my guests. Where's your sister?"

"With Daddy upstairs." Rebecca beamed, looking up at Rayne with obvious admiration. She skipped around me, with Loki following her, just as a man with a massive bushy beard came downstairs. He was carrying a younger girl in his arms, a lopsided pink bow in her hair. She was sucking her thumb and looked half asleep.

"Hey, Andy." Rayne grasped his hand in a familiar way. Even tall as she was, Andy made her look small. He was broad-shouldered and potbellied, with a kind smile. She gave Rachel a gentle touch and said, "Hey kiddo. Still sleepy?"

The little girl nodded groggily, rubbing a small hand over her eyes.

"Good to see ya, Rayne. Rachel just had her nap, she's not quite awake yet," he said, patting the little girl's back. He gave me a nod of acknowledgement. "Mornin', miss. Andy Moss is the name."

"Salem Lockard," I said, shaking his hand.

"Always nice to see new folks around," he said, although he sounded more tired than enthused. "What can I do for ya, then?"

"I've got an unexpected fix. Broken faucet." Rayne's eyes fluttered slightly toward me, and I turned away before I could spontaneously combust with embarrassment.

As Andy and Rayne discussed the repair, I meandered toward the back of the store. The shelves along the wall were locked behind a metal grate, with various boxes of ammo within. A handwritten sign taped to the lock said, *See the manager for ammunition purchase. Conserve your bullets!*

A few yellowed newspaper clippings were framed and hung upon the wall. Headlines extended back through the decades. 1985, *Record Size Black Bear Bagged By Blackridge Hunter.* 1993, *Blackridge Lighthouse Begins Decommission.* 1997, *Grisly Murder Shocks Island Community.*

The final headline made me pause, rising up on my tiptoes for a better look at the article. But the paper was old, and the ink had bloomed from water damage. Besides the date and headline, all that remained was a black-and-white photo of Balfour Manor.

The back door was ajar. Rebecca was outside, humming as she skipped through the grass, plucking dandelions. Poking my head out, I found Loki sitting on the porch, watching the child like a bodyguard. There was a chicken coop to the left, but it was currently being used to shelter a horde of potted tomato plants instead of chickens. Colorful pinwheels were stuck into the pots, spinning in the wind. Several folding chairs were set around a brick fire pit, all of the chairs currently occupied by an assortment of dolls and stuffies.

A small picket fence was the only barrier between the forest and the yard.

"Are you staying at Rayne's house?" Rebecca chirped.

Smiling at her as I spun one of the iridescent pinwheels, I responded in the affirmative.

"Rayne has a whole bunch of people stay with her, 'cuz she has a Better Breakfast," Rebecca said, swinging her arms as she stood next to me. "I wanna stay with Rayne too! Daddy said I can have a sleepover next summer if I'm really good, and eat my veggie-tables, and don't pinch my sister."

Containing my laughter, I let her talk as I wandered around the yard. She barely took a breath between sentences.

"Someday, I'm gonna go to the tower, just like Rayne! She's really brave. She's not even afraid of the dark!"

"Is it dark at the tower?" I said, wondering what exactly she meant.

"It's super dark!" she said. "But you've gotsa go when it's dark, 'cause that's the only way you can see it."

"See what?" I lowered my voice in a conspiratorial way, hoping she'd indulge me.

Rebecca thought for a moment, before she leaned closer and whispered, "The angel." She giggled softly, covering her mouth. "I'm not supposed to say it."

"Does the angel only come when it's dark?"

She nodded. "Yeah. But I'm not supposed to talk about it." She said it a bit more forcefully this time. But when she spoke again, she was as chipper as ever. "We have a lot of goats, did you know that? I help my daddy take care of them. We have Sadie, Daisy, Winnifred, and . . ."

As I peered into the trees, something caught my eyes. A long string extended along the top of the fence, all the way around the yard. Bells were tied to it, rusted from the weather. Curiously, I plucked the string, setting all the bells jingling.

There was an immediate pounding of feet, followed by silence.

Turning, I saw Rebecca had vanished. Rayne and Andy were crowded together on the back porch, looking at me with alarm.

Instead of his little girl, Andy was carrying a rifle.

"Whoa, whoa, is everything okay?" I said, looking around nervously.

"Did you touch those bells?" Andy said. His voice was grim, and it felt like a block of ice settling in my stomach.

"Yes, I—I'm so sorry, I didn't think—"

Andy's shoulders relaxed. He raised his hand, giving me a patient smile. "Don't you worry about it, miss. Caught me off guard is all. They're to keep out the pests, see. Deer, raccoons. Bells let us know if they're trying to get in. I'll, uh . . . lemme put this away . . ." He went back inside, but Rayne stayed, her eyes narrowed as she looked at me.

No, not at me. *Beyond* me, into the trees.

Finally, she sighed. "Try not to touch anything. People around here can be . . ." A hawk screeched as it wheeled overhead and she flinched, eyes darting to survey the trees again before she finally finished. "Edgy."

Rayne

Marihope's Missing

MY HEART WAS STILL POUNDING, THE TINKLING OF BELLS ringing in my head, when Andy pulled me aside. He glanced down at little Rachel, who was clinging sleepily to his leg, and covered the little girl's ears.

"Someone went missing," he said. "Night before last, a fifteen-year-old named Andrea was walking home from a friend's house and never made it."

Instantly, there were chills on my arms. Salem and Rebecca were at the front of the shop, discussing the various flavors of candy sticks available on the counter. Neither of them could hear our conversation as we kept our voices low.

"Did anyone see anything?" I said. "Hear anything?"

Andy shook his head. "Nothing. Sheriff Keatin took out a search party and has been looking for her. But it's not looking good."

"It's too early," I said desperately. "It's never shown up before November. Never."

Andy sighed heavily. Rachel began to whine, grasping her hands at him to be picked up, so he scooped her up again. "I know. Sheriff thinks we should get a lookout up to the tower soon. We need to get the trail cameras turned on."

"I'll ask James to do it," I said, making a mental reminder to stop by my cousin's house while we were in town. "I'd do it myself if I didn't still have guests to look after."

"It could be nothin'," Andy said, watching as Rebecca tried to sneakily stuff candy sticks into Salem's pockets. "That girl might've just run away. Gotten on a boat and gone."

"Somehow I doubt a fifteen-year-old is going to pilot a boat off this island alone. Especially this late in the year."

"Well, we don't know enough to be scaring ourselves yet," he said, lowering his voice even further as he held his daughter close.

Many of the island's younger generation had tried to leave, scrounging together enough money to settle on the mainland or simply leaving with nothing. But they always came back. None of us could tear the island's roots from our minds. Nightmares would exhaust us, disembodied whispers and screams would follow us day and night.

The longer we stayed away, the worse it would become. Even the kids, like Rebecca and little Rachel, weren't immune.

If you were born here, you had no choice but to die here.

⊷⊷⊷⊱❖⊰⊶⊶⊶

INSTEAD OF FAIRY tales, my childhood was full of frightful stories from my own backyard. Floods and snowstorms, mudslides and summer wildfires. I knew the stories connected to all the old houses, the tavern, the tiny library. Who owned them, who built them, and who had died within them.

I tried to relay all this to Salem without sounding too grim, telling her stories of the places we passed, casually neglecting to mention the worst of the tales. She listened quietly—much more quietly than usual.

It made me suspicious, but so did everything she did. Her presence made me skeptical in a way no one else's ever had.

I felt like a creep for watching her. For lingering outside her door and listening to the sounds of her moving on the other side. For longing to bring her into my bed and make her admit to me all the filthy things she desired.

I wanted nothing more than to see that stunned, pleasured look on her face again when I took command. She'd given me something precious that evening near the gardens; she'd trusted me.

I wished I could give the same trust to her.

"Rebecca seems to really like you," Salem said, wrenching me from my thoughts.

Clearing my throat, I said, "I used to babysit for Andy, watch the girls while he worked at the shop. It was really hard for him after his wife passed away. He really needed help."

We shared a similar loss, the girls and I. It bonded us, struggling to navigate a world wherein our mothers were gone too soon. But at least Rebecca and Rachel had a father who would move mountains for them. He'd done everything in his power to protect them, which was more than I could say for my own father.

"Rebecca said she wants to go to the tower, like you." She laughed lightly, and put on a mystical tone as she twiddled her fingers. "She said that if you go there in the dark, you can see an angel."

I nearly tripped over my own feet. Christ, why would she say—she knew not to—it didn't fucking matter, but—

"She has a big imagination. She means the firewatch tower. When I'm not working at the manor, I take shifts in the tower to keep a lookout for smoke."

Thankfully we'd reached the ATV, and I occupied myself securing the supplies I'd purchased before taking out our helmets.

"We're gonna take a drive to the other side of town," I said, clipping the helmet beneath her chin. "I have to stop by my cousin's place, but I'll show you the town square. There's a couple cafes over there, you can grab lunch if you'd like."

With her clinging to my waist, we drove to the east side of Marihope. I was thankful everyone was still in church. If anyone besides Andy saw me driving around with company, it would be the talk of the whole town by tonight. That was the problem with small communities: Your business never really stayed *your* business.

But despite my paranoia, having Salem cling to me was one of the best feelings in the world. Merely the weight of her head against my back gave me such a dopamine rush I felt high.

We parked outside Innsmouth Tavern; the barkeep's old cats watched us through the cloudy windows, waiting for their master to return from the morning's sermon. By evening, he'd serve enough liquor to wash away the town's guilt, then do it all over again next Sunday.

The square wasn't far. In its center stood an old redwood tree, tall, twisted, and gnarled. Its branches bent as if in an eternal wind, and wooden benches encircled its massive trunk. Empty wooden stands, draped with protective tarps, stood waiting for the farmers who would sell their goods here in the spring, summer, and early autumn.

"Is this where the Halloween festival will be?" Salem craned her neck to look up at the massive tree, then spread her arms and did a little spin, her scarf trailing in the breeze. "I'm so excited for it. The photos online looked so cute!"

The Hallow's Festival was Blackridge's last hurrah before winter—before sleet, snow, and an early curfew began. We'd always tried to keep it a strictly local thing. Given that the last ferry off the island left the following evening, none of us wanted to try to herd a bunch of hungover mainlanders down to the docks after the Halloween festivities.

But I couldn't tell her no.

"It'll be here," I said. "The kids have already started carving jack-o'-lanterns for it, I've heard. It's the last night before curfew, so the whole town stays up late. They'll have some bonfires, teenagers will run around in the graveyard and scare themselves. And you can't miss the spiced apple cider."

"I'll buy the first round," she said, and I suddenly realized she had no intention of going to that festival alone.

Frankly, even if she had, I would have found a way to accompany her.

The church bell chimed the hour, and Salem's mouth dropped open as her attention was drawn to the cathedral across the square. Although I had plenty of bad memories from that church, I still had to admit it was breathtaking. It was meant to be.

It was built of light gray stone, with a tall, pointy bell tower and elaborately carved arches. It looked too old, too beautiful to be sequestered in the middle of an island forest. Too beautiful for the wickedness within it.

"My grandfather built it when he moved here," I said. "Just like the manor. He was inspired by the architecture he saw in Europe, and when he came back, he tried to replicate it. The door is always open, if you want to take a look inside."

Salem looked eager to do exactly that, which was my cue to leave.

"Listen, I'll meet you back here in about an hour," I said. "There's a coffee shop and deli there, near the fountain across the street. Great soup and sandwiches, if you're hungry."

"Where are you going?" She sounded disappointed to see me go, and it took physical effort not to immediately offer to bring her along.

"Just need to have a word with my cousin James. He lives up the street. Feel free to explore, but don't wander too far. It's a long walk back to the manor."

"I won't," she said. "I'm not trying to become a snack for bears today. Or angels."

She giggled, but I failed to find the humor.

⸻ ❖ ⸻

THE HOUSE JAMES shared with his parents and brothers had been my second home as a child.

The place was quiet as I walked in, the soft smell of baked bread permeating the air. After my father died, my Uncle Gerard took over as the preacher in Marihope's church. Naturally, the entire family was out attending the sermon—my Aunt Veronica and cousins Mark and Jacob. Only James remained, the black sheep in an otherwise loyal flock. I could smell the vanilla-tobacco odor of his pipe as I ascended the ladder to the attic.

James's room was cluttered floor to ceiling with books, magazines, and specimens—numerous pinned bugs under glass.

But it wasn't the butterflies and beetles that made my stomach turn. It was the newspapers. The clippings plastered all over the walls, pinned to the bulletin board, and stacked in yellowing heaps.

MISSING. MISSING. MISSING. Reward offered, no
questions asked, please bring our baby home.

Dozens of them. Names and faces blurred together in my memory; some of them I'd known, some I'd only heard of. All of them missing from Blackridge.

But they weren't missing, not really. We all knew they were dead, and James's gruesome collection was the only memorial they'd have.

"Let me guess," he said, hunched over his desk with a microscope pressed to his eye. He was examining some kind of insect wing, squashed between two panes of glass. "You're here because of that girl who went missing . . . what was her name? Andrea?"

She'd likely be joining his memorial wall soon.

"I'm surprised you heard about that. Andy said Keatin is trying to keep it quiet so people don't panic." I folded my arms, looking around the dim room. The rest of the house was plastered with yellow floral wallpaper; the walls up here were barren, dark brown wood.

"Mm, yes, well, I think we both know how fast word spreads around here." He sighed as he raised his head, staring at me through thick Coke-bottle glasses. "Besides, I may have given up my hopes of getting a badge, but Keatin still talks to me. Especially when he's worried."

James's dream used to be getting his badge and joining the tiny coalition of officers we had on the island—currently at a grand total of three. But going to the mainland for his academy training proved impossible, so he settled for work as a voluntary forest ranger. Setting up the trail cams had been his idea, allowing the island's residents to watch for approaching danger on the roads and forest paths.

"I think we should get the cameras turned on early," I said, grabbing Loki's collar before he could dart after a white fluffy cat that ran out from under the bed. "Just as a precaution."

His mouth tightened, and he tapped his fingers continually on the desk. "It's never woken up this early before."

"I'm not saying it's awake," I hissed. "It's *just* a precaution."

He stared at me, and I stared back, wordless desperate hope passing between us.

Finally, he nodded. "I can go Wednesday morning. I'll take a walkie with me."

"Thank you. Call me when you go out, I'll verify all the feeds are live. Take someone with you, okay? Don't be stupid and go alone."

The church bell was ringing the end of service. Pulling aside the curtain, I gazed down the hill, watching as people swarmed from the chapel. I couldn't see Salem, and that made me nervous.

Not that she couldn't take care of herself. She clearly could. But there was plenty about this island she didn't know, and around here, what you didn't know could kill you.

Salem

The Tragedy of the Balfours

THE GRASSY CHURCHYARD WAS QUIET, SAVE FOR THE SOFT sound of hymns being sung within the cathedral's stone walls. Tall, narrow windows encircled the building, the likenesses of angels carved into the arches above the glass.

My family had never been particularly religious; my grandma took me to Easter Mass once, but that was the extent of it. My mom was too free-spirited to adhere to any one particular faith, and my father had never taken an interest either.

As much as I wanted to check out the interior, I didn't want to interrupt the service. I wandered through the yard, past several picnic tables and the screeching gulls perched upon them. At the far side of the yard, a curved archway stood within a tall iron fence. A simple wooden sign hung from the arch, carved with the words *Marihope Cemetery*.

Dappled sunlight lit the dirt path leading within. It was overgrown, with dozens of crooked headstones jutting out of the grass, wrapped in the wicked thorns of blackberry brambles. One in particular caught my eye, and as the church bell rang again, I squatted down to have a closer look.

While the other graves stood in crooked rows, this one was alone. The headstone was a simple square block, carved with the name *Picard Balfour*.

"What a pleasure to see you again, Miss Lockard."

I looked up in surprise to find the woman from the market, Ruth, smiling at me. Several other women were with her, all of them around my own age, dressed in their Sunday best. With a sudden burst of adrenaline, I recognized one of them: It was the same woman from the ferry, the one who'd been distraught and crying.

Our eyes met, and hers widened, quickly looking away. Her hair was clean and combed, and her face no longer looked so gaunt.

I straightened up from the grave, nervously saying, "You're—are you—"

"Have you been enjoying your time on the island?" Ruth interrupted. "How lucky you've found your way to our chapel. It's the most beautiful place on Blackridge."

The other women nodded eagerly. It was unnerving how intently they were observing me, as if I was some new kind of specimen they could barely contain their excitement for. The woman from the ferry stepped back among them, as if intentionally avoiding my scrutiny.

"I've enjoyed it," I said. Despite my unease, I tried to smile. But I didn't like being cornered between them and the cemetery fence. "It really is beautiful here. I would have gone inside, but I didn't want to interrupt the service."

Ruth laughed lightly as a gaggle of children ran through the yard, screeching as they played. "Well, you certainly need not have worried about that. Pastor Balfour always welcomes guests."

"Pastor . . . Balfour?"

"Oh, you didn't know?" She laughed again, and her friends did too, and I felt as if I'd missed something. "I'm surprised Miss Rayne didn't tell you. Her Uncle Gerard is our pastor, just like her father was." Her eyes drifted down, and she nodded toward Picard's grave.

"He was Rayne's father?" I asked.

"Oh yes. He had us all fooled into believing he was a worthy shepherd for our flock, but sadly, he was not."

The churchyard was full of congregants conversing with one another, but the four of us were far enough away that our conversation was private. Too private. Ruth's eyes bored into me, as if searching for secrets she could root out.

"What happened?" I said, trying to sidle away from her. But Ruth inched closer again.

"God struck him down," she said. If I didn't know better, I would have said she sounded cheerful. "Right there, in the very church he preached in."

Uncertain, I repeated, "God . . . struck him . . . down?"

"His body was found lying in front of the lectern," one of the other women piped up in a hushed whisper. "Disemboweled. He'd led a sermon only hours before."

"Diana," Ruth snapped. "Let's not sensationalize the Lord's judgment. It's no laughing matter. Picard, like all men, fell to his sin. May God forgive his soul."

I barely registered Ruth's words—I was still trying to process the fact that I'd just found out Rayne's father was murdered.

"Someone killed him?" I gasped. "God, poor Rayne . . . that's awful!"

"Yes, poor, poor Rayne," Ruth said dismissively. "Anyway, what's the matter with all of us? What a depressing subject. How are you liking your accommodations, Salem?"

Still reeling, it took me a moment to answer.

"It's definitely been . . . interesting," I said. "I mean, I got a big surprise when I showed up to the manor and saw Rayne. I'd met her before, actually, in town before I got on the ferry. On the mainland."

The women exchanged glances.

"I see," Ruth said, hiding her mouth behind her hand. "You're one of *those* girls."

This would have been a great time to walk away.

"What do you mean?" I said.

"You had sex with her," she responded, so flatly and clinically that I nearly choked.

"I—excuse me? I don't think that's any of your business—"

"Oh, honey, don't take offense." She clasped my shoulder like a friend, as if she was about to tell me a hard truth. "Rayne is a pervert. She doesn't keep it a secret."

"She brags about it," one of the women interjected, rolling her eyes.

"We all know what she does when she goes to the mainland," Ruth said, and patted my shoulder before taking a step back from me. "She's never brought one of her whores to Marihope before though. How special."

Had she really just said that to me? My heart hammered, my palms becoming slick with sweat. I hated confrontations.

I hated rude people. I hated feeling so purposefully misunderstood.

I wanted to defend myself. It didn't even matter what this awful woman thought of me, yet it still felt like a balloon was swelling in my chest. My tongue was dry and useless, my throat choked with anger.

With a furiously mumbled "excuse me," I hurried from the churchyard. Everyone's eyes were on me, and I wasn't just being paranoid. Every time I looked up, their gazes darted away.

I needed to get the hell out of here.

Nearly tripping on the uneven cobblestones as I made my way across the square, I paused beneath the massive gnarled redwood and caught my breath. The sounds of the churchyard echoed around me: the laughter, the children squealing, the garbled conversation.

My back prickled, and I glanced over my shoulder. People were slowly beginning to disperse from the churchyard, but it was the screeching gulls that drew my attention. They'd found something small, furry, and dead, and were bickering with one another as they ripped it to pieces and swallowed the bloody chunks down.

Heart hammering and appetite gone, I took a quick turn down a wide road. Shops lined either side of the street. A few trucks were parked along the curb, but all the shops were dark, their display windows empty. Which way was the ATV parked? To the south . . . west?

With these cloudy skies, how the hell was I supposed to tell which direction that was?

I shouldn't have left my meet-up spot with Rayne. I shouldn't have left the manor at all. I shouldn't have even come here.

Okay, okay, cool it, Salem.

Taking a deep breath, I clenched my fists and hurriedly kept walking, determined that I would see something familiar at any moment. I rounded another corner, staring all around for a road sign—

I ran face-first into someone coming in the opposite direction. Before I could squeak out an apology, I was seized by my jacket and slammed up against the stone wall. Something cold and sharp was pressed against my throat, immediately freezing my lungs with fear.

"I—Rayne?" I whimpered, realizing who had a grip on me. She realized who I was at the same time.

Her face melted with concern, mouth drawn down and eyes wide as she hurriedly put her blade away. I'd never seen anyone move so fast with a knife, and never been so close to certain death.

God, was this an adrenaline rush? What was wrong with me?

"Salem, shit, I'm so sorry." Rayne tugged her sleeve down and pressed it against my neck, and I realized she must have cut me. I didn't even notice. Her hand was warm as she guided me, leading me just off the road toward a fallen log nestled in the tall grass.

"Sit here," she said, pressing my shoulders down. She tipped up my head to examine my neck and winced. "I deserve a terrible review for this. Fuck, I'm sorry."

"I'll give it a seven out of ten," I said, a little breathlessly. "At least the knife was sharp."

She stared at me a moment before shaking her head with a wry grin. "Well, I try to be prepared."

"For what?" I said, but Rayne was distracted. She stalked through the tall grass, obviously looking for something.

"There we go," she said, and knelt down before a thick bush sporting dark purple berries. She plucked several of the green leaves, then wadded them up and chewed them vigorously as she returned to me.

"This is salal," she said, dabbing the wad of leaves onto my cut. "It's a natural disinfectant. We have a proper first aid kit at the house, but for now . . ."

"I'm sure it's fine. Just a little cut, no biggie."

She frowned. "It's not fine to me. Why were you in such a rush?"

"I get nervous around crowds," I said, waving my hand dismissively. "Church service let out and I'm just not the best with conversations." The look she gave me was incredibly skeptical—or perhaps concerned. Hurriedly, I changed the subject. "What made you so jumpy anyway? Or do you always pull a knife on people who bump into you?"

She shook her head, her mouth pressed into a thin line. "I'm sorry. I should have been more careful."

She peeled the herbs away from my wound, pulled a water bottle from her bag, and had me lean over so she could wash off the blood.

"We'll get proper disinfectant on it at the house," she said. "Let's go. Can you walk?"

"I—yes, I can walk." I snickered, and she looked confused. "It's just a little cut, Rayne! Not a broken bone. Of which I've had plenty, by the way. Mountain biking isn't exactly safe."

Footsteps were approaching, a family coming up the road as they headed home from church. The shutters on a nearby shop clattered open, and it finally sounded as if Marihope was coming to life.

"Alright, Miss Lockard," Rayne said, stepping closer, voice low. The way her mouth held my name made me shiver. Her tone was warm, but the promise in her eyes was as cold as the knife she'd cut me with. "You're no delicate flower. You've shown me that already. But while you are residing under my roof, the only pain you should experience is the pain you want. You didn't ask for that cut on your neck, so it shouldn't have happened."

Any response I could have given was squashed by the sincerity in her voice. She nodded politely to the family as they walked past, keeping her eyes mostly averted from them.

"Come on," she said. "Let's get back to the house. Have you eaten yet?"

Rayne

Closer

I COULDN'T RECALL THE LAST TIME I'D PREPARED A MEAL FOR someone other than myself. I was certainly no chef—that was why the kitchen team always prepared the meals, despite the expense to employ them. As much as I wanted to do it all, I wasn't about to inflict my cooking on a guest.

But considering I'd nearly sliced open Salem's jugular, I figured the least I could do was feed her.

The big industrial kitchen was quiet, other than the sound of my knife on the cutting board. Salem had insisted she could tend to her injury herself, laughing away my concern over it, so she had gone upstairs for now. She had been so eager to explore the square; the fact that she'd left so quickly made me certain something had happened.

Who the hell had talked to her?

When Salem eventually poked her head into the kitchen, I waved her over to join me.

"You look cozy," I said as she walked in wearing what I could only describe as a red fox onesie, complete with a fluffy tail and eared hood.

"I think I've had enough excitement for one day," she said, taking a seat on the shining metal cabinets beside me. "This is my chill time costume." My eyes immediately fell to her throat, and the very obvious bandage pasted there. She hurriedly covered it with her hand. "Stop worrying about me, silly! I'm *fine*."

Part of me wanted to tell her I was sorry again. The other part cringed at the uselessness of apologies. Empty words fixed nothing, so I ducked my head down and kept chopping and mixing until I'd assembled a passable bruschetta.

"What did you think of Marihope?" I said after she'd stuffed her mouth with some topped toasted bread and did a little dance of pleasure. I wasn't any good at small talk. It bored me and took too long. I would have far rather gone straight to the point: Who had sent her running from the square?

"It's beautiful," she said, leaning back on her palms and swinging her legs. "Really quiet. I guess it was even quieter than I expected."

"It's a small community." I avoided the typical "tight-knit" phrase that so many others liked to use. Our community was small, but *knitted* it was not. More like tangled. "Did you meet the pastor?"

She frowned. Perhaps my question was a bit too direct. "I didn't. He's . . . your uncle, right?"

Ah. Someone had indeed spoken to her.

"Yeah. Gerard. He took over at the church after my father passed."

Any time my tongue had to form that word—*father*—it felt bitter in my mouth. But I cleared my throat and said, "Given how morbid people around here can be, I'm guessing someone already told you about my dad, right?"

She frowned deeper, and I realized that came out way more intense than I meant it. The endless mill of gossip had ground down my last nerve, but it wasn't Salem's fault.

"I saw his grave," she said softly. "I'm really sorry, Rayne."

"Please don't be." I stuffed my mouth with bruschetta—too much. I couldn't get a single word out as I chewed.

"Did he—I mean, God, it's so awful, did he really die in that church?" She lowered her voice to ask me, as if the house would be offended to hear her talk about it. "Did someone really—"

"He died in the church, on a Sunday in the middle of January. There was so much fucking snow, no one found him until it was time for the next service. A woman named Ruth found him."

"She did? Wow, she didn't mention that . . ."

I tried not to groan, I really did, but it came out anyway. "Ah, hell, no wonder you ran out of there. Ruth was talking to you?"

She awkwardly rubbed the back of her neck. "Yeah. She's a little . . . well, she's . . ."

"A bitch." I finished for her. "You can say it. Trust me, I know. I had to go to school with her."

She laughed. "She really doesn't seem to like you very much."

"Nope, she does not." Not anymore.

I wasn't sure how to talk about this; I never had, not at any length. But nothing about this situation was familiar to me. I never spent time with guests; I avoided them. People came here for the house and the land, not for me.

But something about Salem made my tongue feel loose. The more I was around her, the more I babbled and didn't know how to stop.

"My dad died when I was a teenager," I said. "Left me the house and a little money. I haven't missed him. Never have and never will. We weren't close. It wasn't sad. We don't know how he died."

She raised her eyebrows at that, and I guessed she'd already been told differently.

"Like I said, there was a bad storm. Animals got into the church and tore up the body. It's gross, but that's just what happens." I talked better when I was moving, so I started assembling my best attempt at a dessert. It also enabled me to avoid looking at her, and I frankly couldn't look her in the eyes when I was lying. "Personally, I think he killed himself. He wasn't well. Hadn't been for a long time."

At least the last part was true.

"I'm sorry to bring it up," she said, but I quickly shook my head.

"Don't be, seriously. It beats talking about the weather."

Taking a glass down from the cabinet, I layered fresh berries, a few slices of pound cake, and whipped cream together.

"Do you always make dessert with lunch?" she said. Her grin told me she knew the answer, well aware I was showing off.

"When I have the time." I wiped a bit of cream from the side of the bowl and slid it over to her. I was pretty damn proud of coming up with it on the spot. It was a simple parfait, but the way her eyes lit up and she pulled her phone out to take a photo felt like winning an award.

She took a bite, and her face melted with bliss. "Oh my God. That is so good. These berries are so sweet."

"They grow at the edge of the property," I said. "I make jam with them too. I'll send you home with some."

She took another excited bite before she realized I wasn't eating. "You're not having one?"

We were out of whipped cream until I could defrost more, but I just shrugged. "I'm too full. Couldn't handle another bite."

"Are you sure?" She held up the spoon. Dollops of cream sandwiched soft, fluffy cake, stained purple from plump berries. Delicious, obviously, but offered from her hand? Ambrosia.

Sitting down on the stool across from her, I let her feed it to me. The berries burst on my tongue, cream smudged on my mouth.

She stared at it. My tongue licked it away, and her pupils swelled.

When her gaze dropped and she took another bite, I was watching too intently. Her lips closed around the spoon, stroking the silver clean but leaving cream on her lip.

I was too close. Staring too hard. Wanting too much.

Obediently, when she offered me another bite, I ate. This time, she wiped my lip clean with her thumb, then lingered with it by my mouth. Turning my head, I closed my lips around her. Stroking my tongue over the pad of her finger, I watched her face. Sweet cream and vanilla melted in my mouth.

Her breath hitched, and I took her finger a little deeper into my mouth. I wanted to see her eyes flutter shut in ecstasy, her chest rise and fall with gasps of pleasure. I teased her with my tongue, held eye contact, and slowly released her finger from my mouth.

She looked like a dream, staring at me with those wide, wanting eyes.

No one had ever looked at me like that. Like a little explorer peering into the dark cavern of my soul, her light shining inside and terrifying everything that hid in the dark.

I wanted to guide her in. Show her the safe places in my shadows. Shelter her behind my walls.

But . . .

She wasn't mine. She never would be. To *want* her to be, to desire her to stay, was so selfish I should have been ashamed.

I wasn't. I was greedily, ravenously fixated.

"Rayne . . ." She trailed off, and my heart sped up. I knew what she wanted. Damn it, I did too. She would taste sweet and soft, like the last remnants of summer. She would feel warm, and shake under my touch.

But I'd already gone too far, hadn't I?

I stood up, even though the disappointment on her face shattered me.

"I need to get back to work," I said. "Take as long as you want; I'll clean up later."

"Oh—okay." She didn't even have a chance to get more than a few words out. I hated myself for it. Hated walking away and leaving her there, with so many words still tangled in my throat.

Salem

Evisceration and Shadows

$\mathfrak{I}$T WAS DUSK, AND I WAS RIDING.

The trail was long and meandering, twisting and turning through the forested hills and down steep gullies. My lungs filled with cold air that tasted faintly salty from the ocean breeze.

It had been two days since I'd seen Rayne. She was in the manor, somewhere. I could feel her presence like a cold fog lingering around the house. But she didn't show up in the dining room for meals, and I didn't see her around the yard or in the halls.

Last night, I sat on my bed in complete silence, straining to hear anything from her room next door. I hated myself for my curiosity, hated that I couldn't stop thinking about her.

But my heart skipped a beat when I heard her shower turn on or her bed springs creak. I listened to her feet pace softly around the room to the crooning hum of her music played at a low volume.

My heart was still an open wound; I knew better than to offer it up on a silver platter to be cut open again.

Skidding to a stop, I climbed off the bike for a moment to stretch my back. The pale blue sky was swiftly darkening, the chirping birds joined by singing crickets. The scent of rain was in the air.

I only had one more week in this beautiful place.

It didn't feel nearly long enough. Going home meant telling the same sad story over and over again to sympathetic coworkers, friends, and family. I'd have to establish some kind of running joke about being left at the altar, because I really hated pity, and would far rather laugh than admit how much it all hurt. I'd eventually have to "get back out there" and dive back into the repulsive dating pool I thought I'd already escaped.

Maybe I should just get a dog.

Shivering as the wind picked up, I rubbed my hands over my bare arms and scolded myself for not bringing a jacket. So long as I was on the bike it was fine, but if I stood still too long, I was going to turn into a frozen-sweat popsicle.

But right as I was about to get on my bike, I saw something strange.

About twelve yards ahead, someone was staring at me from between the trees. My heart jolted with alarm, until I squinted my eyes and realized who it was.

"Oh my God—Martin?" Hand over my pounding heart, I took a step toward him. I'd seen the old hunter at breakfast with George early that morning, laughing uproariously at his own jokes as he ate eggs and scones. But now, the man's expression was odd. He looked at me like he didn't recognize me, as if in a daze.

"Miss Lockard," he finally said, blinking rapidly before he rubbed his head. He had his rifle in one hand; the other was messily bandaged. "Have you, uh . . . you haven't happened to see old George around, have you?"

I shook my head. His expression made me uneasy; he was wide-eyed and pale.

"Are you okay?" I said, taking another slow step toward him. There was an awful smell in the air, as if something putrid was rotting nearby. "Are you hurt?"

He clutched his obviously injured hand, but shook his head. "No. No, I'm alright." He kept looking around; behind, above, side to side. He took off his glasses, tried to clean them with one hand on his shirt, but his hand shook and he dropped them to the ground. As he squatted to pick them up, cursing, I suddenly noticed the source of the smell.

It was behind him.

The corpse of a deer lay in the tall grass. Its belly had been ripped open, its guts strewn about. Pools of blood soaked the dirt around it, buzzing flies swarming over the body. The open, glassy eyes stared at me.

The blood was still wet.

A sudden feeling of trepidation made a cold sweat break out on my back. "Martin, did you . . . how did . . ."

"That wasn't me," he said, jabbing his finger at the mangled deer. "I don't hunt like that. No hunter worth his damn salt would . . ."

He bit his lower lip, kneading it between his teeth. My fingers were clenched tight, and I instinctively began to back away, toward my bike. Some primal instinct inside me was screaming, telling me to go.

"You ain't seen old George around, have you?" he said again. His eyes were glassy.

"No." Slowly, I got back on my bike, never taking my eyes off him. "I haven't seen him. You should get back to the house, Martin. Do you want me to get help?"

"No, no, he'll turn up." His voice turned faint, almost dreamy as he stared up into the trees. "He'll turn up."

I SHOULDN'T HAVE stayed out so late, but I wasn't used to these early sunsets. Riding back to the house in the dark was nothing short of terrifying, especially after my encounter with Martin. I had a headlight on my bike, but its beam of light only made the ride more eerie. It cast shadows between the trees, and in my peripheral vision, those shadows became faceless figures.

Raindrops were falling when I finally caught sight of the manor's glow on the hilltop above me. Unfortunately, I found myself on the backside of the property, gazing through an iron fence at the distant house. I really didn't want to spend even another mile on the trail, and I rode the fenceline until I found a place I could climb over and haul my bike with me.

A massive fallen tree provided me something to climb on. Tossing my bike over the fence with a grunt, I hauled myself over too, half expecting an alarm to sound.

All that stood between me and the manor's warmth was a dark, open field, and a single lonely stone building.

Even in the dark, it was obviously dilapidated. An old shed or abandoned workshop, I guessed. The rain began to pour, and

I took shelter beneath the roof's overhang as I rummaged in my bag for my thin rain jacket.

Tap. Tap-tap.

I paid no attention at first, assuming all I could hear was the dripping rain.

Tap-tap. Scriee-ch!

The undeniable sound of sharp nails on glass set my every nerve on edge, and I whipped my head around. There was a window nearby, the old glass so dirty it was impossible to see through no matter how long I stared.

There was no movement. The sound had stopped.

Swallowing hard, I turned my bike's light toward the window.

Through the filthy glass, all I could see was a large silhouette as it darted away from the light. There was clatter, a crash, and the rapid scuffle of nails on wood.

With a shuddering breath, I peeked around the front of the structure and spotted the door. Or at least, what had *once* been a door. The entrance had been completely boarded over.

"Ooh, nope. Nope, nope, nope." Muttering to myself, I hurriedly got on my bike. My shoes slipped on the pedals and I almost couldn't see a thing with the weather, but I didn't care. Between Martin, the dead deer, and whatever the hell had made its home in that shed, I was thoroughly creeped out.

Rayne

Terrors in the Dark

SALEM HAD BEEN GONE FAR TOO LONG.

My eyes were glued to the clock, my leg jiggling faster with every minute that passed without her walking in that door. I'd sat in the foyer for hours, sorting through files that didn't need sorting and playing solitaire on the ancient desktop. Loki had gone up the stairs to lie on the landing in protest, staring at me as if it was *my* fault we weren't in bed yet.

It wasn't my business what guests did with their time. Salem, Martin, and George were the last visitors remaining for the season, and I trusted that the hunters knew how to take care of themselves out in the forest.

Salem's bike was missing from the shed. I knew because I'd checked, after stalking outside her room for thirty minutes and hearing nothing within. With winter curfew looming over us and paranoid whispers among the townsfolk, I regretted ever accepting Salem's last-minute booking in the first place.

The missing girl, Andrea, had yet to be found. I feared her disappearance wouldn't be the last.

"Goddamn it, where are you?" I paced across the foyer, staring at the door, trying to convince myself not to get on the ATV to go look for her. I hated having my emotions tied up with someone else. The chaos in my brain wouldn't let me rest.

Creeeak.

I flinched, whirling around to face the stairway. Loki's head was up, ears pricked, his attention focused on the upper floor.

Creeeak.

A low growl rumbled in the dog's chest. I stormed up the stairway, heart in my throat and fury making my hands shake. When I reached the landing, I stared up to the dark second floor. Except, it shouldn't have been dark. I kept those lights on for guests, always, and we had a backup generator in case the electricity went out.

But it was black as night. My breath fogged in the air, a shiver running up my spine. Jamming my hand into my pocket, I grasped the tiny earbuds I always kept on me, fighting the urge to stuff them in my ears and make it all go away.

"What do you want?" I shouted, as if I could intimidate the darkness into retreating. Loki whimpered, nuzzled against my leg, and quickly retreated to the lower floor. It made my stomach sink not to have him beside me, but even he knew better than to indulge my madness.

I heard nothing, but it felt as if someone had sharply sucked in their breath, drawing all the oxygen out of the room.

"WHAT DO YOU WANT?!" My voice broke with fury, my hands balled into fists. There was no answer. No footsteps.

Just the cold, stagnant air and the scent of mold. Tightness swelled in my chest as I thought of the long winter ahead, the dark days when I had no choice but to wander these halls alone.

I couldn't bear to stay. But I wasn't allowed to leave, and God, I'd tried.

After twenty-four hours off the island, the whispers would begin. Incessant, hissing cold breath that tickled my neck and wouldn't let me sleep. The island's roots were in me, and they might stretch, but they would never break.

The whispers were my warden; this house was my prison.

THERE WAS ONLY one place I could find peace. The conservatory was almost as old as the manor itself, built by Grandpa Henry for my grandmother, his wife. The plants within had been collected and nurtured through the decades, creating a diverse jungle of flora.

When my father would rage, this was where my mom would send me. She showed me how to propagate plants with simple cuttings and jars of water, how to care for seeds until they were ready for soil, how to pot, plant, and prune. It relaxed me to work with my hands, to set my mind to a quiet task. That was why I spent so many hours tending these grounds, despite it being beyond my capacity to care for.

If nothing else, I'd kept my mom's plants alive when my father would have let them wither and die. I was proud of that.

Despite the rain and cold weather, the greenhouse was pleasantly warm. I lit up a joint and wandered among the plants, touching the leaves like I was greeting old friends. My phone automatically connected to the Bluetooth speaker on my workbench, and Siouxsie's "Love Crime" began to play.

No more whispers. No creaking footsteps and oppressive sadness.

I sank into an old wicker chair and propped my feet up on a bucket as I smoked. Beside me, tucked between the clay pots of several propagated monsteras, sat a framed photo of my mom and me: a selfie she'd taken with an old disposable camera, hugging me close as we stood on the beach.

I couldn't remember that day anymore. I couldn't remember her voice, or her smell; the clothing of hers I'd kept smelled like mothballs and dust now instead of her old perfume. I couldn't remember what it felt like when she hugged me, but I could still recall the tune she would hum to me, gentle and slow.

She was the one I would always go to. The one with an answer for all my questions and comfort for all my pain. When my father spoke of angels in his sermons, I envisioned them like her.

That was before I knew how dangerous angels could be.

"What do I do, Mom?" I said softly. I stubbed out the joint in my ashtray and set it aside, staring at her photo as if she'd speak if I just listened hard enough. But the photo was silent, her smile frozen in time just like mine.

Then, with a start, I saw a light bobbing outside the greenhouse.

Salem

Greenhouse

𝕴 WAS SOAKED TO THE BONE BY THE TIME I MADE IT UP THE HILL
into the manor gardens. Shivering, glancing over my shoulder every other second with fear, I nearly screamed when I heard
a sudden rush of footsteps approaching from my right.

"Salem? Where the hell have you been?"

"Rayne, I—" My words were muffled against her coat as
she threw her arms around me, smothering me in her chest.
Instantly, I melted. She was the warmest thing I'd felt for hours
and smelled so good. The exhausted urge to cry nearly choked
me up as I said, "Something is wrong. I don't know what happened, I saw Martin and—"

"Your teeth are chattering too hard, I can't understand a
word you're saying," she muttered, hurriedly stripping off her
jacket and wrapping it around me. She led me into the greenhouse from which she had emerged, the warm air hitting me

with such relief that I moaned. "You're going to catch your death out there."

Dripping as I walked, I let her guide me through the plants to a small seating area. Soils and fertilizers were stacked in bags on nearby shelves, the damp, rich dirt putting the smell of minerals in the air. A large workbench held a plethora of baby plants, an old photo, and to my delight, an electric kettle.

Rayne promptly turned it on before coming back to me.

"Jesus, you're freezing!" She seized a chunky knit blanket from the back of my wicker chair and wrapped it around my shoulders. She took my hands, holding them tight in hers, even leaning down to blow her warm breath onto me. "Are your fingers always this cold? Am I going to have to knit some mittens for you?"

With my shivering finally under control, I told her about my run-in with Martin, the butchered deer, and George's mysterious absence. I didn't mention the thing I'd seen in the shed. Now that I thought back on it, I suspected it was probably an animal. Or, just like when I'd "seen" something in the bathroom, maybe it had only been my imagination.

Rayne listened with an intent frown.

When I finished, she said, "I'll report it to the sheriff. He'll get someone out there to look for them. Don't worry." She gripped my hands tighter; I was ashamed of how clammy they were. "Martin and George may not look like much, but they're more experienced with the outdoors than you might think. They've been to Blackridge before, they know their way around."

But by the expression on her face, I doubted she believed her own words.

She went to the workbench, picking up a large, brick-like walkie-talkie. "Keatin, come in. It's Rayne." The silence drew out, and she tried again. "Keatin, wake up. A guest is missing."

This time, after another few seconds of silence, a sleepy voice responded. "I hear you. Go ahead."

Rayne relayed everything I'd told her, from Martin's injury to George's absence. The sheriff's staticy voice responded intermittently, clarifying information, until he ended with a heavy sigh.

"I'll get someone out there to search," he said. "This ain't good. This late in the year—"

Rayne abruptly cleared her throat, cutting him off. "I'm not alone. Talk to you tomorrow. Let me know if you find anything?"

"Will do. Over and out."

She returned the walkie to its cradle, leaning against the workbench for a moment in silence.

"They know their way around," she repeated, but I didn't feel as if she was talking to me this time. "They probably just had a little too much to drink and got turned around."

She turned back to me, arms folded, and her eyes narrowed. "Are you still shivering?"

"Yeah, I have the shakes, it's—I'm just a little anxious."

She quickly took down two stained mugs from a shelf and dropped in a couple tea bags. As I watched her prepare the hot beverages, my brain finally caught up with everything she'd said.

"Did you say you knit?" I held up the edge of the colorful blanket. "Did you make this?"

"Yeah. Surprised? I do have some talents besides giving head and being an asshole."

I laughed, thankful for the distraction from my shattered nerves. She finished preparing our tea and pulled over a stool so she could sit facing me. Holding the mug in both hands, I deeply inhaled. Peppermint and honey flooded my head, slowing my pounding heart and shaky breathing.

"Do I make you anxious?" Rayne said suddenly as she stared at her teabag slowly swirling round the mug.

"No. I mean, kind of. A little. A lot." My sweaty hands were evidence enough of that, despite how cold I was. "But it's in a different way than, like . . . bad anxiety, if that makes sense."

I rarely tried to explain this to people. To those who didn't experience it, an anxiety disorder typically didn't make much sense anyway. I just needed to "calm down" or "have a more optimistic outlook."

Fighting my anxiety didn't work. It would beat me down every time.

"I got diagnosed with an anxiety disorder when I was fourteen," I said. As much as I didn't like explaining it, I desperately needed to do so. "It, um . . . explained a lot. And I was able to get on medication, which didn't help, but I've switched prescriptions a few times. It's just something I live with."

"So, I make your anxiety act up," she said. "But it's not a bad thing? What happened to trusting your gut?"

I snorted. "Yeah, my gut is not to be trusted. It's way too paranoid."

Silence stretched until she said softly, "You should trust it about me, Salem."

Immediately, I responded, "I do."

My gut didn't tell me to stay away from her. She drew me in like a magnet, and I trembled as I tried to resist. It was my heart that warned me to stay away, tender as it was. The waves of nerves that washed over me when I saw her, the way my heart clenched when she spoke—I hadn't felt like that when I looked at Colin.

And that scared me.

As I sipped my tea, I took a closer look at the photo on the workbench. A beautiful woman with long brown hair held her child close, cheeks squished together as they smiled for the camera. The beach was behind them; the rocky sand and driftwood told me it was Blackridge's craggy shore.

"Who is she?" I said.

"Melanie Balfour. My mother. She was murdered twenty years ago."

I choked on my tea.

"It's okay," Rayne said quickly, looking at me with alarm. "It's been a long time, and I'm . . . I'm okay." Again, I didn't believe her, nor did I think she believed herself.

My curiosity burned, but I didn't push for more. Instead, after a minute of silence, Rayne continued, "My mom used to walk out to the old lighthouse in the evenings to watch the sunset. She'd climb up to the gallery for the best view. And one day . . . November first . . . she didn't come back."

She recounted it like a history lesson, a tragedy long past. But her eyes grew distant, fogged over with an emotion she wouldn't give voice to.

"She was found by that evening, near the lighthouse. Her throat was cut. She bled out. She . . . crawled . . . before she died. Tried to get away, I guess, or get help. I was eight years old." She cleared her throat. "It was just me and Dad after that. He never wanted to be a father, he didn't know what the hell to do with me. His life was the church, and with Mom gone, that was all he ever focused on. He wrote his sermons as if they were for the murderer themselves."

"Who did it?" I said, and shivered when she shook her head again.

"We don't know. We'll probably never know."

Slowly, carefully, I moved my hand on top of hers, hoping she wouldn't pull away. She didn't.

"Dad thought Blackridge deserved to be punished," she said. "We were all wretched sinners and he hated us. All of us. He used the pulpit like a judge's podium and his Bible like a weapon. Growing up with him was lonely. This island is already an isolated place, but in this big house, it was worse. The quiet is so loud."

She took a deep breath and straightened up. But she let my hand remain on hers.

"Hatred changes a place. It builds up, it festers. All the anger and pain becomes a curse. It's like a scar the island can't heal, a wound we're always ripping open again. Even with him gone, it's still here."

She paused, her finger brushing pointedly over the indent left on my own by my missing engagement ring. "Well, I told you my tragedy. Now it's your turn."

Still absorbed with what she'd told me, I responded slowly. "He didn't die. He just broke off our engagement a month before the wedding. Turned out he was cheating on me."

"Shit." Rayne shook her head in disbelief. "I feel like a tragic accident would have been better."

Shrugging, as if I was entirely over it, I said, "I can't complain. According to the plan, I should be in Las Vegas right now, partying it up as a newlywed. Instead, I'm here."

"With me." Her words were so soft, I barely caught them. "You don't seem like the type to go for a Vegas wedding."

"Can't you tell I'm a total party animal?" I teased, and she gave me a skeptical look. "You're right. Vegas wasn't my idea. It actually made me really anxious. But that was what he wanted." I sighed. "I spent too much time only focusing on what he wanted. But I was afraid if I didn't, he'd leave. Find someone else. Turns out, he did that anyway."

"Then tell me," she said. "Where would you get married?"

I'd thought about it so many times. Still, I almost gave my usual answer: For the right person, I'd get married in a cardboard box. Location and a big party weren't what really mattered to me.

But I still had a dream, a wedding day I desired even if it was unlikely to happen. I'd gotten so used to brushing off the things I wanted, talking about it felt scary. As if merely admitting what I desired was too demanding of me.

"I wanted a small ceremony," I whispered. "Just our family. A few friends. In the mountains, at sunset. That was how I always imagined it. With lanterns and candles to light the dusk. And I'd wear a long dress even though it would drag on the ground." I thought of the wedding dress I'd ordered, then swiftly canceled. Even that dress hadn't been exactly what I wanted, short and tight to fit the Las Vegas theme.

Rayne kept holding my hand, her finger stroking back and forth. I wanted to ask her the same question.

I didn't dare.

Finally, without looking up, she said, "We should get you out of those wet clothes." But she didn't get up and neither did I. I didn't want to leave this moment behind.

Our eyes met. Her hand tightened on mine.

"Don't tempt me," she whispered, words ground out as if in pain.

"I'm not." My heart hammered when she leaned closer.

"Oh yes, you are. You always do, and you know it. You're always . . ." She slid her hand over my wrist, gripping my arm with a desperate hold. "Watching me."

"As if you don't do the same?"

She shook her head, laughed softly—but she didn't deny it. I wanted her to tighten her grip again; I wanted her hungry words.

She had tempted me every damn day from the moment I arrived. The way her eyes lingered when she looked at me, the low octaves of her voice when she spoke. I was a yo-yo in her hands, returning even though she pushed me away, but only because she refused to let me go.

After Colin, I refused to go where I wasn't wanted, or to cling to things that wouldn't have me. But I felt her want, her need. I saw it in her eyes and heard it in her voice.

"You don't understand," she said. Her words tossed me down, but like a string wrapped around her finger, she pulled me right back. "I'm not safe for you, Salem."

"I don't run from risks." I leaned toward her, as much a challenge as I dared to muster. "I learn how to work with them."

Salem

Regret

AYNE'S GAZE WAS BRIGHT AND DANGEROUS IN THE GREEN-house's dim light. "I know. You like the adrenaline rush. The unknown. The fear." She narrowed her eyes, reading me like an open book. "You're obsessed with it. Addicted to it. Just like . . ."

She winced and fell silent, but I couldn't let those unspoken words go. "Just like what?"

She sucked in her breath. Her fingers traced up my arm to the damp sleeve of my shirt, then to the cold, wet collar. Her answer was a whisper, her eyes fixed on my throat. "Just like I'm addicted to you."

This entire island dripped with an eeriness I didn't understand; there were shadows here that no amount of light could erase. But the most mysterious of it all was her. Her hidden feelings, her fears, her desire.

"I'm only here for a few more days," I said. My body was practically vibrating as she stroked her fingers across my cheek, closer to me than ever. Only a few days, and still so much didn't make sense. "I don't want to leave here with regrets."

Her hand closed around my jaw, gripping my face with a possessiveness that made blood rush to my cheeks. "You'll regret me. Everyone does."

The way she touched me, rough yet reverent, was perfect. I closed my eyes, leaned into her hand. "You're wrong. I don't regret you. I regret that I don't have longer."

She touched the bandage on my neck; her breath shuddered as she exhaled. "What's your safeword?"

Without hesitation, I blurted, "Red."

The most delicious predatory smile spread over her face. "Damn, how long have you been waiting to tell me that?"

"Too long."

She made me feral, reduced to need and desire like an animal. Starving, I traced her lips with my fingertip. Wanting, wondering, worrying.

Her words came out rough, as if they were rusty. "If I push you too far, make me stop. Don't regret me, Salem. Please."

Bringing my mouth close to her ear, I said, "I want you. Every mean, dangerous, fucked-up part of you. Right now."

She stood, knocking her stool to its side with a clatter. She held me, fingers tangling through my short hair as she kissed me. She gripped the nape of my neck and I moaned into her mouth. Her tongue slid alongside my own—touching, twining, tasting.

I rose up to meet her and she shoved me back against the workbench, the smooth old wood groaning.

She covered my throat with her palm, and her fingers squeezed the sides of my neck. I giggled in lightheaded bliss as her mouth stole my breath away again. Goose bumps sprinted up my spine and prickled over my skull. She tasted like apples and smelled like the forest—like fresh sap, crumbling wood, blood, and soil. As if she was a part of the island come to life, a wild thing allowed indoors, an untamed creature.

She could hunt me down and rip me apart, but I was willing prey.

She was sex and violence intertwined as she bit my lip, and I eagerly guided her hand between my legs. I was grinding down against her palm and not even the fabric of my shorts was enough to keep me from moaning.

"I love how sensitive you are," she said, leaving featherlight kisses down my neck. I shivered, my entire core tensing at her stimulating touch. "Let me hear you, pretty girl. Let me hear those sweet sounds you make."

"Oh, God, please, Rayne." Mouth to mouth, lips touching, I spoke my desperate words. "Don't stop, don't—"

She swallowed my begging, her tongue playing a sinful game with my own as her hands explored me. She pushed up my shirt, then pulled it off. She kneaded my breasts, pinching my nipples between her thumb and forefinger. Then she lowered her head, and her tongue circled teasingly around one tense bud, then the other. My eyes fluttered closed, breath hitching as her mouth closed over my breast and sucked.

She teased me with gentle bites that made me whimper. Her tongue flicked back and forth, lighting my nerves like sparklers, until my legs were shaking. She consumed me like a feast as her hands were occupied with my shorts, popping the button open and pulling my zipper down.

"God, you taste so fucking good," she groaned. Her hand slipped between my legs, cupping my cunt through my panties. "I know that wet pussy is going to taste even better."

My shorts fell to my ankles. I peeled off her shirt and unhooked her bra, momentarily rendered speechless as I drank in the sight of her. Her breasts were soft and heavy, filling my hands as I cupped them. I traced her stretch mark stripes, enamored with the perfect brown color of her areolas, the blushing maroon hue of her nipples.

"Please, Rayne, can I . . ." I lowered my head pleadingly, wanting so badly to pleasure her. But I wouldn't push without her permission. I wanted to know she desired my touch.

"Such a good girl," she murmured, and guided my head down until I caught her nipple in my mouth.

I looked up, eyes wide as I teased my tongue around the swollen bud. Her lips were parted with pleasure, giving little gasps of bliss. Her hand was warm, her palm rubbing me through my underwear's thin fabric.

Slipping my hand down her joggers, I found her bare—God, she was *dripping*. She inhaled sharply when I touched her, before melting into a moan that made me feral.

Bringing my fingers to my mouth, I licked them clean, and she watched me like she was witnessing an angel descend from heaven.

"Goddamn, you're so sexy." She seized me, gripping my ass and lifting me so I was sitting at the edge of a potting table. The wood groaned beneath me, and I leaned back against the glass wall. Sensations of warm and cool, pain and pleasure collided.

Rayne spread my legs as she pressed herself between them. She hooked her finger around my underwear and pulled it to the side, looking at me so intently my face flooded with heat.

"Look at that beautiful pussy," she said. "Fuck, you're gorgeous, Salem. I'll make this sweet little hole cry for me."

She knelt down, and her mouth closed over me before I could respond, her tongue weaving a wicked spell on my flesh. It plunged inside me and my toes curled, and she lifted her head just enough to demand, "Hold your legs up for me. I'm going to eat you until you scream."

Her tongue pressed hungrily inside me. My eyes rolled back and fluttered shut as she stroked, licked, and sucked. Her fingers dug possessively into my thigh, gripping me tight.

"Mm, so wet for me." The vibration of her words and puff of her warm breath made me tremble. Every time my legs began to lower she would pause, teasing me even more slowly, drawing out my most desperate sounds. "Hold your position, Salem. Be a good girl for me, or I'll tie those beautiful legs above your head."

She must have seen the excitement that sparked in me at her threat. She gave a low, throaty chuckle, and said, "Oh, you like that, don't you? Want me to tie you up?"

I could barely get the words out, but I huffed, "Y-yes, Madam, please . . ."

Metal hooks were affixed to the wall above my head; potted plants hung from some, coils of rope hung from others. She seized one of those ropes and unwound it, watching me all the while.

"Have you ever been tied before?" she said, and I shook my head.

"Unless you can count fuzzy handcuffs, no," I said. She grinned and leaned over me, pressed between my legs.

"Thank you for trusting me to do it," she said. Her words were tender, her voice soft. "Give me your wrists. If it hurts, call your safeword. Are we clear on that?"

"Yes, Madam."

Her breasts were almost close enough to smother me. I opened my mouth, whimpering until she leaned closer and I caught her nipple in my mouth again.

She looped the rope around my wrists, then tied the other end to the hook above my head, extending my arms upward. I savored the feeling of helplessness, tugged against the rope and moaned when the rough fibers dug into my skin.

"That's my girl," she said. "You make me feel so good. How can you have such an innocent face but such a wicked tongue?"

She straightened up and stepped back, folding her arms as she admired me. It lit a fire inside me to be observed like that, her eyes combing over my exposed body.

"Maybe I should keep you like this," she mused, teasing her fingers over my inner thighs and making me shiver. "My very own little pet, tied up to be used whenever I please."

She stripped off her joggers and tossed them aside. She looked like a goddess as she stood over me, tracing her hands delicately over my skin. Then she reached over and lifted a pair of small garden shears. She snipped them slowly, the eerie sound of scraping metal making a chill run over me. Slowly, she dragged the cold metal tip down my arm . . . then between my breasts . . . until she stopped just below my navel.

"Were these expensive?" she said sweetly, caressing the shears along the edge of my panties. I shook my head, and she insisted, "Give me your words. May I ruin these, just like I'm going to ruin the rest of you?"

"Yes, Madam."

She cut my panties off with two quick snips. She brought them to her nose and inhaled deeply, her half-lidded eyes looking straight into my soul.

"I'll never forget the way you smell," she said, tossing the ruined clothing away. "The way you taste . . . how you sound . . . fuck, I wish I could keep you."

Her body cleaved to mine, hot and heavy as she kissed me. My bound arms trembled as she straightened up and guided my leg to rest on her shoulder, while the other hung limp off the edge of the table. I was splayed out and utterly helpless as she massaged two fingers back and forth over my clit.

"That's it, moan for me. You're so soft, Salem. You feel perfect." She kept talking as she teased, until I was twitching, whimpering, *pleading.*

"Please, I need more, please . . ."

"Greedy girl," she crooned. "God, look at you shake."

The table creaked as she lifted one leg up, planted right next to my hip. My short legs could never, but with her height and the new angle, she pressed her soaking-wet pussy against mine. She thrust against me, her breath shuddering, and I made a strangled sound. The heat of her was overwhelming, the sensation of her grinding down on me making my eyes roll back.

She moved slow and sensually at first, her chest swelling with each deep breath. She was mesmerizing, intoxicating. Condensation dripped from the glass I was pressed against, warmth surrounding us despite the cold outside.

"Don't stop!" I begged. That knot of pleasure deep within my core pulsed and I cried out her name.

"Say my name again," she said, breathless. "Let me hear you."

"Rayne, please!" I didn't know what I was begging for, nor did it matter. The feeling of her, so soft and slick as she fucked against me, was nothing short of heaven. She tipped her head back, sweat beading on her chest.

"I'm going to come on this perfect pussy," she said. She turned her head and set her teeth against my thigh, biting down as her entire body tensed and shuddered. Her breath came short and quick. The wet sounds of our flesh moving together were primal, in a deep, dark, wild way that made my soul feel alive.

Her eyes fluttered closed as she came. She gave a guttural moan, the sound so hot that my vaginal muscles clenched and throbbed. I was unbearably sensitive, my clit swollen with arousal, and Rayne kept grinding against me . . .

"Rayne—oh my God—you're gonna make me come—"

My core tightened, tension knitting through every muscle. Ripples of pleasure reverberated through me, and I groaned with abandon.

It was impossible to stay silent. I was crumbling, stuck in a whirlwind of sensation and desire. My self-control shattered, my vision blurred. All that remained was her, watching me break, talking me through the bliss—"That's it, let go. Come for me. Fuck, that's so good, Salem. Just look at you."

The glass was fogged, and we were enveloped in heat. Intertwined, sticky with sweat. Rayne eased my leg down from her shoulder, leaning heavily against the table I lay on, her hair hanging in my face.

"So . . . do you regret it?" she said, in that deep, rough voice that made me feel like squealing and kicking my feet.

"Never," I said.

She leaned down, her soft chest pressed to mine, and kissed me. I could taste myself on her lips, making my afterglow burn even brighter.

A greedy girl, indeed.

Rayne

Awakening

I WASN'T ABOUT TO MAKE SALEM WALK BACK TO THE HOUSE IN her damp clothes. Instead, I wrapped her in the blanket, bundled tight, and carried her through the garden and into the house.

By the time I reached the third floor, her head was slumped against my chest. Her eyes barely fluttered when I laid her in bed. She curled up on her side as I tugged the blankets over her and brushed a few short locks of hair off her forehead. There were hickies all over her throat, violet blooms I couldn't resist touching. Her lips were red, just a little swollen. Her breathing was deep and easy.

Her taste was in my mouth, on my fingers, seared into my soul.

It wasn't supposed to be like this.

She was a cookie stolen from the jar, a slice of cake at midnight. She was temptation and deliverance. Everything I'd forbidden myself to have; everything I'd been told I *couldn't* have.

And it was true: I couldn't have her. She wasn't here for me, as much as I wanted her to be.

These were stolen moments, selfish indulgences. She would leave, and I would stay. She would live the life she was meant to, fall in love, have a career, maybe kids. The pain of her fiancé leaving her would diminish, and she would go on. But me?

I'd be left thinking about her. Clinging to the dream I was allowed to live in for a brief few days. A dream of normalcy, of safety.

But nothing here was normal. There was no safety on Blackridge, and there was no safety with me.

This island was no place for the living.

SHERIFF KEATIN HAD no good news to report in the following days. Martin and George had come to Blackridge before; they were no strangers to hunting here. But when I checked their rooms and found their bags still there, with no sign of them despite it being past their checkout date, a feeling of dread took root in me.

Perhaps they'd lost track of time. Perhaps an injury had stranded them. Or perhaps they'd simply left, abandoning their belongings. I tried to cling to hope, but it was wearing thin.

Blackridge wasn't a particularly large island, but it was densely covered with woodland. It made searching for the missing even more difficult, and the impending storms didn't help.

The forecast showed rain, rain, and more rain, with howling winds and a high chance of thunderstorms.

My unease made me irritable. My one reassurance—and heartbreak—was that Salem was leaving soon. Only a few more days, and she would be off this island for good.

She would be safe, and I could stop living in a fantasy.

"Helloooo, Earth to Rayne? It's fucking creepy out here, sing us a song or something!"

The crackle of James's voice coming through the walkie-talkie made me jump, jolting upright. It was midday, but I'd been struggling to sleep at night and kept dozing off. Stifling a yawn, I grabbed the walkie and seized a paper map of the island from a shelf above my desk. Spreading it out before me, I located the red dots indicating where the trail cameras were in the woodlands around Marihope.

"Where are you?" I said, chewing the end of my pen. I was on call with James and his brother, Mark, while they turned the cameras on. The sheriff usually would have helped the volunteer rangers, but with three people now unaccounted for, he had his hands full.

"I'm on Corrain Trail, just past the fork. Freezing my balls off out here."

"It's barely under forty degrees," I said, tracing the trail with my finger. "Don't be a baby."

"Easy for you to say. You're probably sitting in front of your fireplace right now, cuddled up with that pretty little woman you've got living with you."

Loudly, I cleared my throat. "Watch it, James. Or I'm turning the walkie off."

"Okay, okay, jeez, sorry. It's hard to miss the gossip, that's all."

"Well, start missing it. Or ignore it, like a goddamn adult."

"Damn, okay. Someone's sensitive."

James and several other forest rangers had helped install the trail cameras around the same time we were finally blessed with a cell tower on the island. While cell reception wasn't great, the cameras worked well enough to provide us with delayed live feeds of our most used roads and trails.

Every year, as the weather grew colder and winter crept closer, we'd turn on the cameras and keep them running until spring. It wasn't much, but even a little information about what was out there was better than nothing.

"Alright, lighting it up in three . . . two . . . one . . ." A loud click came over the speaker and James grunted in concentration. "Are we live?"

"Hold on, let's see." Scooting my chair around the corner, I peered at the six small screens mounted to the wall. The first two blinked, then a black-and-white image of the forest appeared with James and Mark in frame, their faces frozen as the laggy feed gave me one mere image at a time.

"Got it. Corrain One and Two are live." The frames updated, my cousins disappearing from view as they continued their hike. My chair creaked loudly as I leaned back, the old springs more than ready for retirement. "We have to kill the damn thing, James. This is the year. We have to do it."

"That's what you said last year." He didn't say it to be accusatory. His tone was mild, but lowered with worry as he went on. "Every year you push yourself harder, Rayne. You're just putting yourself in danger."

"*Living* is putting myself in danger," I snarled. "And I can barely even do that. None of us can." Rubbing my forehead, I could already feel a headache coming on. "I'm going to lose my mind if I have to stay in this house much longer."

Static crackled, his voice warped for a few seconds. "... gotten worse? I thought things had finally quieted down around the house."

"Yeah, it *was* quiet." Until she showed up. Salem's arrival had stirred something up, and the dust from that refused to settle. "I've been seeing her again. Hearing her."

The red woman. My whispering stalker, the curse from which I could never escape. Music could block out the ghostly words, and pumping the furnace chased away the chill. But no matter what I did, it clung to me. That painful presence, the wailing, the fury. Some days it was a quiet roar in the distance, and others, it was drowning me in its riptide.

"Hey, uh, Rayne . . ." Static took over and James cut out. Sighing in irritation, I fiddled with the antenna until his voice came back.

"Can you repeat, please?" I said. "Lost you for a minute there."

Silence.

"James, can you repeat?"

I waited, my leg jiggling impatiently. Corrain Trail curved south along the coast, before forking into either the dockside road or an easterly turn back toward Marihope. They would be coming up on the next camera shortly, positioned only a mile beyond my own property line.

"James, Mark, do you copy?"

I waited. A minute passed, and it felt far too long.

"James, you'd better fucking copy or I'm coming out after you," I said, my voice reduced to a harsh whisper. My shoulders slumped in relief when there was a crackle of static in response. But my relief was short-lived when I heard what he had to say.

"Something is out here."

A shiver went down my back. My heart jumped into my throat, adrenaline making my head spin.

"What do you see?" My fingers ached as I gripped the walkie tightly. "Do you see it?"

"No, I—no, but there's—ugh, God!" There came a harsh sound of coughing, followed by gagging. "There's something dead. Shit, Rayne, it's a mess—it's—"

Static cut in again and my stomach was in knots, my ears were ringing. "James, listen to me: Just turn on the camera and get out. You and Mark need to go."

"Okay. Okay, don't panic, it's—Christ, it stinks. It's a bear, a big one. God, it's just—everywhere. There's parts of it *everywhere.*"

"James, I swear to God . . ." Gripping my hair in frustration, I waited, staring at the screens. The third feed blinked to life, and my entire body shuddered in revulsion.

The black-and-white image showed a large black bear slumped against a tree. It was blurry, but I could see the head was misshapen, the limbs were gone, and jagged pieces of broken ribs jutted from its chest as if they had been ripped outward.

James and Mark stood over it, shirts pulled up to cover their faces from the stench. A cloud of flies burst into the air as Mark nudged it with his boot.

When the radio crackled again, I nearly jumped out of my seat.

"It could've been another bear that killed it," James said, his voice grim. "They're aggressive this time of year."

But we could all see the way that thing died. Ripped to pieces. Broken and torn, limbs and flesh flung around as if whatever killed it had *enjoyed* it.

"Just get home," I said. "Please fucking get home."

My head sunk into my hands. I wanted to believe his theory, that this was simply the result of a natural conflict between large predators. But I could feel it in my bones: The long, bloody winter was here. The wrath of the Angel of Blackridge was coming. No matter how much I anticipated it, braced for it, I never truly felt ready.

With a sudden burst of alarm, I leapt to my feet, nearly knocking over my chair. I had no idea where Salem was, whether she had stayed in the house today or gone out riding . . .

I *needed* to know she was safe. I needed her indoors before dark. If she'd gone out riding, I didn't have a clue where to look for her first, but I'd still try. Loki would track her down, even if I had to search all night.

By the time I reached the third floor, I was completely out of breath, panic set in so deep that my entire body tingled. Pins and needles burst through my hand as I pounded my fist against her door, about to bring out my master key and force it open—

Salem opened the door with her hair mussed, looking sleepy and concerned. "Oh! Rayne, are you okay? You look—"

"Firewood," I said quickly, and she frowned. "I came to check if you needed more firewood."

She was okay. She was safely inside, protected. The rush of emotion I felt just to see her standing there made me unable to speak for a moment.

I wanted to hold her, kiss her. I wanted to take her to bed and swear to her that I would keep her safe, that nothing and no one would harm her.

Instead, I brushed past her without an invitation and went straight to her fireplace. She had plenty of wood, and a few smoldering coals remained to warm the room. But I needed to move my hands, to do *something*.

She approached me, her bare feet padding softly across the floor to stand beside me. She pulled her headphones off and let them drop to her neck, and I could hear Amy Winehouse playing from the speakers.

"I still have plenty," she said. "Thank you, you really don't have to—"

"You're going to freeze up here," I grumbled, flicking my lighter to get the wood lit.

A little voice of madness inside me wanted to tell her everything, to warn her, to make her see why I so desperately needed her to leave. But she didn't deserve to be dragged into the danger we faced; the less she knew the better.

Only a couple more days and she would be gone. It hurt—God, it fucking hurt so much more than I thought was possible, the idea of never seeing her again, never hearing her voice, never touching her.

I stood up, and she said softly, "Do you want to stay?"

She looked so uncertain, hands clasped together, biting her lip. Did I want to stay? More than anything.

I wanted to collapse on her bed and listen to her talk for hours. I wanted to hear about her inspirations, talk about her dreams. I wanted to know her, desperately, in a way that no one else could. I wanted to consume all that she was, treasure and study her.

With every passing year, this island rotted a little more of my soul. But Salem made me want to flourish; she made me think that maybe there could be something more for me.

But . . .

"I can't," I said.

Her face fell, but she tried to hide it with a forgiving smile. "O-oh, um, right, sorry—"

"But I'll see you tomorrow," I said quickly. "For the Halloween festival. I'm . . ." I smiled, and despite everything, it was genuine. I didn't even have to force it. "I'm looking forward to going. With you."

Her face brightened, like a candle lighting up the dark. I took her hand, warm and half buried in the long sleeves of her sweater, and kissed her fingers. Inhaled the soft scent of her skin.

I imagined holding her close until the nightmares in my head were gone, telling her all the secrets that were petrifying me. It would feel like such relief, like setting down the burden I'd carried for so damn long.

But I couldn't.

"Sweet dreams, Salem."

"You too." She stood in her doorway and watched me leave. My dreams would be sweet as long as she was in them.

Salem

Bonfires and Ghost Stories

I *LOVED* HALLOWEEN. IT HAD BEEN MY FAVORITE HOLIDAY EVER since I was a child, when my mom and I would handcraft elaborate costumes that I would proudly wear to school, usually losing bits of tinsel, glitter, and felt throughout the day. Luckily, I had inherited my mom's crafting skills. The costume I'd brought to Blackridge was simple, but I thought it was adorable.

"What are you?" Rayne said, staring at my all-pink getup before I left the house.

"An axolotl!" I said excitedly. "See?" I pointed to my pink bucket hat, which I had adorned with sparkly ruffles and two big googly eyes. But Rayne still looked thoroughly confused. "You know, the little pink amphibians?"

"So you're . . . a salamander?" she said slowly, and shook her head when I nodded excitedly. "Well, you're the prettiest salamander I've ever seen. Good job."

Her awkward praise made me blush the same shade as my clothes. "What are you going to dress as?"

"Myself." She was preoccupied with her backpack, which I'd yet to see her leave home without. She always packed like she was going on an overnight trip instead of a few miles into town.

"Aw, come on, just wear a costume from last year!"

"There's no costume from last year. I've never dressed up."

"Never?" I gasped. "Not once? Even when you were little?"

She shook her head. "Dad didn't approve. We're lucky the festival goes on at all. Certain folks *still* don't approve."

My soul was shaken, but there was no way I was letting Rayne miss out on another year of Halloween fun. "What if I made you a costume?" She raised one eyebrow skeptically. "I'll be quick! I just need some bobby pins, a sharpie, and my makeup bag—wait right there!"

When I returned, she was seated in a chair in the foyer. Her hands were folded on her lap, her face so solemn one would think she was waiting for a doctor. When she spotted the makeup bag in my hands, her eyes widened slightly.

Hoping to reassure her, I promised, "I'll keep it really simple. Just a little eyeliner on the tip of your nose . . . and your cheeks . . ."

"Are you making me into a black cat?" she said as I leaned close with a stick of black eyeliner.

"Of course! It's been the go-to costume for people who don't know what to dress as since, like, the inception of Halloween. And it fits your personality."

"It . . . what?"

"N-never mind, just hold still." I bit my lip in concentration as I steadied my hand to draw on her nose. I tucked my left hand beneath her chin, holding her face as I delicately drew a dot to mimic a cat nose.

She held perfectly still, and when I straightened up to check my work, she said, "I look ridiculous, don't I?"

"You look beautiful."

She blinked rapidly, startled. I'd even startled myself. Flustered now, I leaned down again to complete her whiskers. But the angle was tricky, my legs bumping against her chair. I put one knee up on her seat to balance myself, right next to her thigh. Her hand came around my waist, and the next thing I knew, she'd pulled me toward her and I was straddling her lap.

Our chests touched. With her hand against my lower back, she closed her eyes and said, "You're good. Go on."

How was she so calm? The eyeliner was going to shake out of my hand. Clenching my entire body to steady myself, I drew her whiskers like the final strokes of paint on a masterpiece. Her throat bobbed as she swallowed, and I could feel her heartbeat beneath my hand when I rested it gently against her neck.

"Done," I said softly. She didn't remove her hand from my lower back as she opened her eyes and wrinkled her nose a few times, as if getting used to the makeup on it. "Do you wanna see?"

"That's okay." She smiled. "You already told me how I look."

THE BOOM AND crackle of fireworks filled the air, orange and red sparks twinkling in the cloudy sky. The streets of Marihope smelled of cinnamon, nutmeg, and clove, as if the entire town had been dipped in pumpkin spice.

The town center was buzzing with people, the busiest I'd seen the island since I arrived. Jack-o'-lanterns decorated nearly every doorstep and lined the sidewalks, illuminating our way with their fluttering candles. Red and orange flags were draped between the light posts, waving in the cold breeze. Creepy scarecrows with burlap bodies and button eyes guarded the way, while cardboard cutouts of black bats dangled from the trees.

There were no children in costumes running about. In fact, I didn't see any children at all until we got closer to the church. Tented stalls were set up there in the square, selling baked goods, vegetables, and canned fruits. There were a couple of small carnival rides, including a miniature Ferris wheel where children rode in multicolored swinging baskets as the wheel creaked round and round like a rusty cog.

A group of elementary-aged children were gathered at a particularly lively stall, giggling as they decorated caramel apples with marshmallows and chocolate chips.

"Rayne! Hi!" A little hand shot up from the pack, and Rebecca suddenly sprinted over, a huge smile on her face. Rachel ran behind her, struggling to keep up as her candy bucket swung in her hand.

Rebecca flapped her arms, which were lined with long feathers glued to her sweater. "Guess what I am! Guess!"

"A seahawk, of course," Rayne said. "Just look at those wings!"

"Yeah!" Rebecca stomped her foot fiercely. "Amanda told me I looked like a chicken. I am *not* a chicken."

"Rayne is a kitty!" Rachel giggled, pointing her small hand at Rayne's whiskered face and giving a wide gap-toothed grin. She was dressed as a sheep, with a fluffy white coat, pants, and floppy felt ears. Rebecca's eyes instantly lit up with excitement.

"I love your costume!" she exclaimed, feathers flying from her excited bouncing. She looked at me and shyly added, "I like yours too."

"Salem helped me out with it," Rayne said, adjusting the small cardboard ears I'd made her. I'd cut them out of an old box, colored them with black marker, and glued them to bobby pins to stick in her hair. "What do you think, do I make a good black cat?"

"Yes!" The girls responded in unison. They looked at Rayne with complete adoration, and little Rachel reached up to take her hand.

"Come make candy apples with us!" she said, tugging Rayne toward the gaggle of other children.

Rayne squat down to her level, saying gently, "Maybe later, okay? I'm going to spend some time with Salem."

Rebecca looked between us, and her mouth suddenly formed an O of understanding. She giggled, leaned down to her sister's ear, and in a too-loud whisper, said, "Remember what Daddy said? They're on a date!"

Rebecca dragged her sister back to join the other children as my heart sped up to a gallop. Dating? People were talking about us . . . *dating*? Rayne's cheeks were red, and she folded her arms with an exasperated sigh.

"The struggles of living in a small town, right?" I teased, hoping to laugh off the uncertainty. "Everybody gossips."

To my surprise, she smiled despite her blush. "At least I'm keeping them entertained." She looked at me, her eyes reflecting the bonfire's light. "And at least its not a bad rumor, for once."

An elderly couple were serving cups of hot chocolate, apple cider, and warm spiced rum from a nearby stall, so Rayne and I got in line. She knew everyone by name, chatting with the woman in front of us, then greeting the couple when we ordered. I got a lot of side-eye and long, lingering looks from the people she chatted with, but Rayne never satisfied their obvious but unspoken questions.

As we walked away with our warm beverages, Rayne suddenly put her arm around my shoulders.

"People aren't used to seeing visitors here this late in the year," she said. "Don't mind them. People are just nosy."

I expected her to remove her arm. She didn't.

I was trying not to think about the fact that I had to leave tomorrow. My bag wasn't even packed yet, so naturally I'd probably be panicking in the morning. I just wanted to enjoy my last night here, with the woman I'd probably never see again.

Walking with her like this, winding through the crowd as we sipped our drinks, I almost felt like things could be different. Maybe . . .

"Are you okay?" Rayne said suddenly. I hadn't even realized I'd given any indication of my growing distress. "Why are you holding your breath?"

"I'm not." I took several rapid breaths, trying to hide that I was slowly fossilizing into a little ball of anxiety. "I'm fine. Just a little cold."

She didn't believe me. Her expression made that so obvious my face began to heat, and I gulped my drink just to hide from her. But before she could pry any further, a man approached us from across the square, raising his hand in greeting. His beard was light brown and thick, his skin pale and cheeks reddened.

"Evening, Sheriff," Rayne said, clasping his hand and giving it a shake. "How's the night been?"

With a soft-spoken drawl, he folded his arms and surveyed the crowd. "Been quiet. Just a few kids breaking bottles. I don't believe we've met." He extended his hand to me. "Name is John. We don't often see guests this late in the year."

"She's leaving tomorrow," Rayne said. The man actually looked relieved.

It was doubtlessly just the spiced rum making me bold, but I very nearly demanded to know why everyone was so eager for me to leave.

It was the first time I'd seen an officer on the island. He wore street clothes instead of a uniform, with his badge, number, and name, *John Keatin*, embroidered on his jacket. He wasn't much for conversation though, and kept surveying the crowd like he expected to see something suspicious.

"Hope you enjoy your night," he said, giving me a nod before looking at Rayne. He seemed to finally realize she was dressed up, and stared in silence for a moment before muttering, "Black cat, huh?"

Rayne folded her arms, looking every bit the part. "Yep."

He made a sound that could have been a laugh, but he didn't look very entertained. "Do you have a moment to speak in private, Miss Balfour?"

Rayne clasped my arm, leaning close to say, "Don't go too far. I'll be right back." She and the sheriff stepped away into the crowd, out of my earshot, and I frowned.

It was hard to shake the feeling there was some kind of lurking danger here. The cozy, peaceful vibe was a pretty thin veneer, when it was present at all. Someone or . . . something . . . had killed Rayne's mom. And I had yet to hear any news about Martin and George being found.

As I stood there sipping my drink and waiting for Rayne's return, I spotted a bonfire in the churchyard. Feeling the chill nipping at my nose, I wandered toward it for warmth. The pleasant scent of woodsmoke swirled around me, and I gave an awkward smile to the group of teenagers seated on a bench nearby. They were laughing boisterously, obviously sneaking sips of liquor from flasks they passed between one another. I did my best to avoid eye contact, but I listened intently.

"And when they found him, his eyes . . . had been hollowed out!" one of the boys shouted triumphantly, using his fingers to hold his eyes open eerily wide. The girls in his circle shrieked and giggled; the guys smirked. The boy took a few triumphant bows as he finished his story, and his friends began shouting requests. "Which one should I tell next? Come on, I've got a million of them, give me a good topic, something creepy."

As he looked around, our eyes met. And for some reason, I said, "Tell the story of the angel."

The entire group instantly fell silent. Smiles faded, and they looked among one another with confusion. Two of the girls whispered to each other, eyeing me with suspicion. I regretted opening my mouth at all.

But the boy nodded slowly. "Alright. Okay. You wanna hear about the Angel of Blackridge?"

One of his friends elbowed him hard. "Come on, Michael, we're not supposed—"

"It's Halloween, dude! It's just a ghost story, don't be a baby." Michael cleared his throat and stood up, pulling his jacket's hood up and casting his face into shadow. When he spoke again, he lowered his voice to a dramatic baritone. "This is the story of Blackridge's curse, and it all starts with a preacher."

Salem

A Call from the Grave

"THIS PREACHER LOVED THE LORD AND HIS WIFE IN EQUAL measure. But when his wife was murdered, the Lord was all he had left. The preacher's wife was a beautiful woman, but when they found her, her throat was slit from ear to ear." He made a grotesque motion with his thumb, as if slicing open his neck. "She bled to death. She bled so much her entire body was stained bright red, drenched with it. That was how he found her, with her body broken on the rocks below the lighthouse. They say the whole island heard him screaming. He prayed to God for justice. He prayed and wept, wept and prayed, until his face looked just like his wife's—skeletal and *dead*." Michael lunged at one of the girls with a snarl, laughing when she shrieked and slapped his chest. "But no matter how much he prayed and sacrificed, no matter how great his faith, justice didn't come. His wife's murderer was never found."

He paused to pace around the fire, building anticipation in his audience. I hated to admit it, but I was tense as I waited for him to continue.

"He built her a beautiful resting place, right there, in the graveyard behind me. He had a stone angel commissioned, and placed it over her grave, so she would be watched over forever. No one could ever harm her again. And still he prayed. *Please, God, please. Listen to your loyal servant. Strike these sinners down, Lord God, so my wife's soul may rest in peace. Judge them as they deserve.*"

I cast a wary glance over my shoulder, looking for Rayne. I knew this story. She'd told it to me. Her mother's murder and her father's grief. My stomach coiled to hear it relayed like this, as a spooky tale to scare teenagers instead of a tragedy. I almost told him to stop, but my curiousity hadn't been satisfied. I wanted—no, I *needed* to know what everyone seemed so determined to keep hidden. I couldn't leave here and be left wondering forever.

The crowd of teens, formerly boisterous and playful, had become subdued as they listened to their friend's tale. My rum was gone, and I wished I had more to get through whatever was coming next.

A knot of dread grew inside me as the storyteller turned, his face cast in flickering shadow.

"Finally," he said, "God heard his prayers."

"I think that's enough."

I nearly leapt out of my skin at the deep voice beside me. I turned to find a dark-haired man with a neatly trimmed beard standing there. He was around my parents' age, and he gave the teenagers a look that reminded me of my dad as he said, "Run along, enjoy the festival. Don't scare our poor visitor with your fairy tales."

"Yes, Mr. Balfour."

"Sorry, sir."

The mumbles and apologies as the group scurried away made me realize who it was beside me even before he reached out his hand to introduce himself.

"Gerard Balfour. It's a pleasure to meet you at last. You must be Salem." His smile was friendly, his hand warm. His eyes were the same dark forest green as Rayne's. "Your last night on the island, I assume? I hope you've enjoyed your time."

"Oh, yes. It's been lovely." It had also been weird, mind-blowingly hot, and disturbingly creepy, but I wasn't about to tell him that.

"You'll have to excuse the kids. Wild imaginations, especially when they've been sneaking liquor from their parents' cabinets." He laughed lightly, but I didn't. The story had been about his own sister-in-law, his deceased brother's wife. Had it been so long that the tragedy, and the stories surrounding it, simply didn't affect him anymore? "Surely you're not here alone?"

"Oh, no, Rayne is with me. She just stepped away to talk with the sheriff."

He nodded slowly, the kind smile frozen stiffly on his face. "I wish you a safe journey home tomorrow, Salem. Do be safe tonight. I'm sure Rayne has already told you, but don't wander too far." He laughed again, but it didn't sound as easy as the first time. "The old roads and forests get terribly dark. Easy to get lost."

As he walked away, I could feel eyes on me. Distant strangers in the crowd hurriedly looked away, but it was like I could feel their whispers slithering over my skin. Suddenly self-conscious, I sidled over to the other side of the bonfire. The churchyard behind me was empty now that the teenagers had gone, filled only with the crickets' song. Except . . .

I frowned, looking over my shoulder toward the graveyard. Was I only imagining things? Was it a strange echo? I swore I could hear something like a whimper, a persistent sound of distress that prodded the knot of dread in my stomach.

I really wanted Rayne to come back.

"Please don't hurt me."

A full-body chill washed over me, and I looked back at the graveyard again. The trees creaked, dry leaves rustling. I'd heard a voice, I had no doubt.

"Oh my God . . . please . . ."

My heart sped up in alarm. The voice was distant, and something about it was uncanny, but I couldn't put my finger on exactly what. The cadence was strange.

"Hello?" I took a few steps closer, trying to see into the trees. Leaving my cup on the ground, I dug my phone out of my pocket and turned on the flashlight. "Is someone there?"

No one else was close enough to hear it. The trees were too dense for me to see much at all past the graveyard's fence.

"Please help me . . . somebody, please . . ."

The voice was so small, so weak. The voice of a terrified young woman. My throat tightened with alarm, and I stood still with indecision. Rayne still hadn't reappeared.

"Hello? Do you need help?" I cupped my mouth and called into the trees. The crickets fell silent, but the playful chimes of the carnival rides still played behind me. The silence drew on, until I began to suspect I had imagined it after all.

But then . . .

"*Help me.*"

I startled back several steps. The voice was still muffled, but it was harsher, sharper. Riddled with pain. Hands shaking, I lifted my flashlight and walked to the cemetery gate, shining my light down the path.

No one was there.

"Come on, Salem," I said, trying to hype myself up. "You're not going to walk away from someone who needs help, are you?"

No, of course I wouldn't. But that didn't keep my hands from shaking as I started down the path.

The farther I ventured into the graveyard, the quieter it became. Almost all noise from the festivities was gone, and those sounds I did hear were muffled and eerie: childish screams and drunken laughter.

Gnarled roots grew out of the path, which was rutted with puddles. Blackberry vines tangled in the thick, tall grass, their thorny tendrils catching on my pant legs. Lifting my phone a little higher, I cast my light all around.

Snap.

I whirled to the left, in the direction of the sound. "Is someone there?"

My mouth was so dry. The alcohol had made me brave, but the cold and the dark had chased the last of my warmth away. I couldn't see shit. Why would anyone be out here without a light? Had a small child gotten lost?

Another twig snapped, stopping me in my tracks. Leaves rustled softly, slowly. As if something was creeping through them, moving with silent intent.

"I can hear you!" I shouted. I had to act like I wasn't afraid. "I heard you calling earlier! Where are you?"

The total silence that followed told me whoever was out here did not want to be found.

But I had a feeling they wanted to find *me*.

With chills running up my back, I decided I'd gone far enough. Ready to enjoy the last few hours I had here, I turned around and lifted my light—

Only to come face-to-face with a glowing skull-faced *thing*.

I screamed. Screamed like I'd never screamed in my life. Frankly, I didn't even know I had it in me.

With only my phone in hand, I instantly chucked it at my assailant. I followed it up with fistfuls of twigs, leaves, and more screams. I was throwing anything and everything I could get my hands on. But the more I threw, the more I realized the monster's face was askew and its red glow was flickering. It was laughing and puffing.

"Calm down!" it shouted, holding up a pale white hand. The temptation to pick up a rock and throw that next was strong, but I resisted as the teenager pulled off his mask, revealing his unfamiliar face. "It's just a prank, lady—shit!"

He stumbled backwards as something zipped past his face and hit the tree beside him with a thunk. A large knife protruded from the trunk, and we both immediately looked toward the one who'd thrown it.

Rayne was storming toward us—no, toward *him*. He put up his hands, swiftly mewling some kind of excuse as she put herself between us. She yanked the knife out of the trunk and jammed it back into its sheath, and his shoulders visibly sagged with the blade put away.

But even without the knife, Rayne's voice as she got in that boy's face made me shiver. "Did you fucking touch her?"

"No! No, I swear, I just scared her! It was a prank, just a prank, I swear! I'm sorry, Rayne. I'm sorry, okay?"

He looked at her like she was going to skin him alive. Slowly, she glanced back at me.

"Did he touch you?" she said, jerking her head toward him.

"No," I said quickly. "He just scared me."

She nodded and gave the boy one last disgusted look. "Fuck off then. You know better than to be out here in the dark."

"S-sorry. Sorry." He mumbled the words to me hurriedly before he fled.

Rayne picked up my phone from the ground, its flashlight shining like a beacon. As she handed it back to me, she said, "Did you hit him with it?"

"Yeah. Right in his stupid face."

She tried so hard not to smile that she curled her lips between her teeth for a moment.

"You shouldn't have come out here," she said once she'd composed herself. "I thought I told you not to wander off."

I frowned, folding my arms. "Are you scolding me?"

She folded her arms too, mirroring me. "Yeah. I am. I told you not to wander and you did anyway."

"Well, I *thought* I heard somebody crying! Then that asshole came out of nowhere." I sighed. "I hope he gets a black eye." It was only then I realized Rayne had brought no flashlight. My phone was the only illumination we had, casting her face into deep shadows. "Did you run out here in the dark?"

"I heard you scream," she said, as if that explained everything.

"How did you know it was me?"

She gave a low, humorless laugh. When she stepped closer, her eyes caught the light and I tried to back away, only to encounter the tall stone grave marker behind me. She leaned her hand against the marker, looking down at me with an expression I couldn't fully understand.

"I would know your voice anywhere," she said. "Remember,

I've made you scream for me. While you're on this island, under my roof, I'm the only one allowed to do that. Got it?"

Her closeness left me breathless, but I swiftly nodded my head. "Got it."

"Good girl." She kissed my forehead and took my hand. "Let's get back to the festival. The only people out here are the dead, and if you hear them crying, trust me: It's better to leave them alone."

Rayne

Washed Away

WE STAYED UNTIL THE FESTIVAL CLOSED AT MIDNIGHT. Floodlights lit the path back to the ATV, their harsh glare offering a little protection against the smothering darkness. I listened for any hint of the crying voice Salem claimed she heard, but only the crickets' song filled the night. I hoped desperately that it was only the teenagers playing a prank on her, and not something worse.

Salem rested her head against my back as I drove, and I wondered if she could hear how hard my heart was beating with her hands holding tight around my waist.

I wasn't at ease as we drove through the dark roads, but I felt strangely calm. Maybe it was just the alcohol in my veins, but I let myself fantasize. I let myself imagine tonight truly was a date with Salem, the first of many. I thought about taking her to my favorite cafes, bars, and lookout spots, sharing with her my little sparks of joy. I envisioned trips to the mainland with her by my side, knowing I'd spend the night with her instead of a stranger.

They were fantasies outside of my reality. Because I still scanned my surroundings as we drove, watching every shadow, listening for any strange calls. I still felt relief she would be leaving in the morning.

Salem stayed close to me as we walked up to the house. She talked about everything and nothing, her words wandering as much as her steps. She bumped against my side, and her arm brushed mine, her fingers meeting my own in an accidental touch that felt like so much more.

Was she drunk? She'd only had a couple of drinks. But she laughed so easily at every stupid thing I said.

She was still wearing that pink hat with the googly eyes. I tried to convince myself it was only the hat I was staring at, the silly costume distracting me—not the soft light in her eyes, or the flush on her cheeks, or the breathlessness of her words as we climbed the stairs to the third floor.

She stopped at her door, yawned, and stretched before she turned the knob. I didn't mean to stare, I really didn't. The way her nose scrunched up when she yawned and her soft sigh of contentment when she stretched made my chest feel like it was caving in. My lungs forgot how to work.

"Good night," she said, and smiled at me. It was softer than the wide, wondrous grins she'd been flashing all the way home. Her lips parted with a soft inhale, like she was about to say something else—

"Good night, Salem." I disappeared into my room before the words could come out. Pressing my back to the closed door, I cursed myself silently until I heard her door click shut a few seconds later.

I was a coward.

She was just a woman. Just a gorgeous, intelligent, optimistic ray of sunshine in my dark existence.

"Fucking hell." I rubbed my face as I trudged to the bathroom, casting off my cardboard cat ears on the bed. They were a little damp and slightly misshapen from driving through the foggy night; I could have just thrown them away.

I was going to keep them. The thought of throwing them in the garbage made me irrationally angry.

I turned on the faucet, steaming hot water filling the tub. Gripping the edges of the sink, I stared at my tired reflection. Cat whiskers and a black button nose looked back at me, and my mouth twitched into a smile before I caught myself. Everyone in town had stared at me like I just grew a second head, but I didn't care.

It made Salem happy.

Splashing warm water on my face didn't wash away the makeup; scrubbing it with my hands just smudged it around. But I stopped myself as I reached for the bar of soap.

Maybe Salem had a trick for getting this stuff off . . .

Maybe I was looking for an excuse to go knock on her door.

When I stepped into the hall, however, she was already there. We almost collided, and both stepped back with awkward laughter. Then she saw my face and snickered, hiding her mouth behind her hand.

"I should have warned you: It's waterproof," she said. She held out a bottle of makeup remover and a cotton pad. "This will help."

When I didn't take the items immediately, she said, "Do you . . . want me to do it?"

I didn't need help removing makeup; I was capable of

washing my own face, even when it involved potions I wasn't familiar with.

"Yeah, uh . . . yeah . . ." I nodded, leading her back into my bedroom, into the bathroom. The tub was nearly full and I hurriedly turned it off, the steam fogging up the mirror and making my skin sticky. Salem was looking around, observing the half-empty bottles of shampoo and jars of bath salts.

My room suddenly felt depressingly barren and boring.

"Skincare can be intimidating," she said, dabbing the pad with makeup remover. She probably said it to put me at ease, to reassure me my helplessness in this area wasn't anything to be ashamed of. But I was distracted by her hands: one tucked behind my neck to tip my face down toward her, the other gently swiping the cotton across my cheeks. Her eyelashes fluttered, and she met my gaze for just a second.

Surely she felt me gulp. Did she feel my breath stop too? Did she feel my pulse race?

She had to stand close to reach my face. The inches between our bodies were a chasm I wanted to throw myself into. She'd changed out of her costume, so her hair was mussed, and a little pink glitter gloss remained on her lips. Her shirt was oversized, covered in a muted floral print. The fabric was buttery soft when I pinched it between my fingers, but I was oblivious to my action until she leaned closer.

Her whole body pressed to mine as she wiped the makeup off the tip of my nose. I was suddenly achingly aware of exactly where my hands were—and where they weren't. How they were painfully absent from where they *wanted* to be.

"You don't need to hold your breath," she said softly. Could she really not see what she was doing to me? I didn't have a choice in whether or not my stomach fluttered, lungs froze, and hands broke out in a sweat. Air didn't seem important when she looked at me like that.

Like I was worth paying attention to. As if I was worthy of something so simple as having my face washed by gentle hands.

She lowered her hand, tossed the pad away. But she didn't take a step back, didn't break the warmth between us. A thousand jumbled sentences fought to make it out of my throat, but all that came out was "You're leaving tomorrow."

"Yeah." Her smile didn't reach her eyes this time, and I wasn't sure why. "What are you going to do all winter?"

I traced my finger around the shell of her ear, over the studs pierced through her cartilage and the pink bauble dangling from her lobe. "Think about you."

The moment I saw the longing in her eyes, I wanted to snatch the words back. I was selfish *and* a coward. I wasn't supposed to want her to stay.

But . . .

Her hand remained on the back of my neck, fingers stroking slowly, etching her emotion into my skin. She rose up slightly, on her tiptoes, leaving a kiss as light as a feather on my cheek. Her breath tickled my ear; her face pressed close to mine.

I slid my hand up her side, under her shirt, over the soft curve of her waist, and around her back. She pressed her nose into the soft indent below my ear, her breathing slow but her heart beating hard; I could feel it in her chest pressed to mine.

My hands were too cold against her warm skin. She was the Persephone to my Hades, the summer warmth that could chase away the winter's frost. She didn't flinch away from me; she took my other hand in hers and laced our fingers together, sun and moon intertwined.

"I want you to think of me too," I said, whispering the words between her parted lips. Her kiss was deep, it was slow and divine. Like she was committing it to memory, exploring lips and tongue as if to learn them by heart.

Or maybe that was only my foolish hopes, clinging to a forever that was already at its end.

I couldn't have her . . .

But she was mine.

I couldn't keep her . . .

But my heart would never let her go.

I wanted to live in the warmth of her kiss. Her hands cupped my face and she mumbled something into my mouth, words lost in the heat of lust. She tugged at my belt loops, breathless, and said, "I want to taste you, Madam. One last time."

She ducked her head down, went from kissing my mouth to my neck, my chest, hands exploring under my shirt.

God*damn*, she was perfect, and it wasn't fair. The way she said the title gave me goose bumps—not because it carried any imaginary authority, but because her voice made it so much more intimate than it was ever meant to be.

Her arms encircled me, slid under my shirt up my back. She unhooked my bra and traced her fingers over the skin beneath. She kissed my jaw, her breath so warm, her doe eyes gazing up at me with an unspoken plea.

A plea I couldn't deny.

I kissed her, pressing her back against the wall, molding my body to hers. Her tongue slid past my lips and met mine, caressing in a dance that made me see stars behind my closed eyes. Her hands kneaded my hips, then slowly tugged my pants down. She only got them midway down my thighs before she was gripping my ass, holding me greedily, *hungrily*.

We broke our kiss only so we could pull off each other's shirts. I scooped her into my arms and held her close, losing myself in all her sensations. Her fingers tugged through my hair, her nails scratching ravenously down my scalp. She bit my lip tenderly, then desperately, and groaned into my mouth.

We stripped naked and climbed into the steaming bath together. Her skin became slick as we sank into the water. She straddled my leg, moving rhythmically against my thigh. I braced one hand around her throat and her lips parted, gasping a little harder for air.

She pressed against my hand, even though it strangled her, just to kiss me again. Her nipples were erect, her breasts tender and slippery against my chest.

"May I taste you?" Her voice was tight, full of need.

"Beg me," I said, lips barely leaving her mouth. "Convince me you deserve it, pretty girl."

She didn't need to convince me at all. But God, I loved the sound of her voice, full of longing. I adored her soft sounds as she moved against me, pleasuring herself, breath stuttering.

"Please . . ." Her voice was husky beneath the pressure of my hand. "I want to feel you shake. I want the taste of you on my tongue." I parted my lips for her and she kissed me deeply. Her knee slid to the apex of my legs and I grinded on her, water sloshing around us.

The touch of her skin was pure luxury. She cupped my breasts, her thumbs making slow circles as she lowered her head and flicked her tongue over my nipple.

"I need you," she whispered, the words like a bolt of lightning to my heart. "I want to suffer for you . . . drown in you . . ." I released her throat, and her head ducked lower, leaving a trail of kisses down my stomach.

She gazed up at me, her mouth barely above the surface of the water. "I want you to think of me," she said softly. "I want to haunt your fantasies."

"I couldn't forget you." I stroked my fingers through her hair, now desperate enough that I regretted making her beg. "Missing you will drive me crazy."

She grinned. "Then maybe you'll have to hunt me down, and bring me back again."

She slipped beneath the water and her mouth closed over me. My head dropped back, my knuckles turning white as I gripped the edge of the tub. The suction of her lips and her lapping tongue pulled a moan from the depths of my soul.

She was already a ghost in my mind, a specter in my heart. She had the power to shake all my self-control, to shatter the walls I'd so carefully built. When I said she would drive me crazy, I meant it: I already wanted to abandon my reason, throw away my logic, and keep her despite knowing it was impossible.

She came up for air, but her fingers kept working. My hips bucked up, abdomen tensing. With her opposite hand, she traced her nails up and down my inner thigh, igniting goose bumps on my arms.

"I want to remember you," she said. "Just like this." She kissed my stomach near my navel, her soft lips and warm breath making me shiver. "I want to remember how you sound when you moan my name."

"You're such a good girl, Salem." I ran my fingers through her wet hair, and she grinned.

She ducked her head beneath the water again—but I was the one who wanted to drown and never have to see her leave. My thighs clenched around her head and I sighed her name, every breath coming harder than the last.

She was summer's sunshine, but I was winter's chill, and when we met she made me feel all of autumn's colors. My days were growing shorter, and she was fading away, slipping through my fingers even now. Before long, I'd be left with only the long dark and my troubled mind.

But before that, before the darkness could close in, she made fire burst through my veins. I was rocking against her mouth, grinding on her tongue, arching up when she rose for air again.

"Fuck, yes . . ." I gripped her hair, staring into her eyes as she licked and sucked, my legs shaking. I held my breath until she had consumed every last drop of my pleasure, swallowing my ecstasy like a drug.

If I spoke, I feared I'd say all the dangerous things locked inside my heart. Things like *don't go, I need you, I'm selfish, I'm horrible, I'll drag you to your death just to keep you in my arms.*

SHE LOOKED SO perfect splayed out on my bed. Her wrists were tied to my headboard and her legs were folded, calves bound to her thighs. She looked at me with excitement, with antici-pation, naked body trembling as she watched me spread lube on the pink strap I wore. I took my time, moving slowly, purely because I wanted to stare at her like that for as long as I could.

Her body was bound by ropes I'd carefully tied—safety shears close by in case I noticed she was in any discomfort. Her fingers curled and stretched as she tested the bindings on her wrists, squirming, savoring the restraint.

I had no idea what time it was and I didn't care.

"Ready to take my strap, pretty girl?" I knelt on the bed be-tween her legs, and she whined softly as I nudged the head of the shaft against her. She was slick with arousal, soft and shining in the firelight. My clit was still swollen and sensitive from her mouth, my body floating on the afterglow of orgasm.

She strained against the ropes as I pressed inside her, swearing softly. The lubricated silicone disappeared, tightly swallowed by soft, rosy flesh. I rocked back and forth, in and out, a little deeper each time.

Gripping her bound legs, I leaned over her and pushed them up, opening her up for me. She cried out, the sound dissolving into a moan as I kissed her. My hips hit her thighs and I was buried in her pussy—I could feel her muscles cling to the strap as I pulled back, then slowly sunk back in.

Watching her pleasure was intoxicating. The way she reacted to me, lips parted, breath heavy, body trembling. I dragged my nose along her collarbone and buried my face against her neck, inhaling the sweet smell of her. She turned her head, whispering her pleas and praise close to my ear.

"Fuck, you feel so good, Rayne." Hearing her whimper my name made me shiver and my clit pulsed, pussy clenching. I reached down, massaging the hot, slick nub of her clit. She flinched, legs twitching, abdomen tensing as her head dropped back against the pillows.

"Come for me, baby," I groaned. "That's my good girl, come on this strap." The headboard creaked as her arms strained, and she gave a trembling cry. Her hazel eyes stared into oblivion, her muscles rigid as she peaked.

I slowed down as she dissolved into gasping breaths, eyes half-lidded and lost in ecstasy. But I wasn't done with her. I pulled out, admiring her slick arousal that clung to the strap. I traced my fingers along the toy and slid them into my mouth, consuming her delicious taste as she watched.

"God, you're sexy," she gasped, and I smiled around my fingers. She begged, "Sit on my face. Please. Let me suck your clit, let me taste you."

I laughed softly, half of me wondering if I was dreaming. "Baby, you don't have to—"

"I *want* to," she cried desperately. "I want to taste you. All of you." She wiggled, bound and helpless. But her gaze was sultry and demanding, and I couldn't deny her.

Crawling over her, I released her hands from their bindings. The ropes left beautiful red bracelets on her wrists, and I traced my fingers over the indents. She grasped my hips, dragged her nails down my thighs as I straddled her face. I lifted the strap, groaning when she pulled me down onto her mouth.

"Fuck, baby . . ." Her tongue lapped over my clit, and she suctioned her lips onto me. I was still sensitive from earlier; the sensation of her mouth sent a jolt through me, throbbing in my core. Her teeth grazed me, alternating between nibbling and sucking. I was breathing so hard I was lightheaded. She peered up at me with the wet strap on her face, nose buried in me.

I reached back and sunk two fingers into her pussy. Wet and hot, she clenched around me as I rode her face, her moans driving me wild.

I felt her come, muscles convulsing, tongue becoming clumsy, and it pushed me over the edge. She kept licking, suckling, urging waves upon waves of pleasure from me until I was spent.

I washed her face with a warm, damp cloth—cleaning her glistening lips, wiping my arousal from her chin.

Her embrace was so much warmer than my bed, so much softer than my heart. She fell asleep in my arms, her back against my chest, her breathing soft and slow.

But my heart was still pounding, and my lungs were heavy. I stared at her head on my pillow, inhaled the scent of her on my sheets, and my soul ached.

She didn't understand that I couldn't hunt her down, I couldn't bring her back. There was no escape, there was no path by which I could run. Flight was impossible, so only fight remained.

Slowly, carefully, so as not to wake her, I slipped out of bed. I put on my coat, grabbed a joint and a lighter, and crept out of the room. The stairs creaked beneath my feet as I went up to the attic, the air cold and stagnant in that old, forgotten room above.

A small, round window, the glass frosted with cold, looked out upon the distant, dark lighthouse. I lit up as I stared at the churning sea crashing against those merciless cliffs. When I held the smoldering joint up and closed one eye, it looked like the lighthouse was on fire.

Salem

Where's Martin?

RAYNE'S BED WAS EMPTY WHEN I WOKE. SHE HADN'T SLEPT beside me. We'd fucked and she . . . left.

I'd been too tired to realize it the night before. Now, my heart beat an uncertain rhythm in my chest. Worry dug its brutal hands into my stomach.

I'd done exactly what I wasn't supposed to do. I'd fallen for her.

I thought of her rare smiles and my nervous stomach fluttered. Recalled the sometimes soft, sometimes merciless touch of her hands and shivered. I closed my eyes and remembered the taste of her, then licked my lips to see if any of her remained.

My thoughts spun uselessly, my mind a whirlpool. It didn't feel right, but this was it. I pulled her sheets up over my nose and breathed in, my eyes stinging with unexpected tears.

Not now, Salem. Keep it together. It's time to go home.

The manor was quiet. The kitchen team had already left by the time I dragged myself down to the dining room. I toasted a bagel and ate alone near the window, watching the rain and trying to figure out why I felt so sad.

I was leaving a puzzle half finished. Putting down a book without reading the last chapter.

But it was more than that.

It was the same feeling I'd had after Colin left. That maybe somehow I could have done something different and everything would have worked out. It was the feeling that my loneliness was my own fault.

But I'd known better from the start. Rayne and I simply weren't meant to be; real life didn't work like that. We had jobs to do, our own lives to lead.

I still hated saying good-bye.

Rayne was nowhere to be found. Loki was asleep in the foyer, and I sat by his side for far too long when I should have been packing, hoping his mistress would make an appearance. But the house was still, and colder than ever.

When I finally returned to my room to hurriedly stuff my belongings into my backpack, I listened outside her door for any movement within. I felt pathetic, but I couldn't help it.

Rayne didn't want to see me again. I had to accept that. She'd given me a little glimpse behind that impenetrable wall around her heart, but never opened the gates. My feelings, my curiosity, my questions were all unresolved.

And likely always would be.

I had come here to start over. To erase my past so I could focus on the future. But I'd let myself feel too much. I'd gotten too invested. I'd allowed myself to think there was more to this than there was.

My last hope was to find Rayne at the front desk as I went to check out, but no. A wooden box had appeared on the reception desk, and someone had written on it in black marker *Drop room key here for checkout.*

It felt like a kick in the stomach. This was it, then. The fantasy was over. The clunk of my key into the box felt like the drop of a guillotine, severing my last tie to this place.

I gave Loki a hug, scratched his chest, and told him he was a very good boy. I opened the door, told myself not to look back even though I heard the big dog whine in protest.

It was time to go home.

THE RAIN POURED as I rode my bike along the winding, muddy road toward the docks. I had two hours to reach the ferry, the last ride off the island until the end of winter. Water streaked down the hood of my raincoat, my tires splashing through mud. No one else was on the road; I didn't see a single vehicle. Even the fields were devoid of animals, who had likely taken shelter from the downpour.

Lightning flashed in the distance, followed by the low rumble of thunder. By nightfall, those storms would be directly over the island. I thought of Rayne sitting at her window, a joint in her hand, watching the storm approach with her music playing.

My heart ached. It wasn't supposed to be like this.

Hood up, scarf wrapped around my face, I barely heard the sudden cry of "Help! Please, I need help!"

My tires skid as I abruptly braked. Wind rustled through the trees, limbs creaking and twigs snapping.

"Help!"

Alarm seeped through me as I laid down my bike and stepped off the path. The voice was distant, but familiar: It was Martin.

The area around me was flat but overgrown, tangled with ferns and fallen trees. I couldn't see the hunter anywhere.

"Help! Please!"

His voice fell strangely on my ears. It was recognizable, but something was off. The tone was distressed, strained as if in pain. I couldn't put my finger on what exactly sounded so wrong.

"I need help!"

Stumbling deeper into the trees, I yelled, "I'm coming! I can hear you! Keep talking!"

The forest abruptly fell silent, as if the trees themselves had gone still. I picked my way through the bushes and brambles, my head on a swivel.

"Martin! Keep talking to me!"

The rain increased, rustling the leaves as it dripped to the forest floor. Even with my raincoat, I was drenched, but I kept stumbling onward, calling Martin's name. He'd call back, sometimes close, sometimes far.

It made no sense.

"Help! I need help!"

A fresh wave of fear washed over me, so heavy I immediately stopped walking. My lungs were heavy, and goose bumps covered my arms. There was something eerie about Martin's voice. It was too . . . repetitive. The same tone, same inflection, every single time.

Despite my instinct to turn back, I clambered down an embankment to have one last look around. The man had been injured last I saw him, and the sheriff had been searching for him and George for days. I would never forgive myself for walking away from someone in danger.

Cupping my hands around my mouth, I shouted, "Hello? Where are you? Martin?"

My inquiry was swallowed by the trees. I could no longer see the path where I'd abandoned my bike, and I couldn't delay any longer. I had to get to the docks.

But when I turned to head back, I wasn't alone.

A figure stood between the trees, naked, its back to me. It looked like a man—at first. Its skin was pale like a fish's belly, its waist and stomach shrunken and narrow, its rib cage wide and squat like a bell. I could count its every rib, the bones clearly visible beneath its taut skin.

My eyes struggled to comprehend what I was seeing.

It was hairless, its flesh wrinkled and thick in unexpected places. Sharp shoulder blades—*four of them*—protruded from its back. Its knees were bent, its long, muscular legs ending in cloven hooves.

Four too-long arms dangled at its sides, swaying slowly as it rocked back and forth.

What the fuck was I looking at?

"Hey! I need some help!"

It was speaking—no, it was *screaming*. But it didn't turn toward me; it didn't move. It just screamed, in Martin's voice, the words full of pain.

This wasn't possible.

It wasn't natural.

This wasn't a prank, this wasn't someone in a costume. Its long clawed fingers twitched, and suddenly, it turned.

It was eyeless, with snakelike slits for a nose. But I could *feel* it looking at me as my stomach lurched with a primal, instinctual terror.

Its mouth gaped. Flaps of skin stretched between its jaw

bones as its maw unfolded like a snake's. Spiked, tonguelike appendages coiled and writhed between rows of pointed teeth.

Then it dropped to the ground and crawled toward me with terrifying speed.

I sprinted through the trees with no path to follow. Branches snapped behind me, the cold air ached in my lungs. I had no idea which way to go. My bike was behind me, the road was gone. I vaulted over a log and nearly lost my footing. My adrenaline made everything seem to be moving in slow motion.

Suddenly, I caught sight of a flash of red. A crimson glow that moved distantly between the trees, and I could have sworn I heard a cold voice whisper, "This way."

Every time I dared to glance back over my shoulder, the creature was in pursuit. I caught only glimpses of it between the trees: the sickly white flesh, too many limbs, the gaping mouth.

It couldn't be real.

This couldn't fucking *be real*.

I sprinted toward the red glow, with no other sense of direction. I could have been hurtling straight toward a cliff and the ocean below, but I had no choice, I couldn't stop.

One moment my feet were flying and then they tangled, slipping on mud. I fell, tumbling, my body striking trees and stones, every blow knocking the wind out of me. Down, down, down, until suddenly—

Pain. Darkness.

THE SKY WAS a dark mass of swirling shadow.

Night had fallen.

My mouth tasted like dirt and blood. There was a pulsing pain in my head, made worse when I crawled unsteadily to my feet. Drenched and shivering, I turned in a slow circle as I tried to determine where I was.

Barely visible between the trees, the Blackridge lighthouse loomed above me, pale as the moon and utterly dark within. I was miles away from the manor, and my phone was missing. My muddy, soaked backpack lay nearby.

It had been hours.

The last ferry was long gone.

My stomach churned as I tried to remember what happened. Something had chased me. But my memory of it—the grotesque body, the eyeless face—had I hallucinated? The way it ran after me on six limbs, how its mouth gaped like a snake's. That couldn't be real.

This was a nightmare. I was dreaming, or I'd hit my head so hard I was misremembering.

Despite my dry throat, I called out, "Hey! Can anyone hear me? I need help!"

The forest's silence was my only response. Chills went up my spine as I remembered the cries for help that had led me to this situation in the first place. Cries that sounded like Martin, yet somehow came from the mouth of that *thing*.

My breath came quick and shallow. None of this made any sense.

At least the lighthouse gave me some insight into where I was. The manor was south of me, and Marihope was due east. I needed to find my way back to the road.

As I huddled beneath the trees, rummaging through my backpack for my flashlight, there was movement among the craggy rocks surrounding the lighthouse. Immediately I shrunk, crouching down behind the boulders and plants. Covering my mouth with my hands, I watched as something impossible emerged from a narrow tunnel burrowed into the dirt.

Six limbs. No eyes. Hooves and claws. Over the wind and rain, I could faintly hear its sounds: grunts and gurgles, whispered syllables. And then . . .

"Can anyone hear me? I need help!"

My voice came from that thing's mouth. The beast paused, crouched near its burrow, head up as if to sniff the air.

"Help! Help!" It was George's voice this time. The creature was switching back and forth between our tones, mimicking them perfectly. Like bait. A trap to lure in the unsuspecting.

Holding my breath, I watched the creature until it crawled away into the forest, its cries fading. Only once it was out of earshot did I start moving, stumbling through the trees. I had to get into town. I had to find a doctor, a firefighter, a policeman . . .

Rayne. I had to find Rayne.

Rayne

In the Trees

"COME TO THE CHURCH, RAYNE. WE FOUND BODIES."
James's voice crackled over the walkie on my bedside table, the first words I heard as I dragged myself out of a troubled sleep. Wind and rain had howled all night, thunder rattling the house's old bones. Rest didn't come easy, but I still felt some relief: Salem was gone.

She was safely off the island, back on the mainland, and far away from me. It ached; fuck, it hurt every time I thought about her, every time I breathed too deep. But the pain of loss was one I was accustomed to, one I knew how to deal with.

I hadn't even been able to face Salem to say good-bye, yet I headed out alone into the early morning, armed with my rifle and my knife. I'd hidden from her, I'd watched her leave the manor from the window in the attic and hated myself the entire time.

She frightened me most; the *possibility* of her was more terrifying than anything lurking in the darkness.

But she was gone.

My time with her was done.

I was a fool for letting myself fantasize, even a little bit, about what could have been. I knew better. There was a massive roadblock between me and the rest of my life, and that block was alive and deadly.

All spring and summer, I got to pretend Blackridge was a normal place. I ran my business, fucked around, made the most of the warm season while it lasted. But like a child's game of make-believe, that came to an end. I didn't *live* during the long, warm days of summer.

I waited.

My life was lived in the cold dark of winter. It wasn't tending guest rooms or scraping fireplaces, it was endless nights in torrential downpours, stalking the forest with my gun. It was hunting and tracking in silence, just me and my dog against the long night.

If I didn't find a way to kill that thing, these corpses would be the first of many in a long, brutal winter.

Despite the early hour, the church was alight and the bell tolled the time as I crossed the town square. The flags from the Halloween festivities flapped weakly in the breeze. Smashed pumpkins littered the ground. Windows were shuttered; some had been boarded up.

The church doors were open. Several people sat scattered among the pews, their desperate prayers falling upon the unhearing ears of the golden Christ hanging over the pulpit.

A crowd had gathered in the yard outside the cemetery gate. Someone was wailing, the gut-wrenching sound echoing in my ears as I pushed through the crowd.

Hanging in the gnarled boughs of the pine trees were bodies. One half hanging here, another hanging there. Pieces and parts dangled from the creaking limbs, intestines strewn out like party streamers.

Their heads hung there, eyes glassy and vacant, skin gray and decaying. Two familiar men, and one young woman.

Martin, George, and Andrea. The missing had been found.

Turning away, I gagged as quietly as I could, pulling up my jacket to hide my dry heaving. It never got easier to see, it never became less horrifying. My stomach roiled and I was thankful I'd chosen not to eat this morning.

The wailing, I was certain, came from Andrea's mother. I glanced back to see the poor woman standing beneath the destroyed remnants of her daughter, pulling her own hair so hard it was coming out in clumps. A man, perhaps her husband, tried to hold her, to comfort her, but her grief was too much to be contained.

Hurriedly, I turned away and vomited into the grass.

"We need to pray!" Although I couldn't see her, Ruth's voice carried over the crowd. "In these times of righteous judgment, we must turn to our God and lean upon his mercy. We cannot doubt—"

Someone shouted, "Fuck your prayers!"

The crowd dissolved into shouting. Distress, uncertainty, and anger rippled through them, growing like a storm.

"How do we get them down?"

"The children! Don't let the children see!"

As the people erupted into chaos and arguments, I spotted James smoking a cigarette at the back of the church. He was staring at the ground as I came up beside him, his hair and clothing disheveled.

"You okay?" he said, offering his cigarette. "Those men were your guests, weren't they?"

"Yeah. George Trager and Martin Keen. Martin had two adult daughters." I didn't often smoke tobacco, but I needed something to distract me, so I took the cancer stick and inhaled. "And George had a grandkid on the way."

My hunters came equipped for bears, sometimes deer or wild turkeys. No hunter alive knew how to face a creature that could mimic their own voices and travel in near-total silence. A beast that could take bullet after bullet, heal itself. A monster that learned more about us year after year, becoming harder to predict as it grew more violent.

"Where's your dad?" I said, and James nodded his head to indicate his location.

As much as I hated to look, I glanced over to the trees again. My Uncle Gerard was there, his wife, Veronica, beside him, comforting Andrea's distraught parents. The dead girl's mother had fallen to the ground, and my aunt rubbed her back, singing a soft hymn. My uncle's head was bowed in prayer, one hand on the shoulder of Andrea's father. But the man didn't pray. He just stared at the ground with empty, listless eyes.

"This is new," James said, motioning at the trees. He sounded clinical, and I knew he'd put on his imaginary lab coat as a defense against the horror. "This display behavior, it's . . . odd. It hasn't done this before."

"It's learning how to scare us," I said. "How to make us panic. Make us weak." My hand shook as I lifted the cigarette again, and I glared at it until I could make it stop.

"Do you think it's getting stronger?" James's clinical tone broke.

I shook my head, flicking my ash to the ground. "I think it's getting smarter."

The crowd moved and parted as the sheriff arrived, followed by a middle-aged Black woman, Dr. Tasha Hale. She was the only doctor on the island and, as such, our only medical examiner. She'd obviously gotten straight out of bed, with a trench coat over her pajamas, but her voice was calm and collected as she offered words of consolation to the panicked and terrified people around her.

As I watched the crowd, full of exhausted faces, I spotted something that made my heart stop.

Salem.

23

Rayne

Her Protector

THE SIGHT OF SALEM'S BEAUTIFUL FACE HORRIFIED ME MORE than the corpses in the trees. But it also filled me with an immediate and unwavering certainty.

I had to protect her.

Was I being blessed? Punished? Or was the universe just laughing at me again, laughing at the chaos of bringing me the one woman I desperately—frantically—needed to let go?

She stood at the edge of the crowd, eyes wide, terror written on her bruised face. She had not yet noticed me, even as I charged toward her. She was staring at the trees, the bodies, mouth agape with disbelief. When my fingers closed around her arm, she looked at me like I was a ghost, as if she couldn't comprehend what was happening.

Of course she couldn't. She was never supposed to witness this.

"Rayne!" Her voice trembled as if she was on the verge of tears. Her clothing was filthy, and she was drenched in mud. She was shivering violently and kept trying to speak, but her teeth were chattering too much to form words. I had to get her out of the cold.

I nearly tripped over the threshold as I brought her inside the church, watching her more than I was watching my feet. The nave was blessedly warm, insulated from the yelling outside. Those huddled in the pews were hollow-eyed, hands folded in silent prayer. Salem sobbed, mumbling something I couldn't understand, and I forced myself to stop and face her.

"God, Rayne, please tell me that . . . tell me that wasn't . . ." She squeezed her eyes shut tight and pressed her fingers against them, as if she could force away the awful vision. I wrapped my arms around her, holding her close—but I could feel eyes on us. Those in the pews had raised their heads.

The angel brought judgment. It not only enacted its own, but inspired the judgment of others too. Rumors and gossip traveled fast, with only one thought on people's minds: We were all sinners. We were all due to die; it was only a matter of when.

With my arm around her trembling shoulders, I guided Salem down a narrow hallway at the back of the church.

The pastor's office was unlocked, as usual. It was a small but cozy room, with a simple desk facing the window and a small sitting area in front of a wood-burning stove. Nevertheless, I'd never liked this room, or any room that my father had once inhabited. It looked different, smelled different; but tension lingered in the air, my lungs withering under the weight of memories.

I only ever saw my father behind a pulpit or behind a desk. Behind the pulpit, his vitriol was aimed at the entire congregation, but behind the desk, it was only aimed at me.

Ignoring my discomfort, I sat Salem down in one of the cushy chairs near the stove. Grasping her jaw, I tipped her head up to the light. There was blood around her ear, mud in her hair. My fingers explored her scalp and found a knot that made her gasp in pain.

"What the fuck happened to you?" I said. "Why are you here, Salem? You can't . . . you shouldn't . . ."

She shuddered, blinking rapidly as she tried to find the words.

"I heard Martin's voice. I tried to find him, he . . . he was screaming for help." She began to cry. Her hands kept moving, wringing, clenching, as if all the energy inside her needed a place to go. "There was a . . ." She waved her arms, as if tracing the outline of a tall, disturbingly skinny figure. "There was a *thing*! Talking in Martin's voice! It had no eyes, and . . . and these arms, and hooves . . . it . . ." Frantic, panicked, she grasped my shirt and begged, "You need to believe me. Please. I don't know what the hell it was, but I swear to God, I saw it, I heard it!"

She sniffled, hiccuping on a sob. Her eyes were reddened, tired, and they gazed into mine with a desperate hope.

"I believe you, Salem." My thumb stroked over her cheek as she cried. "Focus on me, okay? Take a deep breath. That's it, good girl." She held eye contact with me, breathing in deeply through her nose. I laid my hand against her chest, encouraging her. "Come on, keep breathing. It's okay to be afraid. It's okay. Don't fight it."

"Tell me I'm crazy," she said, her voice barely above a whisper. "Tell me it's not real, please." She had yet to let go of my shirt; her fingers knotted tighter and tighter in the fabric. "It chased me and I fell. I hit my head. That must be it, right? I just hit my head?" Disbelief shook her voice.

I wanted to tell her it was all a bad dream. A hallucination, a concussion. But no.

She had been dumped right into the middle of my cold, dark, dangerous life. She needed to be ready for what was coming.

"You're not crazy, Salem."

She stopped crying. Her face, for a moment, was unreadable, a mask of shock.

"Have you seen it?" she said.

"Yes. Every winter for almost twenty years."

"Fuck." Her voice broke. Her chest heaved as she took short, rapid breaths. "It can't be real. It can't. Things like that don't exist, they don't, they don't . . ."

Taking her hands, I uncurled her fingers' death grip and held them. Her skin was like ice, and I squeezed onto the chair beside her, wrapping my arms around her and holding her tight.

"Breathe with me," I said, rubbing my hand up and down her back. "I've got you. You're safe, I promise." She rested her head against my shoulder, face buried in my neck. Her warm tears dampened my skin, and my heart ached with every shuddering sob.

Eventually, her breathing fell in rhythm with my own. With every deep, slow breath she took, a little more of the tension melted out of her limbs. Little tremors ran through her when she sniffled, wiping her face with the back of her hand.

"I'm sorry," she whispered. "I'm so sorry, I just . . . I can't believe this is real." She lifted her head, staying as close to me as she could as she met my eyes. "Outside, in the trees . . . those people . . ."

I shook my head. "Don't think about it, Salem. They're gone. Their suffering is done."

I hated to see that void in her eyes: a dark expanse only pain and terror could open.

"The red figure I saw in my room," she said suddenly. Her eyes searched my face. "Was it real too?"

"Yes. It was real."

She gave a gasp of relief that nearly dissolved into another sob. I needed to get her cleaned up; I hated to see her like this.

"You don't need to fear the one in the house," I said. "It scares me too. But it won't hurt you."

"I know." She nodded. "I know it won't. I think it helped me."

This wasn't the time to question her, so I didn't push to hear more, not yet. But there was one more thing I needed to know, and I dreaded speaking it out loud.

"The creature you saw in the forest, did it see you? Did it look at you?"

For a moment, she went stiff and still as she remembered.

"It had no eyes," she said. "It saw me but it had no eyes." She inhaled shakily. "It kept calling me with Martin's voice. It even . . . it used my voice too. It mimicked me. It *knows*, it . . . it . . ." She flinched violently as someone walked past the window, but it was just two grim-faced men carrying a long ladder. "I'm going to be sick. Holy fucking fuck, this is *fucked*."

She clapped her hand over her mouth, squeezed her eyes shut. I knew that feeling of terror, the panic; I knew it all too well, and I knew fighting it did no good. She was whimpering, trembling, whispering denials as the fear racked her.

"Look at me," I said. I cradled her face, moving her hands

down, gently holding her wrists captive in one hand. "Nothing is going to touch you. Nothing—listen to me—*nothing* is going to hurt you. Not if I have anything to do with it. Do you understand?"

She was so close. She nodded, softening against me. The hairsbreadth between our mouths was a canyon, and my stomach dropped when I leapt across it. But she met me before I could fall, pulling me into a desperate kiss. It was a promise, an apology. It was every fear I couldn't speak aloud.

"I'm with you," I whispered, and she frantically nodded. "I'll protect you. I fucking swear it."

Salem

The Angel

WHEN WE RETURNED TO THE MANOR, RAYNE DREW A BATH for me. She helped me peel off my filthy clothes and then gave me my privacy to soak in the hot water. I scrubbed away blood, dirt, and grime, and changed the bathwater three times.

I was so tired, I fell asleep in the water and awoke with a jolt before dragging myself out of the bath. My backpack, along with all of my belongings, was thoroughly soaked. But on the bed I found an oversized pair of sweatpants and a large, soft shirt. When I put it on, it smelled like her.

Luckily, my diazepam pills were still in my bag, undamaged. I popped one and curled up on the bed, managing to sleep for a few hours before nightmares woke me up again.

When I drowsily sat up, there was a note on my bedside table. *Meet me downstairs. I'll tell you the truth.*

With the blanket from the bed wrapped around me, I shuffled down to the first floor. Following the distant sound of Rayne's voice, I soon stood outside the common room, listening through the half-open door to the conversation within.

"Barry, come on, please, I'm begging you. Just one trip back here, I'll pay you whatever you—"

I peered through the crack in the door. Rayne was on the phone, her lower lip clenched between her teeth as she listened to whoever was talking on the other end of the line.

"You'll be fine, I swear, it's just superstitions—"

The response was so loud, even I could hear a furious man's voice as he said, "There's a curse on that godforsaken island and there ain't a seaman worth his salt that will bring a boat back there now. I've got a wife and family to get home to. Call the damn coast guard!"

"Barry—"

Rayne pulled the phone away from her ear and cursed. Whoever she'd been talking to had hung up, and she tossed the phone on the couch before flopping down herself.

But she jumped up when the floor creaked under my feet.

"Who was that?" I said.

She sighed, running a hand through her hair. "Barry, the owner of the ferry that services the island. I asked if he could make an emergency trip back here to take you home, but . . ." She shook her head. "We're in for a stretch of really bad weather, he doesn't want to risk it." She winced and added, "A lot of the shipman are superstitious about Blackridge. In the past, we used to get deliveries by boat through the winter months. But over a decade, half a dozen were sunk. Three others just disappeared. Some of the men say there's a phantom beacon in the lighthouse. Others claim they hear whispers and screams coming from the water."

She sat down again, wringing her hands and staring into the fire. She seized a glass half full of whiskey from the coffee table and took a swig, and I came to sit beside her.

"I need to tell you the truth," she said. Her voice was rough and uncertain. "After Mom was murdered, a lot of things changed. But the first thing was I started hearing voices—we all did. Then, people started dying." Rayne paused, her mouth twisting into a grimace. "Sorry. I'm not used to talking about this. I've never told anyone." She gulped her whiskey without a flinch. "Everyone here already knows."

Even wrapped in a blanket, sitting on the couch across from her, a cold chill went over me. Everyone on this island—except me—was already aware of the horrors. They knew this monster existed. They knew it was capable of killing. Their strange and lingering looks, their distrust of an outsider, their religious zeal; it was all beginning to make sense.

Sap popped and twigs snapped in the fireplace. I stared into the twisting flames, as if I could sear what I'd seen out of my head.

Those bodies in the trees had been living, breathing people. People with families, friends, entire lives. People who felt fear and pain just as sharply as I did. To die like that, so cruelly, so brutally, and then be hung up like some kind of warning...

Fighting back my nausea, I briefly closed my eyes. When I opened them again, Rayne was leaning toward me in concern.

"We can talk later," she said. "You need rest."

But I shook my head and forced myself to sit up straighter. "I'm okay. I want to know the truth. All of it."

She sat back, nodding slowly as she swirled her whiskey in her glass. I could smell the spice of it in the air.

She stared into her glass instead of at me. "I started hearing voices in the house the winter after Mom died. I was lonely. So fucking lonely." She trailed off. I could feel her pain in every word she forced out. "But the voices scared me. They whispered about pain. Blood and bones. I didn't understand. I tried to tell my father and he . . ." She sniffed, bitterness etched into her face. "He told me I was hearing evil things, and if I listened, I would go to Hell. He told me to pray and shut his door in my face."

"Rayne . . ." What could I say? What words could possibly comfort her?

She cleared her throat, finished off her drink, and abruptly got up to pour herself another. As she stood at the bar cart, her back to me, she said, "Dad changed after Mom died. He'd never been affectionate, but he turned angry. And cruel. He didn't even talk about her at her own funeral; he talked about the Devil. About judgment and damnation. He didn't want justice for what happened, he wanted punishment. He would get behind the pulpit every Sunday and remind us that God is judge and jury over all, and that God's judgment was coming."

"God's judgment? What did he mean?"

"I'm not sure he knew. Maybe if he did, he wouldn't have preached that way." She finally looked at me, and in her eyes was the reflection of a years-old horror. "I don't believe in God, Salem. But I believe there are things in this world we don't understand. Some of those things are harmless, but some are predators. And when a predator senses weakness, they'll come hunting." Lowering her voice, she went on: "My father prayed and *prayed* for God to send an angel, a messenger, a holy soldier. He finally got what he prayed for.

"A man died that winter: Greg Kennison. He was found disemboweled and beheaded outside his barn, along with most of his animals. He was kind, a good man. But he struggled with drinking." She lifted her glass in a miserable toast. "Who doesn't? But my father said he was wicked. God had judged him and found him lacking. He was the first.

"More followed every winter. Rumors started that there was a beast in the woods, a predator. A creature that hunted at night, in the rain, in the snow. People said they could hear their dead loved ones calling to them from the forest. Soon enough, a group of hunters got the thing on video. My father called it Blackridge's angel. Sent by God to enact his holy judgment."

I listened with growing horror. "How can they believe that *thing* is holy?"

"It comforts them," she said. "They have faith in their own righteousness. When someone is killed, they can justify it. It's God's will."

Clutching the blanket tighter, I thought of Martin and George, their friendly banter and silly jokes. They didn't deserve to die like that. An act of God couldn't justify such horror.

Rayne put down her drink and scooted closer to me. She put her arm around me, and I leaned my head against her shoulder. My heart rate was rising again, my legs beginning to shake. I needed another pill.

But I wanted the full truth out in the open.

"So you've learned to live with it," I said.

Rayne nodded. "More or less. As the years went on, people learned the beast's habits, its weaknesses, its fears. It rarely comes out during the day, unless clouds are covering the sun. We never see it in the summer. Bright lights and fire can spook it, but won't scare it off completely. It has no eyes, but it can see. And it mimics." She hugged me tighter. "You heard it."

I nodded, recalling that awful voice with a shudder.

"It imitates the voices of its victims, using them like a trap," she said. "The sheriff started a coalition of volunteer forest rangers to patrol the roads, set up cameras. Some of us have tried to fight it. No one could kill it, but we eventually figured out we could injure it. Andy blew one of its limbs off with a shotgun one winter, and we didn't see it again for the rest of the season. But the next year, it had grown the damn arm back."

"If you can injure it, you can kill it," I said, with as much conviction as I could muster. Frankly, I didn't know if that was true. I had no idea if the rules of reality applied to this situation, but I had to believe they did. I had to find hope.

Rayne was nodding in agreement. "Yeah. I think it can be killed. I've tried. So many of us have tried." She sighed. "But there has to be a way."

"Why haven't you left?" I said. "So many people are still here." I sat up, gripping her arm urgently. "We can find a way to leave together. You and me. You don't have to stay here!"

She smiled gently, but the expression was sad.

"I've tried," she said. "Many of us have tried."

I frowned. "Tried?"

"The voices follow us."

She got up and began to pace back and forth, biting her thumbnail. "Others have left. Entire families have tried to escape. Within a few weeks, they come back. Those that force themselves to stay away . . . they die." She released her ragged nail from between her teeth. "I stayed on the mainland for a week. By the fifth day, all I could hear, day or night, was screaming. It's like something was clinging to my back, screeching bloody murder in my ear. I couldn't sleep. Couldn't eat. I would have flung myself into the ocean to make it stop." She looked at me grimly. "It happens to all of us, to anyone who stays here too long. The red woman, the whisperer. The one you've seen. She won't let us go."

A strange sound, like a soft breath, made us both flinch, and we turned to stare at the door leading out into the hallway. Even Loki raised his head, staring with his ears pricked up. I swallowed hard, cold waves of fear running up my back.

"Do you mean . . ." I could barely get the words out. "Even me . . . ?"

She didn't answer at first. The silence was painfully heavy, settling on my stomach like a boulder.

"I don't know," she finally said.

My heart thumped painfully, every beat reverberating in my tight chest. My legs shook, and I tried to still them, but it was no use. I drew my blanket tighter around me, but the cold couldn't be chased away.

"Who is she? A ghost?" I said, the words coming from between my clenched, chattering teeth.

"Sometimes I wonder if it's her," Rayne said. "Or whatever is left of her. My mom." She swallowed hard, taking a deep breath. "Salem, I never wanted you to know any of this, I didn't . . . I know it's taking a risk to bring people here in the first place, to host guests at all, but I didn't know what else to do. This house is falling apart and my father's money was gone long before he died. So during the summer, I pretend everything is fine. I host, I keep up the grounds. Then, when everyone leaves, I start hunting. I help keep watch on the roads."

"What about the police?" I said desperately. "Sheriff Keatin, can't he report it and get help?"

"He tried. He nearly got put on mental health leave for even suggesting to mainland authorities that these aren't simple wild animal attacks. We deal with it alone. Some people don't think we should deal with it at all. People like Ruth."

Confused, I said, "But why? How could she—"

"It's God's judgment. Who are we to question God? No matter who dies, they're sinners. Dig deep enough into their life, and you'll always find a reason they deserved it. Unfaithful. A liar. A thief. Drunk. Pervert. No one can be spared because no one is blameless."

"The angel isn't judging anyone," I said. "It isn't picking and choosing with purpose. It's just hunting."

"Exactly. There's nothing holy about it, it's just a beast. A monster." She took a deep breath. "I'm going to kill it. Somehow. Someday. I'll fucking kill it."

Salem

Stay

I FELL ASLEEP ON THE COUCH, WARMED BY THE CRACKLING FIRE, too frightened to return to my room and sleep alone. I listened to Rayne move about: her soft steps as she fed more logs into the flames, then the *flick-click* of her lighter, followed by the sour scent of a joint. She sat beside me on the couch, and at one point I opened my eyes to find her with knitting needles in her hands, clicking as she worked with pale pink yarn. The sound was soothing, and her face was soft as she worked.

Late in the night, she lay beside me. She grasped my hands and kissed them, and when I stirred, she whispered, "You're safe. I've got you."

When nightmares woke me before dawn, she was still holding me, even in sleep. My heart pounded painfully as I stared at the windows streaked with rain, trembling with the thought of that awful beast appearing beyond the glass. I shuddered, my eyes brimming, trying to not envision those destroyed bodies in the trees.

Near the fire, Loki stirred from his sleep and came closer. He sat beside me and licked my face, and I wrapped an arm around his fluffy neck. Rayne sighed softly, nuzzling her face into my hair.

"I've got you," she whispered, voice groggy with sleep. "I've got you, baby."

My pounding heart slowed. Loki lay down, my arm dangling off the couch to stroke his thick black fur. Somehow, I was able to sleep a few more hours.

By the next morning, a vicious storm had moved over the island. Rumbling thunder startled me out of sleep, as rain and howling wind buffeted the house.

I lay there for a while without moving, listening to the storm. My muscles ached, and my head was pounding painfully. Eventually, my grumbling stomach drove me to get up. My butt had barely left the couch when Rayne violently flinched, her eyes flew open, and she seized my wrist in a vise grip.

"It's okay," I said quickly. "Sorry, I didn't mean to wake you. Do you want some coffee? Or tea?"

She stared at me for a good ten seconds without saying a word, before she mumbled, "I must be dreaming. You're not supposed to be here." She let go of me, scrubbing her hand over her face. "Did you say coffee? I'll get it, you're hurt, you're—"

I firmly pressed her back down when she began to get up, her movements clumsy and half asleep. "I'm fine, I promise."

She slumped onto the couch, shaking her head with a soft laugh. "I am definitely dreaming. Beautiful women don't bring me coffee in the morning."

It made my heart hurt, and I wasn't sure why. Her eyes were closed, and I leaned down to kiss her cold cheek. She didn't open her eyes, but she sharply drew in her breath.

"Well, this one does," I said. "I'll be right back."

With an absence of guests, the dining room had been cleared. The chairs were stacked along the wall, and both them and the tables were covered with white sheets to keep the dust off. It was as if the room was full of silent ghosts, or perhaps that was just my lingering paranoia.

My mind churned with surreal images—the creature, the bodies, blood and gore. I stood in the kitchen doorway, eyes closed, forcing myself to breathe slow and deep. My brain said, *It's not real. Don't think about it.*

But I couldn't gaslight myself out of acknowledging reality, no matter how unbelievable. I'd seen it with my own eyes. I'd smelled the stench of death and blood. I'd heard the wails and cries of horrified witnesses.

The final ferry was gone; no one was coming to rescue me. It felt silly to even think about at this point, but I did feel a sudden pang of fear that a long absence from work would get me fired.

Maybe I could rent a helicopter—empty my savings, max out a credit card or two. Find a rowboat. Call the coast guard. I imagined rescue arriving, saying good-bye to Rayne—and leaving her to face that beast alone.

It didn't feel right. As terrified as I was, I didn't want to leave her behind.

She needed someone. She needed *me*, even if she didn't want to.

Finding my way around the massive kitchen took longer than I expected, but I eventually found a five-pound bag of coffee, nestled among other large bags of supplies. At least food wasn't going to be an issue; Rayne was clearly well stocked and prepared for a long winter without access to a grocery store.

When I returned to the lounge with two mugs of steaming coffee, Rayne was seated in her green velvet chair, holding something in her lap. She had revived the fire, comforting warmth filling the room as rain streaked down the windows.

"Thank you." She smiled at me as I set the mug on the table beside her. At the same time, I got a glimpse of what she was looking at. An open manilla folder lay on her lap, full of newspaper clippings and photographs.

"Is that—oh, God." I hurriedly turned away, heart pounding, lungs constricting. The chair creaked, and the next thing I knew, Rayne wrapped her arms around me from behind, tucking my head under her chin. With a shaking voice, I said, "Those are photos of it, aren't they? The angel?"

"Yes. I took most of them myself. They're all blurry; it's impossible to get a clear image of it. I've tried. You don't have to look."

But I took several deep breaths, and waited until I stopped feeling like my stomach was going to cave in. "No. I want to look. I need to." I turned around, coffee mug shaking in my hands. "I want to see it."

She nodded, taking her seat again and rifling through the papers until she held up an old Polaroid. "This is the first one I took of it."

The photo was blurry; it was almost impossible to distinguish what was a tree and what wasn't. But as I looked longer, I was able to make out the strange, long-limbed being, standing with its back to the camera.

Just as it had looked when I first saw it.

"Fuck." I took a shaky breath, and set down my coffee before I spilled it.

"After it killed my dad, James put together a small posse of hunters to go after it. He didn't want me tagging along, but . . ." She shrugged. "I followed them anyway. I didn't have a firearm of my own, so one of them gave me an old rifle. I started learning to shoot."

There were about a dozen photos, some small, some enlarged. In some, I could barely tell the beast was there at all. But in others, even though they were blurry, it was all too obvious.

"Rebecca almost told you too much," Rayne said, holding up a final photo. It was taken from high above, looking down on the angel as it crawled across a craggy expanse of black rock. "This one was taken from the firewatch tower at the north end of the island."

"You don't go there to look out for fires, do you?"

She shook her head. "This is what I go for: to search for this thing, watch the roads, warn people if I see it. Our only cell phone tower is there too, sometimes it needs maintenance."

She abruptly closed the folder, set it aside and picked up her coffee. She took a long sip and sighed. "Wow, this tastes a lot better when you make it for me."

"My first job was working as a barista," I said. "It's infused with my innate coffee-making skills."

She laughed, and it made me smile. A few moments passed in comfortable silence, until I said softly, "Are you angry I'm here? I know you didn't plan to have anyone here over the winter, and it's probably weird to have someone in your house, and I swear I'll pay you for the food—"

But she held up her hand, silencing me. "I'm not angry. No, I'm . . . fuck, Salem, I'm . . . I want to keep you safe. Don't you dare think it burdens me to have you here. It doesn't, not in the least. It's . . . well . . ." She lowered her voice. "Part of me is happy you're here. I didn't want you to leave. It's hard in the winter, being alone." She put down her mug, rubbing a hand over her face. "I dragged you into this. I'm gonna drag you out too."

Instinctively, I reached out my hand for hers. She took it, lacing her fingers through mine and kissing the back of my hand.

"Are we safe here?" I said. "In the house?"

She nodded. "As safe as we can be. I have cameras and floodlights around the perimeter. I'm going to walk the fenceline today and put up razor wire." She squeezed my hand. "I'll keep you safe, Salem. No matter what it takes."

THE DAY PASSED slowly. Rayne had plenty to do, and disappeared with Loki shortly after finishing her coffee. But I could only sit and worry—draining the coffeepot as I did. I tried reading, but couldn't lose myself in the words. I tried drawing, but my fingers shook and nothing but shadowy scribbles appeared from my pencil's lead.

Instead, I curled up in the window seat in my room and watched the yard, waiting for a glimpse of her. When she walked by pushing a wheelbarrow full of razor wire, coat flapping in the breeze, Loki trotting at her heels, my heart didn't just skip; it sprinted.

Eventually, I made my way down to the library and the computer there. The desktop was old, the connection abysmally slow. Over the next couple hours, I researched everything from renting private helicopters to calling for an emergency rescue from the coast guard. With the upcoming stretch of bad weather, none of them could reach me for a week, at least.

And again, I thought of leaving Rayne. Knowing what I did now—she would tell me to go in a heartbeat.

But I didn't know if I could. This woman who had sworn to protect me, who made me feel seen, who made me feel . . . cared for. Knowing what she faced, how could I leave her to fight it alone?

I was terrified. The fear of what I'd seen was so deep in my bones that no amount of pills would bury it. The fear of what was, and what *could be*. This island's curse could take hold of me. It could infect my brain just like the others.

Maybe it already had.

A shuffling sound made me turn, but the library was empty. The lights' soft glow flickered, and I hurriedly turned back to the computer, trying to ignore the chill running up my spine.

I typed and deleted multiple emails to my mom, before finally managing to write something that wouldn't make her panic. There was no point in frightening her. Waiting for the message to send, I chewed my thumbnail down to a nub, feeling as if I'd just written my own obituary.

"*Stay.*"

The sharp, hissed whisper made me yelp, flying up out of my seat. My leg painfully hit the desk and I clutched it, my back pressed into the corner of the bookshelves as I stared around the room in horror. Empty, just like before. But my neck tingled from the cold breath I'd felt.

"Hello?" My voice echoed around the room. The lit sconce near the door flickered rapidly, then went out. My mouth was so dry; I tried to swallow to no avail. I could barely get my words out. "Rayne? Are you . . ."

My words dissolved into a whimper. Barely visible behind a distant bookcase was a woman's hollow, blood-drenched face.

My throat closed. Lightheadedness washed over me, as if I might pass out. She was staring straight at me with sunken, unblinking eyes. Her long hair dripped thick, dark red liquid; I could hear the ominous *drip, drip, drip* of it hitting the floor.

Blood foamed from between her lips as they moved.

"Stay."

I clutched desperately at the shelf to keep my knees from buckling. "I—I—"

Another sconce, this one right above my head, began to flicker. The woman didn't move, other than the occasional small twitch.

"Stay."

All the lights went out. The computer's screen flashed white, then turned pure red, bathing me in its glow. I couldn't see the woman anymore, but I could hear slow, wet steps shuffling closer. I was hyperventilating now, eyes straining to see in the dark.

"I—I'll stay!" I gasped, voice squeaky with panic. "Please— I'll—"

The lights came back on. The computer turned off. My breath clouded in the cold air, but nothing remained of the woman I'd seen . . .

Except for the faint wet imprint of bare feet, standing right in front of me.

Salem

Make It Burn

SLEEP DIDN'T COME EASILY THAT NIGHT. RAYNE WAS STILL OUT by the time I got in bed, and I tossed and turned in my cold bed. That woman's face haunted me. When I closed my eyes, I was overcome with the sense that she was close by, watching me, close enough to touch me.

At one point, I opened my eyes to see a glow seeping through my curtains. I looked out, and through the pouring rain I saw floodlights lining the property—a ring of illumination to drive away the beast. There was a distant thump, and I wondered if it was the sound of the heavy front door slamming shut.

My anxiety wouldn't let me rest. I only felt worse the longer I lay there tossing and turning, listening to howling wind and pouring rain. So I pulled on socks and a sweater and shuffled downstairs.

Loki was asleep on a rug in the foyer, his thick fur damp from the rain. Flickering firelight emanated from the common room, so that was where I headed.

Rayne sat on the couch, facing the fire. She had a tumbler of whiskey in one hand, a joint in the other. Several candles were set around the room, their flames twisting and dancing to the music playing from her phone. Leaning against the door-frame, the familiar lyrics of "Spiracle" by Flower Face made me smile.

"Can't sleep?"

Rayne's question made me jump. "Sorry, I thought I was . . ."

She turned, the firelight reflected in her green eyes. The blaze threatened to burn me alive.

"You can't sneak up on me," she said with a little smirk. "I've been stalked by far worse things than you."

She watched me approach, gaze raking up and down my body. She took a drink, ice clinking in her glass. She swallowed slowly, and I stared at the subtle ripple of her throat, then the drop of condensation that streaked down her arm until it disappeared into the couch's smooth velvet.

She was hypnotizing in a way I didn't understand, like shattered glass or molten metal. Dangerous and beautiful. When she turned away, the air seemed colder, and I shivered.

"Want a drink?" She held up her empty glass as I came to stand on the rug, my bare feet curling in the soft fur. I nodded, but she was already getting up, trudging over to the drink cart. There was plenty of room to sit on the couch beside her, but the rug was warmer and closer to the fire. Besides, just like the deadly things she reminded me of, sitting next to her was intim-idating, like sharing space with a panther.

When she turned back with a glass in each hand, she snickered to see me sitting on the ground. "Is the couch uncomfortable?"

"No!" I stuttered, hoping I hadn't offended her. "I'm just weird, I guess. The fur is soft, and it's warmer . . ."

My cheeks grew hot as she squatted beside me and offered the glass. "If you're cold, I can make you a hot toddy. It would only take a few minutes."

"This is fine." I smiled as I took the drink. It was a deep amber color, chilled with a couple of ice cubes. The scent was rich, with hints of cinnamon and caramel. "What is this?"

"A temporary cure for your problems." She knocked her glass against mine in a toast, then drained half her glass in a single gulp. It was spicy on my tongue, but warm and smooth when I swallowed. She seated herself on the couch again, and I could feel her eyes on me as I stared into the fire.

"Did you have any luck booking a rescue helicopter?" she said after a few moments of silence. She must have seen my frantic search history on the computer.

"No." I sighed and took a deeper drink. "I emailed my mom. Told her not to worry . . ." My throat choked up, and I drank again to make it stop. Maybe I should have written more; I should have made it clearer how much I loved her and Dad, how thankful I was for them always being supportive of me.

"You'll see them again, Salem."

Rayne's reassurance made me suck in my breath and hold it. My emotions were getting the better of me, but I couldn't hide it: I was scared. No, I was *terrified*. Unfortunately, none of my wilderness survival guides provided a section on dealing with supernatural monsters.

"Do you believe me?"

I turned. Rayne's eyes stared back into mine, cloaked with an emotion I couldn't read. For a few moments, I couldn't form a response.

Finally, I choked out, "It killed Martin and George."

"I wasn't protecting them," she said. "But I'm protecting you."

I turned away, downed my drink, and set the empty glass aside. Trying not to spiral into panic again, I rubbed my hands back and forth over the fur and tried to focus on the warmth sliding down my throat.

"I saw her," I said softly. "The red ghost. The woman. She told me to stay." I took a deep breath, looking back over my shoulder. "So I'm going to. I'm going to help you figure this out."

Rayne's careful mask cracked, and fear seeped through. "Salem, no. No, listen to me, as soon as I'm able to get in contact with the coast guard, I'm going to get you—"

"I'm not leaving."

Her face twitched. When she exhaled, her breath shuddered, and she swore under her breath.

"You shouldn't be alone," I said, before I could lose my courage, before she could argue. "I can help you, Rayne. I want to. And I don't think . . . I don't think I can just leave. I feel her watching me." Even now, I felt it: the cold surety that eyes were on me, watching from the shadowy corners, like an ever-present dark figure in the corner of my vision.

Rayne looked at me for a long while. Her jaw was clenched, as if to hold back all the words that wanted to spill out.

"You don't know me well enough for my word to mean much," she finally said, her voice rough with emotion. "But I'm going to keep you safe. I won't—" She stopped herself abruptly. She wasn't looking at me anymore, her eyes far away.

"I won't let this island take another person from me," she said, her voice barely above a whisper. "Not again. Not you."

I shuffled closer to her until I was kneeling at her feet. She leaned down and traced her finger across my cheek, then down along my jaw.

"I've never gotten a damn thing I wanted," she said. "Until you, until this. It feels like a cruel joke." She sipped her drink, then hovered the glass above me.

"The world is cruel enough," I said softly, resting my hands on her thigh. "I want to stay. I don't want you to face the dark alone. Not again."

I opened my mouth expectantly, waiting for a drink, and she made a sound like a strangled gasp.

"God, Salem. You're the first blessing I've ever received."

She tipped the glass and let the cold whiskey trickle onto my tongue. It wasn't only the alcohol making me hot as I swallowed, never taking my eyes off her.

"What am I going to do with you, pretty girl?"

A cacophony of possibilities stormed through my head. I crawled up onto the couch and into her lap, silent and slow. She never took her eyes off me. When my thighs tightened around hers, her breathing deepened, and she ran her fingers through my hair, making goose bumps run up my spine.

Nervous wings fluttered through my stomach as I leaned close to her ear. I inhaled, my nose barely touching her skin, and whispered, "Anything you want."

To my surprise, she shook her head.

"Wrong. It's anything *you* want, Salem. Every filthy fantasy in your head."

Tingles shot from my head to my toes. "Then I want . . . I want you to remind me how good fear can feel."

I whimpered when she slowly, firmly gripped my hair. She drew me closer, until I was mere inches away from her lips, and said tightly, "I've lived in misery every winter until now. Fucking you on every available surface in this house, until my father rolls over in his grave, sounds like a damn good time."

She flustered me so badly all I could get out was "Oh, shit."

She kissed me slowly, like she was savoring me. Her tongue slipped past my lips, her fingers still knotted in my hair, her grip tightening until it ached. I began to grind against her thigh, whimpering into her mouth. The stimulation made me shake, my breath quickening.

Our lips barely parted, and she whispered, "What's first, Salem? What the hell am I going to do with you?"

A choked sound stuttered out of my throat. "Hurt me, Madam."

"There you go, there's my good girl. That's a start." She gave my face a rough shake before she released me, then winced and said, "Mm, we'll be careful with your head though."

"I don't think I have a concussion."

"Are you really going to argue with me?" she said, and laughed incredulously. "Don't make me punish you, Salem."

"Oh *no*," I said sarcastically. "Anything but *punishment*—"

"Fuck it, you have far too many clothes on."

She tugged my sweater over my head and flung it away. I wasn't wearing a bra, and her eyes grew wide as she released a slow breath.

"You're so beautiful," she said. "Maybe I've seen an angel after all."

Her reference to the beast made me shiver, but that little hit of adrenaline was like fire shooting straight into my veins.

"Do you remember your safeword?" she said. I nodded

hurriedly, carelessly, but she forced me to slow down. "Say it back to me, Salem. Prove you remember."

"Red," I said impatiently, and she seized the candle from the small table beside her chair.

"Fuck, that's—oh, God—" I braced, turning my face away from the flame.

"Don't look away," she whispered. She brought the candle closer, hovering just a few inches beneath my nipple. "You're okay, you can do it. Do you want it?"

"I want it. Please." I whimpered sharply as the fire came closer and the heat grew from subtle warmth to a tingling burn. My nails dug into her thigh, my heart pounding like a drum.

"Let me feel those claws," she said. Her arm wrapped around my waist, holding me in place.

The flame was so close. It twitched and twisted, and I flinched every time it did. Deep, gasping breaths filled my lungs, and I was lightheaded with anticipation.

"Face your fears for me. Show me how brave you are."

I nodded quickly, desperately. The flame licked across my nipple, quick enough to feel but not to burn. An intoxicating cocktail of relief, adrenaline, and desire pumped through my veins, my chest heaving with the effort to stay still.

"Do you want more?" she said, her voice rapid with excitement. She had me in her jaws, a masochistic little lamb begging for slaughter.

"Yes! I want—oh, fuck—"

Back and forth, she moved the flame over my nipples. Every spark of heat made tiny, petulant sounds burst out of me.

Gasping with need, sweating, I groaned when she set the candle aside.

"Fuck off with these clothes," she suddenly muttered, lifting me as she got to her feet. She stripped me naked, before drawing me down onto the rug.

She put me on my knees, my hands clasped on the back of my head as she played with my nipples: sucking, pinching, teasing bites. My hips shuddered, longing for stimulation as her hand played between my legs, stroking my thighs but never going any higher.

"That's my girl." She murmured it so offhandedly, like it was natural. Like I really was *her girl*. "Look at me." Her hand came up and held my face, calloused fingers tracing lightly down my jaw. Her thumb reached my mouth and stroked across my lip—then pressed inside. At the same time, her other hand cupped between my legs, the heel of her palm rubbing against my clit.

Closing my lips around her thumb, I watched her eyes go round as I moaned and sucked. She pressed down on my tongue, forcing my jaw open and holding me like that. Saliva collected at the corners of my mouth, my tongue writhing under her thumb as I instinctively tried to swallow.

She chuckled, drew her thumb from my mouth, and offered her index and middle fingers instead. "Get them nice and wet for me," she said. "Because these fingers are going inside your pussy."

I ran my tongue over the digits and slid it between them, never taking my eyes off her. When she pulled back, a thin string of saliva glistened as it stretched from my lips to her fingers.

"Fuck, you're so sexy, Salem. What did I ever do to deserve you?"

She pressed one finger inside me, slick as it entered. I held my breath, but she grasped my jaw, squeezing my cheeks.

"*Deep* breaths now . . . that's it." She breathed with me. Her forehead pressed to mine, and I fell into the fiery night of her eyes. I exhaled, then sucked in the warmth between us, letting her fill my lungs. Her finger moved slow and deep, curling and caressing until my eyes rolled back.

"Ready for more?" she murmured. I nodded rapidly, then moaned as a second finger slid inside me. She thrust as I rocked my hips, grinding into her hand.

"You're doing so well. God, look at you. Ride my fingers, baby. Show me how badly you want it."

She pulled my face closer and kissed me, fingers and tongue moving in wicked unison.

Her breathing grew heavier as she said, "I'm going to make you come so hard, you won't even remember your own name."

Instantly, for reasons I couldn't understand, my anxiety swelled.

No, no, not now! Why now?

But what if I couldn't do it? What if I couldn't orgasm, what if I took too long, what if she got impatient? My movements grew clumsy and I held my breath again, my eyes darting away from hers.

"Are we still green, sweet girl?" she said, in that tone of voice that made me melt into a puddle. She released her hold on my jaw and stroked her fingers across my cheek. "Talk to me."

You're overthinking. Just stop thinking. What's the matter with you? Why do you always have to complicate things?

Shaking my head, I stuttered, "It's nothing, I'm fine, I'm good, we're green—"

She gently withdrew her fingers from between my legs and brought them to her mouth to suck clean. The sight of her savoring my arousal almost made my brain short-circuit, already near overwhelm.

"I consent only to honest, enthusiastic play from you, Salem," she said, popping her fingers from her mouth. "Do you understand? If you're using me to self-destruct, then we're going to stop. Right now."

My body was coiled like a spring.

"No . . . I'm not . . ." I said. "It's just . . . I got . . . nervous . . ."

There, you've gone and ruined it, haven't you? Because you had to get lost in your head. This is why people can't stand you, Salem. This is why—

"What's making you nervous?" Her voice was gentle, unbothered. But I felt like I'd let her down.

She held my face, one hand on each cheek as she slowly rubbed my tense jaw. It gave me something solid to cling to in the midst of the storm in my mind.

She repeated, "What is it? Be honest with me. It's okay. You're safe with me."

"I . . . um . . ." Swallowing hard, I said, "I'm not sure if I'll be able to come. I just . . . I might not . . . sometimes it takes a while and sometimes it doesn't happen if I've been anxious. And the past few days . . . it's just . . . so much. My brain fixates on things and sometimes it's like . . . like a stuck record. So I keep remembering the awful things." Things like corpses and monsters, blood and specters.

I swallowed hard, still unable to look at her. I wanted to curl in on myself like a bug.

"I understand," she said. "I really do. It's okay to feel what you're feeling. What can I do? What do you need from me?"

My lungs unlocked. I exhaled, a heavy shudder went through me. "What you're doing is . . . perfect. I just needed to slow

down. I like this, I really like this, and I want to keep going . . .
I want . . ." I lifted my eyes, and for a moment, the softness in
her gaze made me catch my breath again. "I want you. I do."

She took my hands and kissed them. She drew me close and
wrapped her arms around me. The warmth of her embrace was a
ray of sunlight piercing through fog, and I sighed as I rested my
head against her.

"Listen to me: I'm perfectly happy to sit here with you all
night," she said. "Whether I'm pleasuring you until you're
squirming and begging . . . or just holding you. If you can't
come, that's okay. It's not going to hurt my ego or make me impatient. As long as you feel good and you're enjoying yourself,
that's what matters to me. All I want is for you to be okay."

I couldn't think straight when I was this close to her. Her
words soothed the trembling knot of anxiety in my chest, loosening it until I could breathe deeply again. She stroked her
fingers through my hair and gripped it, playfully shaking my
head as she smirked with such confident swagger that my toes
curled.

"I'm not trying to rush toward the goal of an orgasm," she
said. "I want to see your pleasure build, slow and easy like the
tide coming in. I want to make those beautiful eyes roll back in
your head from how good you feel. I want you to feel safe and
cared for, just as you are."

She pressed her cheek to mine, talking soft and slow in
my ear.

"My only goal is to explore ecstasy together. To learn your
body like my own. All I need you to do is talk to me. Tell me
how you feel, what you like. Let me worry about the rest."

She kissed me again and laid me on my back on the furs, encouraging me to take slow, deep breaths as she caressed my legs.

"You're safe here," she said. "The gates are closed. The lights are on. Loki is watching the door." She leaned down and kissed my collarbone, then my throat, my chest. "I'll take care of you, baby."

She moved slowly, taking her time to kiss and caress every inch of me. When my breath would stutter with pleasure, she would pause, giving extra special attention to the sensitive spot she'd found. She laid her head against my stomach, traced the curves of my hips and thighs.

"We'll get through this," she said. "You and me. Together."

"Together," I echoed, the word comforting me.

My legs encircled her as she sat up. Maybe it was just the firelight, but the way she looked at me felt like adoration. It was tender and warm.

"Are you okay?" she said, and I nodded. She lifted her hand to her mouth, and slowly sucked the two fingers that had been inside me only minutes ago. I watched her with growing anticipation, heat swelling in my core. She ran her nails up and down my inner thigh, the sensation making me shiver.

"Look at you, dripping for me," she said after withdrawing her fingers from her mouth. "I know that sweet pussy wants more. Remember your safeword. Remember to talk to me. Are you okay to keep going?"

I nodded quickly. She kissed my thigh, then the other, and ducked her head down.

She made me see stars. Fingers and tongue worked in unison, pumping and sucking until I was wound so tight, I felt as if I would levitate off the floor.

But then her movements slowed. She worked her fingers steady and deep, kissing my hips, dragging her nose across my sensitive skin. She locked her eyes on mine as she laid a kiss beside my navel, her breath giving me goose bumps.

She drew out her fingers, slick and shining, and sucked them clean. "Fuck, you taste so good. Like heaven." She wrapped her arms around my thighs as she consumed me. Her tongue drew a devilish rhythm, awakening every nerve until my legs were shaking.

"Fuck, that's it, there you go," she said, her words sloppy with her tongue against me.

I was hurtling toward the edge, unable to stop. All I could do was cry her name as I gripped her hair and my thighs squeezed, orgasm rushing over me like a tidal wave.

She drew my soul out of my body. She moved with me, she praised my reactions. She asked, "Do you like that?" in such a gutturally sexy voice I almost fell apart again.

"I'm looking forward to using my strap on you again," she said, her grin widening when my eyes went round. "And you'll take it like a good girl for me, won't you?" She thrust her fingers deep and slow, working me through waves of stimulation. I whimpered and writhed, and her expression grew wild.

She stripped off her clothes, pausing between every article because my hands were all over her. Touching, exploring, finding the places that made her breath catch. Worshiping her, in awe of her beauty. But she was attentive; she was so focused on me that it continually caught me off guard.

"Let me taste you," I begged.

Taking me by the throat, she pinned me to the ground. She got on her knees and knelt over my face, tempting me, teasing me.

"Reach for it if you want it so bad," she murmured as I strained against her hand, cutting off my own air. But I didn't need air; I needed her, only her, smothering me, filling me, taking all of me.

She was infatuating. The touch of her skin. The smell of her arousal. The soft hum she made when she turned around, her perfect ass filling my entire vision. She swayed, a final sexy tease before she sat on my face.

The taste of her made me groan. I lapped my tongue over her clit, savoring every gasp and tremble. Gripping her thighs, I squeezed them tighter around my head.

"Fuck, you're so good," she groaned. I couldn't see what she was doing, realizing only when I felt her mouth close over me again. My hips bucked up, writhing beneath her.

Wrapping my arm around her leg, I used two fingers to spread her open, focusing the tip of my tongue on her clit. She groaned, body twitching and jerking as I sucked and licked. I carefully pulled back the hood of her clit, which was swollen with need, as I suctioned my lips onto her.

"Ah, yes, right there!" She rode my tongue, and I was in heaven, listening to her moan and feeling her shudder.

I was a mess, drenched with her, drunk on desire, lost in a haze of pleasure. Her muscles tensed; her legs shook. I wasn't so far gone that I wasn't paying attention. She was close, and I wanted nothing more than for her to come on my tongue.

My limbs were shaking, and I was swiftly losing proper control of my muscles. All my will, all my focus, was on chasing her orgasm. She shuddered and said, "God, Salem, you're gonna make me come—"

Her guttural, desperate words made my belly clench. Her arousal was salty-sweet, slick and delicious on my mouth, nose, and chin. The sound of her drove me wild, and when she groaned with her mouth and tongue on my pussy, I lost control.

I came hard, muscles convulsing. She kept licking, sucking, grinding herself on me. My body was possessed, shaking uncontrollably. She seized my legs, curling them up and hooking them beneath her arms as she consumed me without mercy.

The room spun. Time had no meaning anymore. I was a boneless bundle of stimulation, barely human, somewhere between waking and dreaming.

There was a weight on the rug beside me and a gentle touch on my face. Rayne pulled me close, wiping my mouth with the back of her hand.

"We'll make it, Salem," she murmured. "One night at a time, we'll fucking make it."

Rayne

The Stone House

B Y THE NEXT MORNING, THE RAIN HAD STOPPED, BUT COLDER weather was swiftly moving in. Thick fog rolled across the grounds as Salem and I walked along the narrow, winding path leading south of manor, toward the backend of the Balfour property. Loki trotted ahead of us, sniffing here and there as he decided where to relieve himself.

Winter's distinct chill was in the still air. Everything, from the mist to the sky to the brittle grass we walked through, was a pale shade of gray.

Salem stayed close. Her head was on a swivel, and every time there was a sound she didn't recognize, her entire body flinched.

I wrapped an arm around her shoulders, tucking her close against my side. I pointed at the distant fence, topped with thick curls of vicious, sharp wire.

"Not even a monster will drag itself through that," I said. "I checked the cameras this morning. We're okay."

She smiled shyly, but remained close against me. I didn't want her to be afraid, but it made me feel good to comfort her, and that she felt safer with me close.

Maybe it was only her presence, but despite the bitter cold, it was a beautiful morning. Birds were twittering in the trees, the grass glistened with frost, spiderwebs shone with morning dew. It was peacefully quiet.

Until Loki let out a heart-stopping snarl and sprinted across the field.

"Loki!" I yelled out to him, but he was singularly focused. He sprinted straight to the bottom of the hill, to the small stone structure my father had built there: a one-room cabin, with a narrow chimney and filthy windows. Grass and moss covered the roof, and blackberry brambles clung to the walls. He ran up to the boarded door and paced, barking furiously.

I huffed in exasperation. "A raccoon must have gotten inside there. Silly dog . . . Salem? Hey, what's wrong?"

She'd stopped walking. She was staring at the building with an expression of utter terror, shaking her head slowly.

"I told myself it wasn't real," she whispered. "I thought—I thought I imagined it—"

I grasped her shoulders, making her look at me. "What is it? What are you talking about?"

She was so frightened, her eyes reddened with tears. "In the stone house . . . something . . . something big."

AN HOUR LATER, we returned to the bottom of the hill. But this time, we were prepared. I carried my rifle and a flashlight; Salem had my hunting knife. Loki walked ahead of us, ears up, nose twitching, as if he knew we were on a mission.

"Why did your dad build an office way out here?" she said. Her voice was shaky with nerves.

"He built it after I was born. I cried a lot through the night as an infant, and he hated it."

The stone house was where my father spent most of his time when he wasn't at the church. Locked inside, in communion with God, he would sometimes sleep out here for days before setting foot in the manor again. Toward the end of his life, he was locked in there day and night.

I'd always been strictly forbidden from entering. My father couldn't handle the thought of a grubby child touching his belongings, and the fear he instilled in me remained even now. After he died, and the entire property became mine, I couldn't be bothered to destroy the old building. I never found his key, so the door had remained locked for years, until I eventually boarded it up and left it to rot.

As we reached the door, Loki began to circle the house. Nose to the ground, tail curled over his back, he trotted around the entire place until returning to my side and taking a *very* long sniff at the door.

"What is it?" I said, giving his thick ruff a scratch. "What is it, boy?"

He didn't take his eyes off the door, nor did he lower his tail. He just stared, nose twitching.

"Does he usually do that?" Salem said.

Drawing my lips between my teeth, I used my sleeve to clear

the window of grime and peered inside. It was dim, but nothing stood out to me as unusual. Just a dusty old office.

"Keep your knife ready," I said, turning back to her. "Keep it close, hold it like this . . ." I adjusted her hand until she had a firm grip on the weapon. "If I tell you to run, you run. Okay?"

She nodded and swallowed hard. I seized a rusted old ax leaning near the door and swung it down to meet the moss-covered boards. Wood splintered, chunks flying as I hacked my way through. It wasn't the most subtle way of getting in, but it certainly felt good. There was something satisfying about destroying the door my father had used specifically to keep me away.

When only splintered wood remained and the dark interior was revealed, Salem released a slow breath.

"Wow," she said. "That was . . ."

"Sorry. I might have gotten carried away."

"Sorry? No, don't be. That was hot. I'll watch you chop down doors any day."

For a moment, I could only stare at her, speechless. Her eyes sparkled with what I could only describe as awe.

I'd had plenty of hookups who lusted after me, complimented me, but somehow, when Salem did it, it felt entirely different. Like a songbird was in my chest, trying to fly away.

Before she could see me blush, I cleared my throat and said, "I'll go first."

I stepped inside, with Loki following closely, the old wood creaking ominously beneath my feet. Dust cascaded from the rafters, which were strewn with years of thick cobwebs. The interior was dark and smelled musty, the windows so filthy no natural light could penetrate.

"Ugh, what is that smell?" Salem hissed, pulling her sleeve over her hand and covering her mouth and nose. She was right;

beneath the smell of mold and dust was the stench of something rotten and decayed.

"Something must have died in here," I said, clicking on my flashlight. Dust motes swirled in the beam as I swung it around the room. "Looks like the roof has been leaking."

The wooden floor was moldy and discolored, some of the boards bowing as I put my weight on them. Being in here felt entirely wrong. The songbird in my chest had died, leaving a weight between my ribs that only grew heavier as I examined the many shelves lining the walls.

My father had an extensive library, but these books looked ancient. Cracking spines and peeling covers, some with their titles worn away. Melted candles stood entombed within piles of their own wax on every available surface. A single bulb, long since burnt out, dangled from a chain in the center of the room over a filthy square table.

Salem gingerly picked up a rusted metal instrument from the table. I couldn't even hazard a guess what the thing had once been used for.

"So, what exactly was your dad studying in here?" she said. The table was smeared with discoloration, dark stains blemishing the wood. Those dark stains encircled the table too, on the floor, as if something had once dripped off of it.

"He wrote his sermons here," I said. A large desk stood beneath a filthy window, with loose papers, pencils, and books scattered across the surface. A worn leather Bible lay there, its thin pages mildew stained. It was open to the Book of Romans, and a highlighted passage: *We also glory in our sufferings, because we know that suffering produces perseverance.*

"How cheerful," Salem said dryly. She screwed up her mouth as she looked around. "I was so sure I saw someone. But it doesn't look like anyone has been in here for years. Except maybe rats." She made a face as she kicked at some rodent droppings near her shoe. "I don't even see how anyone could have gotten in here."

She was right, but a lingering doubt remained in my mind as I cast my light across the floor. The thick dust showed our shoe prints and Loki's paw prints. But there, near the far window . . . I narrowed my eyes.

"Salem, look over there," I said, keeping my light on the floor. She crouched down for a closer look, frowning. "What do you see?"

"It's . . . um . . ." She shook her head slowly, as if she didn't want to say it. "There's hoofprints. At the window."

Sudden sharp pain seared through my eardrums. I flinched violently, grabbing my head as the flashlight clattered to the ground, my head filled with the sound of screaming.

"Shit, no, no, no, not now!" My breath came rapid and shallow as the horrifying screams overwhelmed me. I didn't have my earbuds, my music, *nothing* that could shut it out.

"Rayne? What's wrong? What is it?" Salem's voice was panicked. The pain was too great to open my eyes. My arms were locked into position as I held my head, teeth clenched, willing it to stop . . . please . . . stop . . .

A sinister voice hissed in my skull, *The blood, the blood, in blood do I call thee.*

"Leave me alone!" I gasped in pain. My upper lip was wet and the taste of blood was in my mouth.

"Rayne? What—what's happening to you?"

It came again, like someone was speaking right in my ear: *To the bones, to the bones, right down to your cracked and rotten bones!*

Bile rose in my throat. The voice was vicious and angry, but the screaming was *agonized*—the sounds of someone in torturous pain.

And then . . .

It's here.

It's here.

It'shereIt'shereIt'shereIt'shereIt'shereIt'shere—

The voice and the screams melded together, becoming a cacophony that shut out all else. I couldn't breathe, blood was dripping from my nose, and when I forced my eyes open, the world was a blurry haze of pain.

"Oh my God, Rayne . . . I'll help you, let me . . ." Salem stepped closer, hand stretched out for me.

It was too late that I noticed the red glow beneath the floorboards.

I could hardly speak. "Salem, don't—"

The moment she put weight on her foot, there was a loud crack and a rending of wood as the floor collapsed.

Salem

The Thing in the Cellar

"**S**ALEM! OH, GOD—FUCK—*SALEM!*"

Gasping, I lay stiff as a board until I sucked enough air back into my lungs to feel alive. Dust drifted around me, shards of wood poking into my back.

First of all: *Ouch*. Second: Where the hell was I?

Groaning, I pushed myself into a sitting position. A shadow moved through the light above me, and I looked up to see Rayne standing at the edge of the gaping hole in the cabin's floor. Loki paced beside her, whimpering and barking.

"I'm okay!" I shouted. "I'm not hurt, I don't think, just sore. Ugh. Really sore." Wincing as I got to my feet, I picked up my knife, which had flown from my hand as I fell. I was lucky I hadn't landed on it. I rubbed the back of my aching head and peered up into the light as Rayne's silhouette looked back at me.

"Can you see a way to get back up? Can you climb?"

Looking around, there weren't many options. I'd fallen about fifteen feet into a dark cellar. The walls were dirt, and crooked wooden support beams braced the house's floor. Copper piping and frighteningly old electrical wiring ran willy-nilly through the space, but there was nothing I could climb on.

"I don't see a way out!" I yelled, then immediately whirled around when I heard scuffling behind me.

"What's wrong? Salem?"

The space was less a cellar and more a dark pit. Tree roots stuck out of the wall like crooked fingers. Splintered wood, collapsing beams, and the petrified corpses of indistinguishable small animals littered the dirt floor. Nothing moved. Nothing made a sound.

But my brain told me something was there.

"It was nothing," I shouted. "But I'd really, *really* like to get out of here."

"I'm going to find something to get you out. Here!" She tossed her flashlight down, and I caught it. "I'll be right back!"

"Okay! I'll just . . . wait here . . ." With a gulp, I swung the flashlight's beam around me. Dust floated through the meager light. The air was stale and musty, making me cough every time I took a breath.

Suddenly, something scurried over my foot. I shrieked, dropping the flashlight as I flailed. But it was just a rat, running away into the shadows. With a heavy sigh, I laid my hand over my pounding heart and took a few deep breaths.

As I bent to pick up my light, I spotted something illuminated in its beam: a dirty piece of red cloth, sticking out of the dirt. I crept closer, crouching down to have a better look. The cloth was stiff with age as I took hold of it and tugged. The resistance told me there was more buried beneath the soil.

Digging quickly with my bare hands, I found something beneath just a few inches of dirt. A slightly squishy, rectangular shape wrapped in red cloth. Peeling the wrapping back, I found a moldy cardboard shoebox within, tied shut with twine. Multiple things rattled around inside.

The hair on the back of my neck stood on end. A distinct feeling I wasn't alone sent shivers up my spine.

Slowly, I turned the light behind me. There, like a gaping mouth in the dirt wall, was a hole.

A *burrow*.

It was narrow, just big enough for me to crawl inside—if I'd been crazy enough to do so. Instead, I stared at it in horrified silence as something moved within.

"Fuck no," I whispered. I hurriedly wrapped the shoebox again and tucked it into my jacket. "God, Rayne, please come back . . ."

First, one long, boney limb extended from the hole. Then another. Then the rest followed, like a spider moving its knobby limbs. A pale, eyeless face poked out, its mouth hanging open, an insect-like chattering sound coming from its throat.

The angel was here.

My eyes stung; I was so terrified I couldn't breathe. The angel moved slowly, its head bobbing up and down as it sniffed the air. It was coming closer; I had no choice but to back away, ducking around beams and squeezing under piping. I couldn't see where I was going. I didn't dare take my eyes off the beast for even a moment.

As I stepped back and put weight on my foot, there was a crunch, followed by a burst of sharp pain. I clapped my hand over my mouth, but not before a shocked cry tore out of me, and the angel's head snapped toward me. Choking on my screams, I moved my foot and saw a bloody nail sticking out of the board I'd just stepped on.

"I'm back, Salem! Where—hey, where'd you go?"

The beast's head immediately jerked upward, looking for the source of the voice. Tears of pain poured down my cheeks as I remained silent, limping slowly backwards. If I could just get around this thing, back toward the gap in the floorboards . . .

"Salem . . . where . . . where . . ."

My heart was in my throat. That wasn't Rayne's voice, but it was close. It was a near-perfect imitation.

A mess of broken wood stood between me and the gap in the floor. Down on my belly, I dragged myself through the mud, squeezing beneath the wooden beams and shoving trash out of my way. Rats scurried over my hands, fleeing in fear. I had to press my cheek to the dirt to make it under a massive beam, the scent of ammonia and rat feces cloying in my lungs.

I had to keep crawling. Just keep crawling.

"I see you, Salem! Hang on . . ." Rayne's boots pounded across the floorboards, her shadow moving above me. For a split second I was filled with hope, the adrenaline rush making me crawl faster.

Then, right behind my head, I heard "Salem . . . I see . . . you . . ."

Trembling, I dared to look over my shoulder. The angel was there, limbs spread between the beams, holding its body suspended in midair as it crawled toward me, mouth gaping open. Splinters jabbed into my palms, my foot screaming in pain as I scrambled away.

"Run, Salem!"

A wooden ladder slammed down, my only hope of escape. There was a crack of gunfire and the beast shrieked, a terribly high-pitched, furious sound. Rayne fired her rifle again, the sound terrifyingly loud in the enclosed space. Loki's barking reached a fever pitch, with vicious snarls and snapping teeth.

Finally out from under the wreckage, I scrambled to my feet—but my ankle was wrenched back, slamming me to the dirt. Gripping my knife, I whirled around and slashed, screaming when I saw the boney, clawed hand holding onto to me. The blade opened a thick, bloody gash across the creature's face and it thrashed backwards.

For a moment, I was a rabbit frozen in front of a predator. My eyes were fixated on its unnatural form, my hand trembling in a death grip on the knife. Time seemed to slow, my heart thumping in my ears. I couldn't get enough air.

Then the moment was gone, and I ran.

I seized the ladder's ancient wooden rungs and began to climb—but the beast was close behind. Its claws raked the wood, shattering the step below me. Only my grip kept me from plummeting to the ground and into its clutches.

"Look out!" I ducked my head at Rayne's warning as she fired again. The bit of wood I was standing on gave an terrifying crack, and I screamed, scrambling for the next rung. My stability gave way but Rayne seized my arm, leaning dangerously over the ledge to keep hold of me.

"Hold on!" she yelled, teeth bared with effort. My sweating hands nearly slipped, but her grip was tight enough to bruise. Loki stood by us, hackles raised, saliva foaming around his mouth as he challenged the angel below, daring it to come closer.

Rayne hauled me up, and I fell into her arms. Gasping, almost sobbing. We peered together into the cellar, but the beast had vanished into its burrow.

Rayne held me tight, one hand slowly stroking my hair as she murmured, "You're okay. Goddamn, just breathe, you're okay." I never wanted her to let me go, and I almost entirely forgot about the strange red-wrapped parcel tucked inside my jacket.

But as we parted, Rayne's eyes drifted down to the squishy bulk between us. She gently tugged down my jacket zipper, frowning as she looked closely at the parcel. "What's this?"

"I don't know," I said, still breathless. "I found it down there."

She took it, curiously feeling the fabric. Her face fell. Disbelief, then alarm, filled her eyes.

"No way," she whispered. "This can't be . . ."

The fabric was ripped and crumbling, but as she unfolded it, it became clear it was a piece of clothing.

"This was Mom's coat," she said. Her words shook, but whether it was out of anger or fear, I didn't know. "I haven't seen it since . . ." She frowned, shaking her head as she swiped her hand across the dusty lid of the box. "This doesn't make any sense. She was buried in this coat. Dad said . . ."

She opened the box. Inside, an old camcorder sat next to a collection of VHS-C tapes.

29

Rayne

Messages Left Behind

Thankfully, Doctor Hale was willing to make a house visit, despite the forecast threatening snow and wind by nightfall. The woman was tenacious, and not one for small talk, which was part of why we got along so well. She administered a tetanus shot, cleaned and bandaged Salem's foot, and was off again within an hour.

"What would we do without you, Tasha?" I said as I paid her and walked her to the door.

She gave a boisterous laugh. "Be dead and buried, no doubt. Don't we have enough to worry about without your girlfriend stepping on nails?" But she embraced me, patting the back of my head in such a way that emotion welled up in my chest, though I didn't let it show. "Take care, hon. Keep an eye on that woman, she'll be trouble for you."

She gave me a wink as she left, and I knew she was right. But Salem was exactly the kind of trouble I wanted.

Returning to my bedroom, I found Salem wrapped in blankets on my bed, her bandaged foot elevated on a couple pillows. She was smoking a joint, and although the window was cracked open, the sour scent wafted around the room and almost immediately soothed me. I'd enjoyed the scent of marijuana for years, probably because it was the one thing that could consistently calm me down.

"How are you feeling, pretty girl?" I said, sitting on the bed beside her.

She gave me a silly, sleepy smile. "Considering I've almost died twice in as many days? Pretty good. It could have been a lot worse . . ." Her voice, and smile, slowly faded away. "Do you think it'll come back?"

I stared out the window, the first fluttering flakes of snow just beginning to fall. The beast had burrowed under the fence, avoiding the lights and the razor wire. It could get anywhere on the property at will, I had no way to prevent it. This island was its domain, and we were all trapped within it.

"I shot it a few times," I said slowly. "I . . . hope . . . that slows it down for a few days. I'm going to destroy the stone house, collapse it. That should plug up the burrow beneath it."

By the way she looked at me, I knew we were both thinking the same thing: It would keep digging. Keep hunting. Keep pursuing.

I took her hand, holding it tight. "While you rest, I'm going to board up the windows downstairs."

"What about the tapes?" she said. We both glanced toward the moldy shoebox sitting on my desk. "What do you think is on them?"

I was trying not to think about it, but simply having the box in here made me feel strange.

As if it was watching me.

"Mom had a camcorder," I said. "I think it was hers. Whatever is on the tapes . . ."

I had to watch them, I had to know. The feeling I got when I imagined seeing my mother's face again was impossible to describe, and uncomfortable as hell.

"They could just be home movies," I said. "But I don't know why my dad would hide them in a cellar I didn't even know existed. And Mom was buried in that coat." The coat that now hung on my doorknob, stiff, stained, and tattered. "That's what he told me. It doesn't make sense. None of it."

Salem offered the joint, and I took it gratefully. She squeezed my hand and then brought it up to her mouth to kiss the back of it. That simple touch meant more to me than she could possibly understand. She didn't know how many weeks, how many *months*, I often went without even touching another person, let alone embracing them. Even when I did get the physical contact I craved, it was usually through sex with a stranger, hot and heavy, over too soon.

I felt pathetic for being so comforted by her slightest touch.

IT TOOK HOURS to barricade the windows downstairs. Loki was on high alert, following along behind me and constantly sniffing the air. I knew he would warn me if it came close again. The snow kept falling, my work illuminated by the floodlights fending off the encroaching night.

My entire body ached by the time I was done, my hands scratched, bruised, and numb from the cold. I sighed in relief when I was finally able to shut and lock the house's thick front door behind me.

I made dinner for Salem and me, canned soup and buttered bread, and took it up to her in bed. I found her sitting at my desk with the old box open, inspecting the tapes inside.

"I'm so curious," she said. "Why would he hide these?"

A combination of dread and resignation made my stomach feel like it was caving in on itself. The same question was on my mind too.

"Only one way to find out," I said.

It took some searching, but I eventually found the VHS-C adapter tape and an old VCR stored away in the attic. I set it up in my bedroom; after fiddling with and cursing at the ancient technology for nearly an hour, I got it to work.

There were six tapes in the box, each with a label, the writing on them too smeared to make out. I inserted one at random, trying to keep my breathing steady and my heart calm.

The sound was warped as the video began to play. It was the beach near the docks, on a rare sunny day. The recording shuddered, lines darting across the screen as it came back into focus.

It was me. Running through the waves, splashing, squealing. Picking up smooth pebbles and hurling them into the ocean. I couldn't have been more than four years old.

"Rayne! Be careful, little love!"

Even warped as it was, my mother's voice made my heart come to a stop. The camera was set down, slightly off-kilter, and my mom came into the frame. She took my hands, twirling with me through the waves, dancing and laughing.

It was only a couple of minutes before the tape ended, leaving me staring back at my own blank expression as the screen went dark.

"Rayne?" Salem touched my shoulder, and I remembered to breathe again.

It had been so long. So painfully long since I'd heard her say my name.

Rayne.

I flinched, causing Salem to flinch too. That voice echoing in my head, dark, bitter, and cold, was too familiar.

Salem followed my suspicious gaze toward my closed bedroom door. As we sat in silence, Loki raised his head and stared too, a low growl rumbling in his chest.

Footsteps creaked past the door, and Salem looked at me with wide eyes.

"Is that her?" she whispered. "The footsteps . . . is it . . . ?"

I didn't take my eyes off the door until nearly a minute had passed without a sound.

"It's whatever is left of her," I said. "Her ghost, her . . . shadow, maybe. I don't know. I don't know what she's become." That thing had none of my mother's love, none of her kindness, her warmth, her gentleness. "She died horribly. She suffered. It's too cruel to think that after all that, she can't even rest. And the things it says . . . horrible things. I try not to listen."

Selecting a tape, I inserted it into the VCR and pressed play. It was jarring when my mother's face filled the screen again. She was in her bedroom: the one that used to be upstairs, in the attic. With its window looking out upon the sea and the lighthouse. Mom used to say it was her nightlight, and the foghorn her lullaby.

Back then, the room was bright and clean. A green blanket covered her bed. It wasn't until I reached my teenage years that I realized it was strange how separated my parents' lives were. They lived in the same house, but beyond that, it was a wonder I'd been born at all.

I'd heard the rumors the pregnancy was accidental, a result of my father's "indiscretion" during a trip to Canada. Some said he only married her, only brought her here, to make right his sinful mistake.

I sometimes wondered if she had wanted to come at all. If she'd truly had a choice.

My mom smiled, waving at the camera. "Hi, Aunt Sophia! I hope you and the kids are doing well. It's been way too long since we had a visit. I've been meaning to write, but um . . ."

She stopped abruptly, turned, and stared at her closed door. Several seconds passed.

"Picard? Is that you, dear?" she said, a high-pitched note of uncertainty in her voice. There was no response to be heard. She slowly turned back to the camera. "Anyway. I really do hope we can have a visit soon. I'm going to send you a phone number where you can reach me. The phones on this island are always going out." She laughed awkwardly, and I paused the tape.

"That's not true," I said softly. "Dad always had a connected phone in the house, and the church. He was paranoid about it."

"Why would she lie?" Salem said.

Pressing play once more, I stayed quiet.

"I might, um . . . I might need some money. For the visit." Mom wasn't looking at the camera anymore, but at the floor, off to the side. She wrung her hands in her lap. "For Rayne too, for her to come along, she would love to see you and meet her cousins. She's lonely, you know? There's not many other kids around here, and any time I mention moving, well, Picard just won't hear it. The church is too important, he ... um ..."

Mom took a deep breath. "God, I hate saying this. We need to get out of here. Picard can't know." Her voice lowered to a whisper. "Something is wrong. He's changed, he ..." She shook her head and closed her eyes. "He scares me. The things he talks about, the sermons he writes. He's always *angry*. The way he talks to Rayne, I just can't stand it. She's only little, but he's so hard on her. He says children are born sinful and need to be trained out of it, and I think it's bullshit. No matter what I say to him, he doesn't care. He doesn't listen. I've tried to write to you, but I think he's ... watching me. I think he opens the letters."

My stomach lurched. I held my breath, dreading the things I felt as I watched my mother break down. Fear contorted her face. It shook her voice.

"We just need to get away for a while," she said, tears welling in her eyes. "Until he gets some help. Please call me. Please. As soon as you can." She leaned forward, reaching for the camera, and the recording ended.

30

Rayne

Polaroid

ACRID SMOKE SPEWED INTO THE AIR AS THE WOODEN FLOOR and roof of the stone house blackened in flames. The cloud cover was thick, but the sparse snowfall wasn't enough to extinguish the fire I'd lit, fueled by the lighter fluid I'd drenched the interior with.

I'd removed the majority of my father's belongings. They were currently heaped in piles around Salem, who was seated in a chair I'd dragged out here for her, wrapped in a thick blanket and sheltered beneath an umbrella. She insisted her foot was fine; I insisted otherwise.

A massive storm had shut down the island for the past twenty-four hours. The temperature plummeted, and the first snow of the season fell fast and heavy, carpeting the ground and blanketing the trees. The cold was vicious; the wind made it worse. It had blown so hard, I'd woken up to several downed trees, branches and debris scattered across the property.

But despite the freezing cold, Salem refused to stay warm in the house as I returned to destroy the beast's burrow, and the building with it. So, after ensuring she wouldn't freeze to death and was properly sheltered, I occupied her with my father's possessions. She was currently rifling through a moldering cardboard box—seemingly his favorite method of storage—her eyebrows drawn together in concentration.

I hadn't kept all his shit for sentimental reasons; I would have preferred to let it burn. But I needed to know what else he'd been keeping hidden away from me.

I couldn't get my mother's words out of my head. The tape had never been sent, and I had a sickening feeling my father was responsible for that.

I'd never seen my mother look so afraid. I knew she and my father weren't close, but hadn't known she feared him, perhaps even more than I did.

We need to get out of here.

He opens the letters.

He's watching me.

I was keeping an eye on the fire, but Salem and Loki noticed something at the same moment. Salem started, and Loki got to his feet.

"Uh, Rayne?" Her alarmed tone made me turn, my back stiffening when I spotted the figure striding toward us. It took me a few seconds to recognize who it was, and only then did I relax.

Andy was bundled up in a thick coat and boots, his beard dusted with snow. "Having a bonfire, eh?" he called out. "Should've told me! I would have brought the girls along with marshmallows." He gave an easy chuckle as he embraced me, then greeted Salem. "Good to see you've survived your first real taste of Blackridge, Miss Lockard. Though not without a bit of damage . . ."

"Just keeping Rayne on her toes," Salem said, entirely too chipper for someone in her position. Andy glanced at me just in time to see me roll my eyes at her. He looked at me for a long moment before cracking a smile and saying, "It's good to find you in high spirits. Lifts my soul a bit." Gazing down the hill toward the smoldering fire, he said, "What's happened with that?"

"It had a burrow beneath," I said. "Nearly took Salem. But it won't be using that tunnel anymore. Doused the whole thing in gasoline."

Andy nodded grimly. "Good. Glad the outcome wasn't worse."

"I know you didn't come all this way for a chat, Andy," I said, my concern growing despite his good mood. Sure enough, his expression grew more serious, his smile gone.

"Last night's storm damaged the cell tower," he said. "The phones are down across the entire island; internet too. With all the snow, it'll take me a few days to get up to the north end of the island and assess the damage. Wanted to ask if you'd watch the girls while I'm gone."

I didn't even hesitate. "I'll go."

"Rayne, you don't need to—"

"Your girls need you," I said firmly. "Besides, I'm a better climber. You'll fall off the tower and break your back, what then?"

Andy chuckled, but insisted, "I'm no doddering old man! Come on now."

"Stay with the girls," I said. "I'll head out first thing in the morning, before the next storm moves in."

We all glanced with trepidation at the dark clouds on the horizon. More snow was coming, but the island needed to have its communication channels running. Neither Andy nor I were professionals, but we'd climbed the tower in previous years to remove massive buildups of ice and snow. When there was no one else to call, we had to learn to do things ourselves.

Andy huffed and puffed, muttering a bit before he finally said, "Alright. There'll be supplies at the fire tower; you can shelter there from the storm. Harness and ropes will be there too. You keep me updated, you hear? If I don't hear anything, I'll come looking for you. We don't need to lose anyone else."

I nodded before I glanced back at Salem. I lowered my voice. "Can she and the dog stay with you while I'm gone? She shouldn't be alone."

"Course she can." Andy patted my shoulder reassuringly. "The girls will probably lose their minds." He added teasingly, "They keep calling Miss Salem your princess. Becca thinks it's the romance of the century."

I didn't have the words to respond to that. My heart was light, and when I looked at Salem again, she smiled at me happily from her mound of blankets. I didn't say it out loud, but I felt like Rebecca was right.

⋆⟶⟶✦⟵⟵⋆

"COULDN'T I JUST go with you? Please? It's only a few days."

God, how had anyone ever managed to deny this woman? With those big eyes staring at me, that sweet pleading look, her downturned mouth—

"No," I said, and it killed me a little. We were in the lounge, with the fire blazing bright, keeping the room warm despite the near-freezing temperatures outside. "You're hurt, Salem. I'm not going to make you hike all the way out into the forest, climb all those stairs, and then sit in a cold firewatch tower. You're safer with Andy. Besides, when that storm moves in, I could be stuck out there even longer. It's not comfortable. You won't like it."

"I can walk!" She immediately cast off her blanket and stood up, but I firmly pushed her back down.

"I swear if you keep putting weight on that foot, I'm going to strap you to the chair," I said.

A fire lit in her eyes, as if I'd challenged her. "Good. Strap me down, I'll be easier to transport that way."

Shaking my head, I said, "Enough. Why don't you tell me what you found in all these boxes?"

She sighed, pursing her lips as if she was debating whether or not to keep arguing.

"Well . . ." She was surrounded by open cardboard boxes on all sides, filled with heaps of books, papers, strange jars, and copious handwritten notes. "Most of the journals are sermons, and related verses. There's a lot of books written in French, which I can't read, but I'm pretty sure they're all religious texts too." She leaned over, grabbed a small box, and dragged it in closer. "This one is cool though. Check this out!"

She reached into the box and excitedly pulled out an old Polaroid camera. Taking it in my hands, I smiled as memories came back to me.

"This was my mom's," I said. Bringing the viewfinder to my eye, I turned it toward Salem and she struck a pose. To my surprise, there was a loud click when I pushed the button, and an undeveloped photo emerged from the slot.

"No way, it still has film?" Salem said excitedly as I waved the Polaroid back and forth. The film was certainly old, and somewhat damaged, if the strange colors and water spots were any indication. But the sight of Salem's silly, smiling face captured on film made me happy.

"I'm taking this one with me when I go," I said, carefully setting the photo aside. Salem pouted.

"Take me with you," she said again. "I won't say anything the entire time." I tweaked up an eyebrow skeptically, and she sputtered, "Well, I'll *try* not to say anything!"

"I should just gag you," I said, grasping her face and giving it a playful shake. "Tie you up and fill that naughty mouth with something else to keep you quiet."

She smiled excitedly. "Does that mean I can go with you?"

"No."

"But what if it finds you?" Her voice cracked. "What if you're trapped up there in the middle of the night, and—"

"You want to know what I'd do?" I said, surprising her as I seized her, squishing her back against the couch. God, the way her eyes widened as she looked at me drove me wild. The excitement on her face, the lust, was enough to make me ravenous. "Do you think I can't defend myself, pretty girl?"

Grasping her jaw, I tilted her head back, baring her throat. A slight, thin red scratch still remained from where I'd accidentally cut her. Reaching down, I unstrapped the same knife from my thigh holster and held it up.

She stared at the blade as its metal caught the light, her pupils enlarging. Her breath hitched, and the small movement of her throat made my belly do somersaults.

"It's sharp," I whispered. I pressed closer, my thigh squeezing between her legs. Her hips moved in slow, hypnotic thrusts against me. "I can use this knife like it's an extension of my arm. It wouldn't be the first time I've defended myself." I came close enough to trace my lips over the shell of her ear, grinning when she shivered. "I know how to kill. I've done it before."

Delicately, I kissed her temple, her cheek, her jaw. My breath ignited goose bumps on her skin. Her body drew closer to mine, her hands grasping my hips. Her breathing quickened, a silent plea on her face.

"God, you really trust me, don't you?"

"Of course I trust you," she said. Why did those words hurt, like darts piercing into my chest? "You showed me I can."

She touched my face, in that gentle way that made me feel transcendent. I was not on this cursed island, in this haunted house, facing down the dark and lonely night. I was in my woman's arms, and she in mine.

She traced my mouth, fingers shaking slightly, as if committing my features to her memory. She took hold of my wrist and moved my hand, which still gripped the knife, closer to her. She opened her mouth, extended her tongue, and held my gaze as she slowly licked the sharp tip of the blade.

"I trust you," she whispered. "To come back to me."

Swiftly, I replaced the blade with my mouth, kissing her deeply. She tasted like the hot chocolate she drank, like the strawberry jam on her morning toast. Soft and so bittersweet.

She made me weak in all the ways I never dared to be.

I endured the winters because I had no choice. Never dying, but never truly living, either. I went through the motions, but I had no real reason to fight. Instead, I stood at the edge of the darkness, refusing to retreat, waiting to be swallowed.

But Salem changed everything. She'd shone a light onto my

path without even meaning to. She made the darkness not seem so deep. She'd given me the wild hope that maybe there truly was a way out for me, a way in which my heart still beat and I had a life worth living.

She lay back on the couch with a sigh, looking up at me with desire softening her eyes. Her fingers delicately traced up my thighs, over my hips, dipping into the curve of my waist. She pulled my sweater over my head, tossed it away, her smile wide and mischievous when she saw I wasn't wearing a bra beneath.

My body was a tool, but she treated it like a work of art. Like something beautiful and rare.

But it was she who embodied those things. She giggled as I stripped her out of her clothes, trying to be gentle while still giving her the roughness she craved. Entirely naked, she spread out on the couch, contentedly stretching her beautiful body over the velvet. Straddling her, I picked up the camera once more and focused on her.

I caressed my free hand over her breasts, her stomach. I wanted to memorize the way she felt, keep that look in her eyes frozen in my mind.

"Look what you've done to me, pretty girl," I said, almost breathless, when I snapped her photo. "You make it so damn hard to leave."

"Then don't," she said. "Stay." She caught my wrist again and kissed the back of my hand.

No one had ever asked me to stay. No one had ever wanted me to. For a split second, I almost pulled away. Her desire had to be a trick, her kind words a trap.

But that wasn't true.

She drew my wrist down, between her legs. Her lips parted when I pressed inside her, the softest sound escaping her. Her core clenched around my finger.

I would do anything to protect her.

Even leave her.

"I'll think of you every hour I'm gone," I said, desperate words growled low in her ear as I bent over her. Chest to chest, I pumped my finger inside her. Our bodies moved together in a slow rhythm of push and pull, those tiny sounds whimpering out of her every time I rocked into her.

"I swear I'll come back to you." Those words felt heavy, stones dropping from my back and rolling away. She nodded eagerly and wrapped her arms around my shoulders.

"You'd better," she gasped, writhing as I squeezed a second finger inside her. Her nails dug into my back, crescents of pain that made me groan. "Don't you dare abandon me." She growled the words, but they hitched with sincerity.

"Never." I added another finger and she cried out, dragging her nails down my back. She rocked her hips, encouraging my fingers to go deeper. My hair fell around us, framing her face in its shadow.

The fire crackled, the only sound besides our own heaving breaths.

"I'll come back to you, even if I have to haunt you." I straightened up, still deep inside her, and reached for the camera again. Her cheeks were flushed, mouth in an irresistible pout.

"Can you take another finger for me?"

She squirmed as she nodded, and whispered, "Please."

The camera flashed as I squeezed a fourth digit inside her, capturing the ecstasy and agony on her face. Immortalized, deified for my own personal worship. Devious, blasphemous, and holy in her beauty.

"Do you like how I feel inside you, pretty girl?" I said, and she groaned her affirmation. "Do you want me to fill you even deeper? Should I fuck this pussy until you come all over me?"

"Yes, please, Madam," she gasped. I pumped my fingers inside her, deep and slow, relaxing her muscles and opening her up for me.

"In just a few minutes, I'm going to put on my strap," I whispered, and her pupils dilated. "And you're going to take every inch. I'm going to fill you up, fuck you deep and slow. And after you've come so many times you can't see straight, I'm going to lick up every delicious drop of you."

"I want you so bad," she said, in a voice that was pure ambrosia for my ears. She reached for my hips, leaving bright red, passionate scratches. "I want you inside me."

"Don't you fucking move." I almost tripped over my own feet in my hurry to get off the couch. "Stay right there." The smile she gave me ensured I *ran* upstairs. I needed to start keeping toys stashed in more convenient places.

When I came back, fastening the harness around my hips, Salem had repositioned herself. She was sitting up on the couch, legs spread, one hand between them and the other holding the camera. She snapped a photo, and for a moment I was rendered speechless and frozen. She sighed softly as she put the camera down, and moaned so prettily that my brain was zapped into action again.

"Getting yourself ready for me?" I said as I walked in front of her. She spread her legs a little wider, looking me up and down appreciatively. God, she was beautiful. I knelt down in front of her, and she used her fingers to spread herself apart. I kept my eyes on her as I opened my mouth, allowing saliva to drip from my extended tongue. She inhaled deeply as I rubbed her, and my core clenched with heat every time she twitched and whimpered.

"That feels so good," she said.

"It's about to feel even better."

I swirled my tongue around her clit, her flesh engorged with arousal. She thrust against my mouth and I shoved her hips back down, smacking her inner thigh hard enough to leave a cherry-red mark. She shuddered, biting her lip and demanding petulantly, "More, please . . ."

"More pain?" I teased, and she nodded rapidly. I slapped her other thigh and she jolted, smiling as she hissed.

"God, Madam, please!" She gripped the couch cushions with shaking hands as I closed my mouth over her clit and sucked, flicking my tongue against her sensitive bud. Then, after a few seconds, I lifted my head and smacked her again, once on each thigh. The marks of my fingers looked beautiful against her skin, and I kissed each one before eating her out again.

"Fuck, pleeeaaase . . ." she groaned, body trembling, nerves wound tight. She was close but I was edging her carefully, keeping her teetering on the brink of oblivion. Her pussy was so wet, feeding me a taste of the gods' ambrosia every time I licked her.

"Are you ready for it, baby?" I crawled up onto the couch, teasing the strap against her opening.

She bucked her hips eagerly, rubbing herself against the silicone as she begged, "Please, God, I want your strap. Fuck my pussy, please, fuck me deep—"

I grasped her throat with one hand and gripped her hair with the other. I pulled her down so she was lying on her back, splayed open: One leg I rested against my shoulder, the other dangled over my thigh off the couch. I eased the toy inside her slowly, thrusting a little deeper each time.

"Do you feel that stretch, baby?" I said, watching her face, drinking in her soft moans. "Do you understand how deep I own you?" The sounds I drew out of her were beautiful, desperate and greedy. "This pussy is mine. This beautiful body is all mine. Mine to please, mine to fuck. It doesn't matter who's had you before. I'm going to erase every trace of them. I'll show you pleasure like they never could. All—fucking—mine." I thrust with every word, driving my point home as her eyes rolled back.

I was consumed entirely by the way she writhed for me. She made me thankful for every spark of life in my body—every shock of pain, every moment of pleasure. She was so wet, taking the entire length and groaning in ecstasy. Every time I drew out of her, the strap glistened with her arousal, and I was breathlessly enraptured when I sank into her again.

Watching the toy disappear inside her was almost too much, and I groaned at her little gasps of pleasure. She was massaging her swollen clit, her eyes half-lidded as she looked up at me. Her cheeks were flushed, her lips parted to whimper my name.

I curled over her and kissed her neck, salty with sweat and sweet with her scent. She tangled her fingers in my hair, tugging as she moaned and begged me for more. I maneuvered my hips until I found an angle that made her eyes roll back.

"Keep breathing," I reminded her. Reaching down, I moved her trembling hand aside so I could touch her. I rubbed her clit until she bucked desperately against my hand, driving the strap in deeper. Her movements were clumsy, her body moving beyond her control and into mine.

"That's it, beautiful," I murmured, kissing her throat as her body tensed, her muscles throbbing in wave after wave of building pleasure. "I've got you, every perfect inch of you. Come for me, there you go."

Watching her fall apart until she was limp and trembling was sheer heaven. Working her through it, I slowed my pace to draw out her pleasure, keeping the strap deep inside her.

"God, Rayne, that feels so good." Her eyes were open but unfocused, an orgasm-drunk smile on her face. "I want—want to feel you—please."

She gasped as the strap pulled out of her. I fumbled in my hurry to get it off and climb back on top. Unable to resist, I dipped my head down one more time and tasted her, sucking her clit and pressing my tongue into her throbbing hole. She mewled, thrusting against my mouth, babbling her pleasure in a string of words I could barely understand.

Lifting my head, I grabbed a pillow and wedged it under her lower back before I straddled the apex of her spread legs. She laid her leg on my shoulder, and I moved against her, side to side, up and down.

There was nothing better, nothing more perfectly *right*, than the sensation of our bodies coming together. Gyrating against her, skin to skin, her clit swollen and tender as it met my own. Every movement of my hips sent pleasure jolting through my core, like lightning to every nerve. I found my rhythm, tension building inside me as her face went slack with bliss. Her throbbing against me was perfect: slick and deliciously warm.

"You're gonna make me come, pretty girl," I said, my words tight. I gripped her hips, lifting her just a bit—the perfect angle for my clit to flick over hers.

I rarely lost myself in pleasure, but with her, I did. I floated into that mind-blowing orgasm with not a thought in my head except the image of her, her eyes looking up at me, her body cleaved to mine. Perfectly beautiful and entirely my own.

Salem

Photos of the Dead

EARLY THE FOLLOWING MORNING, AS THE FIRST RAYS OF THE sun peeked between the trees, Rayne drove me through the snow to Andy's farm. The freshly fallen powder crunched beneath our boots as we walked up the driveway toward his two-story farmhouse, chickens clucking and goats bleating from the nearby barn.

"Mornin', Rayne. Mornin', Miss Lockard." Andy was already up and about, and waved a gloved hand at us from the veranda, a steaming mug perched on the railing beside him. "Coffee is in the pot if ya need it. I can take your bag there . . ."

"I got her." Rayne smiled as she hoisted my bag over her shoulder and led me inside, Loki following behind us. The interior was delightfully warm, and Loki quickly settled by a wood-burning stove near the couch. Children's books and toys were scattered across the floor, and there was a half-finished puzzle on the kitchen table. To judge by how quiet the house was, Rebecca and Rachel were still asleep.

"Got everything you need?" Andy said as Rayne and I re-emerged. Rayne patted the large backback she carried and nodded. "You're taking a gun, yeah? You got ammo?"

"I got enough to get by," she said, but the answer didn't satisfy him and he traipsed inside. He returned minutes later with a box of .45s.

"That should do it," he said, patting her shoulder. "You be safe out there."

"I'll try to be back by tomorrow night," she said. I'd been doing my best to hold my emotions in check, but the moment she turned to me, the struggle to hold in my tears made me hiccup.

She embraced me, tucking my head beneath her chin. I tried not to cry, and when that didn't work, I at least managed to cry silently.

"I'll be okay," she said. "I promise. Don't worry about me."

"I'll miss you," I said. She drew back, just enough to press her forehead to mine.

"I'll miss you too. Just a couple days. That's it. Then I'll be back." She kissed my cheek, and whispered close to my ear, "I've got your pictures in my pocket. I'm going to keep them by my bed and think of you."

I hurriedly wiped my face, the tears already freezing on my cheeks. She kissed my mouth, holding my face in her gloved hands.

All too soon, she was gone, walking away back toward the ATV, then disappearing into the forest.

ANDY WANTED TO treat me like a guest, but I insisted he put me to work. I needed my hands busy and my brain distracted, otherwise my anxiousness over Rayne's absence was going to eat me alive.

We fed the chickens and put down fresh straw for the goats. When the girls finally woke up, I took Loki for a walk around the property while Andy prepared breakfast. Rebecca and Rachel were ecstatic to have company, but I was struggling to keep myself in a happy mood. All I could think of was Rayne, alone on her journey to the northern tip of the island. At the least, she'd told me there was a radio there, so I'd have a way to contact her.

It was freezing outside, so I couldn't stay out there forever. Eventually, I had to put on my happy mask and go inside. I forced myself to eat the bacon and pancakes Andy had prepared, despite my nervous stomach's protests. Rebecca and Rachel were eager to talk; Rachel kept bringing various toys to show me, while Rebecca wanted to hear all about the mainland.

They were sweet kids, and I wished I had more energy to entertain them. My worry was a constant distraction, an itch in the back of my brain, especially when the wind began to blow and the snow started falling.

The day passed slowly. I helped Andy as much as I could, although he insisted I didn't need to. I helped Rebecca with her vocabulary worksheet, and read a storybook to Rachel when it was time for her nap. All the while, the wind and snow howled outside. By evening, Loki was sitting expectantly at the front door, even though he'd already been let out to relieve himself.

"She's not coming back tonight, boy," I said. He looked at me for a long moment, took one last forlorn look at the door, then returned to his spot in front of the fire.

Andy ushered the girls upstairs for "quiet reading time," and I was left alone. The soft, cushy couch had been made up as a bed with comfortable pillows, and the fireplace kept it warm. The farmhouse creaked in the wind, but it didn't have the ominous feeling of Balfour Manor. I didn't feel watched.

Swirls of snow drifted down outside, the windows frosted with ice. The sun had nearly set, and the growing darkness made my heart pound painfully in my chest. Rayne had assured me that Andy was well armed; all the windows were barred, and the front door was equipped with a thick bolt lock. But it wasn't my own safety I was worried about.

Andy had shown me around, so I knew his CB radio was located down the narrow hallway, in his office. I shuffled inside, partially closing the door so I wouldn't disturb the girls upstairs. I curled up in the chair behind the desk, the old springs creaking beneath me. Loki lay down at my feet; he'd been glued to my side since we arrived.

I tuned the radio's channel to the station for the northern firewatch tower and picked up the mic.

"Rayne?" I said softly. "You there?"

My heart pounded sickeningly hard as I waited for a response.

"Hey, pretty girl."

My sprinting heart leapt into my throat at the sound of her voice. "I miss you. I wanted to make sure you're okay."

I could hear the smile in her voice. "I'm all good. I have a fire going in the stove, keeping it really toasty in here. I'm wrapped up in my favorite crocheted blanket. Even got some instant hot cocoa."

I snickered. "With the mini marshmallows?"

"Of course. I'm sure Andy has some there at the house too."

"The floor is too cold to walk to the kitchen," I said, sighing dramatically.

"Tell you what, I'll hike back real quick and make it for you."

My eyes stung. I truly was exhausted, to be moved to tears so easily by the thought of her coming back.

What if she never came back? What if she fell from the cell tower, or the beast found her, or—

"Salem, are you still there?"

"Yeah! Yeah, I'm—" I cleared my throat. "Sorry, I'm a little tired. Was the trip out there okay?"

"Not too bad. It was quiet and cold," she said. "Almost peaceful. There's a helluva lot of snow, but I can see the issue with the tower. There's debris caught on it, but it should be easy enough to remove."

"Oh, good, yeah, that's good . . ."

Childish laughter came from the upper floor, then Andy's loud guffaw. The sounds of a happy household surrounded me, but I felt so lonely.

"Are you okay, Salem?" Rayne's voice was tender, and it wrapped around me like an embrace.

"I'm anxious," I said. "There's a pit in my stomach. I'm just . . . I'm afraid."

She was in far more danger than I. I felt silly for complaining, but these feelings consumed every part of me. Like a monster, anxiety waited in every dark corner of my brain, in every unknown, in every painful memory. It lurked in dangers both very real and imagined. It dredged up every worry, made it into a neon sign, and plastered it at the front of my brain.

"I understand, baby. I don't blame you. It's a scary fucking world. But I've got you. I may not be there with you right now, but I promise, I'll drop everything and come back to you the second you need me."

Her words surprised me so much that I fell silent for several moments. Equal parts guilt and joy made my watery eyes over-flow, and I quickly wiped my cheeks.

"Hey. Did you hear me?"

"I heard you," I whispered, so she wouldn't hear the words shake. "Thank you."

"Don't thank me. I'm happy to do it, Salem. I want to . . ." Her voice faded away for a few moments, and I waited with bated breath. "I want to be there for you. This whole situation is so fucked up, but having you here . . ." She trailed off again. "I should be saying this to you in person. Guess I'm too much of a coward."

"You're not a coward," I said. I held the microphone close to my ear and closed my eyes, almost able to imagine that she was there beside me.

"You gave me hope again, Salem. Who knows if anything will change? But I've been alone for a long time, and after a while, you lose sight of what you're fighting for."

"Did you find it again?" I said. "The thing you're fighting for?"

"No, not again. But for the first time, yes. I have something to fight for now."

I FELL ASLEEP curled up in the chair with the radio in my hand. At some point, Andy came in and draped a blanket over me, so I didn't shiver too much during the long night.

When I woke in the morning, I let Loki out to do his business and watched him from the veranda. An endless expanse of black clouds was gathered overhead, although the snow had stopped for now. Puffy white drifts were piled against the barn, and I helped Andy clear them so we could give the animals their feed.

I popped a pill to keep myself calm, despite how drowsy it made me. After feeding Loki and eating a late breakfast of soft-boiled eggs and toast, I returned to my mission of cataloging the junk we'd removed from the stone house before it was burned. I'd only managed to stuff one small box into my backpack to bring with me, but it was enough to keep me occupied.

I spread out its contents on the desk in Andy's office. There were dozens of childhood photos of Rayne, many of them weathered, stained, and faded from years of being poorly stored. Some of her and her mother, and some of Melanie Balfour alone, clearly self-taken.

Not a single photo of Picard. Not a shred of evidence he was even remotely involved with his own wife and child.

At the very bottom of the box, a large, dirty envelope was encrusted to the cardboard. Groaning in disgust, I used a tissue to peel it up, finding it covered in rings of black mold. There were even more photos within.

But these were different than the others.

The first few were so dark, I could barely tell what I was looking at. But the longer I stared at the strange photos—bloody red, fatty white, pale splintered bone—the more my stomach churned. I didn't know what I was looking at, but I knew there was something very wrong with it.

The first clear photo I found, I dropped as I clapped my hands over my mouth in horror. Dead animals, so mutilated I couldn't determine their species, spread out across a familiar wooden table. The table from the stone house.

"Oh my God . . ." I picked up another, and another, my eyes scanning the photos with growing horror. Flesh and bone, blood and organs. Some photos were so grotesque I was nauseated, and I dry heaved suddenly, doubling over as I tried not to vomit.

The last few photos were the worst. It wasn't an animal they depicted.

It was a person. There was one photo of a wide-open, glassy eye—ringed with blood. Another depicted a woman's naked body laid out as if for dissection, her face not shown. Her throat was gashed open, a deep and vicious slice. Her torso was marred with gaping wounds.

The last photo was of a pile of bloody bones, some with bits of flesh clinging to them. Stained hands held a femur aloft from the pile, showing a row of tiny carved symbols in the bone.

My hands were shaking as I set everything down, got to my feet, and began to pace in circles. I had a terrible feeling I knew whose body that was.

Melanie was supposed to be buried; Rayne said her mother had been laid to rest.

But I didn't believe that was true anymore.

RAYNE HAD PROMISED she would radio me before she began her drive back, but the hours were passing too slowly. Those awful photos festered in my mind, so much so that I looked at them again just to assure myself I'd truly seen them.

I wanted to believe they were fake, but my visceral reaction told me they were real.

How could I tell Rayne? *What* could I tell her? The very thought of her having to see those photos made me ill.

"You feeling okay, Miss Salem?" Andy said, looking at me from across the kitchen table in concern. I'd barely been able to touch the food he'd made. "Don't you worry about Rayne. She's made the trip up to that old tower plenty of times. She's a smart woman; she'll stay up there if the weather is too bad to travel back."

I was thankful for his reassurance. I almost blurted out to him what I'd found, desperate for a second opinion, but the girls were sitting right there. Instead, after poking at my food for a while, I curled up with a cup of tea near the radio, waiting desperately for Rayne's call to come through.

But evening came and darkness fell, still without a word from her.

A knock at the office door made me jump, and Andy poked his head in. "I'm gonna hit the hay. You should try to get some sleep. The weather has been rough; it's probably keeping her busy."

Maybe it was just my anxiety talking, but his assurance didn't seem so *sure* anymore.

Hours later, Loki's sharp bark woke me from a fitful slumber.

I'd fallen asleep at the desk again. I stretched my aching neck, and shivered as I tucked my hands into my sleeves. While I was almost positive the radio would have woken me, I picked up the mic and said softly, "Rayne? Are you there?"

No response. Loki wasn't lying by my feet anymore either; he was probably at the front door, waiting to be let outside to pee. God, it was freezing. Cupping my hands around my mouth and exhaling to warm them, I hurried to the front door and grabbed one of the warm coats hung near the door.

Loki was pacing and whimpering, so I hurriedly opened the door for him before shoving my arms into the coat sleeves and tugging on my boots.

Stepping out onto the veranda, I peered out into the dark night. The snow was falling again, twisting in flurries and massive gusts of wind. Floodlights ringed the house with their illumination, but I still didn't want to stand out here any longer than necessary.

But as I scanned the yard, I realized Loki was nowhere to be seen.

"Loki?" I expected to see him come trotting from around the side of the house, but no. My eyes followed his tracks through the snow, across the yard . . . and away.

Into the forest.

Distantly, carried on the freezing wind, came the sound of a barking dog. It was a frantic snarling sound, full of fear. My heart pounded against my ribs, my throat swelling with fear.

"Loki!" My call was swallowed by the howling wind. His barking sounded even farther away.

Panicking, I hurried inside to my backpack and rummaged through until I found the hunting knife Rayne had left with me. Ripping it from its sheath, I sprinted out into the stormy night.

The freshly fallen snow weighed down my feet like anchors. The wind whipped around me, flurries obscuring my vision.

"Loki!" I kept calling for him, following his prints through the snow as best I could. My lips and fingers were turning numb from the cold, but I couldn't abandon the poor dog to death out here. Why would he run off, what had possesed him?

I couldn't hear him anymore. I couldn't see the farmhouse either. All around me was nothing but a maze of tall trees and frozen brambles.

My heart plummeted, terror racing through me. I needed to go back and wake Andy for help. But as I turned in circles, I quickly realized I might not even be able to find my way to the house again. My prints in the snow, and Loki's, were swiftly being covered.

My breath came faster, my lungs aching with the cold. Damn it, where had the dog run off to? It wasn't like him. I cupped my hands around my mouth, yelling uselessly into the howling wind.

Faintly, distant barking answered me. Desperately, I ran, following the sound. But my foot caught on something I couldn't see beneath the snow, sending me sprawling to the ground.

As I pushed myself up, I could see a faint red glow in front of me.

Long, dark, bloodstained hair flowed in the flurries of wind. Hollow eyes watched me as blood dripped from too-long fingernails, stark in the white snow. I gasped, and it was as if I inhaled a wave of sadness that hit me like a kick to my stomach.

Everything hurt. I could hardly breathe.

It was less than a second, the blink of an eye, then she was gone.

The wind was full of whispers, strange voices overlapping. My chest felt so heavy, my head dizzy. I needed to get inside, but where . . . how . . .

I turned back, and she was there: face contorted, bloody arms outstretched, mouth gaped open in a horrifying scream.

My own scream was swallowed by the storm as I was thrown down. I landed in deep snow and tumbled, sliding down a steep slope into a gully.

The air I desperately needed was squeezed out of my lungs. It felt as if my chest was caving in.

Again and again, the awful feeling of constriction came. I couldn't scream, couldn't get up. It was as if my throat was full of liquid, and I was choking on its gross metallic taste. A shadow wavered before me, forward and back, forward and back. Crushing me with every swing. Pounding my chest, so that bubbles rose in the bloody pond filling my mouth.

Someone in the distance was screaming. Such a wretched, pitiful wailing. The whispers persisted, surrounding me, infecting me.

The bones, the bones, to the bones I bind thee. With flesh, with flesh, with this flesh I feed thee. In blood, in blood, in blood do I call thee.

32

Rayne

Lights Out

MY HANDS WERE STIFF AND COLD AS I PEELED MY GLOVES off, dumping them into the storage container alongside my climbing harness. It had taken me even longer than I expected to climb up the cell tower, thanks to the freezing temperatures making the metal slick with ice. A massive branch had become entangled on the transceiver, but with it removed, the ghostly green glow of the live trail cameras had returned to the fire tower's square room.

The old monitors were stacked precariously on the desk, their glass cracked and their old plastic bodies brittle. Blackridge wasn't swimming in tax revenue; the tools we had were community-funded, but they were old and breaking down. Every winter, I begged them to last just one more year, and so far they had clung to life.

My body ached with exhaustion, and I collapsed face down on the bed. The sun was just setting, but the storm clouds made it so dark, it may as well have been night. There was no way I was making it back home tonight. More than I wanted food, more than I wanted rest, I wanted to talk to Salem. To hear her voice, to know she was okay.

No amount of exhaustion could dampen how much I looked forward to simply hearing her voice.

Was something wrong with me? Was this just an obsession, or was the warmth I felt when I thought of her something else entirely? The memory of her smile made my stomach feel like it was shaking. When I reached under my pillow and pulled out the Polaroids of her, all the heat rushed to my face and instantly, I was smiling like a fool.

Click.

The room suddenly plunged into darkness. Rattled, confused, I sprung out of bed and hurriedly flicked the light switch off and on. Nothing. The monitors were off. The CB radio was too. Zipping up my coat, I went out onto the walkway and peered down to the pitch-black forest.

The floodlights surrounding the tower, meant to dissuade the angel from approaching, were off.

"Goddamn it, the electricity is out," I muttered. Grabbing my flashlight from the table, I opened the breaker box near the door.

"Come on!" Turning on and off the breaker did nothing. My only option was the backup generator at the base of the tower.

Snow was falling heavily now. With my gun loaded and ready, I slowly made my way down the tower. The stairs creaked, the tower groaning in the storm. Cold wind whipped my face and I kept my head ducked down, swinging my flashlight across my path. Even if something was waiting for me at the bottom of the tower, I couldn't hear it over the howling wind.

I couldn't see it in the dark.

The generator sputtered when I tried to turn it on, and I swore as I swung the flashlight around, looking for the supply shed where I would hopefully find fuel.

Snap.

The crack of a twig instantly drew my light. The beam reflected off the glittering snow, barely piercing the shadows. The trees swayed in the wind, and beneath them, the darkness was so thick it was like a physical wall.

"Honey?"

My back knotted with tension, but I didn't dare move a muscle. Had I actually heard someone? Or was it just the wind, the creak of the trees?

"Where are you, honey? I can't see you."

That voice reached deep into my subconscious, piercing into a wound I didn't know was still open. I held my breath. I didn't speak, nor move my light even an inch.

"Come back to Mommy, honey."

My teeth were gritted so tight, I expected them to crack. It was my mother's voice. But it shouldn't have been. It *couldn't.* She died before the beast arrived, it couldn't have known her voice.

And yet . . .

"Rayne? Don't upset Mommy."

From the shadows, just a few feet to the left of my flashlight's beam, a long, sickly pale limb reached out. Then another. Then two more. Joints popped in and out of place, crackling grotesquely. As its bizarre body contorted to stand upright, its ribs rippled unnaturally, as if they could move of their own accord.

Its eyeless face looked up, as if toward the stormy sky, its hideous mouth gaping open as pincerlike teeth clawed at the air.

Slowly, I moved my weapon into position.

"Oh, God . . ." Her voice contorted with terror. It was not the beast's usual monotone mimicry. It sounded far too real. "Where are you?"

Dropping the flashlight, I snapped my hand up to brace my weapon and fire. It couldn't have taken more than a second, but my bullet shot through open air, finding no target.

"Shit!" I sprinted for the stairway, but abruptly stopped myself. There was only one way down, and the door up there wouldn't hold forever. With only a flashlight and limited bullets in a confined space, I was as good as dead if I climbed the tower again.

Snap.

The angel charged for me, loping through the snow with terrifying ease. It rammed into the stairway railing, splintering the wood as its claws tore through the back of my jacket. I tumbled, desperately clinging to my weapon, and scrambled to my feet just in time to fire off another bullet as it leapt at me again. It screeched as the shot pierced its chest, reeling backwards and swiping at the wound.

There was no time to aim. There was no other choice.

I sprinted for the ATV. Close behind, the angel screamed my name as I turned the key and pressed the ignition, hoping frantically that the old engine wouldn't fail me. It roared to life, and I pressed the throttle, snow spewing from beneath my tires as I sped off into the darkness.

Salem

Screams in the Dark

WHEN I CAME TO, I WAS SHIVERING VIOLENTLY. MY BODY ached with the vicious cold, and every breath I drew felt laborious. I couldn't move, and several long seconds passed in terror as I wondered if I was dying.

Disoriented, I suddenly realized something warm and heavy was pressed against my back. When I groaned, the thing moved, and something wet and cold nudged against my neck, then my cheek. There was a snuffling sound, then a warm, wet tongue licked frantically at my ear.

"Loki . . ." My vision swam as I tried to look at him. I had no idea how long I'd lain there in the snow, but it was only thanks to his body heat that I was still living. I wrapped my arms around his fluffy neck, clinging to his collar to drag myself to my feet. He stood patiently as I leaned against him, barely able to stand straight.

My body was too heavy, my limbs numb, and I slumped over the big dog's back. Loki started walking, dragging me along as I clung to him. He moved determinedly, ears up, maneuvering us carefully through the snow. Then he paused, one ear forward and one back.

All I could hear was the roar and tumult of the storm. Loki stared into the darkness, his tail sticking straight out as a low growl rumbled in his chest.

"Salem! Help me!"

Chills went over my body. Panic churned in my stomach. That was Rayne's voice—faint, but undeniable. Instantly, adrenaline shot through every limb. I went from sluggish to red alert in mere seconds, but my body didn't want to cooperate. I tried to stand, walked only a few feet, and collapsed again in the snow.

Loki began to pant and bark, jerking against my hold on him. But I refused to let go of his collar. The voice sounded like Rayne, but memories of the angel and its mockery kept me rooted in place.

"Salem! Please! Help me!"

Her distant voice was sharp with agony. As panic rushed through me like a cold river, I yelled, "Rayne! Rayne, can you hear me?"

The wind snatched my words away, drowning them in the storm.

Loki lurched forward with a furious snarl, overpowering me. His wet collar slipped out of my grip and he ran through the trees and out of sight, his barking getting farther and farther away.

"Loki! No!" I had no light, and only a knife for a weapon. I had no idea where I was. Adrenaline alone kept me upright as I stumbled forward.

"Salem!"

"Oh, God, Rayne..."

What could I do? Every second of uncertainty was too long. I had to find Rayne, *I had to*. It was foolish to go on without help, but I didn't even know if I could find my way back. I shouldn't have come out here, I never should have left the house...

It was dangerous. Likely only death waited for me out there in the trees. But if I ignored her voice, if there was even the slightest chance that Rayne was really out there, I would never forgive myself for abandoning her.

My entire body ached with the cold, as if I were walking on needles. Loki's barking was distant and vicious, as if he was in pursuit of something. Every few seconds, Rayne would call, but I didn't dare answer. I moved as silently as I could, my head on a swivel.

I was not the hunter. I was the prey, and every step could be my last.

My flashlight cast its eerie beam through the swirling snow, but shadows were all around me. My paranoia made me see things that weren't there, as if dark figures were darting between the trees. I swore I could still hear whispers on the wind, the soft sound of weeping making the hair on my neck stand straight up.

It was impossible to tell what was real, what was imaginary, and what intended to kill me.

My light flickered. Something was moving nearby, but I couldn't see it no matter which way I turned. Loki's barking was closer than ever. Despite my throat swelling with panic, I called softly. "Loki? Rayne? Are you... are you there?"

My neck tingled with the horrible sense of being watched.

From the dark came a whisper, "Salem . . . please . . . help me."

The vague outline of a figure was crouched in front of me, my light flickering rapidly as I faced it. The air was sharp with a fleshy, metallic scent. Like an open, rotten wound.

I couldn't speak. I didn't dare. I held my knife at the ready, even knowing it wasn't enough to defend my life.

Slowly, the figure stood up, and the angel turned its eyeless face toward me.

"Oh . . . God . . . no . . ." I backed away, arms shaking, knees threatening to buckle. The angel's head twitched eagerly as it crawled toward me, rancid breath clouding in the air. Its nostrils flared and it screeched, the sound so awful that my heart clenched with terror.

In a perfect mimicry of Rayne, it said, "Help me, please . . . help me . . ."

My brain kept telling my legs to *run . . . run . . . run . . .* but they wouldn't obey. Screams were caught in my throat, my body rigid with terror. I couldn't move. Couldn't breathe, couldn't think.

The creature's mouth gaped open, revealing a void-like maw full of teeth. It lunged, slamming into me and sending me sprawling to the ground. I slashed the knife wildly, hoping desperately to feel it pierce into flesh. Putrid saliva dripped onto me, claws raking into the snow around me, and as the blade made contact, something wet and hot splattered across my face.

But the next beastly scream I heard wasn't from the angel. It was Loki.

He was like a shadow sprinting from the trees and flying through the air. He barreled into my attacker, jaws snapping closed around one of its long limbs. In a flurry of snow and horrific sounds they tumbled to the ground, and it was impossible to tell beast from dog in the chaos.

A gunshot rang out. Loki had not come alone.

Rayne stepped into the beam of my shuddering light, her clothing soaked, her hair wild. Blood was splattered on her face and had drenched her coat, but she moved swiftly to take aim and fire again.

The beast screamed as it rose up on its hoofed hind limbs. Bloody wounds peppered its chest, but it roared its defiance and slashed its claws at the dog as he danced around its feet, snarling and snapping. It was dangerously close to me, and as it swung around to face me again, I lunged forward with a scream and plunged the knife into its thigh.

The angel flailed, its wretched shrieks threatening to burst my eardrums. One of its long limbs struck me as it turned to flee, and I was knocked to the ground. Dizzied, I watched it disappear into the darkness, leaving a trail of dark red blood.

Strong arms wrapped around me, dragging me to my feet again. "Salem! Come on, get up, we have to go, we have to go *now*!"

Rayne held me tight, one arm around me as the other held her gun. She whistled, one quick, sharp sound, and Loki came bounding to us.

Stumbling in the snow, we made our way through the dark. Loki followed close behind us, stopping every now and then to stare back into the shadows. The eerie shrieks of the injured beast were frighteningly close. We hadn't defeated it; we'd only made it angry.

"Rayne . . . where are we?" I said.

"I don't know, exactly," she said, gritting her teeth. "We just have to keep moving. I crashed the ATV. Couldn't fucking see

271

where I was going." She tried to whistle again, but her lips were chapped from the wind and cold. "Loki! Home! Go home!"

The dog cocked his head as he listened to her command. He put his nose to the wind, then to the ground, and started off determinedly through the trees.

"Follow him," Rayne said. "He'll find the way."

We kept going, trudging through fresh snow as Loki guided us. The arm Rayne wrapped around me was soaked with blood; I could smell it, feel its stickiness, and when I looked down, her hand was stained with it. Fresh, bright, and cherry red.

"Rayne, you're bleeding . . . you're hurt . . ."

"Never mind that." Her eyes had the look of a hunted animal, wide, wary, and feral. "What about you?"

"I'm not hurt." I wasn't entirely sure that was true, but my own injuries didn't matter to me right then. "God, Rayne, there's so much blood."

She suddenly stumbled, barely catching herself against a tree. Swooping under her arm, I supported her as she bared her teeth, cursing in pain.

"We can't stop," she said. "How did you get all the way out here? You shouldn't . . . shouldn't have left Andy's house." Her strength was fading fast. Her eyes rolled back and her legs buckled, nearly taking both of us to the ground. Loki whimpered, coming back to Rayne's side and nuzzling his nose into her limp hand.

"Go home, Loki," I said, dragging Rayne upright. The dog barked, looking over his shoulder as he trotted ahead. Without his guidance, I would have had no clue which direction to go. We kept moving, one painful step in front of the other, until we reached the gates of Balfour Manor.

"Good boy, Loki," I gasped. I wanted to collapse right there inside the gate. The stairs looked like an impossible task. Sheer force of will propelled me up them, even as I nearly slipped countless times on the ice-slick stone. Rayne was barely keeping her feet. She hadn't said a word, and I wasn't sure if she was fully concious.

My fingers were so cold, I barely managed to hold the house key steady to unlock the door. We stumbled inside, and as if crossing the threshold flicked a switch, Rayne collapsed, one hand clutching her injured arm.

I swiftly slammed and locked the doors, then knelt at her side. "You need a doctor."

She shook her head, eyes squeezed shut. "Can't make it to town. Not without the ATV. North side of the island . . . doesn't have electricity. It went out . . . that's how it got to me."

My anxiety was going haywire, but my brain had found its override: I could ignore my panic for the sake of helping her. Dissociating but bizarrely calm, I closed my eyes for a moment and forced myself to put my next actions into a logical sequence.

"We need to get that wound clean," I finally said. "Do you have a first aid kit? Needle and thread?" She nodded. "Alright. We need to get you warm too, so . . . okay, let's do this, come on."

My hands were shaking and my stomach was in knots as I helped her to her feet and up the stairs. She was shivering violently; every step made her breath catch with pain.

What if her wound got infected before we could get the doctor out to the house? What if I couldn't clean it thoroughly enough, or what if my hands shook too hard when I tried to plunge the needle into her skin?

She stumbled on the final step, gripping me tighter for balance. "It used my mom's voice. It . . . fucking mimicked her. I don't . . . don't understand . . . how it could know . . ."

I had to carry her on my back down the hallway. Her head lolled limply as I dragged her into the bathroom and propped her against the wall. As the tub filled with hot water, I scrambled through the cabinet for supplies.

"Need a drink," she groaned.

"Let's focus on stopping the bleeding before we start the liquor infusion," I said. I hadn't meant it as a joke, but she laughed softly, and I almost wept at the sound. How it hitched with pain. "I need to get your clothes off. Can I . . ."

"I thought you'd never ask, sweetheart." Her slurred words ran together, her head hanging tiredly. I peeled off her sweater and unbuttoned the shirt underneath. A deep, swollen gash ran from her shoulder to her bicep.

"You need stitches," I said, pulling off her boots. Mud spattered across the floor as I tossed them aside, then pulled down her trousers. Her skin was like ice as I helped her into the bath. She lay back, eyes closed, dirt and blood tinting the steaming water.

"I'll do it myself," she whispered. "Don't need help, I'm . . . fine . . ."

"Don't be ridiculous," I said. Using a soft cloth, I washed her body and took extra care around the wound, cleaning away dirt and blood. I drained and replaced the water, then rummaged under the sink for a first aid kit.

Rayne kept her eyes closed, her breathing slow and deep. For a few minutes, I thought she was asleep.

Then, "You came looking for me. You thought . . . thought you'd save me."

"But you saved me instead," I said. "Loki knew something was wrong. He ran off to find you." Her wound was still slowly bleeding, a bright red stream in the white porcelain tub. If I didn't take care of that now, she wouldn't be conscious for much longer. Sheer willpower could only win against biology for so long.

"Rayne." I crawled close to the tub, and her eyes were unfocused as she looked at me. "I need to . . . to, um . . ." Gulping down the nausea, I forced myself to calmly say, "I'm going to stitch up your wound to stop the bleeding. I need to get you out of the water to do that."

She forced her eyes open wider, drawing in a breath. "Okay."

She grasped the edge of the tub, unsteadily, refusing to glance at my hands as they hovered around her. She stood up straight, dripping water and blood, a goddess returning from war. I swallowed hard, staring at her for a moment, at the stone-cold determination in her eyes.

She held out her arm and said, "I can't step over alone."

She looked straight ahead as she said it, as if the words were a knife in her own guts. I steadied her, but her knee buckled as she stepped onto the tile. Catching her under the arms, I eased her to the floor, hurriedly dragging over towels to wrap around her and keep her warm.

Her eyes drooped, her expression listless as she murmured, "I shouldn't have left you. What would I do . . . what I would I fucking *do* if you . . ."

"Save your strength, please," I said. "Be quiet."

I dabbed disinfectant around her wound, trying not to think of what had to come next. There was a curved needle and sterile thread in the kit, but my hands were already trembling.

Rayne opened her eyes. They were reddened and glassy with

exhaustion as she raised her arm, bringing her hand to my face. Her fingers traced over my cheek, slow and tender.

"You shouldn't have come for me," she said, but the words seemed to exhaust her, deflating her like a balloon. She slumped toward me and I propped her back up, bracing her against the tub.

"Stop being a martyr," I said. "Focus on staying awake so you can tell me how to do this."

My stomach churned as I threaded the needle. My fingers jumped and trembled, and I gritted my teeth.

"Okay, okay, I . . . I can do this. I've sewn some things before, um, little things. Stuff for costumes."

"Nerd," she whispered, eyes nearly closed again. I pursed my lips, my hands shaking a little less. "You can do it. I'll tell you how."

Rayne

Caretaker

Salem didn't stitch me up the way I would have. She was slow and careful, whispering apologies when I swore in pain. She was gentler to me than I ever would have been, and I didn't know how to thank her for that.

I didn't know how to thank her for any of this.

She sat cross-legged beside me, jaw clenched, focused solely on her work. Jab, tug, jab, tug. Despite the cold tile floor beneath me, I was sweating bullets from the pain. Fortunately, or not, I'd lost enough blood to feel high, shock offering me some mild relief.

"I'll get you food," she said, glancing worriedly at my face. I was willing to bet I looked as bad as I felt. "As soon as I'm done with this."

"I need whiskey, ibuprofen, and zolpidem," I said. "I—oh, fuck—"

"Sorry." I grimaced as she tugged the thread through. "I'm not very good at this."

"You're doing great," I said, gritting my teeth. Loki nudged into the room, peering at me with his ears pricked up. Weakly, I reached out my hand and rubbed his muzzle, then scratched under his chin. "You shouldn't have come after me, silly boy. You shouldn't have either." I looked at Salem, but she just shook her head.

"Even knowing that thing is out there, when I heard your voice, I . . ." She paused, running her finger gently over the stitching before tying off the end. "I couldn't ignore it. I *couldn't*. Could you? If it was me?"

With a knot growing in my chest and an ache behind my eyes, I said, "If it was you, I'd go to the ends of the Earth to bring you back. But I'm not worth your life, Salem."

Fiercely, she said, "That's not fucking true. You deserve to be saved just as much as I do." She gripped my arm and I winced, but she was too upset to notice. "You don't deserve to be abandoned, Rayne! I would never, I . . ." She took a deep breath, and I braced myself as if she was going to hit me.

She did strike—not with her hand but with her words. "I'm sorry you were made to feel that way. When you were little, and you were scared, you shouldn't have been alone. But you're not anymore, remember? I promise you, I'm not going anywhere."

My chest felt as thin as an eggshell, about to crack. I was thankful she kept talking, babbling to calm her nerves as she bandaged me. She talked about her mom—"She was a little witchy, I guess. As if you couldn't tell by my name"—and about how she should have listened more closely to her recipes for poultices and tinctures. I drifted in and out of consciousness, her voice like a song drawing me back to reality when I floated too far away.

I was a kite, bobbing over the sea, dipping and diving on the wind. Almost free.

When she helped me into bed and my head hit the pillow, it was the closest thing to a religious experience I'd ever had. I was warm. My hands didn't shake and my mind was blessedly slow. My eyes were too heavy to open, but her voice was still there, gentle and calm.

"Just sleep as long as you need to. I'll be here. I'm right here."

THE NIGHT WAS cold and dark, and I couldn't see where I was going.

Rain pelted my face like the vicious bites of invisible spirits. My thin clothes were soaked, my empty hands slick with water.

Where were my weapons? My light?

Stumbling in the dark, a prickle went up my spine. Something was creeping through the trees close by—I couldn't see it, but I could hear its heavy steps, grass crunching, twigs snapping. I could hear its harsh breathing.

"Salem . . ." I gasped her name aloud. Where was she? Why wasn't she with me? Had she gotten lost?

Her name filled my throat, and I wanted to bellow it into the dark, but I didn't dare.

"Salem!" I whispered instead, too loud, and the movements nearby suddenly went quiet. It knew I was here.

"Salem . . . no, no, where are you? Salem!" I ran, my panic growning. The trees went on and on, the darkness so deep. The footsteps were getting closer, the harsh breathing becoming faster.

"Salem!" I screamed for her, sprinting now, dodging around trees and leaping over stones. "Salem, where—"

—◦—◦◦●◦◦—◦—

"I'm here. I'm here, Rayne."

I woke with a start, gasping for breath. My fingers were clenched, gripped tight around something.

When I realized it was Salem's hand I was crushing in my fist, I swiftly let go.

"Sorry." I rubbed my face, but my limbs were shaky and weak. The room was dark, illuminated only by the smoldering glow of the coals in the fireplace. My head swam when I tried to sit up, and I slumped back onto the pillow. The sheets were soaked with my sweat, and I was entirely naked.

"What time is it?" I said. "I need to . . . to check on . . ."

But Salem laid her hand against my forehead, easing me back, murmuring to me softly. "You don't need to do anything. You're okay. I called the doctor. As soon as the storm lets up, she'll come. It's okay. You're safe."

Nothing was safe. Neither walls nor doors could protect me. So then how could I ever hope to protect her?

I was crushing her hand again, but this time, I couldn't let go.

"Don't leave." I don't know why those words escaped me. I hadn't planned them; they'd leapt from my heart to my tongue before I could stop them.

"I'm not going anywhere." She lay down beside me, head resting on the pillow as she gently stroked my cheek. She was wearing my sweatshirt; it was bunched around her wrists, loose around her chest. "I've got you. I'm here. You were just having a bad dream."

All dreams were like that.

Staring at the ceiling, counting my heartbeats, I waited for them to slow. All the while, Salem talked to me. Her voice was soft, as tender as her touch. She stroked my cheek and trailed her fingers down my throat. She drew patterns on my bare chest. Her touch wasn't sexual; it demanded nothing yet gave everything.

The last thing I heard her say before I drifted off to sleep again was "I'm with you, Rayne. I'm with you."

Salem

Good Girl

RAYNE SLEPT FOR NEARLY TWENTY-FOUR HOURS. BUT EVERY few hours she would flinch, startling awake with a cry, sweat pouring down her face. She would look at me with panicked, half-asleep eyes and I would talk her down, hold her hands, and kiss her cheeks. It broke my heart to see her thrash in her sleep, her mind unable to rest, her fingers gripping the sheets like there were enemies all around her.

I didn't leave her side, other than to tend to Loki's needs and answer the radio when Andy called in a panic.

"Thank God you're alright," he said when I answered his frantic call and explained what happened. "I about had a heart attack when I woke up and found you gone. You need anything? How's she holding up?"

"She's still sleeping," I said. "Dr. Hale is going to try to make it out to the house today, when the snow lets up."

"You give me a call if there's anything you need," he said. "In the meantime, I'll go out and have a look for the ATV, see if I can get it hauled back to the house. I don't want to leave you without transportation."

Knowing Andy was looking out for us eased some of my worry. I'd barely slept since finding Rayne, and hadn't managed to stomach even a bite of food. It would be a relief to have Dr. Hale finally take a look at her.

I spent the next few hours at Rayne's side. Her brutal nightmares had finally stopped, and she lay still. The worry fell away from her face; her mouth softened. I lay beside her, resting my aching body. I watched her, memorizing the subtle lines at the edges of her eyes, counting the freckles on her cheeks.

My chest tightened with the thought of how vulnerable she was.

We both were.

Last night could have so easily gone differently. If I'd hesitated for another second, or if Rayne had, or if Loki hadn't been there, one of us would be dead now. It made my mind run in circles, an endless what-if. With every cycle, I ran into the same wall: Either we would fight to survive until spring came, or . . . we'd put an end to the beast.

But I was no hunter. I wasn't a fighter. I could barely even stand to kill a spider. When I charged the angel and jabbed that knife into it, I'd been running on pure panic and adrenaline. What could I hope to achieve that Rayne hadn't?

Together. We had to do it together, we had to find a way. And, perhaps, that way lay in the bizarre photos I'd found, photos that Rayne still hadn't seen. The thought of showing them to her made a cold pit grow in my hollow stomach.

Eventually, hunger drove me out of bed. Rayne had numerous supplies stockpiled in the pantry, and even more in the kitchen's massive walk-in freezer, although I didn't dare open the door for fear of somehow locking myself inside. I settled for a cold bagel with cream cheese and a cup of chamomile tea. My anxiety was too high to risk giving it any caffeine for fuel.

Regardless, my adrenaline spiked through the roof when I heard a distant knock, then the alarming chime of the doorbell ringing through the speakers in the kitchen. Loki was instantly on his feet, growling as he trotted from the room.

Seizing a large knife, I headed for the front door. Loki was already there, nose to the crack, tail wagging slowly. But I felt no relief until I looked through the peephole and saw a familiar face.

I cracked open the door, smiling tiredly to see Andy standing there, bundled up in a coat with snow in his beard. He was carrying my backpack.

"Thought you might be wanting this back," he said, handing it over.

Loki nudged his way out to pee in the yard, and my heart was in my throat the entire time. Even though it was daylight and Andy was there, armed with a rifle, having the front door open made me sick with fear.

"I found the ATV," he said as he folded his arms against the chilly wind. "One of the tires burst and it's a little banged up, but it'll still drive. I got the tire changed out, and a full tank of gas in it."

"Thanks, Andy." I sighed with relief to have the vehicle back. "I really appreciate it. You didn't have to do all that . . ."

"Neighbors have to look out for each other," he said, giving Loki a pat as the dog came back inside. "Rayne has always gone out of her way for me and my girls." He stared at me silently for a moment, a look I didn't entirely understand.

"No one has taken care of her, you know," he suddenly said. "Not since her mom was killed." He rubbed his hand over his face, as if to wipe away an unwelcome memory. "I've known her since she was young. She was a serious kid, wasn't interested in games. She wanted to be out in the woods, or in the garden. Wanted to sit with the adults and hear them talk. She was lonely. Never really got to be a kid."

To my surprise, he hugged me. I squeezed back until he let go and patted me on the shoulder. "You're a good woman. She's been moving like a zombie for years, Salem. But not since you got here."

THE SNOWFALL STOPPED by noon. Although the weather was still cold, Dr. Hale reached the house swiftly, arriving on horseback.

"You can never underestimate the value of a good horse," she said, stomping snow off her boots before entering the house. The bay mare she'd arrived on was sheltered at the base of the hill, beneath an awning connected to the shed. "She's gotten me through worse weather than any vehicle!"

Rayne barely stirred as the doctor looked at her, examining her wound with a frown.

"You did good work," she finally said. "First time?" I nodded, and she said seriously, "Did you vomit trying to do it?" When I shook my head, she laughed gently. "Then you did better than me the first time I stitched someone up. I used to have a senstive stomach. Not anymore!"

She left me with ointment, extra bandages, and a bottle of antibiotics.

"Try to make sure she actually rests," she said as she zipped up her coat and prepared to leave. "I know she's stubborn as hell, but she'll tear those stitches open if she goes right back to working." She looked up at the house, eyes narrowed. "I see she got the windows boarded up. That's good. Keep the lights on too. Damn thing doesn't like the light."

When she left, the house felt too quiet. I paced in the hallway, uncertain what to do with myself until Loki whimpered for food. As I fed him, the subtle creak of footsteps began upstairs. Pacing, back and forth, slowly up and down. Could Rayne possibly be walking around already? Trepidation slowed my steps as I made my way to the third floor, expecting to see a red glow at any moment.

But I made it to the bedroom without incident.

Rayne was out of bed, half dressed in an unbuttoned white shirt and gray cotton underwear. She had braced herself against the liquor cabinet in her room, legs trembling as she tried to hold a bottle of whiskey under her arm to uncork it. She tossed the cork to the floor and sucked in her breath as she tried to hold the bottle steady to pour.

It slipped out of her grasp. The amber liquid sloshed and the bottle nearly fell, but I managed to catch it just in time.

"Are you okay?" I said quickly as Rayne sank into the chair at the foot of the bed, rubbing her head. "You should have called me. Are you in pain? Do you need water? Your stitches—"

"Easy, girl," she said gently. "I'm fine. It's all fine. Can you, uh . . . will you . . ." She cleared her throat. "Whiskey. Will you bring me whiskey, please? Not the shit in your hand. It was the only bottle I could reach."

Putting that bottle aside and grabbing another glass, I said, "What's your preference?"

"I'm a sucker for spunky femmes and short-haired brunettes—"

It was a relief to see her smirk as I rolled my eyes at her. "I meant whiskey, you ass."

"Blanton's. Look for the round bottle."

There was no ice, so I simply poured a couple fingers. When I turned around, she was watching me. Chin resting on her palm, elbow positioned on the arm of her chair, legs splayed wide. Even injured, she exuded an air of confidence and authority that made my belly quiver.

She took the glass from my hand without breaking eye contact. She still stared as she brought it to her lips and took a slow sip.

"What are you looking at?" she said. It wasn't accusatory. It was curious.

"You're just, uh . . . you look . . ." *So goddamn sexy, even scraped, bruised, and wrapped in bandages.*

She leaned back in her chair, and winced slightly in pain before swirling the liquor in her glass. "I look like shit. I feel a little better though. Thanks to you." She took another sip, a bigger one this time.

She'd been entirely helpless in bed for the past twenty-four hours, yet she still made me feel like the tiniest squirming mouse when she spoke to me, in the best kind of way. "I'm glad to see you awake. I missed you."

"You missed me?" She repeated the words in a whisper. There was sincerity in the quiet, and I nodded.

Her voice dropped, and hit a shiver-inducing guttural tone as she said, "God, I fucking missed you too."

She pulled me down onto her lap, but I was already coming closer. Straddling her on the chair, it took a conscious effort not to be too rough, too desperate. I wanted to grab her, grip her, hold her tight so she'd never leave again.

"I thought I might lose you," I said, my voice catching.

She paused as she looked at me, cupping my face with one hand. She swallowed hard, and I was surprised to see emotion clouding her eyes.

"When I saw that thing on top of you . . ." She drew in a trembling breath, closing her eyes for a moment. As if she could still see it, even now. "Fuck, Salem, I thought it was going to kill you. That was worse than any nightmare. I couldn't . . ." She stopped and took several slow, deep breaths. "I couldn't watch that happen. I can't even describe what that felt like. Seeing you on the ground and knowing that if I didn't hit my shot—"

She made a soft sound and lowered her head. I took her face in my hands, and her eyes glistened when they met mine.

"I can't lose you," she said. "I've made it through a lot of shit, but that's not something I could survive. You shouldn't have looked for me. You shouldn't—"

I kissed her, stopping her words. Her arms wrapped around my waist, touching me like it was the first and last time.

"I will *always* come after you," I said. I pressed my cheek against hers, savoring her warmth, her closeness. "And I know you'd come after me too."

I expected her to feel frail, but it was the opposite. The way her calloused hands explored me was strong, *hungry*.

"You should eat," I whispered as she kissed and sucked my neck, sending shivers down my spine.

"Don't worry," she said. "I intend to."

She kept kissing, teasing, biting until she made a small sound of pain. She didn't want to stop—but I forced her back against the chair.

"Let me," I said. She didn't seem to fully understand what I meant until I sank to my knees at her feet.

She combed her fingers through my hair, gripped the short tufts, and pulled my head back.

"Look at those eyes," she said. "So beautiful. Open your mouth for me. Open wide, tongue out." Her voice was delicious, irresistibly authoritative. Obeying her made a hot rush of lust scurry down my back, but I sucked in a deep breath and held the position. Mouth open, tongue out, eyes fixed on the woman leaning over me.

"That's it. Look at me." I hung on her every word, my stomach fluttering when she smiled. "I'm never fucking leaving you again, Salem. My good girl."

She sipped her whiskey and slowly, carefully, brought her lips to mine. The liquor flowed between us, fiery over my tongue and burning down my throat. When she straightened up, there was a blaze in my chest and sparks in my heart.

"I'll be your good girl," I said, reaching for the waistband of her underwear. She let me pull them down, standing and leaning on my shoulders as she stepped out of them. She wore only her white shirt, unbuttoned so her chest was laid bare. Her nipples pebbled as I traced my hands over her stomach, kissing her slowly, tenderly.

Her legs were beginning to shake, so she lay back among the big pillows on the bed, legs spread. As she watched me, I stood at the foot of the mattress and peeled off my sweater. One item at a time, I stripped for her, tossing my panties at her face as a final cheeky tease.

She grabbed them and gripped them between her teeth. Her one hand was between her legs, her fingers creating a rhythmic movement over her clit. For a moment, I could only stare. Lost in her sensuality, in every curve, every scar, every dimple. Every perfect human flaw I wanted to touch, kiss, and memorize.

Crawling up the bed, I kissed her feet. Her breath hitched when my lips touched her, moving reverently along the arch of her foot to her ankle.

"Don't tell me you have a thing for feet," she teased, and I laughed. I lingered there, kissed each toe, massaged my fingers into her sole.

"I have a thing for *your* feet," I said. "I have a thing for all of you."

She grinned playfully and pressed her foot against the side of my face. She pushed me down against the bed, holding me there, heel squished into my cheek as she looked down at me.

"Such a pretty face," she said, digging her heel in a little more. The sensation of being crushed by her was delicious. My belly tingled, heat flaring through me the harder she pressed me down. "You'll look even better between my thighs."

I whimpered, reaching out to caress the soft, dark hair on her legs. I turned my head, just enough to inhale the heavenly smell of her skin and kiss her sole. When I looked up at her again, she was staring at me with hooded eyes as she pleasured herself.

"Squirm for me, baby," she said. I did, struggling under her heel, groaning when she pressed her other foot into my face. Her breath came harder. "Can't get away, can you? Just look at you, such a desperate little slut for me."

"Need you," I mumbled, words muffled as she crushed me. "Need you in my mouth . . . please . . . want you so bad . . ."

"Open up," she said, nudging the ball of her foot against my lips. I obeyed, licking and sucking her toes, savoring her sharp gasps at the stimulation. She kept my head pressed down, her soft sounds of ecstasy winding me up until I was unbearably turned on. She pressed two fingers inside her core and groaned, which made me struggle more, mumbling pleading gibberish around her toes.

"Aw, what is it, hm?" she said. "Is that not enough for you, pretty girl? Do you want more?"

"Mm-mmph!" Watching her touch herself was throwing more fuel on the fire inside me. It felt as if my insides were coiling with need, tension winding ever tighter until I was ready to burst.

Finally, she let my head up and said, "Get up here. Put that mouth to work."

"God, I missed waking up next to you," I said, crawling up between her legs. "I dreamed of you." I kissed her stomach, traced my nose across the hollow of her hip bone. "I thought of you all day." I nuzzled against her thigh, in awe of the stretch marks on her beautiful golden skin. I kissed them slowly, softly. "I won't let you go alone again. I won't."

I pressed my face into the curly hair covering her mons, eyes rolling back with the scent of her arousal. I extended my tongue, flicking it over her clit as she pumped her fingers inside.

"God, you're perfect," she said, voice tight. "It kills me, Salem, to want you like this. It's not enough."

"What would be enough?"

"You, always." She said those words like they scared her. Her eyes widened and the words shook.

She withdrew her hand, holding up her glistening fingers for me.

"See what you do to me, sweetheart?" she said as I sucked her fingers clean. She pressed my head down, her thighs squeezing as my tongue plunged inside her. "So good for me. Just looking at you gets me so wet."

She guided my head, keeping a tight grip on my hair as she instructed me, "Just like that, keep going."

She looked like a queen, lounging in pleasure, legs spread. Flicking my tongue back and forth over her clit, I slid two fingers inside her and practically melted at the sound she made. I stroked her inner walls, shivering as she clenched around my fingers. She tasted so good—a little salty, a little sweet, all her.

"Just like that, baby. Holy fuck." She arched on the bed, only to cry out in pain and fall back again. "Shit, shit. Don't fucking stop, Salem." She paused, her tight grip on my hair loosening for a moment. "If you need to stop, tap my leg. Okay?"

"Okay," I said, right before she shoved my head down again, using my mouth for her pleasure. She ground on me until her thighs tensed, every muscle squeezing as she came. God, she tasted so good. I was drunk on her essence and only wanted more.

Her legs were limp and trembling with the aftershocks, but that didn't stop her from flipping me around, grasping my hips, and pulling me back onto her mouth.

"I might hurt you!" I moaned, unable to help it as her tongue found my clit. She pressed her hand against my back, shoving me down, and I couldn't resist burying my face between her legs again. I tried not to mistakenly bump her injuries, but she didn't seem to care.

Her tongue wove poetry on my flesh, moans of pleasure rumbling in her chest. Slowly, I pressed two fingers inside her again, my stomach fluttering when she gasped and said, "Good girl, fuck, just like that . . ."

Her thighs tightened around my head, and I moaned against her. Her nails dragged along my back, leaving burning rivers behind, her passion seared into my flesh.

Locked together, entranced, all I could see, feel, hear—was her.

Her inner walls throbbed, squeezing around my fingers just like her arms squeezed around my waist, locking me in place. Her tongue curled around my clit and I quivered, breath coming in quick gasps.

"Ah! Rayne!" I half cried, half moaned the words. My motor control was nearly lost as I came, the only movement that remained in me was my lapping tongue and shaking legs.

I rolled off her to lay beside her, pressed close. Her skin was sticky with sweat; her lips glistened as she slowly licked the taste of me from them.

"Promise me," I whispered. "We're in this together now."

She nodded, her arm tightening around me. "I promise, Salem."

Rayne

A Father's Wickedness

𝕴 COULDN'T RECALL THE LAST TIME I'D RESTED LIKE THIS. IT wasn't entirely willing; I was eager to get up but Salem watched me with ruthless determination, not even allowing me out of bed to go down to the kitchen. She brought food to me instead, a plate piled high with scrambled eggs, sausage, and waffles.

I was used to doing things for myself. My first instinct—hell, my *only* instinct—was to accept no help and fend for myself. But Salem hovered over me, anticipating my needs sometimes before I even realized them myself.

Her stomach rumbled loudly as I ate, and I looked up at her in alarm. "Did you have breakfast?"

"O-oh, it's okay, no—"

I slapped the mattress next to me, pulling back the blankets for her. "Get your butt over here. I'm not going to let you sit there and starve."

She snuggled up beside me and said shyly, "I've been anxious. My stomach has been sensitive."

"Just small bites then," I said, slicing off a piece of buttery waffle.

She chewed slowly, but after she swallowed, she perked up a bit and said, "Can I have a sausage?"

We cleared the plate together. We spent the rest of the day in bed, napping and playing cards, with her getting up only to get us more food and let Loki outside. I didn't like her opening the door without me, even during the day. With clouds covering the sun, I simply didn't trust that it was safe.

"Do you at least know how to shoot a gun?" I said, offering her mine. But she stared at the weapon awkwardly.

"I, uh . . . shot a BB gun once," she said, and I sighed.

"I'm coming down with you. Don't—" I held up my hand to silence her protests. "I need to stretch my legs anyway. I'm just going to stand there and watch, that's it."

She let me do that, at least, but she looked at me worriedly every time I breathed too hard. It was . . . cute. It was *sweet*. It made my heart flutter in a way I hadn't experienced before. I didn't know how to react to being taken care of.

Mom would have loved her.

But our comfortable laziness couldn't last forever. Salem had found something she wanted me to see, and I could tell by her face that I wasn't going to like it.

The next morning, she brought me a mold-stained manilla envelope.

"There's photos inside," she said softly. "I don't really know how to explain them."

The first Polaroid I pulled out made my stomach churn even before I figured out what I was looking at. The texture of it made a revolted chill run up my back the moment I touched it. Coated with rings of black, crusty mold, it was still remarkably preserved, the photo clear.

Stained hands held a bloody human bone etched with strange carvings. The blood was fresh, bright red. As if the victim had only just died. As if it might have still been warm as their body was skinned and hacked to pieces.

"Rayne?" Salem grasped my forearm in concern, and I slowly inhaled. "Are you okay? You look . . ."

"I'm fine."

Setting the photo aside. I picked up another. There were so many. At least a dozen had been hidden away in the envelope Salem found. Mutilated animals, offal placed in bowls, surrounded by candles.

"What the hell is this?" I muttered, my eyes moving from one horror to the next. "Why would he have these? Why would he keep them?"

Salem listened to me, biting her lower lip. I was used to talking myself through my problems; usually, the only one listening to me was Loki. But he lay asleep near the fire, as if he was relieved to have finally passed me off to someone else.

I paced back and forth, pausing only to pick up my whiskey glass and take a generous sip. Only then was I able to pick up the photo of a dead, naked woman lying on a table.

It was the table in the stone house, I recognized it instantly. The body looked unreal, gray and waxen. The slender throat was cut, gashed open so deep it was almost a decapitation. Her face wasn't visible, but even so, a cold feeling swept through my veins.

"How would your father have gotten that body?" Salem said, but her voice seemed to drift to me from far away. As if she was shouting to me from across a long, dark field. "And those symbols. What could they mean? I've never seen anything like . . ."

Those slight hands, rigid in death. Fingernails painted a defiant shade of red. My stomach clenched, and I couldn't get enough air. I finished off my whiskey, but it didn't help.

Tossing the Polaroids down on the coffee table, I muttered, "I'm sorry, I need to think. I can't . . . these . . . I can't."

She didn't say a word as I walked from the room. My body felt like it might explode, my hands and teeth clenched so tight it hurt. I wanted to run. To scream.

I didn't want her to see me like this.

On the third floor, at the end of the hallway, was the locked door leading to the attic. My mom's old bedroom. Turning my key in that lock always made my heart pound. When I was young, I would sit at the bottom of the attic stairs after her death, earbuds in, pretending she was just up above, singing softly as she rouged her cheeks and sprayed her perfume. I fantasized that she would come down at any moment, wrap her arms around me, and kiss my cheek a dozen times.

What shall we do today, honey? Would you like to come to the garden with me?

On the stairs, I caught myself on the railing as I choked on a sob, forcing it down. The dust couldn't cover the scent of her perfume; I could still smell it in the air.

Or maybe I only wished I could. Maybe it was my own grief turning the smell of damp and decay into the sweet floral scent of lily, mandarin, and grapefruit. She used to hide the bottle from my father, and when she died, I hid it too so he couldn't take it away.

The attic was exactly how she left it. A green-and-black blanket, crocheted by a grandmother I'd never met, was folded neatly near the footboard. Lacy curtains framed the round window that looked out upon the lighthouse. Books of poetry lined her shelves; she used to read to me, but most books were too difficult for me now. It broke my heart to think she would be disappointed to know I hadn't picked up a book since my last tutor left when I was fifteen.

Her vanity had been cleared off by my father, all the makeup and nail polishes thrown away. I caught sight of my face in the dusty mirror, bruised and tired. My eyes looked a hundred years old, older than hers ever had.

There, in solitude, I broke down.

Arms wrapped around myself, I sobbed until I fell to my knees and bent with the weight of grief, my forehead pressed to the floor. I hated the sound of my own weeping, I wanted to curse myself for being weak.

Funny, the voice that cursed at me for breaking sounded so much like Dad.

He'd always been a distant parent, but I saw him offer affection to others, to his congregants. His flock. Everyone who got to pray with him, be led and guided by him, everyone who felt the light of his love; I hated them all. How dare they take him? How dare they have him when I couldn't? He would barely even look at me, talk to me, but he would preach to them for hours.

What was wrong with me?

Why wasn't I enough?

"I needed you here." I didn't even recognize my own voice. "I needed you, Mom. I still need you. I don't know what to do. I don't know . . ."

For a second, I swore I felt a cold breeze move over my back, an eerie whisper too faint to make out—but then, instead of the phantom's chilling presence, the warmth of Salem's arms wrapped around me.

I hadn't even heard her come up. She didn't say anything. She just held me as I knelt there, her weight on my back. She held me tight, and at first, I desperately wanted to pull myself together, to show her I was strong.

But I couldn't. I was broken, and I couldn't hide the cracks anymore.

When I was finally able to raise my head and look at her, her face was wet with tears.

"Why are you crying?" I said, hurriedly wiping her face, worried that I'd somehow hurt her.

But she took my hands and kissed them and said, "When you hurt, I hurt too. And I know it hurts so much."

In her arms, I was raw, more vulnerable than I'd ever allowed myself to be. Guilt and fear waged war in my head, but grief was more powerful than either of them. Usually I could ignore it, shove it into the dark recesses of my mind and pretend it wasn't there. But even healed wounds left scars, and mine had never healed in the first place.

For a while, we just sat on the floor, facing each other as she held my hands. I touched the polish on her nails, chipped away over the weeks she'd been here, but still a beautiful shade of green.

"My mom would have liked this color," I said softly.

She smiled. "I think she would have too. It's the same color as your eyes."

I kissed her forehead, then her beautiful mouth. "I think she would have liked you too. I think she'd be happy you're here." Taking a deep breath, I let the sadness wash through me and away. I let it rest, curling up in my heart like an exhausted creature.

Salem leaned into my hand as I cupped her face. "There's something else I need to tell you," she said. "Something that happened while you were gone."

As I listened, she told me about her search for Loki in the storm. As she described the specter, its long hair, its distorted face, the whispers began again. I resisted covering my ears, but when she suddenly fell silent and looked around, I realized.

"You hear it too?" I said, and she nodded quickly.

"Whispering, screaming, crying," she said. "And Rayne . . . I felt it. It touched me."

The specter had never attacked me; I had long believed that it was only capable of hurting me with the madness it induced. But to hear Salem describe the awful sensation of choking, the taste of blood, the certainty she was going to die—I could hardly bear it.

How could I protect her from something I couldn't fight?

It had whispered the same words to her it had long whispered to me. *Blood and bones, blood and bones . . .*

"What could it mean?" she said. But I was already trying to piece it together, trying desperately to understand why this was all happening *now*.

"You said you tasted blood," I said slowly. "That it felt like choking . . ." She nodded. "My mom's throat was cut. She would have died choking on her own blood."

Salem's eyes went wide, and she covered her mouth in disbelief. "Rayne . . . you don't think . . . you don't think really *that's* your mom? In the photos?"

"I don't know. But I know my father did something he kept secret, something he took to his grave." Thinking back, I recalled the verse he had shouted so many times from behind the pulpit. "*He cast upon them the fierceness of his wrath by sending evil angels among them.* My father always said the beast was God's judgment for Blackridge's wickedness, and that my mother's murder was the catalyst."

Even the dead could still speak, and they had the answers I needed.

"Salem." I turned to her, jaw clenched around the vile thing I was about to tell her. "We need to dig up my mother's grave."

Salem

Grave Digging

A N EERIE QUIET DESCENDED WITH THE RED SUN AS IT PLUNGED toward the horizon. I clung to Rayne on the back of her ATV as we sped along the muddy road, dodging potholes and lumps of icy snow. As we drove, and dusk fell, the streetlamps popped on, flooding our path with light.

The streets of Marihope were empty, shops shuttered, doors locked. Almost every door had a cross hung upon it and floodlights blazed on front porches, beacons of fiery brilliance that fought against the encroaching night.

Somehow, it only made the darkness beneath the trees seem deeper.

Rayne carried her gun; I carried the shovels. We'd left Loki at home, despite his protests. But we needed to move as silently as we could; his barking could give us away to the locals.

As we passed beneath the rusted iron archway into the cemetery, the temperature dropped. Overgrown, mossy headstones were scattered beneath the trees, years of decaying leaves and piles of dirty snow obscuring them. Some stones were so old the trees had grown over them, roots engulfing any record of the dead that lay beneath.

Generations of families were buried together here. Parents and their children. Elderly couples. Beloved daughters and sons, aunt and uncles. It was an echo of another time, when Blackridge was a quiet community which found peace in its isolation, not horror.

Numerous narrow paths twisted beneath the gnarled trees, and I never would have found my way if Rayne hadn't been leading me. She walked close, her arm occasionally brushing mine. We didn't speak, we just listened, heads swiveling from left to right in constant surveillance.

Suddenly, Rayne stopped and said, "She's here."

The grave before us was newer than the others. The creeping vines had yet to swallow it, and patches of bright green moss adorned the pale gray headstone. A statue of a weeping angel was draped over the stone, her head buried in her arms, shrouded in a long veil.

For a few moments, neither of us said anything. We just stood before the grave, shovels in hand, the weight of what we were about to do suddenly crashing down.

Soon the sun would set completely, and it would only be us against all that lurked within the darkness of night. We were running out of time.

"Should we . . . ?" I motioned toward the grave.

Rayne nodded sharply. "It's just bones. Just a coffin."

A pang shot through me as my shovel pierced the dirt; a sense of wrongness made my stomach churn. But I kept digging, minutes turning into an hour. The sounds of our shovels spearing the earth and tossing it aside were the only breaks in the eerie silence. Rayne had to pause frequently; it was obvious she was in pain, but refused to let it show.

"Take a break," I said when she stopped yet again and leaned against her shovel. She sucked in her breath as if through a straw, and glared at me when I made my suggestion. I insisted, "It's getting dark. You should keep watch."

Luckily, she accepted my logic, and faced the forest with her weapon as I kept digging. My back and shoulders ached, and it seemed as if the hole would never end. Was there a coffin here at all? Was it even really a grave?

Thunk.

My shovel struck wood.

Bile rose in my throat unexpectedly, an alarming feeling of unease filling me.

"Rayne." I said her name softly, and she came immediately to the edge of the grave. "This is it."

She extended her hand and helped me climb out before hopping down herself. She straddled the coffin, shovel in hand, but she didn't move.

"It was a closed casket funeral," she finally said. "I was so scared of this coffin when I was a kid. Walking past it in church, I imagined all kinds of horrible things. I imagined Mom's face completely destroyed—beaten, bloody. I didn't know. I couldn't know . . ." Her shoulders sagged for a moment, and I wanted to reach for her, to somehow let her know she wasn't alone.

Harley Laroux

Then she braced herself, and wedged the shovel under the edge of the lid.

Dirt shifted as the lid was pulled open. Rayne's figure blocked my view, so I couldn't see what she was staring at until I walked around the edge of the hole.

Empty. The coffin was empty. Except . . .

Only one thing lay within, and it wasn't a body. It was a tattered old book.

38

Rayne

Sanctuary

THE BOOK WAS WRAPPED IN CRUMBLING LEATHER AND SMELLED strangely smoky, as if it had been through a fire. I loathed holding it. It was heavy, damp, and musty. I tucked it under my arm as I unlocked the iron bar gate guarding the chapel doors, with Salem watching me in surprise.

"Dad's old keys," I said. "I kept them just in case. The chapel is one of the most secure places in Marihope. We can stay here for the night. It's already too dark to drive back, I don't want to risk it."

The gate's old hinges creaked as I pulled it open, then unlocked the sturdy wooden door within. The nave was cold and dark, the only light spilling in from the tall narrow windows lining the walls. I locked the gate and the door behind us, sealing us inside.

As Salem headed to the back storeroom to find wood for the furnace, I laid the book on the pulpit, then dug around in my bag until I found my old bottle of painkillers. I downed one with a swig of water, and took a moment to collect myself.

The pain was deep, breathtaking. I tried to stay on my feet and breathe through it, wait for shock or adrenaline to kick in and spare me.

"You've got this," I whispered. "Just breathe. It'll pass. It's only pain."

I squeezed my eyes shut tight. Only after a few minutes did I gather myself enough to open them and straighten up.

A shudder ran through me as I opened the book and the spine cracked. The pages were stiff and thick, yellowed with age. The text was difficult to read, a calligraphic script I first thought was Latin—but then guessed was Old French. Written in the margins, my father's familiar handwriting joined that of much older writers. Expanding upon centuries of notes with his own translations.

One must call using the proper offerings. ONLY offerings guarantee success—what does it require?

Binding must be immediate.

Use EVERY bone—no excuses.

Painstakingly, I uncurled my fingers from the edges of the pulpit and shook them out, rubbing my clammy palms on my trousers. My father had never given any indication he was interested in the occult. He was a holy man, a man who put God above all else.

But these notes showed an intent not merely to learn, but to practice.

In one of his notes, he referenced a "creature of the heavens, harbinger of holy judgment." My blood turned to ice, but I couldn't bear to stand still. I paced behind the pulpit, needing to read on but sickened at the thought.

My father had been a man of God. A cold, uncaring man, yes—but a holy one. He devoted his life to the church, he loved the Lord more than he ever could have loved me or my mother. When she died, at least, I saw his affection for her. How her murder broke him, turned his coldness to fiery hatred in the depths of his grief. Part of me had even believed that, perhaps, in his desperate prayers for vengeance he had somehow called the beast here to Blackridge.

But my father's interest in this creature had begun even before Mom's death. The translations in this book alone represented what was surely years of work and study.

Where was her body? What the hell had he done with it, if not lain her to rest?

I feared these notes told me, in graphic detail, exactly what he'd done with it.

The bones. The symbols. The reference to an "offering."

"Did he kill you, Mom?" Even whispered, the words were as heavy as boulders.

Dropping my head into my hands, I rubbed my eyes. I was too tired to think. My body ached all the way through my bones, and my head was light. I stumbled into a pew right as Salem returned with an armful of firewood.

Every breath I took reminded me of the wound on my side, and how goddamn fragile I was.

"Rayne? Are you okay?"

I lifted my head, and she was staring at me with those wide brown eyes. Eyes that made me think of warm summer days, when we were safe and monsters didn't stalk the woods.

Maybe I could walk beneath the trees with her in spring, and hold her hand. Maybe I would forget about practicality and take off my shoes, and she could wear some cute little summer dress. I could laugh with her, and close my eyes, lie in the grass. I would know she was safe.

"I'm fine," I said softly. "Just thinking."

She frowned. She knelt in front of the furnace and opened the old metal door, loading the wood inside but never taking her eyes off me.

"Did you read it?" she said, casting a dubious glance toward the open book on the pulpit.

"As much as I could stomach. It's instructions . . ." She needed to know, even if I didn't entirely understand what it meant yet. "For how to summon something."

"*Something*?" The old building creaked, and Salem's entire body flinched. When she spoke again, her voice was low. "What kind of something? Like *the* thing? Out there?"

"I don't know. There's a lot of text, and not all of it is translated." I rubbed my hands together, but the cold was merciless. "But I think so. I think it's the same creature: the one the book talks about, and the one on the island."

Salem was silent as she finished lighting the furnace. The logs caught flame, the old metal creaking and groaning as heat spread through it. "Do you think your father summoned it?"

I was afraid she'd ask that question. I was even more afraid of my answer.

"Yeah. I think he did." It was a lot. Too much. The implications went so deep, I feared I'd never find my way out. I raked my fingers through my hair, then abruptly tried to stand, shoving myself up from the pew—

"Shit, ow." I sank back down, holding my shoulder as throbbing pain shot through it. Almost instantly, Salem was at my side.

"Here, let me," she said, easing my jacket off. She sucked in her breath when she saw the growing red stain on my bandage.

"I'm fine," I said quickly. I wasn't. I'd popped at least one of my stitches, but the pill I'd taken was finally easing the pain. "I've had worse."

The way her eyelashes fluttered as she looked at me was nothing short of miraculous. "Have you? Really?"

I shrugged, irritated to have my lie called out. "Pain is pain, Salem. It's all the same."

She *tsk*ed, reaching for the small bag she'd brought with her. I hadn't stopped to think earlier about what she might have brought, so I was surprised when she pulled out fresh bandages, ointment, and a flask.

"It's Blanton's," she said, handing over the flask. "Just don't overdo it."

God, the way she looked at me made me want to die for her. But, more frightening than that—when she leaned closer to unwrap my dirty bandage—I wanted to *live* for her too.

"You really thought of everything, didn't you?" I said as she tossed the bloody bandages into the furnace. She laughed softly, and the sound made a sudden, unfamiliar feeling burst in my chest. It felt like adrenaline—like the beginning of a panic attack, but no—this was gentler. It exploded into sparks, made my chest tight and warm.

"My dad used to tell me I was a little squirrel-brained, like my mom," she said. "I'd forget big important things but remember silly little details. I didn't think of everything . . ." She squirted a bit of ointment on her finger and gently dabbed it around my wound. "I just thought of you."

The nave began to warm as she worked. She wrapped me with fresh bandages, frowning in concentration.

"Tell me about your mom," I said suddenly. "What's she like?"

Her emotion was evident as she smiled fondly. "She's a kindergarten teacher in Colorado. She says she never wants to retire; she loves working with kids. She and my dad met in college, and *she* proposed to *him*. When I was little, I wanted a romance like theirs. They're still together. He's retired and spends a lot of time fishing. She taught herself how to do taxidermy so she could mount some of the fish he caught. She sews little outfits for them sometimes."

I burst out laughing, even though it hurt. "You're kidding. She taught herself taxidermy? She sounds amazing."

"She is! I . . . I really miss her." She cleared her throat, her words shaking a little. "I'm usually getting ready to fly out to see her at this time of year. She's not a very good cook, she gets distracted and ends up burning things, so Dad usually cooks dinners for us." She fastened my bandage, stroking her hand across my shoulder. "They'd like you."

"You think so?" My belly flopped nervously, and I took a little sip from the flask. "I'm excited to meet them, someday."

I couldn't read the way she looked at me, and I worried I'd assumed too much. She laid her hand against my face. Her breath was warm and soft as she leaned close, her lips brushing mine in a touch that wasn't quite a kiss—it was so much more.

"I'm excited too," she said. "I know you'd like Colorado. And you'd like San Francisco too. There's so many places I want to show you." Her eyes welled, and she shuddered as she exhaled. "I hope . . . I hope we . . ."

"We will." I kissed her soft mouth, my heart racing when she sighed and leaned into me. She was my escape from all this. The salvation I never believed I'd find. "We'll make it out of this. You and me. And you can show me everything."

Salem

God's Judgment Comes

WE CURLED UP TOGETHER NEAR THE FURNACE. WE HAD NO blankets, but Rayne laid her coat over me and held me close, her warm arms around me. She hummed to me as I watched the snow fall through the windows, white drifts piling against the glass. I didn't recognize her tune, but it was gentle and slow. She kept time with her hand, rubbing up and down my back.

Between the warmth of the fire and Rayne's gentle touch, I was soon asleep.

Scritch, scritch. Scritch, scritch.

Barely concious, I groaned. Loki was digging a hole, and the slow, persistent sound made me twitch.

Scritch. Scritch.

Creak.

Perhaps Rayne had woken up and was going to make him stop . . .

My eyes flew open as I remembered where I was. The dog wasn't with us, but something else was.

Rayne's fingers were digging into my arm, her face lit by furnace's orange glow. Her eyes were wide, and her head was turned. She was staring at the window beside us.

"Something's out there," she whispered. Goose bumps ran up my spine as we stared at the dark window, the glass frosted with ice. "Don't move. Don't make a sound."

Creak. Scritch-scritch.

I covered my mouth to hold in the terrified whimper that wanted to escape. Something was outside the window; the noise was so close. It was walking around the exterior of the church, sniffing, scratching at the stones.

Screeeech.

Rayne flinched and I held my breath as long, clawed fingers dragged across the glass, leaving a trail through the ice. My heart threatened to burst out of my chest and run away. Could it hear the organ pounding? Could it smell the blood rushing through my veins?

Rayne tapped my arm and silently held a finger to her lips. Slowly—painfully slowly—she rose to her feet and picked up her gun. She looked at me and mouthed the words "Stay down."

Adrenaline begged me for oxygen, but even my shallow breaths felt too loud. A high-pitched chattering noise, like the buzz of a cicada, sounded from outside. Biting my lip hard, I focused on the pain instead of the fear, holding Rayne's jacket tightly against my chest.

Footsteps crunched in the snow. They moved, and paused. Moved, and paused again.

Then came the ominous creak of the gate swinging open.

My voice was panicked as I whispered, "It can open gates?" Rayne didn't take her eyes off the door as the knob jiggled. She hurriedly lifted her gun, taking aim.

"When it gets in, run for the back door," she said. "Run and don't stop. No matter what you hear, don't stop."

My heart was in my throat. The hinges creaked as the door opened, sending a cold draft rushing into the nave—and Ruth Miller stepped inside.

Rayne sharply exhaled, lowering her weapon, and I almost cried in relief. But Ruth shrieked when she saw us, her hands flying up to cover her mouth.

"Rayne! What are you doing—what's going on here?"

"Be quiet, would you?" Rayne snapped. "Close the damn door, it's out there!"

"It?" Ruth closed the door but didn't lock. Rayne marched down, slamming the bolt into place as Ruth eyed her with suspicion. "You mean the angel? I didn't see anything."

"Then you weren't paying attention," Rayne snapped. "What are you doing here?"

"I should ask you the same question." Ruth pursed her lips as she took off her coat and folded it over her arm. "I always come early on Sundays to light the furnace for service. Although it seems you've already done that. It's warm in here."

"We've been here all night. We didn't make it home in time." Rayne peered out the window nearest the door. "Curfew hasn't ended yet, the sun isn't up. You shouldn't be out at all."

"I shall fear no evil," Ruth said with a small smile. "I have faith, Rayne. God protects his most loyal."

"Hm. Tell that to Job."

Ruth's eyes narrowed, her mouth pursing tightly. Her shoes clicked on the floor as she came farther inside, her eyes scanning the pews as if she suspected we'd damaged the place. Rayne came back and helped me to my feet, moving me farther away from the windows as she eyed them fearfully. When she protectively wrapped her arm around me, Ruth scoffed.

"While the rest of us pray for forgiveness, for mercy, you bring your little whore into the house of God," she said, her voice deathly quiet. "And we wonder why these deaths keep happening. There can be no mercy for those who spit in the face of the Lord."

"Come on, Rue," Rayne said softly. "Don't do this."

"Do *not* call me that!" Ruth practically screamed, startling me. "Get out. Go home. You're not welcome here."

"The sun isn't up yet." Rayne sounded calm, but her tone had gone cold. Her arm tightened around me. "We'll leave as soon as it's safe."

To my shock, Ruth immediately withdrew a knife from the sheath on her belt. It was a small blade, but sharp, and she held it determinedly. Rayne stiffened.

"I said, *get out*." Ruth bared her teeth in a snarl, but she and her knife didn't seem very threatening.

Not when I spotted the thing standing behind her.

The angel was here.

It towered outside the window, its skinny limbs pressed against the church, its eyeless face bobbing eerily at us through the glass. Rayne saw it at the same moment, and she began to whisper frantically, "Ruth, listen to me, you need to—"

With a terrifying crash, glass exploded into the church as the window shattered. Ruth screamed, and suddenly Rayne was yelling, "Go, go, run! Salem, we need to run!"

Scrambling for the door, I tried to pull it open—but was violently shoved to the floor by Ruth. She threw back the lock and wrenched the door open, then ran shrieking into the gray pre-dawn light, leaving a shocking trail of blood in the snow.

The sound of gunfire made me flinch, covering my head. Rayne stood over me, and took aim again as the beast squeezed itself through the narrow broken window, knocking aside pews, its hooves clattering on the floor.

"Run, Salem!" she yelled, and fired another shot. Scrambling to my feet, I fled into the churchyard. Rayne was close behind me.

The morning air was sharp with cold. Drops of frozen dew clung to the leaves, ice crunched beneath our feet. The sun had yet to crest the massive trees, and we were in their shadow. The streetlamps provided meager pools of illumination as we ran through them, drawn to the light like desperate insects.

"It's coming!" Rayne screamed. "Faster, go—"

With a scream, she was torn from my side.

"Rayne! No!" The beast was on top of her, clawed limbs swiping at her as she rolled out of the way, her rifle dangling uselessly from the strap around her neck. I picked up a stone and hurled it, then another, and another. "Hey! Over here, you piece of shit!"

The beast paused as the rocks hit it, bouncing harmlessly off its morbid body. But those few seconds were all Rayne needed. She jabbed her knife up to its hilt in the angel's side, and dark blood erupted from the wound. It thrashed and coiled, its limbs flailing like a spider drenched in poison.

It leapt away, fleeing into the trees, and I rushed to Rayne's side.

"I'm alright, it's okay," she said, panting for breath as I helped her to her feet. "We need to keep moving, quickly."

She'd left her jacket behind, but her skin felt feverishly

319

warm. She had bled through the bandage covering her stitches. I didn't dare say it aloud, but I worried if she would even make it to the ATV parked at the edge of town.

The streets were filled with the eerie sounds of dogs barking and howling, as if every canine in the village was aware of the creature's presence. Rayne remained alert, holding her gun at the ready, but her steps began to drag.

"Just a little farther," I said, as much to myself as to her. "We're close, we're almost there, we—"

Sudden movement ahead made Rayne seize me by the sweater and drag me against a wall, the both of us ducking down.

"Holy shit," she said. "Is that Ruth?"

The woman was crawling on her hands and knees on the side of the road. We ran to catch up with her, but at the sound of our footsteps, she got to her feet and tried to run, screaming raggedly as she did.

"What the hell are you doing?" Rayne hissed as she seized her arm. "Stop screaming! That thing is still stalking us!"

But as Ruth turned toward us, there was only sheer panic in her eye.

Her *one* remaining eye.

Her face was split open. Her forehead had a dip in it, as if her skull had caved in. Blood foamed around her lips as she mumbled incomprehensibly, her gored eye socket staring at me like a void straight into Hell.

I clapped my hands over my mouth in horror. Rayne was shuddering as she stared, her arm outstretched for Ruth but no longer touching her.

"We have to get you help," she said, taking one cautious step closer to the injured woman. "We'll get you to Dr. Hale—"

But Ruth began to scream. Her words ran together incomprehensibly, and I had no idea if she could even tell who we were.

"Please be quiet!" I begged. I looked up and down the foggy streets, certain I could hear something beyond her babbling. A peculiar echo of her voice . . .

Rayne backed away as Ruth fell to her knees again. "She's not lucid, she's going to call the thing right down on us again—"

Tightly, I clutched her hand and whispered, "She already did."

The angel crawled over the stone wall beside the road, mimicking Ruth's voice in an eerie cadence—"God protects . . . God protects . . ."

Its slit nostrils flared, its eyeless face somehow looking straight into my soul. Its mouth gaped open, thick saliva dripped from its teeth. Rayne's knife was still lodged in its side, but it didn't limp nor favor it, as if the wound wasn't there at all.

It stood directly in our path.

Rayne forced her body in front of mine, backing us away one painfully slow step at a time. Ruth stared at the beast as it stalked toward her, her mouth gaping open listlessly.

"Ruth, *move!*" Rayne hissed desperately. She moved us even more hurriedly backwards, but refused to turn her back on the horrific scene as it unfolded.

The creature was staring at Ruth, cocking its head from side to side as it muttered, "God protects. God protects." People were pulling aside their curtains, cracking their doors, daring to peer outside.

Ruth's head slumped weakly to her chest.

When the beast lunged, Rayne and I ran.

My heart was pounding so hard in my ears, almost overpowering the horrific sounds behind us. But when Rayne yanked me around a sharp corner, I glanced back and realized what I'd heard.

It was the sounds of Ruth being ripped apart. The sounds of tearing flesh and snapping bone, of agonized screams. It was only a split second, but the image remained branded into my eyes, my mind.

My limbs were too sluggish, too heavy. The world moved in slow motion, like a nightmare in which my legs turned to lead and the air to quicksand.

I didn't dare look back. My vision had tunneled, and all I could feel was the grip of Rayne's hand, the only thing holding me tethered to reality. Where could we go? How far could we possibly run?

"Here!"

An open door. A waving hand—and the face of an older man urging us toward him.

"Run! Come on!"

The angel shrieked. The ground felt frighteningly unsteady as we sprinted toward the door, toward safety.

We collapsed inside, and the door slammed shut—only to rattle on its hinges when the beast smashed into the other side.

Rayne

The Devil's Book

"**H**OLD THE DOOR! HOLD IT BACK, DAMN IT!"

My shoulder ached as the door slammed into it again. Pain exploded through my chest, but adrenaline numbed me enough to endure it. Claws scraped and scratched against the other side, as if a massive dog was trying to dig a hole through the wood. Even with me and my cousins all holding it back, the beast was stronger.

"Watch out!"

My uncle slammed a thick wooden beam across the door, barricading it as my cousins and I leapt back. Gerard's hair was disheveled, a wool coat thrown over his night clothes. "The lights now. All of them! James, get the rifle!"

As he and my cousins began flipping on the house's external floodlights, I found Salem standing in the hallway. She was gripping the staircase railing with both hands, staring at the door with wide, terrified eyes.

With the lights turned on, the banging stopped. The boom of gunfire sounded from upstairs as James fired at the creature from an upper window. There was a high-pitched shriek and a clatter as the beast fled, before bone-chilling quiet fell over the house.

In the silence that followed, Salem's eyes met mine and filled with tears. Her knees trembled, but I caught her before she could fall.

"It's okay, it's okay, I'm here." I held her tight as she shook, tremors racking her tense body.

"Ruth was—God, did you see her, she—it ripped her apart." She took several rapid, sharp breaths. Stroking my hand up and down her back, I rocked her slowly. "Did she . . . oh, God, can't someone do something . . ."

"Don't think about it, Salem." I kept rubbing her back, trying to pretend Ruth's screams weren't echoing in my head too. The smell of blood was cloying in my nose. No matter how many times I witnessed death, it never got any easier.

It wasn't normal to see these things. It wasn't something we were supposed to get used to.

Kissing the top of her head, I murmured the only lullaby I knew: the one my mom used to sing for me as a child, whose words I didn't know but tune I could remember.

Bringing my mouth close to Salem's ear, I said, "I've got you. Just like I promised. I won't let anything hurt you. You're okay. The sun is almost up. We'll be safe here."

⊷⊷✦⊶⊶

THE POP OF gunfire echoed throughout the town. James kept a lookout from the second floor, and I would occasionally hear the crackle of his walkie, other lookouts providing updates on the beast's movements.

A short time later, I was able to move Salem into one of the bedrooms. Aunt Veronica brought us water, then mugs of tea and a plate of cookies. My younger cousins, Mark and Jacob, both in their early twenties, stood awkwardly in the hallway for a while before shuffling upstairs to join James.

"Thanks, Aunt V." I took a cookie, eating it in two bites. Although I wasn't hungry, I needed something to keep me going. It was a struggle to keep my eyes open.

Salem sipped her tea slowly, glassy-eyed. I kept one arm around her, and she leaned heavily into my side. If only I could take those images away from her. She'd have to live with those horrors now, and I couldn't protect her from them.

"Poor thing," my aunt murmured, hovering in the doorway with concern. Salem didn't seem fully aware she was there. She just sipped her tea in silence, shuddering now and then, wordless.

"Sheriff Keatin and his men are on their way from Dowton," my uncle announced, coming to stand in the doorway beside his wife. "They'll figure out what to do with Ruth."

Salem made a small sound—a hiccup or a sob, I wasn't sure. I wanted nothing more than to be back at the house with her, back in our bed, safe behind those haunted stone walls and boarded windows. I wanted to take her away from this, shelter her from the horror.

"Are you badly hurt?" Aunt Veronica said, catching her breath at the worsening bloody stain on my shoulder.

"I popped a few stitches," I said. "I'll be fine—"

"She needs a doctor," Salem said suddenly. Her voice was strong, but calm. "I do too. I don't know if you have a pharmacy on this fucking island, but I need diazepam. Please."

Aunt Veronica nodded determinedly. "I'll call Dr. Hale immediately. Sit tight, dears."

My uncle, too awkward to stand there and talk to me without her, mumbled something about checking the locks before he followed her down the hallway.

With our privacy at last, I took Salem's face in my hands. Her skin was cold, her eyes reddened. She looked at me with such tiredness that my heart ached.

"I can't forget," she whispered. "It's all I see."

I kissed her face as the tears rolled down her cheeks. I pulled her into my lap and just rocked her as she sobbed. To my surprise, my own eyes stung too. Her pain ran through me as surely as if it were my own.

After several minutes, she wiped her tears. I held her as she slowly ate another cookie and sipped the remainder of her cold tea.

"This used to be my room when I'd sleep over," I said, running my hand over the bed's familiar quilt. Salem looked around, taking in the plastic glow-in-the-dark stars stuck to the ceiling, the board games piled on the old bookshelf. "Me and my cousins would drag all the kitchen chairs in here and cover them with blankets to make a fort. I would pretend I was the warrior queen and made them my soldiers. James would always argue with me that he wanted to be king, but I never let him."

To my relief, a smile spread across her face. "I miss making blanket forts," she said.

"When we get back home, we'll make the most epic blanket fort in the world. We'll cover the whole house in blankets."

"Home." She repeated the word with fondness, but with sadness too. She was silent, plucking at a loose string on her sweater, before she asked, "Did Ruth used to be called Rue?"

The sound of her nickname sent an unexpected pang through my chest. "Yeah. That was what I called her in middle school."

"You were friends?"

"Believe it or not, we were close. Our last summer in eighth grade, we did everything together. She was different when she was a kid, she was . . . well, she was . . ." Shit, this hurt. I didn't let pain linger like this; I pushed it aside or left it behind, I had no time to dwell on it. But I think Salem needed this. Maybe I did too. "She was the first girl who ever kissed me."

Salem gasped. "What? *Ruth*? But she . . . the things she said . . ."

"She inherited a lot of hatred," I said. I could remember that summer only faintly now, like a bizarre dream. Ruth and I separated over the winter, and when I saw her again in spring, she had changed. Those long, cold days locked in the house with her family had warped her perspective.

"Ruth lost herself a long time ago," I said. "I already saw part of her die, and today, I saw the rest of her go too." I sounded flippant, but the words were only a shield against the pain battering my chest. "This island eats people, Salem. It chews up your life and spits out the husk when you've been sucked dry. And when you're finally dead, it rots your flesh and disintegrates your bones. But you and I, Salem . . ." I laid my forehead against hers. "We're not going to die here. I promise you that. Blackridge will never have you."

By the time Dr. Hale arrived, Salem was asleep. I sat on the old floral-print couch in the living room as the doctor cleaned and re-stitched the gash across my chest, then applied disinfectant to the numerous other cuts and scratches covering me. Luckily, besides the popped stitches and fresh bruises, the beast hadn't injured me this time.

"Do you want to wake her?" Dr. Hale asked, nodding her head toward the bedroom where Salem slept.

But I shook my head. "Let her sleep. She doesn't get enough of it. Do you have pills for her?"

She nodded, withdrawing an orange pill bottle from her bag and handing it over.

Turning the bottle over and over in my hands, I said, "When my mom was murdered, did you perform an autopsy?"

"No. Your father was very adamantly against it," she said, peeling the vinyl examination gloves off her wrinkled hands. "He made it clear to me from the start that he wanted a private wake in the home. He didn't even want Eddie touching her."

Eddie was Dr. Hale's late husband, the previous mortician and manager of Blackridge's only funeral home. I couldn't remember him well; he'd been at my mother's funeral, but that day was a nightmarish haze in my memory.

"A private wake?" I said, and she nodded. "I see. Thank you."

"Look after yourself," she said, hoisting her backpack onto her shoulders. The horror of Ruth's death was spreading outside. The muffled sounds of weeping and screaming could be heard, but I tried to block them out. "Try to take it easy." She held up her hand before I could give a snarky response. "I know, I know. You're fine. But *take it easy*, okay? Take one of your girlfriend's pills and relax for a while."

"Alright, alright. I've had enough of getting beat up by angels this week anyway."

I stayed on the couch long after she left, alone with my thoughts and the echoes of grief.

A soft knock on the doorframe announced my uncle's presence. "May I join you?"

I nodded. "It's your house."

He sighed heavily as he sat in the large green chair across from me. He looked too much like my father, although his face was softer and his eyes were gentler. He'd always been kind to me—distant, but kind.

He wore his church vestments, looking stiff and uncomfortable in his white collar. "I'll be going to the church soon. The people need comfort, especially now. Perhaps you—"

"The church is full of broken glass," I said. "That's where all this started. In the church. Salem and I stayed there last night, and when Ruth came in this morning, the angel came too."

He nodded slowly. "Well, it seems I may be doing damage control instead of preaching. It's not like you to be caught out in the night, Rayne. Why the church?"

Wordlessly, I got up and went to the bag I'd discarded by the door when we rushed in. I'd had time to grab only one thing before we fled the church. I pulled it out of my bag and held it out so my uncle could see it.

His face stiffened as he beheld the book in my hands.

"Where did you find that?" he whispered.

"In the coffin you buried in my mother's grave."

"Good God." His voice cracked. "You dug her up?"

"She wasn't there." To judge by the obvious horror on his face, this was new information for him. Walking back to him, book outstretched, I paused when I saw him tensing, drawing back. "What is this thing? My father's handwriting is in it, I recognize it. Is it magic? Witchcraft?"

He closed his eyes for a moment, taking a deep breath. "It is, I believe, a very ancient magic."

To hear him admit it stunned me. Part of me had hoped for a logical explanation, a harmless one.

My uncle rose from his seat and paced to the wall where there hung a wooden crucifix. He took it down and held it in his hand when I passed the book to him. He sucked in his breath as it settled in his palms.

"Ah, it's heavier than I expected. I've never studied its pages. It was acquired by your great-grandfather during World War I." He brushed one hand over the cover but, without opening it, hurriedly handed it back to me. "When your father and I were children, he would tell us the story of how his battalion came upon a burned house in the French countryside. He discovered the book under the floorboards. He believed it was a gift to the God-fearing, meant to be protected so it wouldn't fall into the wrong hands. When he returned home and followed his faith to lead a congregation, the book was at the heart of his devotion. It was his miracle."

"Why?" The thing felt grimey and repulsive in my hands. I couldn't fathom being inspired by it.

"Who knows?" My uncle paced, tugging at his collar. "The untreated effects of PTSD took their toll on him. He was not well when he returned home. The book was never seen in our house; he kept it put away. Hidden. But it would seem your father found it."

"And did he use it?" I said.

My uncle's frown deepened.

"Don't hide what you know from me," I said furiously. I leaned forward, jabbing my finger toward the barred window. "I need to know how the hell that thing ended up here. I need to know what he *did*."

"Rayne, I assure you, I'll tell you all I know," he said. "But I don't know much. It won't satisfy you."

"Nothing ever does. Just spill it."

Carefully, my uncle hung the crucifix back on the wall. "Four months after you were born, your father came to visit me. He wanted to talk about a . . . crisis of faith, as he called it. He was struggling with family life. The pregnancy was unplanned, as was the wedding, but your father believed he would feel more satisfaction with his new family. Instead, he was exhausted and bitter."

He shook his head, as if even now he was left aghast. "I had no children of my own yet. I could only sympathize. But it struck me as strange; Picard kept insisting that God meant for him to do more, something greater, something bigger. He said he was being called to act."

"What did that mean?" My knee was bouncing, my fingers tapping. Like a kettle boiling over.

"I wish I knew. He seemed nervous when I spoke to him, almost frantic when he would speak of the church or his congregation. But calm, always calm, when he spoke about your mother. He said he feared your mother was going to abandon you."

"Abandon me?" I laughed. "She would never. Never. Why would he say that?"

He didn't answer right away. He was staring at the washed-out old photo of himself and my father standing side by side on the chapel steps.

"Picard made many wild claims about your mother," he said slowly. "Yes, I'll call them wild. I didn't believe half the things he said. He claimed she would wander in the woods late at night, that she'd fly off into rages, smash things, threaten to harm herself or you."

I was almost too choked with rage to speak. *Almost.*

"Fuck no. Never. Mom was gentle. She was kind. She was the only person who ever gave a shit about me! She *loved* me. She would never hurt me. Never."

"I believe that," he said. "I truly do. I suggested they seek counseling together. He could leave the congregation to me and take time off, go to the mainland, and tend to his family."

"What a horrifying idea for him," I said sarcastically. "Time alone with his family."

"That was the last time he sought my advice. When your mother died years later, your father's grief was so great, I truly believed they must have repaired whatever rift was between them."

"And now?" I said. "What do you believe?"

My uncle stared down at the vile book in my hands. "I don't know what to believe, Rayne. If your mother's body wasn't in her grave, then—"

"He had photos of her corpse. In an envelope in his office. Old Polaroids of her, naked, dead."

My uncle looked as if he was going to be sick.

"Why would he have that?" I said desperately. "Why would he have photos of bones with marks carved into them? Why did he bury the book instead of her?"

"I wish I had your answers. I know . . ." He sighed heavily. "I know the church failed you—"

"I didn't need the church! I needed my *family*. I needed my mother alive, I needed a father who gave a shit—"

I was about to rage, but a sudden, tiny sound caught my attention. Hurriedly, I went straight back to the spare bedroom where Salem was sleeping and cracked open the door. She was twitching on the bed, eyes closed, making soft sounds of distress in her sleep.

Immediately, I was at her side. I ran my fingers through her hair, caressing her until she was still again.

When I looked up, my uncle was standing in the doorway.

"You've never been one for close friendships," he said, keeping his voice low. "She must be special."

Looking down at her, her fingers clinging to mine even in sleep, I felt that peculiar dip in my stomach again. Like teetering on the edge of a cliff and being terrified to fall, but knowing I needed to make the leap.

But I'd already fallen.

"She's changed everything," I said. "She's the reason I need answers. I'm going to kill it. I'll find a way. I haven't believed in God for two decades, Uncle. But this . . ." I lifted Salem's hand, kissing her knuckles. "I believe in this."

Salem

Our Fort

))) HEN I WOKE FROM MY TORMENTED SLEEP, RAYNE AND I left her uncle's home. My heart was hammering just step-ping outside; I was so anxious I kept stopping to dry heave as we walked. Rayne hovered over me, close at my side, comforting and encouraging me to keep going until we made it to the ATV.

The sun was shining but the air was still sharp with cold, and my entire body was trembling. I hugged close against Rayne's back as she drove, and only felt a little relief when we passed through the gates of Balfour Manor.

Still, I started crying again when Rayne shut and locked the thick doors behind us.

Rayne held me, right there on the floor in the middle of the foyer. I couldn't calm myself down; all my emotions, all my fear, had bubbled over. Again, we'd been only seconds, mere inches, away from death.

Rayne carried me up to bed, tucking me into her warm blankets. She gave me a pill and lay beside me, talking to me gently as I apologized for breaking down.

"It's okay, baby. I'm here. I'm not going anywhere. Don't be sorry, you have nothing to apologize for." She kept her arms around me as I shook, panic engulfing every part of me. My chest hurt; shots of adrenaline kept coming, as if my body couldn't understand I was no longer being chased.

It seemed like an eternity before the pill began to work, blanketing my anxiety with a strange and uncomfortable numbness. My stomach still churned, but at least I stopped shaking. Exhaustion settled over me. My eyes were too heavy to keep open anymore.

When I woke the next morning, I was lying in bed alone.

Rayne's empty pillow and flung-back blankets were the first things I saw, and my heart lurched into my throat so rapidly, I thought I might vomit.

Still half asleep, I attempted to guide my brain out of the fog of alarm, back to reality.

Like a dream, I had a faint memory of Rayne rising from bed that morning and giving me a gentle kiss on the cheek before she left the room. She had only woken up before me; there was nothing to fear. But her absence was like a cold needle through my heart. Where was she? What was she doing? Was she safe?

Squeezing my eyes shut tight, I curled up and wrapped my arms around my head. The deep, awkward pressure was soothing somehow. The more I focused on my breath, the more I felt as if I might faint. But I reassured myself, again and again.

I was safe in bed.

Rayne was safe downstairs.

We were safe . . .

The memory of the angel bursting through the church window shattered my attempt to cope. Nothing was safe here. Maybe nothing would be safe again . . .

There was a jingle, and sudden pressure on the bed. I recognized Loki's familiar snuffle before I opened my eyes, the dog's big head right in my face, staring at me.

"Where's your mama?" I said softly, scratching his fluffy chest. He licked my hand and, to my surprise, lay down beside me with a heavy sigh. I'd only ever seen him lie down when Rayne was nearby. The fact that he felt assured enough to lie with me lifted a huge weight from my lungs, and I released a trembling breath.

"I don't know how to handle this," I whispered, burying my face against his fur. "I'm so afraid. I'm scared to die. I'm . . . fuck . . ." I muffled a sob against him, thankful for his big, warm body to cling to. "I'm so scared of losing her."

For a while, I had to let the emotions out. I let myself feel the despair, the fear, all of it.

Then I took a deep breath. I sat up and wiped my face, and Loki looked at me with his deep brown eyes as he rested his head on my lap.

"We'll just get through the day, won't we?" I said, forcing my voice to be strong as I shoved myself out of bed. Everything shook. I felt like a wet, wrung-out rag. "One breath at a time."

I took a shower. Moisturized my face. Ran my fingers through my hair and lamented how shaggy it had gotten. Loki stayed with me all the while, guarding me like he usually guarded Rayne. When I finally left the room, we went together downstairs toward the dining room.

Sunlight peeked through the boarded windows. There was birdsong in the garden. The kitchen had already been used; the room was warmly scented with butter, vanilla, cinnamon, and coffee.

Music was playing softly somewhere nearby. Leaving the dining room, I followed its sound into the lounge.

But the room had been transformed.

Blankets, pillows, and chairs had been heaped into a soft, glowing castle. Stevie Nicks was playing from a Bluetooth speaker placed near the castle entrance, from which Rayne was just emerging.

She smiled shyly when she saw me and it set my heart fluttering.

"Good morning," she said. Her loose white T-shirt teased me with the stark outline of her breasts, and I almost melted when she wrapped her arms around me and kissed me. "How are you? Feeling okay?"

"I'm okay." I melted into her embrace. Just having her near me made it easier to breathe. She kissed my forehead, then both my cheeks, my nose—I was giggling by the time she reached my mouth.

"How long have you been working on this?" I said, marveling at the fort. "It's incredible!"

"Just some blankets, pillows, and Christmas lights," she said, and although she averted her eyes, I could hear the pride in her voice. "Trying to get the Christmas boxes out of the attic without waking you up wasn't easy. But wait, wait." She held up her hands excitedly, barely restraining a smile. "Close your eyes."

I laughed, but did as she said. She grasped my hands and guided me a few steps forward, turned me, and said, "Okay, you can look."

In front of the pillow fort was a breakfast spread, laid out like a picnic on a big knit blanket. Stacks of pancakes glistened with butter and syrup alongside bowls of fruit and whipped cream. Loki was staring at a plate of crispy bacon and fragrant sausage with longing.

My jaw almost unhinged when a glass of bubbling mimosa was thrust into my hand.

"Rayne, you . . . this is . . ."

"Do you like it?" She kissed my neck, gentle and slow. She looked soft and relaxed in her T-shirt and baggy jeans, and something about her serenity made my heart swell.

"I love it. I don't even know what to say, I—"

"You don't need to say anything, you need to eat," she said, flopping down on a heap of pillows. "One benefit of owning a bed-and-breakfast is that I naturally have all the supplies for an epic pillow fort."

She wasn't kidding, and I desperately wanted to crawl inside and look around. But my stomach was demanding food, so I happily dug in. I heaped my pancakes with berries and cream and rolled them up to eat in my hand. It made for a very messy plate, but it also made Rayne laugh, and I would gladly have sticky hands for a treat like that.

"How early did you wake up?" I insisted, nudging her with my elbow. "Be serious. This must have taken you hours!"

Rayne just shrugged. "I've always been an early riser. It didn't take that long."

But I knew. There were hours of work in this. Hours of care. Even when she was injured and should've been resting, she—

"Salem."

Blinking rapidly, I looked up from my plate to find that Rayne had leaned close to me.

"You deserve all of this and more," she said. She touched my face, tracing her fingers along my jaw and then combing them through my hair. "I wish it was more. I wish I could give you everything. I know this has been hard, but I'm . . . part of me . . ." She sighed and held my face as she said, "I'm glad you're here. It's so damn selfish to be happy about it, but I can't help it. I look forward to waking up now, just because I get to see your face."

For the second time that morning, she rendered me speechless.

"I wish I could take all your fear away," she said. Her lips were close enough to brush mine as she spoke, and it somehow still wasn't close enough. "I wish I could promise you safety. I'll give you everything that's mine to give . . ."

I shook my head, giggling quietly. "All I want is you." Her eyes went wide, and wider still when I kissed her. "Just you."

Plates of food forgotten, she pulled me into the shelter of our blanket fort. We collapsed among heaped pillows, warmly lit by electric lanterns. She kissed me all over, tugging up my clothing to caress my bare skin. Her hair was still damp from showering, and I shivered and gasped when the cold strands trailed over me.

"You taste like syrup," she said as she kissed me, licking her lips and grinning like a cat with her prize. "So sweet." Her tongue explored my lips, my mouth. Lying on my back, with her above me, I wrapped my legs around her hips. My breath hitched when she began to grind on me, her entire body moving in a slow rhythm.

She kissed my neck, her lips lingering on my skin, her breath warm and tickling. A nibble at my earlobe sent a spark of sensations all the way down my spine. Her fingers ignited goose bumps on my arms with her gentle touches. She pulled off my shirt, smiling widely as she straightened up and looked at me, and I at her.

Her messy hair fell around her face. Her soft skin smelled like fresh soap. She looked like a dream, my safety in this nightmare.

To my surprise, she suddenly averted her eyes, rubbing the back of her neck. I laid my hand against her cheek and brought her back, her gaze like morning sunlight peeking through the trees.

"You're so beautiful," I murmured. Her cheeks flushed the most gorgeous shade of pink. "Ever since I first saw you, I couldn't stop thinking about you. Your eyes. Your smile. Your voice."

"You don't mean all that," she whispered. I pulled her down to me, hands framing her face. I kissed her slowly, taking my time to appreciate her every breath, to savor the sweet softness of her lips.

"Your eyes remind me of the forest," I said, speaking the words in between kisses. "When the sun first touches the trees, and the shadows are still deep, and the morning feels quiet and wild. Your voice is a song I never want to end. Your mouth . . ." I giggled as she kissed me hard and shoved my pants down, her hand coming to rest on my thigh. "Your mouth is wicked in the best ways I can imagine. Your hair—"

"God, stop making me blush!" She laughed, tossing my pants away and trailing her fingers over my legs. "No one has ever looked at me the way you do, Salem. No one has ever . . . seen me . . . like you do."

I never knew kisses could enrapture me like hers. The way her mouth hovered so teasingly close over mine made the barest brush of her lips an electrifying sensation. She touched my breasts, gently squeezing, caressing, fingers flicking over my nipples until they were erect. I found the edge of her shirt and pulled it over her head, breaking our kiss for only seconds before her mouth returned, hungrier than ever.

As her tongue pressed into my mouth, her fingers stroked between my legs.

"Mm, already wet for me?" she said. She teased around my opening, spreading my arousal and making her fingers slick. "Do you want me inside you, baby?"

"Yes, please . . ." I moaned as she entered me.

She mirrored the motions of her fingers with her kiss, working me in unison. When her tongue slid alongside my own, her fingers slid deeper too. When she stroked deep and hard inside me, she kissed me like she was starving.

While I was still dizzied and breathless, she suddenly switched our position. She lay on the pillows and pulled me on top and, with a wicked grin, said, "Undress me, pretty girl."

I did, eagerly, pulling down her pants and tossing them aside. "Holy shit," I said softly. "Are you wearing a thong?"

"Just for you," she said, and rolled over so her bare ass was on display. Something short-circuited in my brain; I was instantly a drooling bimbo who wanted nothing more than that perfect butt smothering my face. I grasped her cheeks, one in each hand, marveling at the thick muscles of her thighs. I bent down, peppering soft kisses, biting here and there. Dragging my nails over each bouncy cheek, I giggled and scratched a design.

She glanced at me over her shoulder, smirking. "What are you doing?"

Seizing my phone, I took a picture and showed it to her: S+R scratched inside a messy heart. With a twinkle in her eyes, she said, "Damn, you really are trying to make me fall in love, aren't you?"

My heart leapt. I set aside my phone and ran my finger underneath the thong buried within her cheeks, pulling it up and out of my way.

"Hmm, maybe I am," I said. "I think you're trying to do the same thing."

I spread her ass, and swirled my tongue around her puckered entrance. She moaned softly, spurring me on. I trailed my tongue up and down, burying my face in her soft flesh. She reached back, her hand coming to rest on the back of my head as she bucked up her hips.

"Fuck yes, just like that," she said. The sounds of her pleasure shot straight to my core, arousal making my thighs sticky. I thrust my tongue against her tight hole, listening to her sounds and letting her hand guide me.

She arched her back, lifting herself a little higher and giving me access to lap my tongue over her clit.

"God, baby girl, you're gonna make me come," she said, and I groaned my encouragement against her. Her core pulsed, muscles throbbing as I thrust my tongue inside. With her sweet arousal on my lips, I let her grind back against me, using me for her pleasure until she cried out and shuddered.

"How can you have a face so innocent and a mouth so dirty?" she said, rolling onto her back to look at me. I licked my lips clean and grinned in triumph.

She still had another surprise for me.

She reached up, under a mound of pillows near her head, and held up my vibrator.

"Remember this?" she teased. "Remember being a very naughty girl and breaking my faucet while you got off in my bathtub?"

"Oh, God, don't remind me," I groaned, but she curled her finger at me to come closer, and of course I obeyed. She butterflied her legs and positioned me to straddle her thigh. She clicked a button and the vibrator came to life, buzzing like a hornet. She dragged it slowly along her inner thigh, shudder-ing with the vibrations. Then she did the same to me, teasing it across my abdomen.

As I rubbed against her thigh, her skin was velvety soft and warm. She brought the vibrator to my breasts and swirled it around my nipples, the stimulation going straight to my core and pulsing inside me.

"Just look at my dirty girl, so desperate for more, aren't you?" she said. She reached up, cupped her hand around the nape of my neck, and dragged me down to kiss her. She moved the vi-brator between us, her thighs tensing the moment it touched her clit. "Grind on me, baby. Just like that, I wanna see you come."

She didn't have to tell me twice.

Grinding against the vibrator pressed it harder against her, and as I moved, her breath caught. She praised me, her words the sweetest aphrodisiac I could imagine. I kissed her deeply, hips gyrating, thrusting down onto the vibrator with desperate abandon. She murmured increasingly breathless curses, gripped my short hair and held it tight.

"Look at me," she said, and I fell into her eyes as my pleasure peaked. "Tell me who you belong to."

"To you, Madam," I gasped. When her eyes fluttered closed in ecstasy, it pushed me over the edge. The orgasm crashed over me in waves, my body flooded with euphoria.

For a few moments, my entire world was only her. Our bod-ies in perfect unity, locked together in primal abandon.

"This is all I want," I whispered, caressing her flushed face. "Just you and me. Together and safe."

She laid her hand over mine, leaning into my palm as she closed her eyes. "Me too, pretty girl. Me too."

Salem

Follow the Light

WE LAY IN OUR FORT ALL DAY. WE ATE SLOWLY AND GREEDILY, mounds of syrup, butter, and jam on everything we pleased. We licked cream off each other's fingers and lay naked on the pillows, touching and kissing.

We napped off and on, waking when we wanted and shuffling to the kitchen wrapped in blankets for our lunch and dinner. Anxiety crept up on me as the windows grew dark, but I took another one of the pills Dr. Hale had given me, and it tempered the worst of my fear.

We lay in the fort, our hands interlaced, trading stories of our lives in quiet voices. We listened to Chelsea Wolfe and TV Girl, and I laid my head on Rayne's chest as she sang, losing myself in the echoes of her voice.

When I slept, it was soft and dreamless, and for hours I lay just on the edge of awakening.

But I must have slept deeper than I believed.

A cold chill woke me. For several moments I lay still, eyes closed, trying to sink back into peaceful slumber. But despite Rayne laying close beside me, Loki at my feet, and the blanket covering me, I was so cold I began to shiver.

The world was washed of color when I opened my eyes. Everything was in black-and-white, from the blankets to the walls. Even Rayne, lying sound asleep beside me, had a strange pallor to her face, and it made my heart lurch.

"Rayne. Rayne, hey, wake up." I shook her shoulder vigorously, but she didn't move. Her breathing didn't change from the same slow and steady pace. "Rayne!"

Nothing. Not so much as a twitch. Scrambling out of the fort, I tried Loki next. But the dog didn't move either, no matter how much I shook him.

"I'm dreaming," I said suddenly, and the weight of those words made a little color come back into the world.

The Christmas lights. Someone had unraveled them from around our pillow fort and dragged them out of the room and around the corner. They twinkled, their colorful glow the only illumination in the hallway.

The strand was moving, as if something was lightly tugging on the end of it. Despite the cold trepidation washing over me, the feeling that I should follow the lights needled me until my feet began to move. The hallway was pitch-black: All I could see was the colorful lights, leading away into the darkness before they twisted out of sight.

The floor was strangely damp beneath my bare feet. Pulling my phone from my pocket, I turned on the flashlight and stumbled back in horror. The hall was covered in thick, muddy sludge that reeked of rot. The beautiful filgreed wallpaper was flaking away from the walls like ash in the wind. It wasn't wood beneath; it was bone-white metal, crusted with rust.

The crash of the ocean waves was impossibly close, as if they were beating against the house. A buoy clanged as if in a storm, and the crying of gulls filled my ears. Water lapped over my feet, cold and sticky with salt.

As I reached the ruined foyer, I finally laid eyes on what was holding the other end of the strand of lights. I barely swallowed my scream.

Driftwood and seaweed were tangled over the deathly pale body of a woman, who was gripping the lights in a frail, bloody fist. She was naked, drenched in the blood pouring from her sliced throat. Her body was unnaturally twisted and broken, as if she had fallen from a great height and landed in a heap.

She was looking straight at me, with eyes that looked so eerily like Rayne's.

"Melanie," I whispered. "Are you . . . Melanie Balfour?"

A rattling groan emanated from her throat, and the lights began to flicker.

"Help . . . me . . ." she croaked. "The bones . . . my . . . bones . . ."

It wasn't only driftwood piled around her. It was *bones*. Misshapen, cracked, and etched with strange symbols. They surrounded her like a cage, pierced into her flesh.

"Please . . . I can't . . . stop . . . help me . . ."

As I stepped away, horror shivering through my veins, the woman's cries grew more frantic and her eyes bulged. "Help me! *Please!*" The sound was so terrible I covered my ears, my stomach churning, eyes stinging. She writhed in the bones surrounding her, shrieking as if she were being burned alive.

"HE WON'T LET ME GO—HE WON'T—WON'T—"
Her voice distorted more with every word. It became thick and
deep, harsh and grating. "Find me—he won't let—"

With the vile sound of ripping flesh and cracking bone, the
woman transformed before my eyes. Her skin burst open, moist
sinews engulfing the etched bones. Extra limbs grew; black
claws distended from long, gnarled fingers.

The angel rose up, jaw unhinged, maw of grisly teeth gaping
at me. It screamed, rotten spittle flecking my face. Adrenaline
flooded me but it was like my legs were knee-deep in tar. I
couldn't move, couldn't breathe.

My head swam, my world tumbling. The beast stood over
me, two flesh voids staring into my quivering soul. Its spine
crackled as it bent down to look into my face, and from its
dark throat came a choked woman's voice: "Destroy me—before—I—kill her."

I closed my eyes, breath frozen in my lungs, certain I was
about to die. I braced for pain. I imagined what Ruth might
have felt in her final moments and thought I might be sick from
the fear.

But only silence came.

"Salem? What are you doing?"

Blinking rapidly, I looked back. I was standing in the lounge,
and Rayne was looking at me sleepily from the entrance to the
fort. There was no water on the floor, no rusted walls. When
I turned back around, breathless, neither the angel nor the
woman was there.

A box of Christmas decorations was spilled open at my
feet. Shattered glass ornaments sparkled on the floor, heaps of
tangled lights flung about. Rayne came to stand next to me,

rubbing my back slowly. "Were you sleepwalking? I heard a crash. Be careful, there's glass everywhere."

"I had an awful dream," I said breathlessly. "I think I saw your mom. She said . . ."

Her wide-eyed expression silenced me. She stared, and so did I, as we both realized at the same moment what had been buried at the bottom of the box, beneath all the old decorations.

A VHS-C tape, labeled simply *For Rayne*.

43

Rayne

The Final Tape

IN THE VIDEO, IT WAS SNOWING. THE SKY LOOKED GRAY AND cold, flakes drifting gently between the trees. My mother wore her bright red coat, with a thick scarf wrapped around her beautiful long hair as she walked through the woods. She held the camera in her hand, unsteady. Her eyes were reddened, with deep dark circles beneath, as if she hadn't slept in days.

She looked exhausted. Defeated. But she tried to smile at the camera.

"Hi, honey. It's Mom."

In silence, my heart broke. Salem squeezed my hand.

"If you're seeing this, I'm probably not with you anymore." Her voice trembled, and she looked away from the camera for a moment. "Maybe it's been a few years now. Maybe you're grown up. No matter how long it's been, I want you to know how much I love you. From the very first time I held your little tiny hand,

I've loved you so much, Rayne. And I've always wanted nothing but happiness and safety for you. I would do anything to keep you safe." She smiled, but it was sad. "Anything in the world."

Crows squawked overhead and she flinched, the camera going out of focus. For a moment, the only sound was her deep and panicked breathing. When she finally lifted the camera again, her back was against a tree and she lowered her voice, as if she was afraid someone was listening.

"This is important, honey. You need to listen to me. You need to believe me. If I'm dead now, it's because your father killed me."

Like a knife in my gut, her words ripped me open. Salem made a horrified sound, but edged closer to me, wrapping her arms around me. Shielding me.

"I promise, I did everything I could. I'm doing every-thing . . ." She trailed off. Her head swiveled, and she stared off into the woods. Her eyes were wide—the expression of a hunted animal. "Your father has gotten involved in things he doesn't fully understand. I told him not to involve you. Just a child . . . his own child . . ." She closed her eyes, exhaling heavily. "He thinks God is speaking, but all I hear is the Devil."

Cold chills ran over my arms. She started walking again, slowly, every step crunching in fresh snow.

"He's intercepting my letters," she said. "He has been for months. He watches whenever I leave the house." She kept glancing over her shoulder. I'd never seen her look so afraid. Even as a child, I'd seen the rift between my parents, but I never knew it was this deep.

Mom was terrified of him. How could I have never seen it? How had nobody else—not my aunt, not my uncle—noticed what was happening?

But then I recalled what my uncle said, the "wild" stories my father told him about Mom. He was setting her up, sabotaging her, seeding the poisonous roots that trapped her here.

A rage more deep and cold than any before settled in my heart.

"I'm going to hide this tape where he'll never find it," she said. "I love you, honey. No matter what he tells you about me, please believe that. I wish I could protect you from all the awful things in this world."

My nails dug viciously into my palm. I was biting my lip so hard I tasted blood.

Mom came closer to the camera. A feeling of claustrophobia crushed my lungs. "No matter what he told you about me, don't believe it. No one believes me, but you . . . *you need to*. He isn't a holy man, Rayne. I don't know what he's trying to do, but I promise you I tried—I'm *trying*—to get us out of here. He tells people I'm crazy." Her eyes welled with tears.

The tapes. The book. The photos and the whispers. The long breadcrumb trail led straight to my father's guilt.

"I won't go without you," she said fiercely. "If I'm gone, please know this: I never wanted to leave you."

Static filled the screen.

He killed her. The murderer who took her from me, who stole my hope, my dreams, my love—was my own father.

I stared, unmoving, trapped in the limbo of anger and grief. All this time . . .

"She was trying to tell me," I said. "I didn't want to listen. I shut it out, I couldn't look at her. I couldn't stand the whispers. I ignored them until they turned into screams." I closed my eyes, remembering all times I turned my music louder, plugged my ears, closed my eyes. The echoes of her dead voice were more than I could bear.

353

My father had fooled so many, only to be killed by his own hubris in the end. I still didn't fully understand how he'd done it, or what wicked bargain he'd struck to bring the angel here. But that creature was tied to both my mother, and the book we'd dug out of her grave.

"It's not your fault, Rayne." Salem's voice was full of all the gentleness I'd spent my life longing for. "You buried your childhood with her. You've been trying to protect the scared kid inside you all this time, because no one else would."

I squeezed her hand as the guilt rose inside me like a tidal wave. It created a whirlpool with my anger, threatening to drown me, but Salem kept me from sinking. "I couldn't hear her over my own fear. So she went to you instead."

Salem wrapped her arms around me, and I immediately did the same to her, squeezing her close.

"All these years I've wondered who killed her. My father lied. He lied to me . . . to everyone." I didn't care about crying, for once. There was relief in this sadness, validation in this agony. I knew the truth now.

"She wants to protect you," Salem said. "She told me so. She said we have to stop her before you get hurt. I don't know how, but I think the angel is a part of her. Or she's a part of it."

She wiped the tears from my face. It ached to look at her, in a way that was too beautiful to put into words.

"You've protected me," she said. "I'm going to protect you too."

Her promise lit a fire in the darkness of my pain. She'd chosen me, again and again, and even after all the horror, she was determined to be here. She'd faced her own fear, risked her life . . . for me.

"I love you," I said, and watched fireworks light up her eyes. Her breath stuttered, her fingers tightening around me.

Leaning close, her breath was mine. A little shiver ran through her when I tipped up her chin and whispered into her mouth, "I adore you." Her lips were so soft. The way she sighed, the way she *moaned*, fuck. "I look at you, and I finally understand why I've stayed alive. You broke me open and found something I didn't think I had anymore. When I said you were mine, I meant it. But what I should have told you . . . what I should have said . . . is that I'm *yours*."

"God, I love you too," she said. "I love you so much."

How strange to smile, laugh, and weep all at once. How odd to feel hope in the midst of terror, to feel joy despite my grief. For the first time in so long, my hollow heart was full.

Curled against me, she said, "What are we going to do now?"

And, without a shadow of doubt, I said, "We're going to get off this island. We're going to live."

Rayne

It's Come for the Children

B Y EVENING, ANOTHER SNOWSTORM MOVED IN. BUT NOT EVEN the chill outside could destroy the warmth Salem filled me with.

She loved me. This beautiful, intelligent, brave, miraculous woman loved *me*. For the rest of the day, I kept catching myself staring at her, wondering how, why? What did I do to deserve her, to be chosen by her?

All my mistakes, my faults, seemed so brazenly obvious. Yet she faced them like they were nothing, mere dips and bumps like the same ones she effortlessly flew over on her bike. The terror she had endured here should have had her begging for a way to escape, desperate to get as far away from me as possible.

I'd always felt like a burden. Every breath I took felt stolen, every beat of my heart was in defiance. I strived to need nothing and depend on no one.

But God, I needed her like the trees needed the sun, like the tides needed the moon.

Part of me believed she would vanish by morning, disappearing like dawn's thick fog. But she was real enough to kiss when I woke, real enough to laugh with as we ate breakfast. She fed me slices of apple from her hand and squealed when I put her fingers between my teeth.

She held my face close and told me she loved me. After so many years in Hell, it felt like I'd finally found the stairs to Heaven.

But those stairs were gated, guarded by an angel of death.

I needed to find my mother's body. She was connected to this creature somehow; perhaps her remains held the secret to its destruction.

My father must have hidden her somewhere he believed she would never be found, just as he had with the tapes and photographs. But where? Blackridge wasn't massive, but it was dense, covered in thick forest and harsh terrain. How many weeks, months, years would I have to search to find her final resting place?

Even if I had to search and dig until I was old and gray, I would end this. I would find a way. It wasn't only the dead that cried for justice; I did too.

NEXT TO THE lounge, the overcrowded library became my constant refuge over the next few days. I kept my father's wicked old book there, cracked open on the wooden table, where I would study it for hours. With multiple French dictionaries on hand and the assistance of the internet, I did my best to translate, but reading had never been my strength. I didn't have the patience, and few things made me feel so incapable as staring down at that black-and-white page, all the letters blending together.

But with Salem there, I kept calm through the long, frustrating hours. She refilled my coffee before I even realized it was gone, made sure I ate when my hands became shaky from neglected hunger. When my eyes grew so tired they could no longer focus, she took over with the book, her brow furrowed in concentration as we slowly uncovered the mysteries within.

The details for elaborate rituals filled its pages. Our translations were crude at best, but it became clear this was not a book of worship. It contained no mythos or parables, only instructions. Much of it was impossible to decipher, but my father had already done some of the work for us, and left his notes in the margins.

These rituals demanded horrifying sacrifice. The torture of innocents, the killing of children.

My father's notes were sprinkled throughout a chapter that called for the sacrifice of one's firstborn. They were clinical and cold: Did the composition of the candles matter? Or the kindling used for the fire? Did the sacrifice need to be conscious?

Blood draws it near, death gives it power, he wrote. *Flesh must be stripped from the bones and left to be consumed.*

It made me ill to read, but I pushed on. Somewhere within these pages was the answer I sought: If it told how to summon the beast, surely it also told how to send it back.

Finally, scribbled in the margins, I found it. A note from my father, which read, *Bones are its tether. The script must remain intact. If the bones are broken or burned, such that the runes upon them are indecipherable, the beast will be sent back. Hide them well within its nest. It will guard them.*

I had to step away, pacing up and down the library. *It will guard them within its nest.*

My freedom lay in the lion's den.

I poured myself two fingers of whiskey, my mind running a million miles an hour. I'd need help, of that I had no doubt. The sheriff could get a search party together; we would go armed and ready. We would search the woods, until—

The soft crackle of static caught my attention.

Moments later, Salem poked her head into the library and said, "I think someone's trying to call you on the radio."

When I reached the foyer, an almost imperceptible whisper was coming from the speakers. Quiet as it was, I recognized it, and sprinted the last few steps to pick up the mic.

"Rebecca, I need you to repeat," I said, keeping my voice slow and calm. No response came.

Frowning, I held the button and repeated, "Rebecca, come in. Do you hear me?"

Faint noise came from the speaker. Crackling. Slow, desperately shallow breaths.

"Rayne?" The child's voice was the tiniest whimper. "Help me."

My blood ran cold. She was keeping her voice low, obviously afraid of being heard. For a few seconds, I didn't dare to even speak into the mic again.

"Where are you?" I whispered. My hand shook, and I flinched violently when Salem walked into the foyer. Her face fell when she saw my expression.

"In the shed. Me and Rachel were helping Daddy get the chickens inside, but he heard something and told me to go inside but I got scared and . . ." She sniffled, her voice shivering with cold. "I hid in the shed. I have his walkie-talkie. Rachel is with Daddy in the barn but the animals are all upset. Missy was screaming."

Missy. Their friendly potbellied pig. There was an awful feeling inside me that it wasn't the swine she'd heard screaming.

Suddenly, another voice came through the speaker. Even more muffled than Rebecca's, as if it was sounding from the other side of a wall, Andy's voice yelled, "Becca! Where are you? Becca! Come outside."

"That's not Daddy," Rebecca whispered frantically. "I know that's not my daddy!"

"Stay where you are." I was already gathering my things. Backpack, gun, GPS . . . "Stay inside, no matter what you hear. Understand? No matter *what* you hear."

"Rayne, what's happening?" Salem's voice was thick with alarm. Loki could tell something was happening as I put my backpack on, and began to whine at the door.

Heart pounding, stomach sick, I turned to Salem and said, "The angel took Andy. The girls need our help."

"Please hurry," Rebecca whimpered. "It keeps calling me. It knows I'm inside."

"Stay where you are, Seahawk," I said. "I'm coming to get you. Just hang on. Hang on, please. Please." I kept repeating the words even as I let the mic go. She didn't need to hear my begging, but something in this cursed world had to.

If there was a God, he was a fucking dick if he didn't spare these poor kids.

I turned, ready to sprint for the door, but Salem was already there, zipping up her jacket. Her boots, beanie, and gloves were on. She had my hunting knife strapped to her belt, and she really must have sprinted, because she also had a small pitchfork from the garden shed.

361

"Salem . . ." I shook my head as I went to her, cradling her head in my hands. "Please, sweetheart, please stay here, I can't—"

"You're not going alone," she said, unflinching. "They need our help. There's no time." She wrenched open the door, a rush of cold, snowy air billowing into the foyer. "We go together."

※

WITH SALEM CLINGING to my back on the ATV, we sped into the storm.

Loki ran ahead of us, sprinting over the snowbanks the vehicle couldn't navigate. The blinking light on his collar guided my way as we headed north along the road.

I parked the ATV along the wooden fence that surrounded Andy's farm. In the distance, I could see the subtle glow from the house's front porch light. The sound of goats bleating in fear carried on the wind. Cows were scattered beneath the trees, eyes glowing eerily in the headlights. Despite the storm, they had all shunned the warmth of the barn.

"Loki, heel." The dog came instantly to my side, watching me for his next command. "Salem, stay close to me. When we get into the yard, stay low and quiet. Follow me."

Salem nodded. Only her eyes were visible beneath her hood and wrapped scarf. She trusted me. She would follow me into the storm, into danger, without hesitation.

Now was my last chance, so I pulled her close. "I love you."

She yanked down her scarf, throwing her arms around my neck to kiss me.

"I love you too," she whispered. "We're going to make it, Rayne."

The howling wind, although frigid, drowned out the crunch of our footsteps as we ducked under the fence. The barn doors were ajar, and I thought I could make out a faint light within. The house was lit, the curtained windows casting a warm glow. About fifty yards from the front porch stood the shed.

The wind died down for a moment, and only the nervous lowing of the livestock and the crackling of the trees in the wind broke the eerie silence. I readied my weapon, nerves making it difficult to keep still. Where was the damn thing? My stomach churned with thoughts of what could have occurred in the time it took us to get here.

"I need you to get to the shed," I whispered, pointing Salem toward the small building. "Your only goal is to get Rebecca, and get to the house, okay? When you get inside, take her straight down to the basement and wait for me, got it?"

She nodded slowly. "Where are you going to go?"

"Into the barn." We both glanced toward the dark, ominous entrance. "If Rachel is alive, I need to find her."

Her eyes welled—whether from the cold or grief, I couldn't be sure—before she rapidly blinked the tears away.

Then, holding her pitchfork like a spear, she said grimly, "Let's fucking do this."

My heart was in my throat by the time we reached the shed. I was constantly moving, turning, watching, just as Loki was. Salem tried to ease open the shed door, but it was barricaded on the other side. Pressing her mouth close to the door crack, she whispered, "Rebbecca, it's me! Salem! It's Salem and Rayne!"

There was no response from within, so Salem began to force the door. Bracing her shoulder against it, her feet kept slipping in the snow as she tried to open a crack wide enough to see through. Finally, she was able to shine her phone's light inside, and there was a small gasp of relief.

Rebecca was wedged beneath a workbench, her wide, terrified eyes only visible when Salem's light shone on them. She crawled out when she saw us, her nose and cheeks bright red from the cold, her eyes swollen from crying.

Salem took her hand and helped her climb over the mountain of things she'd piled in front of the door. She was trembling violently, looking around the yard with an expression of confused horror.

"Where's Daddy?" she whispered, but I shushed her quickly.

"Go, Salem. Go," I hissed, pushing her toward the house. Keeping low, tightly gripping Rebecca's hand, Salem sprinted to the house. I covered her escape, scanning my surroundings through my gun's sights. But Loki's attention was fixated solely behind me . . . on the barn.

The tension around my lungs loosened as Salem and Rebecca disappeared into the house. Safe. They were safe.

Loki matched my pace as I crept toward the barn, his head low. The snow was disheveled with prints, some of boots both large and small, and some of hooves.

"Easy, now," I whispered, but I wasn't sure if I meant it to reassure him or myself.

A single electric lantern hung from a hook just inside the barn doors, illuminating the wide, frightened eyes of the horse in the stall next to it. The mare flung her head, squealing in fear. Chickens were squawking and fluttering, wings beating against their coop sending plumes of dust and feathers into the air. The goats were restless, milling about in their stall, wide-eyed and bleating.

Before me, lying face down, was Andy. Blood pooled around his still body, dark patches of gore ripped through his clothing. My stomach clenched, my chest tightening as I stared, hoping for any sign of life.

His chest didn't move. There was too much blood.

My instinct was to run to his side, try to wake him, try to drag him to safety. But I forced myself to be still, crouched just inside the barn doors. I couldn't help him now. Making the wrong move could cost me my life.

He was lying on the broken remnants of the ladder that once led to the hayloft. He'd been ripped down as he tried to flee to higher ground.

No ... no, that wasn't right ...

There was an ax, fallen near his right hand. To judge by the remains of the ladder still hanging above, he'd used to the ax to chop it down.

He hadn't died while trying to flee. He'd died trying to protect someone.

Unclipping my flashlight from my pack, I clicked it on and aimed the beam into the rafters.

Something scurried about near the back of the barn, and I went still as stone as Loki began to growl. He didn't move—he just stared straight ahead, ears flattened, teeth bared. The shadows were too deep to see within. Chains dangling from the rafters swayed slowly, but there was no breeze in here to move them.

Suddenly, there was a soft footstep above me, and Rachel's terrified face peered at me through a crack in the hayloft floor. Her hair was mussed, tangled with straw as if she'd been hiding beneath the piles of hay. She was crying silently, and began to whimper when she saw me, but I hurriedly put my finger to my lips.

Then I heard something that made my veins run with ice.

"Come here. *Come. Here.*"

Loki's growl deepened. That eerie voice was Andy—but it wasn't. He would never call his own child with such coldness.

"Where are you, sweetheart? Come here."

Rachel squeezed her eyes shut tight and covered her ears with her tiny hands. I trusted Loki not to leave my side; we crouched behind plastic barrels full of animal feed, with the voice of the beast emanating from the darkness. If I could get on top of the horse's stall door, I could get a leg up on the rafters and pull myself into the loft.

Peering cautiously around the barrels, I watched as the angel emerged from the darkness. It crawled about on its six long limbs, coming to eagerly sniff at Andy's corpse. Its jaw gaped open, gore and pink-tinted saliva dripping from its teeth. Chattering excitedly, it took the poor man's limp arm between its teeth and—

Suddenly, with a flurry of squawking, the chickens were released. The birds flew in a panic, feathers filling the air. Loki barked and the beast startled, swaying its head side to side in confusion at the noise. It swiped at them, but with a dozen frightened birds fluttering around it, it was thoroughly distracted.

Now was my chance.

As I hurried to climb up into the loft, I spotted Salem crouched near the chicken coop. She gave a thumbs-up and a wicked grin, and my heart beat harder but not out of fear.

"I love you, pretty girl." She couldn't hear me but I said the words anyway, hoping she could read my lips before I disappeared into the loft. Loki remained obediently hidden below.

The angel stalked in a slow circle as the chickens fled, snapping at them with half-hearted aggression. The birds clearly weren't its preferred prey. Salem was out of my sight, but I hoped she was making her way for the exit.

Little Rachel was huddled behind a pile of hay bales, clutching a ragged plushie in her arms. Her eyes were wide with shock, and she was frighteningly cold as I picked her up. But as I did, the wooden floor groaned, and the angel's attention snapped toward us. It began to chitter, and as I remained crouched and still, I could see the shadow of its long arms reaching toward the loft, looking for a way to climb up.

Seizing a rusty hand spade from the ground, I threw it to the back corner of the loft. The beast shrieked, pursuing the sound from below, its head lifted as it sniffed intently. Moving painfully slow to remain silent, I made my way to the front of the loft, Rachel held tight in my arms.

The hay door was silent as I eased it open; thank God for Andy keeping the hinges well oiled. The icy wind hit my face, flurries of snow blowing in. It was a long drop, but I hoped the snow would cushion our fall.

When I looked down, Salem was waiting below. Her arms were outstretched, her gaze darting between me and the barn as she watched for the angel. She motioned with her arms and I squeezed Rachel tight, whispering to her, "Salem is going to catch you, baby, okay? Don't be scared, it's going to be okay. But you have to be quiet, alright? Do you understand?"

She gave a tiny, timid nod of her head. She didn't make a sound as I lowered her down, and allowed her to fall the last few yards before Salem caught her. Salem stumbled with her weight but didn't fall. I followed, lowering myself until I dangled from my fingers, then dropped to the ground and landed in a crouch.

"Don't look, it's okay, just close your eyes," Salem was saying, covering Rachel's eyes so she wouldn't see what had become of her father. I could no longer see the beast in the barn; it had crept away somewhere, and without a line of sight, we were vulnerable from all directions.

I whispered Loki's name, and the dog immediately came to my side. But he kept staring off into the trees at the back of the barn, where the cattle were huddled together against the snow. Their wide eyes glowed in the darkness as my flashlight moved over them, but they were still and silent.

"Where did it go?" Salem whispered. Loki was growing restless. He caught my pant leg in his teeth, tugging and whimpering.

Like a deer in the headlights of an oncoming semi, I didn't dare move. We were the prey, standing vulnerable in the middle of the yard. If we ran, it would chase. If we didn't . . .

We would die.

Still surveying the darkness beyond the barn, I cast my beam over a large, huddled form just at the edge of the trees. No eyes caught the light.

"Run, Salem," I whispered, the flashlight shaking as the angel rose to its feet. "Run for the house."

She sprinted, and in the same moment, Andy's voice called out, "Don't leave, Rachel. Daddy is here."

"Run, run, go!" I yelled, bringing my rifle up and firing off a shot. The bullet barely missed the angel's head as it charged for me, long limbs sending it loping over the snowy ground with terrifying speed. It was almost on top of me, and I ducked down as I braced myself—but a dark blur flew past me.

Loki met the beast head-on. He dodged around its long limbs, snapping and snarling before he caught one of its hind legs between his teeth. He wrenched his head back and forth and the angel shrieked, swiping him with its claws and sending him tumbling through the snow with a yelp.

My hands were almost too cold to fire the gun. I shot it in the back as it stalked toward my dog, who had limped to his feet, snarling and snapping his teeth. The beast stumbled and thrashed, and I screamed for Loki to come as I fumbled to reload.

He limped toward me, slowed by his injury. The angel was swiping at the bullet wound in its back, dripping blood into the snow. It gave me just enough time to fire again.

The gunshot rang out and my bullet hit its mark, piercing the beast between its upper shoulders. It roared, lurching forward before whirling around to face me.

It wasn't intimidated. It was *angry*.

Loki stood in front of me, barking furiously as the angel charged. We didn't have time to run. I couldn't reload quickly enough. All I could do was crouch over my dog and cling to him, as if I could somehow save him.

A long object sailed over my head and speared into the angel's chest.

Putrid blood spurted across the snow and the creature gave a horrendous scream, tumbling backwards as it clawed the pitchfork out of its torso. Grabbing Loki's collar, we ran. Salem was standing near the shed, already armed with another gardening tool. Rachel was safely inside, but she had come back for me.

"Go, Loki! House, go!" I yelled, and the dog limped ahead of me with all the speed he could muster. The snow was powdery and deep, my boots dragging through it. I didn't dare look back, but the angel's snarling breath was close behind.

Salem began to scream. "Hey! Come on, fuckface! Come get me!" She swung her arms, jumping up and down, drawing as much attention as she could. Loki reached the house's front porch and began scratching at the door, which opened just enough to allow him to slip inside before it slammed shut again. I reached the porch just behind him, but instead of rushing inside, I turned back to make sure Salem had followed me.

She hadn't.

The angel was now between her and the house, blocking her path, stalking closer with terrifying intent.

My fingers were numb as I tried to reload, and the bullet slipped from my grasp.

Salem was still yelling, making herself as loud and threatening as she could. She jabbed her shovel toward it, and at first, the angel seemed hesitant. Almost as if it couldn't understand why this small thing was yelling so much and not running away.

For a moment, I felt hope.

I thought that maybe, just maybe, I could be fast enough. I could reach her.

I couldn't.

The next thing I knew, the angel was on top of her. Her leg was in its mouth and she was screaming as she was dragged, hands scrambling for something to grip.

"Rayne! Help me!"

Those words would haunt me. The terror in them. The pain.

It dragged her into the trees. Her screams echoed out as I followed, my chest hollow, my lungs like blocks of ice. I couldn't feel the exhaustion in my limbs or the numbness in my extremities. All I could feel was the terrifying pounding of my own heart.

Her screams were distant. I couldn't see her anymore. I was following only the awful, bright red trail of blood starkly visible against the snow.

"Salem! Oh my God—Salem . . . Salem!"

My throat was raw, my hands and feet numb. No amount of willpower could force my limbs to sprint another step, and I stumbled to my knees . . .

Only to find myself staring into the gaping maw of a dark burrow. Nearby, Salem's torn and bloodied boot lay abandoned in the snow.

Rayne

Into the Burrow

ON MY HANDS AND KNEES IN THE DARK, I SCREAMED UNTIL MY throat felt flayed. When I could no longer get the breath to scream, panicked gasps overtook me.

"Please, God, no . . . please . . ." I screamed again, beating the snow with my fists as if it would make this all stop. As if it would make her come back.

If I was loud enough, drew enough attention to myself, then surely it would come back.

I yelled for it. I braced my hands against the dirt piled around the burrow and cursed it, begged it. I cried out prayers to any god that would listen.

"Don't take her! I'm right here! Isn't this what you want? I'm—right—fucking—here! Bring her back! Come back and face me! *Salem*! Salem, please God, no . . . don't take her . . . don't take her away . . ."

Snow fell around me. The forest was mercilessly cold and far too quiet. My voice was gone, my screams silenced.

I knew what I had to do.

I was going to get my girl back, no matter what it took.

The burrow looked and smelled like a pit to Hell. Taking a bandana from my backpack, I tied it around my face, covering my mouth and nose. I discarded my bag, and my rifle too, when I realized I wouldn't be able to crawl through the small opening with them.

I had only my knife, my flashlight, and a lighter in my pocket as I crawled into the darkness.

The tunnel was narrow, just big enough for me to get through nearly flat on my belly. The dirt was wet and sticky—not damp enough to be mud, but enough to make the air thick with the smell. Roots stuck out everywhere, brushing against my face like fingers. I dragged myself over bits of broken bone and lumps of rotting flesh.

"I'm coming, Salem. Hold on. Please hold on."

I couldn't consider a possibility wherein she didn't survive. I couldn't fathom the absence of her life from this world. But wasn't that exactly the kind of nasty trick fate would play: offering me everything before brutally taking her away?

"Fuck no," I snarled. Fate could do as it pleased with me. I'd always believed I would die on this island, that my flesh would be consumed by its dirt. And it could take me still. I would gladly go in her place.

If God needed another death so badly, then it would be my own. How the hell would I go on without her? What light would I find if hers was snuffed out?

I refused to be her curse. Blackridge wouldn't take her.

It would have to kill me first.

Salem

The Nest

THE ANGEL WAS GOING TO EAT ME ALIVE.

Its jagged teeth were embedded deeply in my leg, the pain reverberating throughout my body as I was dragged through the darkness. Dirt filled my screaming mouth, my head knocked about on invisible obstacles as the creature moved with unnatural speed through its narrow burrow. The seconds felt like hours as my flesh was torn and pierced, my bones splintering with unspeakable agony.

I wasn't sure if I fell unconscious, or merely sank into shock. For a while, I was only aware of darkness and pain.

Slowly, the cold crept over me, and I became frighteningly aware that I was freezing. As if I lay on a block of ice, the cold seared through my flesh and ached in every muscle. Violent shivering spasms brought me hurtling back to reality.

I was alive, somehow, but I didn't dare to open my eyes. I feared that if I did, I would see my own death approaching.

I took a deep breath—and gagged. The smell was putrid. A hundred different kinds of rot collided in my nose. It stuck in my throat like bile, too awful to swallow. A cough exploded out of me and I curled into a ball, frantically covering my mouth as the coughing continued.

The sudden movement caused sharp and splintering pain to shoot through my leg and foot, as if my bones were made of needles.

The pain made lightning flash behind my closed eyes, and I almost screamed. My head swam, and I lay there listlessly for a while, drifting away into semiconsciousness. All my willpower was devoted to remaining silent and blocking out the pain.

Finally, I opened my eyes just slightly, taking in my blurred surroundings through my lashes.

Red, black, and gray. The surface I lay on was squishy and damp, and the awful smell was emanating from it. Straining my ears for the slightest sound, I held my breath.

The roar of the ocean's crashing waves echoed around me. Water dripped and the wind howled. But I didn't hear the angel's voice.

My heart beat a little steadier, and my head felt clearer. But with my return to reality, the pain also felt sharper.

Opening my eyes completely, I moved my head just enough to survey my surroundings. It was a tower of some kind—filthy, dank, and dark. There was a rusted spiral staircase, draped in moss and debris. There were old crates, barrels, and rusting machinery, all covered in a thick layer of filth and grime.

I was lying on a compressed layer of putrid rot. It covered every surface, even the walls, as if plastered there intentionally. Like a swallow, building its mud nest . . .

But this nest was built of flesh and blood. A decayed collection of victims, both human and animal. I lifted my shaking hands; they were coated in the stuff. Mud, slime, and blood.

The smell was horrendous, but I forced myself to take slow breaths, as deep and steady as I could. I needed oxygen. I needed to *get up*. So long as I didn't move my ankle too suddenly, the pain was bearable. A result of shock, I guess. My brain felt numb but my body was electric.

Slowly, I managed to crawl to my hands and knees, then to my feet. I could barely put weight on my leg without wanting to scream.

The boot on my injured foot was missing, and in the dim light I could see the damage the beast had inflicted. Deep lacerations curved around my ankle, which was swollen, red, and purple. My foot was stiff, two of my toes positioned at odd angles.

God, it hurt so badly I wanted to cry. But I sucked it up, biting my tongue as I shuffled my way toward the staircase. I didn't even want to think about the amount of bacteria in this place. What if I made it out of here alive only to die of sepsis?

One fucking problem at a time, Salem.

Gritting my teeth, I lowered myself to the ground and crawled behind some old barrels near the stairs to hide. Where had the creature taken me? This was clearly a human structure, but the angel had made itself at home since the building's abandonment. Sticks, twigs, bones, and leaves were piled in the corners and on the stairs.

Strange items were strewn on the stair railing and stuck on the gory walls. Jewelry—wedding rings and cross necklaces. There were torn and bloodied jackets, and random scraps of clothing. There was even a rusted old gun, and what appeared to be matted clumps of hair.

Like mementos, decorating a nest.

There was an old door, but mounds of mud and petrified gore were blocking it. The faint light came from above, and I suddenly realized where I was.

The old Blackridge lighthouse.

There had to be a way out of here. Cautiously, I crawled out from behind my barrels again. My hand squelched into something black and slimy, releasing more putrefaction into the air, and I choked down my gag.

I didn't have to crawl far before I reached the jagged edge of a hole in the concrete floor: a tunnel, burrowed deep into the earth below. This was how the angel brought me in. If I was brave enough, it could also lead me out.

Or it could lead me straight back into the jaws of the beast.

I had to be cautious. I had to *think*. But God, my mind was racing. Panic was creeping up and I began to hyperventilate. I crawled back behind the barrels, squeezing myself into a corner and making myself as small as possible. I was too terrified to cry, to move, to act.

But if I didn't do something, the angel would return to finish me off. I would become a part of its morbid nest. My family would never know what became of me, they wouldn't even have a body to bury.

I thought of Rayne, of Rebecca and poor little Rachel. At least they were safe, at least it had taken me instead of one of them. I didn't regret it. Even scared as I was and in so much pain, I would do it again. I would put my life on the line for those kids, and for the woman I loved.

Thinking of them brought back a little of my courage. I

wasn't dead yet; neither was my will to fight. I couldn't allow myself to rot here until death came for me.

Still hidden behind the barrels, I examined the mass of fleshy webbing beneath the stairs. It clung to the walls, forming what appeared to be a large cocoon. Peering through thin gaps in the sticky, wet substance, I spotted something lying inside. Believing it to be the branches or pale roots of a tree, I unsheathed the knife from my belt and began slicing through the webbing. Perhaps I would find a way out.

But it wasn't an escape I found within.

It was a skeleton, perfect and complete down to every finger bone, surrounded by the melted remnants of six black candles.

"Oh my God . . ." I whispered. "Melanie . . ."

Her bones were completely stripped of flesh, intricately carved with row upon row of unrecognizable symbols. The amount of time it must have taken to carve this, I could only imagine—hours and hours, bent over these bones while they still smelt of the acid used to clean them.

She had lain here for years, cold and exposed, surrounded by the macabre nest of the angel she'd been used to summon. Abandoned in the very lighthouse she had once gazed upon from her window, entombed below the beacon she used to watch for in the darkness.

Suddenly, above the sound of the wind and waves, I heard scratching. A scraping, like something being dragged. An ominous, throaty clicking sound echoed around the tower.

It was coming from the burrow.

In a panic, and with no idea where to go, I dropped to my belly and crawled farther under the stairs. Stretchy, sticky webbing was everywhere, and I slashed through it with my knife, wedging myself into the tightest corner I could, my back pressed to the wall. I clapped my hands over my mouth right as a pair of long spidery limbs emerged from the ground.

The angel clicked and chattered as it entered the room. Random words, all uttered in different voices, fell from its horrid mouth. It passed close to the stairs, hooves squelching in the muck.

It came to the place where I'd been lying and paused, nose to the ground.

Its high-pitched shriek made me cover my ears, my teeth set on edge. It rose up on its hind legs, sniffing the air, its mouth hanging open. Then it began to scurry about with frantic speed, climbing over mounds of bones and rot.

It was searching for me. It was only a matter of time before it found me hiding here.

"Come out, sweetheart." It tried Andy's voice again, and my stomach churned as I thought of the poor man lying dead in his barn. "Where are you?"

Its voice was like a skipping record, repeating the same phrases again and again. What could I do? The only way out of here was back through the tunnel. But the thought of trying to crawl some unknown distance through that tiny space, with the angel in pursuit—I'd never survive. I'd be killed before I ever saw the light of day.

Think, Salem, think.

I had to get out of here, and my only other option was up.

The angel continued its rampage, eventually scuttling through a narrow crack in the floor down to the cellar. Now was my chance. Maybe the only chance I'd get.

Keeping an eye on the crack, I crawled for the stairs. I tried to hurry, but when I braced myself on a blackened piece of wood, it snapped in half under my weight.

It wasn't wood at all. It was a human arm.

Bile rose in my throat, but I forced myself to keep crawling. As I reached the stairs and cautiously put my weight on them, something brushed against my leg, and my heart nearly exploded from my chest.

Scrambling forward, I tried to drag myself upwards as my uninjured leg was grasped, pulled back, and suddenly as I was being grappled, held tight but gently. A familiar voice whispered urgently in my ear, "Don't scream, it's me, I'm here."

"Oh my God! Rayne!"

Her face was streaked with tears as she held me. She was covered in mud, as dirty and cold as I was, both of us trembling as we wrapped our arms around each other. She kissed my hands, touching me all over as if in disbelief I was truly there.

My words barely audible, I gasped, "How did you—"

"I crawled." She mouthed the words, pointing back toward the tunnel.

She crawled through the dark, into the unknown and alone with a monster, just to find me.

"You're alive," she whispered again and again. She kissed my face, regardless of the filth. She cupped my head in her hand and held me against her chest. "I've got you, Salem. We'll get out of here."

If only that moment of relief could have lasted an eternity.

Like a bolt of lightning striking down, the angel shrieked and we both flinched. It would return at any moment, searching for its lost prey. Our wide eyes met, a silent promise in her gaze: Whether we lived or died, we would go together.

Pressing my finger to my lips, I motioned for her to follow me. We crawled back under the stairs, toward the cocoon, and I pointed within. She frowned, and used her knife to cut a larger opening.

Her face went slack with disbelief. Her breath came faster, and she shot a worried glance toward the crack through which the beast had crawled. It was scurrying about below us, claws scratching, hooves clicking.

Silently, we crawled into the cocoon. Rayne knelt beside the bones, her eyes far away and glossy. She reached out slowly and reverently laid her hand on the skull, marred with etchings but perfectly intact. She touched the delicate finger bones and bowed her head over the hollow rib cage.

"Mom," she whispered. "I'm so sorry."

Edging closer, I wrapped my arms around her and laid my head between her shoulders, listening to the sound of her beating heart.

Her fingers squeezed around mine, and she whispered. "Let's end this."

Rayne

Up in Flames

After so long, Mom and I were together again. I had once believed that the sight of her body, her bones, would frighten me. But they didn't. Even in this terrible place, her remains emanated her gentle spirit, her kindness, her love.

For all these years, she'd waited, hidden here, guarded by that creature and enshrined in its gore. But not for much longer. I would put her to rest, destroy the blemished bones holding her spirit captive.

My father's curse was at its end. I refused to live another winter in fear. I wasn't going to lose the woman I loved to the monster born out of his hatred.

The book said her bones were the tether. The runic script upon them had to be destroyed. But crushing the bones would attract too much attention and take too long. Burning them—I had a lighter in my pocket, but I had no fuel. Whatever small fire I managed to create wouldn't be enough.

Surely this lighthouse had once used fuel to feed its light . . .

Stripping off my jacket, I handed it to Salem and whispered in her ear, "Gather up the bones, tie them together in this. I'm going to find the furnace."

Nodding, she laid out the jacket and hurriedly collected the bones on top of it. I crawled out of our hiding place and took my first cautious steps up the stairs.

I tested my weight with every step, silently begging the rusty old metal to hold. The structure creaked and groaned ominously. Keeping low, I was able to remain mostly hidden behind the moss and gore draped over the railing. But the angel's voice echoed around the tower, impossible to escape.

It was looking for Salem, trying to lure her out. It tried Andy's voice, then Ruth's. It cycled through the echoes of a dozen victims, their voices stolen and repurposed as bait. The eerie sound of my own voice being mimicked sent a shudder up my back.

This was the end. I wouldn't let this damned creature live another day.

Finally, after what felt like an eternity of crawling, I reached the topmost room beneath the light, the watch room. Among the dusty old barrels and chests, I found a large metal tank with a distinct smell.

Kerosene.

I wouldn't be able to produce a fire hot enough to reduce the bones to ash. But we could break and blacken them, enough to render the runes upon them unreadable. If the old book was to be believed, that would be enough to sever the angel's tether to them.

Working quickly, I found an empty metal barrel. I collected dry pieces of wood from around the room, the remnants of old crates and firewood, and dumped them into the barrel before soaking them in kerosene. Then I filled a bucket with the fuel, hoisted it up, and headed for the stairs.

Every step made the metal give an eerie creak. Rust flaked away beneath my feet, and the entire staircase shuddered when I moved. The oil sloshed, dripping through the grate and streaking down the wall.

There was an ear-piercing shriek, and I nearly dropped the bucket. Peering below, I spotted the creature sniffing along the wall, inspecting the dripping liquid. Tentatively, I tipped the bucket, allowing a little more of the kerosene to spill out and splatter onto the beast's head. It flailed, swiping at its skin as if to flick off the substance.

I could only hope the smell of the oil would hide my own scent.

I seized a broken bone and threw it over the railing. It bounced off the opposite wall before clattering to the ground, and the beast leapt for it. It was snarling, its breathing harsh, its movements becoming increasingly erratic as it searched for its prey. Its distraction gave me time to make it back under the stairs.

Salem was waiting for me there. My mother's bones were bundled up in my coat, the sleeves tied tight around them to make a makeshift sack.

"Can you walk?" I said, eyeing her injured foot. It was painful just looking at it, and it was clear she was avoiding putting weight on that leg.

Her jaw was clenched in obvious pain. "I will. I have to."

"I found kerosene up above." I kept my mouth close to her ear so I could speak as quietly as possible. "If we can break up the bones and get them burning, it should destroy the runes carved into them."

She eyed the bucket I brought with me. "What's that for?"

"Distraction." I pulled my lighter from my pocket. "I'm going to light that motherfucker on fire, while you head up the stairs. Can you do that?"

She nodded firmly, bravely. "Yes. But I might be slow."

We both took a deep breath. The angel had gone ominously quiet. The crashing waves and howling wind made the tower echo and groan. The light was almost too dim to see Salem's face as she stood there, clutching my mother's bones, preparing to face her fate.

I stepped close and kissed her bruised face. "You're the bravest woman I've ever met." She shook her head, but I kissed her again before she could deny it. "No matter what happens, Salem, I'm glad I got to love you."

Her eyes said what her mouth couldn't. Her lip trembled for just a moment. Her breath shook, and she said, "Let's end this. Together."

She tore a sleeve off her shirt and hurriedly wrapped it around her injured ankle, providing herself with a little more stability. Then she picked up her parcel of bones and we crawled out of the cocoon.

For a moment, I believed we would get lucky. The space was quiet, the beast nowhere to be seen. Salem limped hurriedly for the stairs, but the moment she put her weight onto the first step, the old metal creaked.

From behind a mound of rot and broken bones, the angel emerged. It walked on its hind legs, a grotesque hybrid of human and beast. It faced me, then turned its head toward Salem, and I swore the thing moved its mouth into something like a grin.

"Salem, run! Go!"

I needed to buy her time. As the beast stalked closer, I lifted the bucket of kerosene and threw the strong-smelling fuel. It splashed onto the creature, drenching its sickly pale skin. It seemed momentarily confused, and halted its approach as it sniffed its dripping arms.

Salem was climbing the stairs, the sound of her frantic steps echoing off the metal. I pulled out my lighter, and was about to flick it to life—but my own hands and shirt were drenched in kerosene. If I lit it . . .

My second of hesitation was a fatal mistake.

The beast lunged, closing the space between us before I could force my limbs to move. It slammed into me, and my lighter went flying, vanishing into the piles of junk.

"Shit!" I covered my head, and screamed as its claws tore deep lacerations in my forearms. It struck my side, tumbling me over onto my back. Agonizing pain richoted through me as its teeth sunk into my shoulder, piercing muscle and tendons.

I ripped my knife from its sheath and swung wildly. The blade met a soft spot and sunk up to its hilt in the creature's face.

It screamed, rearing back and flailing. I took my chance and ran.

My body hurt in ways I hadn't thought possible, but adrenaline kept me moving. Every step I took, sprinting up the stairs, felt disturbingly unsteady. I swiftly caught up with Salem, relieving her of the bundle of bones so she could steady herself against the railing.

But the beast was crawling after us, shrieking and wailing. It galloped up the stairs on six limbs, every step rattling the entire structure.

There was a sudden pop, and a distant tinkling sound of metal—to my horror, the staircase leaned away from the wall, its bolts unmoored from the old plaster. Salem reached frantically for something to hold onto, crawling up the stairs as I lost my balance and fell into the railing, nearly dropping the bones.

"It's going to collapse!" Salem screamed. I turned just in time to see her leap up several steps as an entire section of wall gave way. The wind and snow rushed in, and the old metal snapped—the section of stairway upon which the angel and I stood swayed, about to plummet to the ground.

I scrambled. I tossed the bundle over to her, and she caught it before it fell. The stairs gave way beneath my feet, and I threw myself with all my strength, one arm outstretched as I leapt.

She caught me. She gripped my arm, and I gripped hers; her other arm was wrapped tightly around the remaining railing beside her. She was panting, eyes wide with panic.

"It's coming," she said. "It's crawling back up!"

Snow rushed in through the gaping wall, peppering me with the cold. There was a heavy crash as the lower staircase hit the floor, more bricks rattling loose from the wall. Salem pulled, and I managed to get a hold on the railing and drag myself up. Panting, arms and shoulders aching, I had no time to rest. One glance down showed me the angel had crawled halfway up the lighthouse wall, its claws digging deep into the filth for its grip.

We reached the workroom at last. I slammed the door closed, barricading it with anything I could get my hands on. Salem unwrapped the bones, seized an old mallet from a nearby shelf, and slammed it down. The bones cracked and splintered—

So did the door. The beast slammed into it, one skinny arm clawing through the gap.

It was going to get in. I had no way of stopping it now.

I grabbed the bones Salem broke and dumped them into the barrel, atop the wood I'd already loaded inside.

"I lost my light," I said frantically. Salem pulled a damp packet of matches from her pocket, handing them over with a trembling hand as the angel tore away slivers of wood from the door with claws and teeth.

"Get to the observation deck! I'll be right behind you!" I pointed to the narrow stairs, leading up one final level to the exterior of the lighthouse. Salem limped up them as I stripped off my shirt and used the dry patches to wipe my hands.

I tried desperately to get a match to light. "Come on . . . please, just work!"

Finally, the match lit. I tossed it into the barrel, relieved to see the kerosene-drenched wood quickly catch. Before I fled for the stairs, I opened the tap on the kerosene barrel, allowing it to spill across the floor. I partially filled another bucket and hauled it with me to the observation deck.

"Rayne!" Salem was waiting for me, snow swirling around her. The sea churned viciously below, massive waves slamming against the peninsula's rocky cliffs. As I slammed the door to the workroom shut, the beast was sprinting for it. It rammed into the other side, repeatedly. The bolts holding the door in place were wrenched halfway from the wall. "Oh, God, Rayne, you're hurt!"

"It doesn't matter." I sloshed the kerosene over the deck until the bucket was empty. A sudden *boom* made the lighthouse shudder as the fire in the workroom escaped its containment and spread.

"There's no way down," Salem said desperately. "What are we going to do?"

Smoke seeped from the breaking door as the beast destroyed it. Salem clung to me, both of us pressed against the railing. A monstrous death before us, and the cold, merciless ocean below.

Bolts clattered to the floor and long, spidery limbs emerged. There was nowhere else to run.

I took Salem's face in my hands and kissed her. I blocked her view so she wouldn't see the creature coming. Her eyes were full of tears, wide and frightened.

"Salem, my beautiful girl." I smiled, only so she wouldn't see my heart breaking as I flicked another match and held up its flame. "I love you, until the end of time."

Then I shoved her, hard, sending her plummeting over the railing toward the ocean below. As she screamed my name, I closed my eyes, and dropped the light.

The last thing I saw before the heat engulfed me was the angel, consumed by flames. I smiled, but this time, it wasn't sadness.

It was triumph.

Salem

From the Ashen Waves

STRIKING THE WATER, I BLACKED OUT.

Conciousness came and went, terrifying moments of painful reality. The waves beat me, tumbling me end over end. Seawater rushed into my mouth and nose. Choking, flailing, I tried to right myself. The waves and the sky were the same deep void of darkness, except one shone with stars and the other reflected the flickering orange light of the flames.

The cold was making my muscles freeze up. I had mere minutes before hypothermia dragged me down to a watery grave. The majority of the shoreline here was a sheer cliff face, but I could see a narrow, rocky beach over the waves, and I swam for it.

Dragging myself onto the smooth pebbles, I coughed until I vomited the water out of my lungs. My breath rattled in my chest as I gasped for air, but with every gasp I yelled, "Rayne! Rayne, where are you?"

The waves crashed relentlessly against the shore. The churning ocean gave me no answer. Up on the cliff, the lighthouse's flames were spreading. The bricks were so hot they were glowing from within. A giant funeral pyre.

"RAYNE!" I screamed her name until my throat was hoarse. "Rayne, please! Please . . . where are you?"

Dragging myself to my feet, I took my first agonizing steps. My ankle was broken, surely, but it didn't matter. I could reach her. I could get back to the lighthouse, I—I could find her, I—somehow—somehow, I would—

My ankle gave out, and I went down. Sobbing, shaking my head, I curled up in the sand. "No, no, no, please—fucking, God, *please*—"

She deserved better than this. We were going to escape this island together. She was going to explore all the places she'd always wanted to see. She was going to experience so much more than the isolation she'd always been forced into.

She fought for years to be free. She fought so hard.

I watched the lighthouse burn. I couldn't look away. I stared until it felt as if my eyes were burning too.

She didn't want to die here. She'd always feared she would. And now . . .

Tears or screaming weren't enough. This grief was too heavy, this void of cold darkness was too great. Every time I whispered her name, my heart cracked a little more. But her name was all I had left.

As I watched the flames, another faint red glow caught my attention. I thought it was only a reflection on the waves at first, but no. It was a figure, surrounded by crimson light.

Melanie Balfour, standing in the waves, watched me.

She didn't look like the haggard, rotting spirit that had stalked me in the manor anymore. She looked like the woman in Rayne's photos, with long, dark hair, skin the same golden brown as her daughter's, and a gentle expression.

"I'm sorry," I whispered as tears poured down my face and my voice broke. "I'm sorry I couldn't save her."

Melanie raised her arm, her finger pointing to the south. I looked, scanning the dark shore and the crashing waves. Nothing but driftwood and tangled seaweed.

No . . . there was . . .

"Oh my god." I struggled to my feet. I tried to run, but every step felt like glass shattering in my leg and I stumbled. Heart pounding so hard I thought I might collapse, I crawled the last few yards toward the soaked, limp body lying on the shore.

Rayne was face down, and when I turned her over, her face was deathly pale and her lips were blue. I couldn't think, I couldn't speak. She must have leapt after me, following me into the waves only once she was sure the beast was burning.

I started giving chest compressions, begging her all the while, "Please wake up, please, please start breathing . . ."

Suddenly, in a fit of explosive coughing, Rayne's eyes opened.

She gasped for air, choking on the water she'd inhaled. One side of her face, including her hair, had been burned severely. Her skin was red and blistered, her hair singed away.

But she was alive. Heart beating, lungs breathing.

She looked at me, and it felt like awakening from a dream. Like shedding the veil of a nightmare.

"I'm sorry," she whispered. "God, Salem, I didn't want to do it, I didn't, I just—"

I threw my arms around her, collapsing into the sand beside

her. Our bodies entwined, tears of joy and relief overflowed as the cold waves lapped over our feet.

"I had to make sure you were safe," she said. "If I killed it, but lost you . . . I would have rather burned alive."

Relief made me weak, my muscles like jelly. But even as battered as she was, Rayne still held me.

Part of the lighthouse collapsed, sending plumes of sparks into the night sky. Like spirits fleeing this cursed place.

Faintly, among the waves, a crimson light glowed. But it was fading, melting into the flames reflected in the water. Rayne sat up, holding me close, and together we watched until the light was gone completely.

"She knew you'd save me," Rayne said softly. "She knew it all along."

There was something I'd known all along too. I kissed Rayne's cold, rough fingers, resting my head against her chest. Her heart still beat like a war drum, but the battle was at an end.

Our love had won.

Epilogue

Salem

An Important Question

Three Years Later

"**G**IRLS, COME ON! THE CAR IS ALREADY PACKED!" I shouted up the stairway, zipping my jacket up over my bike shorts. "Rayne and Loki are going to leave without you!"

Right on cue, a bullhorn sounded from outside the house: "Attention Seahawk and Little Chick: I am leaving in five minutes whether you are in this car or not. Your bike tires are already aired up, so you can bike up the mountain with Salem!"

Roused by the terrible threat of mountain biking, Rachel and Rebecca came sprinting from their rooms, duffel bags in hand and backpacks on.

"Don't make us bike!" Rachel shrieked dramatically as she ran past me and out the door.

"Noooo!" Rebecca gave an equally dramatic protest as she followed her sister into the front yard. Walking out onto the porch, I smiled as Rayne secured the girls' bags to the roof of our Jeep, which was laden down with camping gear.

As usual, Rayne had insisted on packing everything herself. The woman would hardly let me lift a finger since we moved in together. We were busier now that the girls' adoption had officially been approved. But if something needed to be built, repaired, torn down, replaced, cooked, or cleaned, Rayne usually did it before I even realized it needed doing.

I worried she would be overwhelmed, but when I brought it up, she said it was the opposite.

"This is what makes me happy," she told me. "Taking care of you, taking care of the girls—there's nothing else I'd rather do."

No exaggeration, I almost swooned.

With the bags secured, Rayne sauntered up to me on the porch, glanced back to make sure the girls weren't looking, and slapped my ass.

"You jerk." I laughed as she held me. "I have to be on a bike seat for the next few hours, remember? Take it easy."

"Or you could sit in the car and let me drive you to the campsite like a normal person," she said. "Then I could spank you more."

"You'd better turn down the horniness, or it's going to be a very long weekend in a very small tent," I teased. She rolled her eyes before she kissed me, and it was only a matter of seconds before we heard a long, drawn-out "eeeeewwww, stop kissing!" from the Jeep.

"Your passengers are getting impatient," I whispered. I laid my hand against her face, over the scars left behind from where the fire had burned her. There was a patch of her hair that had never grown back, but she'd never tried to hide the marks left behind. She had started shaving the side of her head, wearing her long hair up so the scars couldn't be missed.

"Yeah, well, I might have promised to get them ice cream on the way there," Rayne said. "I figured we'll be waiting for you all day anyway, may as well take our time getting there."

"You guys can still bike with me," I said, laughing at the horrified protests from the girls. They would happily bike with me on the trails, but riding for hours up a steep incline was a bit more than they were ready to handle.

Rayne said riding a bike made her feel like "Mary fucking Poppins" despite the fact that I couldn't recall the character ever riding a bike.

"You know, we'll pass on that." Rayne kissed my forehead, waving as she backed away toward the Jeep. "I'll pick up a pint of ice cream for you. Be careful, okay? Call me?"

"I will," I promised. "I'll see you in a few hours!"

IT HAD BEEN about six months since we made the move to Colorado. Rayne's new landscaping company was growing steadily, and she had a handful of regular clients. When she first left Blackridge, she'd been utterly lost as to what to do.

She worked at a coffee shop for about a month, until a customer was rude and she threw a bagel at him. I was a little worried about the fact that her new job gave her constant contact with sharp, pointy gardening tools, but she hadn't stabbed anyone yet.

She no longer heard the whispers, and neither did I. She'd been scared, when she first left Blackridge, that she would still be haunted, that she couldn't possibly be free. But days, then weeks, spent on the mainland proved it to her.

All that haunted her now was the trauma of her past, and that was a monster on its own. Therapy was an imperfect solution, given that there were some things she couldn't share.

Rayne still spoke with some of the folks from Blackridge. Dr. Hale hosted monthly video calls for the survivors, and having that outlet of conversation helped her, even though it wasn't easy to open up.

Working with the land made her happy, and she was confident in it too. Our new house's yard had been nothing more than a weed-infested empty lot when we moved in. Now, our front yard was full of native species of bushes, grass, and flowers. Our backyard had been transformed into a garden, and our vegetables were already sprouting.

It made the events of three years ago seem like a distant nightmare.

Distant, but not forgotten.

It had taken a long time for me to feel comfortable going into the woods again. For almost an entire year afterwards, I didn't even touch my bike, let alone go riding.

But I loved the mountains, the twisting trails, the crisp, fresh air. I loved the birdsong and the wind rustling in the leaves. I loved to remember when those things didn't carry any anxiety for me, only peace.

The dread crept up in me slowly, once quiet suburbia was behind me and the trees blotted out the sun. I focused on the subtle burn in my thighs, the cold air in my lungs. But I was braced for something to happen. For the birds to stop chirping and the trees to fall silent. For the cold awareness of being watched to wash over me.

But the feeling remained as only dread, nothing more. I passed other cyclists, cheerful hikers, and early-morning joggers on the trail. People who had no idea what kinds of things lurked beyond the shadows of their imaginations.

About halfway to the campsite, I stopped at a small gas station to stretch and eat my snack. My phone's signal wasn't very good, but I was able to call Rayne and update her on my location.

"Thank you for calling, beautiful," she said, the relief evident in her voice the moment she picked up the phone. "I was thinking of you. You—hey, no, Becca, do *not* light that match, hold up—"

I laughed at the sound of Rayne's phone dropping to the ground. She'd broken three screens this year already and swore that if she broke one again, she was trading in her smartphone for a flip phone.

"Sorry." Rayne was puffing when she got back on the phone. "The girls have been running wild since we got here."

"Go play, have fun," I said. "I'm a little more than halfway, I should be there by sunset."

"Are you sure you don't want me to come pick you up? I don't mind."

"I'll be okay. I promise." She was silent for a beat too long. "I have my bear spray. And I think this is good for me. To do this."

"Yeah, you're right." I could imagine her running her fingers through her long hair, circling the camp restlessly and watching the girls like a hawk. "I know you're right."

"You can't worry about me forever, babe."

"Don't underestimate me."

As I smiled, I almost told her to come pick me up after all. "I love you. Give the girls kisses for me. I'll see you soon."

Sunset colors were painting the sky by the time I reached the campsite. I'd intended to hurry, but the last stretch of my ride was a steep incline that slowed me down. The camp was quiet, with a few other families scattered throughout the trees around their own tents and fires. I followed the winding path until I reached the site number Rayne had given me.

As I walked my bike around the bend and got my first glimpse of the camp, I halted in shock.

Electric candles and lanterns were everywhere: dangling from the trees, placed on the hood of the Jeep, and forming a meandering path into the camp. Laying my bike aside, I followed the candles under the trees. The gargantuan pines' gnarled boughs swooped over the camp, forming a canopy of branches and leaves. More lanterns hung from those boughs, swaying slightly in the breeze.

If it weren't for the familiar Jeep, I would have been convinced I'd walked into the wrong camp. Then I saw Loki lying nearby, the old dog lifting his head and wagging his tail at the sight of me.

"What's going on here, boy?" I said, squatting down to pet him.

The sound of whispering, childish voices came from nearby, drawing my attention. Suddenly, with hushed giggles, Rebecca and Rachel ran out of hiding to greet me, holding bouquets of flowers that they excitedly thrust into my hands.

"Welcome back, Mama!" Rachel beamed, and I struggled not to let my breath catch. She rarely called me that—and I'd never asked her to—but occasionally it would slip out. Every time, it caused the sweetest ache in my chest.

"We've been waiting for you!" Rebecca was jumping up and down, practically bursting at the seams. She'd never been good at keeping secrets, so I couldn't fathom how I hadn't heard about whatever this was.

Even though I didn't know what was happening, a warmth bloomed in my chest when I looked up from the girls and saw Rayne. She was standing in front of the crackling fire, her long hair loose and wild around her face.

Beautiful. How the hell had I gotten so lucky?

"Thanks, girls," she said softly, and gave them a little nod. They scurried off again, giggling, holding hands as they crawled into the tent and zipped it up.

It was just me and Rayne, surrounded by twinkling lights in the middle of the forest, bathed in the warmth of the fire.

"You must have really missed me today," I said, but I was too breathless to laugh. She took me in her arms and kissed me slowly. From inside the tent, Lana Del Rey's "Say Yes to Heaven" began to play.

Her body swayed with mine, a gentle dance in the middle of the forest.

"I did miss you," she said. "I miss you every second you're away from me. When I wake up in the morning and get to see your face, I forget every nightmare. You chase all my shadows away."

Laying my hand against her cheek, I smiled as I kissed her again and said, "What's got you so romantic tonight?"

She laughed softly. "I was inspired by this gorgeous woman, with a smile like sunshine and a laugh I'll never get enough of hearing. A woman who believed in me, and who's been by my side no matter how damn hard it was." She stopped swaying and ran her fingers through my short hair. "I'm not perfect, I know. I have a long way to go, I have a lot of wounds I still need to heal. But I want you there with me, Salem."

She was fumbling for something in her pocket. When she got on one knee, I began to sputter in disbelief, and she was laughing when she flipped open a little blue box and held my hand.

"Salem, will you give me the honor of being my wife?" I was nodding before she even got the whole sentence out. "Will you be my forever?"

"Yes! Yes, Rayne, of course, yes!"

She slipped the ring onto my finger, the diamonds glistening in the lantern light. She kissed me, and I pulled her up, arms around her, crying and laughing all at once.

It was only a few seconds before the girls weren't able to hold in their excitement anymore, and excited squeals came from the tent. They ran out to us, jumping up and down as they both breathlessly told the same story of keeping the biggest secret ever. Loki barked and circled us, matching the excitement.

Rayne wiped her eyes quickly, but I caught her hands and stood up on my tiptoes to kiss her again. The girls giggled and ran to get water from the creek for my flower bouquets. When I settled back on my heels, Rayne let the tears fall as she smiled.

I wiped them away and said, "Forever, my love. Always and forever."

Her arms wrapped around me, and I rested my head on her shoulder. The darkness beyond the camp was growing deeper, and for just a moment—I swore I saw a crimson glow.

Acknowledgments

House of Rayne was one of those books that felt *almost* too easy to write. Not to say it wasn't a struggle—there's always a struggle, at some level, in some way, to get a book just right. To make sure you're doing justice to the characters, the story, the audience. But this story came to me easily, and these characters worked together in a romance that flew onto the page.

Rayne and Salem waltzed into my brain one day and promptly made themselves at home, and now, finally, I get to share them. I've been wildly in love with this couple from the beginning, and I'm so incredibly grateful for those who've been hyping my idea for the "sapphic gothic romance" since I first mentioned it. Your excitement and enthusiasm kept me going even when I doubted myself. I know it's felt like ages of teasing waiting for this book to come out, and I'm thankful to every single one of you who have been looking forward to Rayne and Salem's story.

To my husband, my forever muse and biggest supporter, thank you for your endless encouragement, for being my personal chef and keeping me away from kitchen knives, for being my HR department, tech department, and therapist. I love you.

Liz, and the entire editing team, thank you for making this book the best it can be. Thank you for stopping me from switching Rayne's eye color every other chapter, and making suggestions that led to four hours of in-depth research on lighthouse fuel and burning human remains. I'm sure my FBI agent is used to this by now.

Bethany, thank you for your tireless work and guidance. I don't know where I'd be without you.

To every single reader, new and old, thank you for picking up this book. I'm so grateful that you chose to spend your time with Rayne and Salem.

I'll see you in the next adventure . . .

Harley